SPI
EGE
L&G
RAU

RUBY'S
SPOON

RUBY'S
SPOON

A Novel

Anna Lawrence Pietroni

SPIEGEL & GRAU
NEW YORK
2010

Published in the United States by Spiegel & Grau, an imprint of The Random House Publishing Group, a division of Random House, Inc., New York.

SPIEGEL & GRAU and Design is a registered trademark of Random House, Inc.

Grateful acknowledgment is made to Houghton Mifflin Harcourt Publishing Company for permission to reprint an excerpt from "The Hollow Men," from *Collected Poems 1909–1962* by T. S. Eliot, copyright © 1936 by Harcourt, Inc., and copyright renewed 1964 by T. S. Eliot. Reprinted by permission of Houghton Mifflin Harcourt Publishing Company.

Library of Congress Cataloging-in-Publication Data
Pietroni, Anna Lawrence.
  Ruby's spoon: a novel / Anna Lawrence Pietroni.
    p. cm.
  ISBN 978-1-4000-6868-5
  eBook ISBN 978-1-58836-921-5
1. Black Country (England)—Social conditions—20th century—Fiction.
2. Factories—England—Fiction. 3. City and town life—England—Black Country—Fiction. I. Title.
PR6116.I63R87 2010
823'.92—dc22   2009034841

Printed in the United States of America on acid-free paper

www.spiegelandgrau.com

9 8 7 6 5 4 3 2 1

First Edition

Title-page photograph copyright © iStockphoto.com
Maps by Anna Lawrence Pietroni
Book design by Caroline Cunningham

For my grandad, Norman Coley

to Muckeleye

THE LUDLEYE ROAD

Blicks' House

nailers' cottages

Tenter Lane

Isbourne

THE BREACH

To the Lean Hills →

Tail Lane

The Ludleye Gutter

Cradle Cross
near Muckeleye

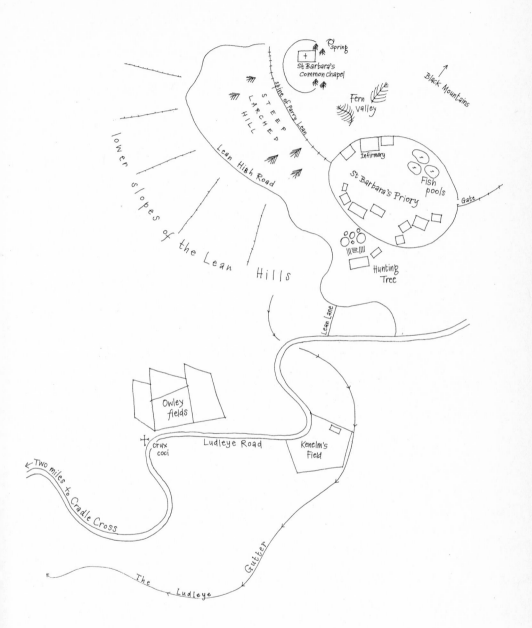

spring

St Barbara's
common chapel

STEEP LARCHED HILL

spine of Parry Lean

Fern valley

Black Mountains

lower slopes of the Lean Hills

Lean High Road

Infirmary

St Barbara's Priory

Fish pools

Gate

Hunting Tree

Lean Lane

Owley fields

crux coci

Ludleye Road

Kenelm's Field

Two miles to Cradle Cross

The   Ludleye   Gutter

Anna Lawrence Pietroni

RUBY'S SPOON

CRADLE CROSS was locked in tight by land, as far from sea as you could be. It squatted—red brick, dull slate—cramped up between fat chimney stacks and blind factory walls in the pit of Ludleye Valley, west of the steep slopes of the Lean Hills; south of the prouder, sprawling town of Muckeleye. Even in midwinter, there was always somewhere close to warm your fingers: by the greedy ovens out the backs where nailer-women hammered; or by the horn oven in Blick's roasting shed (big enough to burn a cow) if you could stand the stink; brazier fires in the folds behind, between the houses, lit to purify the air. Midwives passed their freshborn babies over open hearths to burn off evil spirits and to make their peace with fire. And if they didn't take the baby to the flames, the flames would take the baby: it happened every winter. A hungry furnace, crouching, till a nailer-mother, parched like kindling paper, leaves the fire unguarded for a second. She tells her toddling child to "sit right theya; doe move" and goes to wet her lips on a jug of beer at the door. Then while her back is turned, the furnace springs and snatches up this overreaching bit of boy while his mother screams and throws her bitter at the flames. (The thirsty mother weeps and tells the magistrate how she only left him for a second. He shakes his head and holds up neglect and Holloway in her face. While she stoops in court, her husband's in the foundry, naked to the waist; he strikes on, skin bleached and pocked with little slug trails, silvery and raised, where beads of molten iron have seared the skin.)

Each May, with blazing brands they'd plaited from the first felled birches of the spring, the nailers and the chainmakers walked the streets; sang thanks in dumpty songs for their life-labor—their furnaces that spat out nails, spewed monstrous ropes of chain. The hammers were so delicately named: some chains were "dollied," some were "tommied." And the nails had brisk and merry titles: spike and scupper; hob and tenter; rose and mop and fine-knee; clinker. Dog-and-ugly was the only name that fitted with the nail; the snarling fury of the fire.

But even here in Cradle Cross where the streets breathed fire, they never thought they'd gather in Horn Lane at the dead end of that long scorched summer, 1933, to watch a witch-burning. Word got out, and someone struck the bell at Blick's Button Factory; men spilled out of the Leopard, sloshing ale; from the chapel, a scattering herd of women hobbled down towards the factory, lit by flames, and men called out their "fogging hells," not troubling to keep their cursing quiet. They all smelled the fire before they saw it; the clawing stench of scorching fat and bone. Some came to souse the flames, others to stoke the fire—either way, they were all shocked by what they saw and stood in a shifting curve around the fire, held back by the heat and bleating at each other, nudging, shuffling, leaning on each other's backs and jumping for a peep.

The witch's name was Isa Fly, and the children had a rhyme for her:

If yoom wiser
Doe cross Isa
Or her'll split un splay un splice ya.

There was no stake, no rope, no stack of seasoned elder. The whole street was on fire: the horn sheds and the factory and the little row of houses in between; the Fried Fish Shop, Blick's Button Shop, and upstairs, backlit at the window, stock-still and watching the crowd, stood the witch. With her, tugging frantic at her sleeve, a young girl who wasn't meant to be burned up.

You might have thought the sight of Ruby Abel Tailor, trapped beside the witch, her knotted fists both flailing, would be enough to shift the crowd from warming up their fingers on the witch-fire. Some started, staggered off towards the Breach; some battered at the high gates of the factory, crying out for firemen, fetching water, ladders, axes. But others stayed put, for the sight of Ruby proved to them they had been right about the witch, right all along—so evil that she'd let an innocent die with her—and this ignited a new passion in the crowd: spitting, hawking, swiping, calling livid curses down on Isa Fly, screaming at each other that the witch would get a burning.

When they turned back to the window, there was no one there— just wild flame, red and gold.

THIS IS the tale of Ruby Abel Tailor, who could not cross the water but dreamed of an easy plenty by the sea. This is the tale of three women—one witch, one mermaid and one missing—and how Ruby was caught up in between.

Chapter 1

Fly, *a.* 1. Knowing, wide-awake. 2. Of the fingers: Nimble, skillful.

CRADLE CROSS was circled round with water, and Ruby could not cross it. To the east ran Ludleye Gutter, a brook that carved a broad but shallow conduit through the clay. To the north and south and west, canals curbed Cradle Cross—filthy slits of water called the Cut; beneath the waterline, wood rotted down to slime, and wire and rusted iron. Not like the sea, where you don't know what the tide might bring—a whale, off-course; a raft; a barrel full of something rare and bright—the Cut brought barges loaded up with steel tubes, salt and coal and rivets. And two weeks before the fire that burned Horn Lane, the Cut brought Isa Fly to Cradle Cross.

The Cut ran right behind Horn Lane—it kinked round at the southern end of Blick's and swelled out to a basin where the barges turned when they'd unloaded heads of Russian cows or picked up sacks of blood-bone fertilizer for the farms. The Cut then narrowed and ran straight for half a mile behind the vast vaulted horn shed, behind the little row of houses, up and under Wytepole Bridge and on for Lapple. For years now Ruby hadn't dared to walk along the towpath, but she could just manage sitting above it, on the top of the three steep stone steps out the back of Captin's Fried Fish Shop, with her back safely pressed against the doorframe. This night—the night the Cut brought Isa Fly—was hot even for July and Ruby came out every now and then, just when the shop was quiet, and sat with Captin's best knife and a bucket, starting on potatoes for the next day. She could peel potatoes without looking down, angling the knife so when it hit her thumb it wouldn't slip into her skin, and from her top step she watched the inky, shifting waters—the Cut could not be trusted and it *needed* watching. Captin's narrowboat, his *Ferret,* nodded gently at its mooring. Looking left, she could see as far down as the gas lamp in the wall on Blick's Kink, and right, to the lantern hanging from a ring sunk in the capstone on Wytepole Bridge. Not much traffic on the Cut on Friday nights.

She'd worked for Captin (Fridays, Saturdays) since she was ten, and she was saving for a boat. Three years she'd stood beside him at the counter, dishing up fish suppers to the well-off women, serving out chip ends and skate knobs to the rest. The pattern of the evening, every week: first off, little boys with a penny between them, asking for a bag of bits. Later, courting couples wanting to share a packet so they could stand elbow to elbow. At closing time, the young men from the Leopard would come, taking swigs of vinegar for bets when they thought she wasn't looking. She'd want to lean across the counter with her spatula and smack their sticky fingers; shout, "I saw that, Alf Malpass! Bog off, Jimmy Male!" But instead, she knew, she'd look away and take her pinny to the fat, blind jar of pickled eggs and polish up the glass.

That half-hour lull before the pub closed, Captin and Ruby enjoyed the easy quiet and didn't talk much while they worked: he checked the range and flicked a glob of batter in to test the fat; she scoured the counter and put out fresh greaseproof squares beside the paper, ready to wrap chips, then Captin wiped the counter down again. "It ay as I doe trust yo, Ruby, yo knows that. The only way as fish-friers thrive—"

"Is if weem cleaner than a queen."

This was not the whole truth, Ruby knew: brushed fingernails, ungritty counters—they would keep your reputation clean enough. The test was, Captin taught her, in the stomaching, in the buying of the fish up at the wet market in Muckeleye; cheap fish, but not rotten. There was a woman, Ruby read in Captin's *Muckeleye Gazette,* been jailed for selling poison fish; a man, for trying to fry his chips in motor oil.

"S' all right, Captin. It woe be your countertops as see yo banged up in Winson Green," said Ruby. "It ull be for flogging fish that's green under the batter."

"Ay I taught yo nothing, Ruby?" He reached over for the broom and swept at her feet while she jumped and giggled. "Who will I leave me fishy empire to if Ruby plays so light and careless wi it? If her goes bringing me good name to disrepute?"

Ruby wouldn't play this way in front of other people, and there was no queue yet, but when a bent-up woman came in and tried to stand up tall against the counter, Captin shooed Ruby out. Ruby knew the bent-up woman wouldn't ask for anything, not while *she* was there—the woman never did. With care, eyes fixed on Captin, she would place whatever coin she had to spare flat on the counter, and Captin Len would smile and then be gruff and say that he was sure he'd fetch her something, like a bag of cods' heads to stretch out with mash into a fishcake. But he would pack it up with extras, like some chips in with her bits. Been doing this for years. It was Captin Len's Fried Fish Shop kept the Cradles fed, since the hungry winters of the War and women driven to cobbling War-loaves fit for only pigs (more potato in than wheat) to keep their children from being starved into coffins small enough to carry on their laps.

So, when Captin started wrapping up jellied roe and a whole scoop of batter-bits, Ruby went when she was told, no hesitation, through to the back. This, Ruby loved in Captin: how he was so careful with the dignities of strangers and the dignities of friends, how he cradled them so lightly, yet weighted down his pockets with responsibilities that were not his to bear.

"I doe mind a cup of tea either, Ruby," Captin called to her. "Bring it back wi yo when yoom finished out the back."

Ruby left the door between the fish shop and the back room slightly open. She stopped by the shallow sink in Captin's scullery to rinse scourings from her fingers and fill the kettle; she started at the spit and fizz of fresh chips dropping in the fat. (A lesson Captin taught her early: never leave your range too long without some chips to cool the fat. "Yo doe want the chip fat catching else we'll all go up." All that grease sunk deep into the wall, and bowls of rendered fat about the place.) She took the top sheet from the pile of old *Gazettes* that Captin kept for wrapping up bad fish, and pulled on Captin's sweater—big on her, but something between her and the low wind that brought the sulphur in off the canal. It was treacherously dark down by the Cut, but light swung out through the doorway and flung Ruby's shadow long across the water. Eyes flicking up to keep the Cut in check, she steadied herself (a hand on each side of the doorframe, the paper pinched between a finger and thumb) and lowered herself down onto the top step.

She reached into the pocket of her pinny and pulled out a small book bound in soft, scratched leather. It was tied shut with a shoelace, and when she undid the knot, the book eased open, pages splayed. The book had been her mother's, and Captin's before that, passed down to Ruby when she had turned seven. Inside the cover, a tidy, careful "Leonard Salt, Cradle Cross," and underneath, in a looser hand, "given over by Captin to Bethy for her Birthday." Despite the binding, Captin's book was cheap and not meant to be kept beyond the year—the print bled on damp fingers, the pages tore, and on the title page, *The Coastal Companion, Severnsea, Almanac for 1899* was set askew. Within, the times of tides; a chart of all the stars; the lunar calendar. Some pages—registered importers and their agents, best bait for sea trout, the breeding patterns of the slob trout in the estuary—were obscured with pasted lists of "Places I will Go when I have got a Boat," or maps, "From Cradle Cross to Ludleye Port, by water," drawn on scraps of sugar packet, flattened out, or advertisements: "Clamp a Johnson's Sea-Horse to your boat"; "Our spring-knit slims even the most amorphous mermaid."

She laid her Almanac—she liked the way that sounded—on her lap, shook out the sheet of newspaper and held it up so it would catch the light. She read the headlines and no more ("Miss Brenda Paul to go to Prison," "Criminal Libel: Verdict in Mr. X Case," "New Orchid Named 'Lady Mayoress' ") until she came to one that caught her: "Sleepwalker's Fall into the Sea." Ruby read enough to be sure this was what she wanted ("they traced the wet footprints to the forecastle, where they found a heap of wet clothes and Alexander Middleton, a young deckhand, lying naked in his bunk."), and with a pair of trimming scissors from her pinny she clipped the two-inch square of story out and slipped it in between the pages of her Almanac for pasting later. Nothing on the breeze to show this night was different. Not quite yet.

She had put her book safely away and crumpled up the paper for the fire—the kettle singing, now, and Captin wanting tea—when she heard dislocated voices on the Cut, resounding hard and clear, and then she saw the swinging light approaching around the kink as it curved behind Blick's. She stood up quickly and stepped back inside the doorway, leaning out and peering at the lurching lamp, but holding to the frame. Boats, Ruby loved. It was the water that they traveled on that troubled her. Each time a boat passed by she'd fix herself to something firm on land because she would be, suddenly, afraid that if she moved from where she stood she might step out towards the water. So as the light swayed side to side along the Cut, Ruby set her back against the frame and pressed her feet hard down against the stone. It looked to Ruby like a common barge—room for the payload, with a little one-man cabin at the back. But this boat didn't pass. It veered in to take a mooring behind *Ferret*. And on the platform up next to the skipper stood a slighter figure with an arm out on the bar for holding steady.

The bow light glinted on a woman's face and fierce white hair that gleamed, half coiled, inside the lowered hood of a deep crimson cloak. Ruby drew back further as the woman disembarked and stumbled on the towpath. She found her footing; glanced up and caught Ruby's eye. As she did so something started deep in Ruby, and for a moment Ruby felt she was about to spew up all the life she knew. Her eyes grew wide. She darted back inside and closed the door and shrank down below its window to wait for the woman to pass by.

"Is my tea ever coming?" Ruby flinched at Captin's voice behind her. "What yo up to, Rubygirl? Boiled to dry, that kettle has, all but." He took up the thick cloth by the grate and lifted off the kettle, shaking it to see that there was water still inside. "Just enough," he said, but seeing Ruby was still crouching by the door, he set the kettle, clank, down on the hotplate and crouched beside her, pressing the warm flat of his hand to her forehead. "Am yo all right, our Ruby?"

"There's someone out there." She tried to tug him, keep him down, voice low—too low for Captin.

"Is it them kids again? Better not be messing with my *Ferret*, they had better not."

Before Ruby could pull him back, he'd raised himself up, yanked open the door and thrown his chest out and his hands wide like a bear ready to growl and roar at felons. Ruby could not stop him, and that's how Isa Fly got in.

In the days and weeks that followed, Ruby tried to work out when she'd found the breach in her own history (the breach that's stitched in every story: run your fingers over it and you will find a clumsy nub where someone tried to darn across the slit). Ruby could not stop him. Captin, tamed and gallant and seeming younger than his fifty years, asked the woman in. And looking back, Ruby knew this was when it started; the slow unraveling of all that she had held as sure and true.

The stranger said she had to find a cheap room, just for a night or two. Watching her, sat cautious and unsteady on the edge of Captin's one-armed sofa that sprouted horsehair around the studs and buttons, Ruby could see what had made her afraid of this woman. She was guarded, Ruby thought, as if within she held at bay a secret— jumpy, yappy, like an untrained hound that could leap free and knock the air from Ruby, knock her to the ground. The scarlet cloak, the salt-white hair that settled heavy on her shoulder like a pelt—the hair of an old woman on the head of a young soul, for the woman *was* still young, and her skin lambent and unlined. And more than this, the strange unbalanced eyes—one dark as coal, the other gauzy, white. Everyone avoids a white, white eye. You can see further with a white eye—see the scabs and pits and scars that mark our hearts. *This blind eye it was, catched me out,* thought Ruby, but while Captin brought fresh chips out for the stranger, she decided to be civil.

She introduced herself, and the woman said her name was Isa Fly. Pouring tea out in the good cups, Ruby told Miss Fly how the Leopard had a room upstairs as they kept spare so they could rightly call themselves an inn. Captin said he'd see the lady there, but not now when last orders was being rung. Closing time, too rough, too busy—she'd be nudged and elbowed into bruises. "Wait till our chips is done, and then walk yo down, I will." Chilly Fox, the landlord at the Leopard, never went to bed before the dawn.

The shop filled up with shouting boys who leered and jostled: Captin and Ruby left the stranger in the back room, sat still with her traveling bag held two-hands on her lap. Captin lifted battered fish, fresh, golden, out of the fat and slapped them down while Ruby shoveled hot chips onto paper, shook the salt out and dispatched the boys with open parcels, dangling their fingers in the greasy bags and licking salt off fingers in the street. At half-eleven, Captin locked the door, sending out the last boy with the fattest packet, topped with shards of crisped-up batter, rocky chippings from the bottom of the pan.

When Captin Len had strained the fat and wrapped the grainy sediment in paper, and Ruby'd swept the floor and mopped it, they went through to the back. Ruby tried to keep her eyes from Isa Fly, but she couldn't. Isa was perching on the couch with a book that Ruby knew she must have brought with her—it wasn't one of Captin's. (Besides his daily study of the *Muckeleye Gazette* from front to back each morning, Captin wasn't one for reading. Two books he had, up on the high shelf above the grate, and Ruby knew each page. When the shop was quietest, she'd switch on Captin's wireless, then reach up and pull down a book and fold herself up to read at the high end of the couch. The first, *Ashore and Afloat,* a Sunday School prize for good attendance, and the second, *The Child's World of Knowledge, Vol. II: Boa to Con.* Always at the same page, it would open. She never read the ponderous text, "Canals Around the World," but sat and wondered at the bold girl-skipper leaning on the long, arched tiller of the *Walnut.*)

And now she couldn't help but look at the stranger twice. Her emerald skirt was sewn with tiny glinting mirrors like a thousand hungry eyes to snatch up souls. Isa Fly straightened her skirt—beads of light caught up, tossed, caught and tossed—and pushed her book inside her bag. "You have both been kind to me."

Ruby tried to smile a little but said nothing and set to, filling up a deep bowl in the scullery with borax and hot water for soaking all the tools.

"We woe be a minute here, Miss Fly." Captin lathered up his hands on a thin green slip of soap. "Has to be done first, this does, and take yo afterward, I will, back round the Leopard."

In turn they each stripped off their aprons, dropped them in a bucket. "Cottonseed woe shift." Captin took the nailbrush to his fingers. "Seeps in, it does. Woe shift wi scrubbing, or wi soaking half the night in Jeyes. Come far, have yo, Miss Fly?"

"All day, I've come, and all the night before."

What would bring her—anyone—to Cradle Cross, Ruby could not grasp. She knew its bounds as if they were marked out by the tide, and all the crossing points to get beyond: Wytepole Bridge across the Cut, the hinged drawbridges by the Deadarm, the shallow section of Ludleye Gutter where you could step across the width of it on rocks and keep your feet quite dry. Even though she knew these places, lingered near them, drew them on a map, it had been seven years since Ruby crossed the water.

Captin took a rough towel from the hook beside the grate and rubbed his arms and hands. "Exhausted, yo must be, wi such a journey!" He reached up to the shelf above the grate; took down a pipe, pulled up a chair and turned to face the couch. In no hurry to get Miss Fly down to the Leopard. The woman watched him closely as he knocked his pipe against the heel of his hand; emptied out the ash into the bucket by the grate. He twisted in the chair to talk to Ruby. "Make us some fresh tea will yo, Rube? Yo can put new leaves in out the tin."

People trusted Captin easy. But Captin trusted easy too, and later, when things started to unravel, the Ruths and the Naomis would say Isa Fly'd bewitched him, feeding him with salted bread and butter every night and keeping back a special silver laugh for him alone. And this Friday night was when it started up.

"All day and all night?" he said. "That wor an easy trip."

"I missed the Thursday bus, or maybe the bus didn't come at all. It was only three o'clock, but nearly dark. I left home in a rush, but even so . . ."

Captin nodded, waited, locked his pipe between his teeth, lower jaw stuck out; he struck a match against the worn sole of his boot. It didn't catch first time. He threw the spent match at the grate and looked over at Miss Fly.

"The wind was high," she said.

Ruby saw he wanted nothing more than to listen close to Miss Fly. If Ruby could work out how to silence her, then Captin would be free. But Ruby didn't want her to be silent.

"The wind was high," said Isa. "The oaks were bending low and the doctor, seeing that the horse could barely stand, let alone make up lost time, urged me not to go, but I had no choice."

This way of telling tales that Isa had—poised, precise and crafted— it caught up Ruby from the start. Not like the ugly natter Ruby heard on Thursdays from the Ruths and the Naomis, hurling out their spiky little miseries. Ruby's fear of Miss Fly slackened, just a little.

"Doctor Brammeier had offered to drive me to the docks, but the engine wouldn't start, so he rode with me. Brammeier said that with the winds this high we should find some dry rooms for the night, and maybe I could try again tomorrow. He thought the risk too high. He tied the horse up to a post outside an inn, and while he was inside bartering with the landlord, I left and kept on walking till I got back to the quayside. I bought a ticket for the packet boat at six o'clock, but by the time I found the embarkation stand, the boat was gone. The last boat of the night."

"What about the doctor?" Ruby said. "Day yo try to find him?"

"*Day?* You speak like my father."

"*Didn't* yo try to find him? Day yo even try?"

"No," said Isa Fly. She was not impatient, Ruby noted, with these questions and her still and staring eye unnerved Ruby, but she pressed on, thinking about Brammeier, wet from waiting on the quay.

"So is he looking for you now, the doctor, back where yo left him?"

"He will have gone back home."

"But woe he be worried sick about yo, not knowing where yo am? Swept away, yo might be. *Drownded.*"

"I had no choice. I had to come."

"Day yo even leave a note for him?" Ruby was perplexed, but Captin seemed impressed.

"So yo hitched a ride up on an emptied flyboat . . ."

Isa nodded. "I found a man willing to take me, and he was heading up for Muckeleye. I needed to find him, and I was lucky."

"Persistent," said Captin with a laugh, "if a little reckless wi your-self . . . Now put me right, Miss Fly, but I'm thinking from the lilting of your words as yoom from Severnsea."

Ruby dropped a fish slice in the sink-bowl with a clang and glanced at Isa. "Yoom from Severnsea?"

"Yo cor deny it!" Captin wagged a finger toward Isa. "I know the sound of Severnsea!"

Isa Fly was startled into something Ruby could not read; curiosity, or fear.

"Which part am yo from?" In Ruby's Almanac there was a printed map that showed the villages and towns that lay along the length of the Severn Sea Shoulder. Ruby spoke the names out like a rhyme:

Whalemouth, Ebbscombe, Marcombe, Lee;
St. Shirah, St. Stephen, Filvercombe, Gleed.

And as she spoke she sketched the coastline in the air and with a stab-bing of the finger marked where each place lay. "Which one is where yo live?"

"Hush, Rube!" Captin frowned at Ruby. He took the fish slice from her and rubbed at it fiercely with a cloth. "Her's tired! Her's far from home! Look how yoom vexing her!"

Isa looked between them, back and forth. "How do you know this?" She spoke slow, reined in. "All these places?"

"My sister Dil moved to Whalemouth a good forty years back, when I was just a boy. Her got married to a man who took the trawlers out to sea."

"And do you go to Whalemouth often?"

"Well, Dil died . . ."

"I'm sorry."

"Oh, Miss Fly, doe be so sorry, please," said Captin. "A long time now—thirty years, it is, since we lost our Dil." Captin smiled at Ruby. "But her girls have growed up and they've got girls now Ruby's age, and bigger."

Isa pressed a finger to the corner of her white eye. "But do you go to visit them, your nieces?"

"I ay been down for years, to tell the truth."

Isa closed both eyes, and Ruby wondered if she disapproved and Captin must have read her the same way, because he added that he *couldn't* get away. "People wants their chips, yo see . . ."

"A riot, there ud be," Ruby slipped her arm through Captin's, "If he day open up to give um chips."

"But I write to um," Captin said, insistent. He unhooked Ruby's arm from his. "I write to the girls, doe I, Rube?"

"And they send Captin things."

"In the main, to Ruby."

Ruby made a list out loud of all the sea-things Captin's grandnieces had sent him, and the things he'd passed to Ruby: kelp soap, fruit scones, blue-rayed limpets pierced and hanging from a string; a twisted limb of driftwood now sitting on the mantel shelf. Ruby's inventory of these findings from the seashore seemed to lull and comfort Isa Fly. She settled back into the corner of the couch, and Ruby told her about buttons that Dil's girls'd found along the beach; toggled horn and dappled pinbow, buttons made of ivory, apple coral, corozo. Ruby said she liked to think that one of Blickses barrels had been washed overboard and crashed up on the rocks at Whalemouth strand, and Dil's grandchildren were posting them back home.

She poured Isa more tea, sat down at the far end of the couch and asked her questions while she sipped, questions gleaned from cuttings Dil's girls sent her, or from Captin's books, or from the Almanac. "When yo go about in Severnsea," she asked, pressing the map-page open in her Almanac, "dun yo go by sea, or by the road? Cause look! From *here* at Whalemouth" (she planted her finger on the southern tip of a hooked bay) "to *here*" (she placed her thumb on the spur at Filvercombe) "is only *this* far!" She held up her finger and her thumb, not an inch apart. "But if you go by land there's all them wiggles!"

As Isa listened and then answered (Ruby thought, approvingly, with due attention and with gravity), Ruby's fear of her slid out the back door and down onto the towpath. A rangy stray, this fear would stalk Ruby through the coming days, and although she smartly shooed it from her heels, there'd come a time when it would pounce and she would see, too late, that it was trying to guard her, not attack her, and she'd be sorry then that she'd neglected it.

For now, a buoyant recklessness rose in her like hiccoughs. She showed Miss Fly her mother's writing in the Almanac; the lists of what she'd take with her to sea; the pasted timetables of packet boats from Ludleye. She asked if Isa had seen for herself the rib cage of a whale at Gleed, tall enough for a grown man to walk through. She asked about the tunnel through the rocks at Filvercombe and if it was true that convicts had been made to carve it out; and did she believe that story about mermaids off the coast at Sawdy Point and if you hear them singing you will drown?

Isa passed her hands across her eyes and Captin said, "Enough now, Rube, her's tired! All these saft questions!"

Before Ruby could make her own protest, Isa spoke for her. "No. They're not *saft*." She smiled at Ruby. "They are wise questions" (Captin raised his eyebrows), "but I am not sure how best to answer them." Isa shunted down the sofa, close to Ruby. She reached out for the Almanac, settling it on her lap and tracing up along the coast, her fingers stopping on a straight stretch. "Now . . . they celebrate the solstice here, at Marcombe. Is that marked in here?" She tapped the page. "Have they marked the Marcombe solstice in your Almanac?"

Ruby shook her head and looked at Miss Fly's hand, covering the map. She listened while Isa spoke: flags up, braziers lit; hot potatoes cooking in a pan; herrings fried in pepper flour. All there; fishermen, their boys. The boats all hulls-up on the beach. Someone had got a fiddle out; got them all dancing to keep warm . . . and Ruby was caught up in the salt-wind and the spray.

"Now here, at Ebbscombe, see, the sea retreats and leaves a mile of mud. And I go fishing there." She told Ruby how she'd stand there for a full day in the spring, chilled and firm and still in reed beds, with a rod made up of blackthorn, hazel, ash; fingers sliced from paying out a line coated in silk.

Ruby said, with a curling of the lip, "Yo doe use worms in cans to catch your fish, like them blind men who fish the Cut, do yo?"

"No," said Isa, reaching in her bag. "It's flies I use. I tie flies." She pulled out a wooden box and invited Ruby to flick up the hook that kept it shut. Ruby smiled at Miss Fly; raised the lid. With delicate precision Isa lifted something out—a little flash of red and gold, feather, bead and thread—and held it up to Ruby on her palm. Ruby reached a finger out to touch it, but Isa drew her hand back and quickly set the fly back in the box. Before the lid was shut, Ruby saw a row of hooks laid out, cruel and clean.

"What dun yo catch wi um?" Ruby whispered.

"They're strong enough to hook a full-grown pike. But I don't fish for pike. *'The pike is a good fish but for he devoureth so many as well of his own kind as of others, I love him the less.'* "

"What's that mean?"

"He eats his relatives."

Ruby grimaced and Captin said, "Miss Fly!" and they all laughed, together.

"Doe say as yo come to Cradle Cross for fishing?" said Captin. "We got water—plenty of it—but fish most choke on it."

Isa shook her head, her hands around the box. "I haven't come for fishing, but I never go without my hooks and flies."

"What about a rod?" said Ruby. She tried not to yawn. It was late and it was warm. "Hooks ay much use without a rod, am they?"

"I can always find the makings of a rod." Isa tucked the box deep in her bag. "But hooks and flies don't come so readily."

"There *is* a bit of fishing to be had, up close to Lapple," Captin said. Ruby heard a tautness in his voice and looked at him. He was folding and unfolding his handkerchief; not looking at Isa. "I can show it yo tomorrow, if yo like."

Ruby yawned so widely Captin said he could see what she had et for tea. "Come on, Rube," he said. "Yo'd better get off home." He reached down Ruby's cardy from a peg and said to Miss Fly, over Ruby's head, "Her grandmother will worry."

"Her woe!" protested Ruby. "Nan Annie doe worry about me. Not if her knows as I'm wi Captin." She stood up and fastened her arms around him. "Captin Len, the best of men!" And Captin muttered, "Leave off, Rube."

Captin packed up peelings in a paper for Ruby to take home to feed her pig. Ruby pulled on her coat and patted the pocket to check she'd put her Almanac in safe. Captin chided Ruby for not doing up her buttons and by the time they'd turned their attention back to Isa Fly, she was sleeping.

Gently, Ruby tried to wake her, tentatively reaching out a hand and squeezing Miss Fly's cloaked shoulder. She tried to ease the bag from Isa's hand, but even in her sleep she clasped it tighter. So they put a blanket on her where she sat, and turning down the gas light, left her there, Captin going to his bunk on *Ferret,* Ruby going home to Nan Annie, still not knowing why Isa Fly had come.

Chapter 2

Ravel, *n.* 1. a tangle, complication, entanglement. 2. A broken thread, a loose end.

EARLY NEXT MORNING, the mist still clagging around her ankles, Ruby let herself into the Fried Fish Shop with her own key. She hadn't slept well, wondering what Isa Fly might have seen with her white eye and wondering what had brought her all this way inland.

Miss Fly was already awake and sitting on the back step with her cloak pulled around her, her bag bundled in her lap. She didn't stir, so Ruby coughed to show that she was there. Isa turned sharply, but seeing that it was Ruby, she settled back against the doorpost. "You've missed your grandfather."

"My grandfather?" Ruby frowned.

"He said that he was going to Muckeleye. Does that make sense?"

"Muckeleye makes sense; the wet fish market's there. But Captin ay my grandad. I ay got one." She explained how there was just her and her grandmother, Nan Annie up at home; her father, Jamie Abel, down the Deadarm with his workshop on the Cut; somewhere safe and quiet to test his boats and see that the leaks were stopped. "He is so good at boats, yo see, so busy wi um that he has to sleep down there just to get his work done, all the mending." He bedded down on horn sacks underneath the long bench in the workshop, an old tar-paulin hanging from the side to keep the drafts at bay.

Isa glanced quickly up at Ruby and she squirmed. She had, as ever, told more than she was asked, and Nan Annie was always chiding her for being garrulous. She tried to remember where they'd started. "Yo was asking about Captin. He ay my grandad in true life, but as good as." She looked anxiously at Isa, but Isa did not seem to be annoyed: curious, she was, and calm and held together.

"Len said that you'd be down."

"Len? No one calls him Len!" *No one,* Ruby thought, *except my Nan.*

"He came in at first light. He made tea for me." Isa turned back to the water. "He said that I should call him Len."

Ruby stared at the stranger's back; this Miss Fly was sat in Ruby's tater-peeling spot, and for just a moment, Ruby felt affronted. She dropped the basket she'd brought with her on the table and the noise made Isa start and turn around.

"I thought as yo'd be hungry." Ruby took out a pound of bread, an end of lardy cake, two fingers of butter in a greased-paper twist and two eggs on top, wrapped in an old towel. "Dun yo want sommat to eat or did Captin—I mean Len—already feed yo?"

They ate eggs soft-boiled in the kettle, sitting on the back step, with Ruby naming chimneys and their factories with her spoon: Bissell's Rivets; Tolley's Bolts; Rudge's Tube and Pipe. "The whole of Horn Lane from up there" (Ruby pointed up to Wytepole Bridge), "to there" (she pointed down to where the Cut curved left beyond the fac-tory) "is Blickses. *And* they owns half the town. Well, not *they* now. Just one Blick left, there is, now Hector Blick is dead. One Blick. Serves her right."

She told Miss Fly the little that she knew of Truda Cole Blick. Ruby had made a study of the heiress; she wasn't like the other Cradles women. Truda had been to Oxford for an education; she said *don't* instead of *day, I'm not* instead of *ay.* These days Miss Blick worked away in London, and on the rare occasions when she came back home, Ruby would watch for her from the bread queue at Maison

Hester's. (The baker, Dinah, used to say that Truda walked "as if her owns the town. It ay as if her'll have it until her uncle's dead, and we all know them Blicks is long livers, unless there's a war on. Her ull be an ode maid afore her gets her hands on any money." Dinah's daughter Glenda would put in that Miss Blick, though not yet thirty, was the kind who'd always be a "shall-we-call-it *spinster*?" as sniggers gently shook the ladies waiting for their custards and their bread. And Ruby would stand high on tiptoes until Truda dipped down with the Breach and Ruby couldn't see her any more.)

Ruby and Miss Fly salted their bread, their eggs, their fingers, but sitting by the Cut they still tasted oil, hot steel, and diesel, horse-dung. "Makes yo want to keck, it does, even when it ay a roasting day," said Ruby. "Get used to it, yo do, except when it's been raining. It ay the Cut that smells so bad, then, but smell um burning all the fat up off the bones, yo can, all round Blickses, where they make the buttons. They need um for the horn and for the bone."

Miss Fly stretched her head back, bent it forward; pushed her fingers hard along her neck, along her shoulder.

"Yo got a crick from sleeping on the couch? We need to make sure yo gets a proper bed for later."

Isa ignored her and pointed up the Cut. "What's that way?"

Foundries, chain-shops, Ruby said, and Isa wanted to know what came next. Ruby drew the Cut's path on her leg, up through the Cradles, and then through Lapple. And after that, a fork and right to Muckeleye.

Isa leaned forward, looking toward Wytepole Bridge. "And from there to the north?"

"Why, am yo traveling that way?" She glanced at Isa's bag, tight in her hands. "Yo ay going already?" Isa shrugged and Ruby's throat grew tight in indignation. "Yo said last night yo needed a bed for a night or two!"

"I don't know, Ruby." Isa worked a finger in the corner of her eye, the gauzy eye, as if there was a speck there irritating her. "We will see."

Ruby's shoulders slumped. "We'll see?" The answer adults gave when they wanted to evade or to placate.

"Why would I want to leave? You and Len: you're so—"

"What?" *So zealous,* Ruby thought. *So keen. So eager to please.* "What am we?"

"Hospitable." Isa glanced at Ruby—just a moment, then switched back to the Cut. "This generosity—it's more than I deserve."

We could bear down on her too strong, thought Ruby, *me and Captin. And then she'd leave us.* Ruby was glad that Captin had gone to get his fish. She had Isa to herself and didn't have to vie for her attention. She and Isa, side by side, sitting on the step; Isa asking questions; listening; Ruby leaning just a little into Isa's shoulder. Still, Isa was, but not inert. Fleet and deft, just like the golden-feathered fly she had held up on her palm: poised, intent.

When they'd finished with the eggs and each drank down two cups of tea and had an extra slice of bread, Ruby washed and dried the spoons and plates and cups, and Isa helped, her bag beside her feet. Ruby watched as she reached to hang their cups on hooks inside the tall cupboard beside the grate. "What ud bring someone like yo, Isa, to a place like this?"

"Someone like me?" Isa paused, her arm stretched up. Eyes on her own hand as she slipped the cup over its hook. "You know nothing about me, Ruby. You don't know *what* I'm like."

Isa did not reprimand, but Ruby spoke quickly, panicking. "I know yoom from the sea." *I have offended her,* she thought. "That's all I meant. Someone from the sea is all I meant. Yoom used to waves and salty water that is clean, not like the cack that's in the Cut."

"You imagine that the sea is clean?"

"Yoom used to rocks and cliffs and caves!" She'd been there, just that once; not Severnsea, but to the southeast shore. When it got late, she'd refused to come home. Her dad had scooped her up and held her firm; walked inland with her kicking at his thighs, Ruby sobbing hard into his shoulder. "Around here's all hills and dips filled in with bricks and sheds and chimneys." She couldn't think of anywhere in Cradle Cross that someone from the sea could bear to be, except perhaps the Lean Hills rising modestly above the town, and at the top, St. Barbara's, the high, dry little Ararat of a priory. "There ay no sights to see. This ay Paris."

"Tell me," Isa took up a rag from a saucer by the sink, "why do *you* think I'm here?"

Ruby frowned.

Isa held the rag taut across the neck of the tap, pulling the rag back and forth to polish it. "I'm not trying to trick you. Last night you asked me all those questions: whale-carcasses; tunnels . . . Can it be my turn now? Why do you imagine that I'm here?" Isa's words were tight, reined-in, and Ruby was not certain whether Isa Fly was mocking her. "I'm sure you've given it some thought."

Ruby's speculations had kept her from sleeping. She didn't care what had brought Isa Fly to Horn Lane and to Ruby, but she'd willed it to be compelling enough to keep her here. "Well, yo must of needed to come here quick because yo said last night as when yo missed the packet boat yo hitched up on a barge."

Isa nodded.

"Yo was in a rush to get here. And then yo said that the Doctor Something come wi yo to the docks . . ." Ruby peered at Isa, anxious. "Am yo ill, Isa? There's good doctors at the QV at Muckeleye, Nan Annie always says."

"The QV?"

"The hospital. The Queen Victoria. Is that why yo come? Is it for your eye?"

"My eye?"

Ruby felt her cheeks prickle and blush. She dug her fingernails hard into the fleshy heel of her palms. Her words slipped out, too often, like soap from wet fingers, and she couldn't snatch them back.

"No. That's an old wound." Isa folded up the rag and laid it on the saucer. "I lost that when I was a child. Someone threw a stone and it hit me."

"It's just I thought as your eye hurt. I seen yo pressing it. I can warm a flannel, if yo like . . . But that ay why yo come? Yo ay come to see a doctor up at the QV, to see if they can mend it?"

"It has been sore since last night."

"Since yo come to Cradle Cross? The smoke, it is, probably."

"I bathe it, usually, in saline. I've been too lax, these past days . . ."

Ruby offered to make up a bowl of salty water if that would ease the stinging. She poured boiled water into a jug to cool and Isa took a broad and shallow dish down from the shelf. "So if yo ay ill," said Ruby, "why ud a doctor escort you to the docks? Unless—" She blushed. "Is he promised yo?"

"Promised to me? You mean betrothed?" Isa laughed. "Brammeier? No!"

"Is he your friend, then?"

"He's a good doctor, Ruby. A good man. He didn't need to take me to the docks."

"Have you brought bad news for somebody? Has somebody passed on?"

Isa's levity dispersed so quickly that Ruby thought she would fall over; she grasped Isa's arm. "Oh, Isa! What is it? Dun yo need to sit down?" She pulled a chair out at the table (scoured clean, but hatched with little nicks from cutting chips) and Isa sat down heavily. Ruby offered more tea, but she declined and laid her hand on Ruby's arm. "Is there any salt?"

Ruby laughed. "It's a chip shop."

"I'd like to make up my solution."

Ruby brought the salt-pot with its spoon, and set it by the jug and the broad dish. She watched as Isa measured out the salt, tipping the grains slowly from the spoon into the dish. "What is it, Isa? I day mean to upset yo," she whispered. "Has somebody passed on?"

"It's my father."

Ruby watched as Isa let the salt fall from the spoon and held the spoon above the dish even after the last grains had fallen in.

"When did yo lose him?"

"Lose him? I haven't lost him. Not yet. But he is gravely ill."

She sat down next to Isa and laid her clasped hands on the table in the way she'd seen Nan Annie do. She wondered if there was something she was supposed to do, like say that she was sorry to hear that, or make some tea. "What's wrong wi him? Cor that doctor help?"

Isa took the jug and poured cooled water on the salt. "He says there's nothing he can do." She stirred up the solution, the spoon clinking on the enamel as the water clouded up then cleared, and Isa Fly told Ruby how she'd never known her father truly *well*, but these past months he had become this curved man, head down, as if he carried something on his back. Loose hand always picking at the stitching on his shirt. He had never been that comfortable with his height, always stooping, even with the lintel plenty high, or sinking low into his shoulders like a sullen vulture. He was always skinny, Isa said— round flat face lolling unsteady on a scrawny neck, and wrist knobs poking out of cuffs, gaunt and spindly. He was pale, "Paler even than I," she said. But these last days he had lost the light behind his pallor and grown sallow. Loose, light jowls; startled fish eyes bulging, blank and liquid. His skin a pile of old papers sat in a sunny window; parched and yellow. A thin wisp of reluctant life, husked out; dried up; rattled.

"And now he has grown frantic," Isa said. "He will not leave the house, will not sit still. He does not speak except to babble dark things; hollow things. He thinks I am against him. 'You will take me up,' he keeps on saying. 'You'll take me up and cast me forth into the sea . . .' I kissed his fingers, tried to smooth his hair . . ." Isa's words were slow and each was labored; Ruby kept her own lips battened tight lest she say something clumsy that would stem the flow. "But each time he swept me off and kept on, muttering as if it were a charm, 'So shall the sea be calm unto you, so shall the sea be calm.' "

I know those words, thought Ruby. *They're from the Bible. A ship, caught in a storm.*

Isa let her breath out, tight and measured. "I tried to lead him to the window, to show him how the sea *was* breathing gentle, but he would not look." She dipped the tip of her little finger in the water. "He kept screaming out that it was for my sake that this great tempest was upon him."

"For your sake? He's raving?" Ruby asked. "But yo cor die of that, surely?"

Isa sat still for a moment. She held her thumb and forefinger together and pressed them to her gauzy eye. She opened them into a round that drew her eyelids back. She lowered her head, tilting it a little, with her white eye startled wide. She dipped the right side of her face into the water with her eye held open. Ruby squinted and did a sympathetic blink.

Isa sat up straight. Drops of water ran down her face; her tongue dabbed at the corner of her mouth. "A thirst has grown in him. He drinks water by the tankard without pausing for breath, but he cannot slake the thirst. And white stains have appeared, like splashes of something acid and corrosive on his neck, his hands, his cheeks." She raised her hand to her own cheek, where salt water was shining. "These stains, they caused him to scream and I called Brammeier out to the house against my father's wishes."

"What did the doctor say?" Ruby tried to keep her voice properly grave and unexcited, her eyes fixed on the bowl so Isa couldn't see her fascination.

"It is a rare condition, Brammeier says. He could not find a cause in the body for the sickness. He claims that my father is being consumed by remorse: a disease of the soul . . ."

Isa took a spoonful of salted water and tipping her head back, she poured the water onto her white eye. The tendons were stretched taut in Isa's neck and Ruby wanted to lean over and stroke the smooth skin under Isa's chin. Isa tipped her head upright again and pinched her white eye closed. "Brammeier may be right. There are wrongs he has concealed. It seems that my father had a daughter here."

"In Cradle Cross?"

"He left her, thirty years ago; her and her mother."

"So yo got kin here? Kin yo never met, in Cradle Cross?"

Isa shrugged. " 'Other people's bile and spit,' that's what he said he left behind. We always thought he had no family."

"And yo was wrong!" Ruby grinned. "Yo got a sister! A part-sister, anyway!"

But Isa wasn't smiling. "There is no joy for me in this discovery." This *was* a reprimand, and Ruby bit her lip. "His fraudulence, his duplicity. He is guilty of the worst kind of deceit." Isa pressed her hand into the dish; she turned it over, water pooling in her palm. She closed her eyes. *No wonder Isa Fly looks confused,* thought Ruby. As if she wasn't certain how her features should be arranged; how she strived to find some stillness, some composure. But when Isa opened her eyes and pulled her hand out of the water, she turned decisively to Ruby. She spoke more quickly now; her words were light and barbed.

"So, Ruby, my father would like *her,* his daughter, to be aware that he has paid a great price for leaving her. He wants her to know that God's vengeance has been brutal and sustained."

"What's that mean? He wants her to know as he is sorry that he left her?"

"Does that make sense to you?"

Ruby nodded. "He wants to put it right before he dies. That's it, ay it? And does Doctor Brammeier think as this ull help him? Is that why yo come? Cause if feeling bad for what he's done is what's making him ill, making his amends might make him better . . . Doe yo reckon?"

Isa looked down at her hand. "She absolves him and his symptoms disappear?" Isa twisted her hand like a conjurer. Little drops of water flecked the table. "It sounds like a trick, doesn't it, when you put it like that."

Ruby flushed and shifted in her seat. "I day mean to be glib."

Isa stood up and took the bowl to the sink. "I don't think you *are* glib, Ruby. You're trying to be helpful. I can see that."

Ruby screwed her eyes up tight. She felt that she was irritating Isa when she wanted to be indispensable to her. "I could help you find her, if you want."

"You don't have other things to occupy you? Lessons? Errands? Friends to meet?"

"Nope. It's holidays. No school for a month. I can be at your—" She groped for the right word. "Discretion, is it?"

Isa laughed, but not unkindly. "You'll be at my disposal?"

Ruby grinned. "So what's her name, your sister?"

Isa poured the salty water out. "He wasn't very clear."

"He day give yo her name?"

"He shouted about 'Lil.' 'Tell Lil,' he said. 'Tell Lil as my dues am being paid.' "

"Lil? What, short for Lily?"

Isa shrugged. "Perhaps."

"Lily Fly?" Ruby shook her head. "I cor think of anyone named that. Mind, her could of married; her could of changed her name." (*That* wouldn't matter, not in Cradle Cross. The older folk were always talking about "Annie Trent, as was," or "Dinah Basterfield" instead of Hatchett Harper.) "How old ud her be?"

"Older than me by a year or two, I suppose. Somewhere in her middle thirties."

Ruby shook her head. "That doe help. What was her mom's name? Nan Annie might know um, both on um."

But her father wouldn't speak about the mother, Isa said, even when she urged him to say more. She'd used harsh words—abandonment; desertion of a wife—but he'd said it didn't count as a desertion: he had cause enough to think the mother dead.

"But the little girl? Was her left on her own? Maybe someone took her in—the Priory, perhaps, or someone wanting for a child themselves?"

"I don't know, Ruby."

"Yo ay got much to go on, then, have yo?"

"It's not as if he gave precise instructions."

"How can he expect that yo ull find her? He day say where they'd lived, the three of um?"

Isa shook her head.

"He ay made it easy for yo."

"No."

A daughter, left behind! Ruby thought of all the things she'd left at school or chapel or up on the Leans; the things Nan Annie'd chided her for this week alone: a handkerchief, a new unbroken chalk, a hair slide done in tortoiseshell. " 'Seek and you will find,' Nan Annie says, but that doe always work. Losing a whole daughter!" *That would fetch you quite a beating,* Ruby thought, and scratched at the ribbed worm of a scar that crawled across the inside of her wrist. " 'Seek and you will find!' " she said. "It's like a spell, ay it? 'Ask, and you shall receive . . .' "

"A dare, perhaps. Live bold, expectant lives and see what happens . . ."

Ruby's eyes widened. That wasn't what the preacher said in chapel: Jesus, daring them! She thought of the Ruths and the Naomis in the queue outside the bread shop; the cautious ones who nudged and talked behind their hands; the brash ones who thought boldness was in calling out across the street. And Ruby, bold, expectant, striding past them . . .

She asked Isa her father's name, her father's business—someone might remember him; the family he'd left. Isa said his name was Moonie Fly and Ruby saw him sitting idly in the crescent of the waxing moon, legs swinging. "I never heard of any man called Moonie around here, and that ay a name as yo forget too quick!" Isa wasn't sure about Moonie's business back in Cradle Cross—at Severnsea he'd bartered with the merchants who came in to Whalemouth docks; he'd tried to sell their stock on for a profit. And when that business foundered, he began to patch up boats, she said, but wasn't very good at it. No matter what he tried, his boats would sink.

"Weem starting wi the boats, then." Ruby, brisk and purposeful, took the basket. She slipped her hand in Isa Fly's and said that they should start with her own dad, Jamie Abel. She had to take his dinner, anyway. Isa was reluctant ("I do not want to trouble anyone.") but acquiesced when Ruby insisted; allowed herself to be led through the shop. Ruby glanced back over her shoulder to show encouragement to Isa, to show her that it would be fine, that they would find Lily, that this would make her father well again, but Isa Fly was frowning at the distance. Her gaze snapped back to Ruby, and Isa tried to flash a smile, but for that instant Ruby was disquieted. She felt indulged, a child playing a game that Isa went along with. If Ruby had seen fit to ask the wise unworldly widows, they would have told her that this was a sign. If Ruby hadn't caught the sea-breath in her lungs, if she hadn't looked full on at Isa Fly—that white, white eye—then she would not have been hooked in. Too late, already. This was her sport, and Isa Fly had caught her.

Ruby closed up the shop behind them and led Isa out onto Horn Lane. A narrow, sloping lane, with the high green gates through to Blick's Fine Horn Button Manufactory blocking off the bottom and the factory building continuing in an L along the full length of the street—a tall windowless wall that, in the mornings, cast the lane in shadow. "It's Blickses road, by rights," she said. There were wrought-iron gates at the top end of Horn Lane, but Blick's never closed them. A narrow pavement and a high curb down to cobbles good for ankle twisting, "So take care," Ruby said. Past Gertrude Cole's old button shop next door. (Old Mrs. Cole a year dead now, at least, said Ruby, and the shop shut up.) She led Isa past the pork lawn, hemmed with railings, where pig trotters were laid out to dry before they were minced and mixed for spreading on the fields. Ruby said this mix, sent down on covered carts to Evesham in the World War, was shaken on the fields to grow potatoes for the National Kitchen. She said the bonemeal won the War ("The only good thing Blickses ever did.") and pointed out a painted sign up on the wall in letters three feet high: BLICK'S BEST BLOOD AND BONE—FOOD FOR YOUR FIELD. Past the high sheds, up onto the Breach.

Not yet eight o'clock—although to Ruby it seemed she had lived half the day already—and Cradle Cross had woken. Saturday, a working day (except at Blick's), and every chimney spewing smoke and flakes of smut. The factories along the Cut were stocked with hungry furnaces and men worked there all week to keep the fires well-stoked. A gaggle of small boys, throwing sticks down from Wytepole Bridge into the Cut, turned to watch as Isa Fly and Ruby started up the Breach. One, straggling, shouted after them, "Can I have some chips in wi me bits, please, Ruby!" and the others called and cackled, "Who's the ghost, then, Ruby?" She shook her head indulgently. "Doe mind them," she said. "Theym only boys." She appraised Isa and, though she looked less startling by day—her white hair held back with a clasp, her cloak folded and stowed inside her bag—there was still the eye, the mirrored skirt, the skin pale as stripped bone. Ruby, protective, slipped her arm through Isa's. And Ruby (who had made an island out of Cradle Cross and never ventured off it, except once) smelled the sea breeze Isa Fly was steeped in. She breathed it, and she was enchanted.

Her fingers tightened around Isa's arm—too tight. "Take me back wi yo!"

Isa loosened Ruby's fingers but she didn't laugh at Ruby to dismiss her. "What, to Severnsea?"

"Take me back there, when yo've found your sister."

"You'd like to go there with me?"

Ruby nodded. Isa took her hand, and Ruby took this as consent that Isa Fly would take her to the sea.

Isa walked toward the steps beside the bridge that led down to the towpath, Ruby lagging a step or two behind her. Isa turned her head to ask which way they should go along the Cut.

"Not that way. I ay allowed."

"Children may not walk along the towpath?"

"I ay allowed. This way. Come on."

She pulled Isa by the hand and led her past the dimpled windows of the Leopard. Past a low brick building, arched windows like expectant eyes, with MISSION TO CANAL FOLK stenciled out in white above the door. In front stood a dark wooden post with *"Services Provided to Canal Folk"* painted in an energetic script on the black paint board: "Monday, Lessons; Tuesday, Clothes washed; Wednesday, Friday, Correspondence (free); all week, Hot Coffee, Newspapers, Metered Bath (2d.) with Towels." Past Dodd's Chemist, and already next door there was a shifting queue up the steep slope outside Maison Hester's. ("I doe know why it's 'Hester's' on the sign," said Ruby. "That was Dinah's mother, but it's Dinah is in charge of all the baking.) Dinah took the custards out the oven, eight o'clock, said Ruby. Dinah Hatchett Harper had a heavy hand—too warm for pastry but suited to custards—and she sold the wrinkled, brown-skinned eggy wedges as fast as she could carve them.

The women in the queue twisted round as one to watch them pass: heads together, elbows, hands cupped round hissy whispers. Ruby leaned up to Isa's ear. "We'll talk to that lot later. They ull wait." But just before they crowned the high point of the Breach, Ruby heard her name bellowed behind her. A deep woman's voice. Ruby knew that if she turned around she would see Dinah Hatchett Harper frowning in the middle of the street, hands planted on her hips and sleeves billowing above her doughy elbows.

But this time, Ruby didn't turn around when Dinah called her. She walked on up the hill and tugged at Isa. Pulled her through an entryway that tunneled between two terraced houses. Quick as Ruby could, they threaded through arched entries in between the houses that stepped in winding lines from Stower Street, through the little yards ("We call um folds," said Ruby); past a woman with a shovelful of coal, children hammering on tins; ducking under sheets and underskirts. Every minute, Ruby turning round to reassure: "not far now, just another fold or two." In their wake, women heaving buckets stopped what they were doing for a moment, stood up straight and, hands on hips, stared after Isa Fly. Then, a thin slit of a passage with an ending so abrupt that Isa staggered back a step or two as they came out high above the towpath on a steep and scrubby bank, a good mile upstream from Horn Lane.

"Weem here. My dad ull help us."

This was an offshoot of the main thrust of the Cut, one of a network of many smaller arms. Ruby didn't draw these off-Cuts, as she called them, on the maps she made of waterways in Cradle Cross, because they couldn't take her anywhere—they shunted coal or rivets between factories and wouldn't take her nearer to the sea.

Just below them on the towpath stood two signs worked up in iron: THIS WAY FOR SILAS TOLLEY: MAKER OF TOMMIED & DOLLIED CHAIN. CABLE CHAIN SUPPLIED TO THE ADMIRALTY. HOOKS AND SHACKLES TO ORDER. OTHER ITEMS OF ODDWORK. The second sign was simpler: TRENT NAILER TAILOR. BOATS. EST. 1863 and beneath it, hammered to the signpost, a small wooden plaque with PROP. ANNIE NAILER TAILOR painted on in black.

Ruby skittered sideways down the bank but Isa did not follow her till Ruby took her hand and tugged her down. Across the water, there was a little island with a channel running around it. A dry dock underneath a vaulted, open shed. Beneath the roof, a dark and splintered hull lay in the giant outstretched fingers of a cradle. You could smell the cooking tar from here and Ruby sucked the air like licorice. When she was younger, before Nan Annie stopped her crossing water, Ruby spent her hours at the Deadarm, watching Jamie Abel as he showed her how to bend an elm with steam or slice a skin-thin lining for a hull. She liked to do the grotty jobs for him—cooking tar and counting roves and spinning out the oakum into threads; making caulk with horse muck she'd fresh-shoveled from the towpath, slapped wet in a trough and stirred up with hot pitch. And when the work was finished for the day, he'd throw her up beside the Cut and step aside as if to let her fall into the water, then, as she drew breath for shrieking, he'd scoop her up and flip her over his shoulder, charging around the edges of the Deadarm.

Now, whenever she smelled tar, her stomach rolled and more than anything Ruby wanted to reach out for her father and to moor herself to him.

"How do you get to him?" said Isa Fly.

"There's bridges." Ruby pointed to a wooden gangway leaning up against the shed leg on the island and loosely tethered to two posts; matching posts were sunk into the towpath. "But I doe use um. I leave his dinner and he ull fetch it when he wants it."

She set the basket down, and, gripping the sign for Silas Tolley, she drew up from the basket a bowl tied up in cloth. She held it by the bulky knot and raised it high above her head and called, "I got your dinner, Dad!"

While they waited, Ruby pointed to the boat set in the cradle and explained how it had been beached a few weeks back when those flash floods made the Cut breach above Lapple; that if any man could make it float again, it would be Jamie Abel.

"And he lives there?" Isa asked.

"He sleeps there," Ruby corrected her. "And he works there." There was something questioning, pitying, in the way that Isa looked at Ruby, something that made her protest, "It ay as if he cor get off the Deadarm, just that he's got used to it. Everything he needs, I bring it." She tried to make herself stand proud and tall. "He works too hard. He ay got time to come back over here." She looked away as Isa raised her eyebrows and called out, "Dad! Can yo come up a sec?"

A lithe man with his shirt sleeves rolled emerged from the belly of the boat and climbed down a ladder set against the side. Like Ruby, Jamie Abel was neither tall nor skinny, and like Ruby, he had wiry rust-brown hair that sat in solid, sculpted waves; eyes like muddy puddles showing every mark, every little hurt a fallen leaf. Like Ruby, his cheeks started up with freckles when he blushed. (If Nan Annie saw this happening to Ruby, she would press cold fingers flat on Ruby's cheek and promise to buy powder when she'd grown so Ruby would look less of a speckled hen and find a man prepared to marry her.)

Jamie Abel took a cloth out of his apron and wiped his hands and face, stepping out toward his island's edge. "Everything all right, Rube? Is it Annie?"

Isa took a step back up the bank. "We should not be troubling him with this. I can see that he is busy. We're interrupting him."

Ruby shook her head and gripped Isa's hand. "Nan Annie's fine," she called back to her father. "This is my friend, Isa Fly. Her's looking for someone named Lily. Her'd be your age, thereabouts. Dun yo know her?" She explained that Lily's father was called Moonie, if that helped; that they had reason to believe he worked on boats in Cradle Cross; and as she spoke she felt pride swelling in her. She was assisting Isa Fly. She was looking for a lost girl and finding her would make Isa's father well.

"I cor help yo, Rube. I'm sorry."

"But, Dad! Ay no one ever mentioned Moonie Fly?"

"No, Rube, and if that's it—" he looked behind him at the boat. "I got to get this pitch on." Before he turned away, he looked at Isa with a searching curiosity that Ruby'd never seen in him before. "But Dad! A man called Moonie; cor yo ask Silas and the others if they knowed him?" But Jamie Abel had already scaled his ladder, swung his leg over the top, and now he had disappeared into the hull.

Sometimes, later in the day, she would come back to make sure Jamie Abel ate up all his food; there was no one else to watch out for his welfare. She'd wait unseen in the shelter of the high-up passageway and watch her father sinking down and sitting on his island, dangling his feet over the edge where in fuller years (this year was such a dry one) the water would be lapping at his toes. Head down, elbows up, spooning up his dinner.

Not today.

Ruby always felt a sinking in her stomach, leaving him. But today her guts clenched up in agitation. "I am so sorry, Isa," she said as they climbed back up the bank. "Saft, I was, to think as he ud help." *What does Jamie Abel know but fixing boats for other men to steer?*

Ruby threaded through the folds and entries, slower than they'd come, and Isa followed. *How kind Isa is,* she thought, as Isa tried to reassure her, said it didn't matter. Her father had been rude; he had been curt; he had embarrassed her, so she told Isa that she wanted to get a boat but not like those her father mended. She wanted a small one with a curved hull, not an ugly flat one for the Cut. "One that I can take on rivers; to the sea." She asked Isa about the boats her father worked on (how different Moonie sounded!); they were sea boats, weren't they? And did he build them up from nothing or just mend them? Did he take Isa out into the ocean?

.   .   .

By eleven o'clock that morning, not one of all the people Ruby asked—not Mr. Dodd, not Grocer Foley nor the women in his queue—had heard of Moonie Fly. And Lily? "Lilies am ten a penny," they were told, but nobody remembered Lily Fly. Quiet and enclosed, Isa had stopped telling Ruby that she didn't need to do this, and instead she waited, watched, a few steps behind her. Some people said, "Who's asking?" and peered at Isa; most of them would not meet Isa's gaze, or meeting it, would flinch a little and then turn away.

They gave up before they got to Maison Hester's: Isa was too hot, she said—this inland heat without a breeze from off the sea to temper it—and Ruby was happy not to argue. She wasn't ready to face Dinah yet—she knew she would be in for it, but more than that, she dreaded Dinah meeting Isa. Dinah was the one person who wouldn't drop her eyes.

They headed down the Breach towards the Fried Fish Shop, but Isa didn't turn onto Horn Lane. She walked up onto Wytepole Bridge and waited high above the Cut, to see if the air was any looser there. Ruby waited at the foot of the bridge and tried to dampen down her own impatience. Captin would be back home from the wet markets at any time and Ruby liked to get to the shop before he did and fill up the kettle, setting up a pan for warming up his dinner in its bowl, laying out a knife and fork for him and cutting two thick slices of a loaf for wiping up the gravy. She liked to take her time and cut the bread up into strips and lay them in a flower on a plate, then leave before he got there, contentment in her belly like a settling cat. More than this, today, she needed Captin's help: the doctor had given Isa a 'phone number; she was to call him to find out how her father did. But the public 'phone was two streets behind Rudge's on the other side of Wytepole Bridge; she didn't mention this (she could not take Isa *there*, over the water!) yet neither could she name a single household with a private telephone. She felt a surge of fury; so far, she'd not been *any* help to Isa. And if she couldn't help her find the missing sister, then Ruby wasn't going to the sea. She nursed a dull and pressured ache low in her belly, and her feet felt rash and twitchy as if they might kick out without permission.

Sullen, Ruby looked towards the Cut. Her impatience dropped away like sand grains in a funnel: in its place a crane-necked curiosity. The dredge-boat was skulking down toward Blick's, the black-ened steam barge with the shallow sides that crouched low on the water, that sieved the Cut with a vast scoop tilting on a pivot. She'd seen it before many times through Captin's kitchen window, but she never paid it much attention. A woman worked the dredger. Ruby saw her now as the boat eked closer, fully into view, its name done out in a simple unscrolled script along the prow: *Cassandra*. Ruby had never seen a name more mismatched to a boat, or to its pilot. The men who came for chips out of the Leopard called her "The Blackbird," because she was one of those few boatwomen who still wore the full black barge dress, with the frilled front and the bonnet trailing like burned plumage down the neck to ward off the sun. The Blackbird kept another boat to live on, up on a dead-arm on the other side of Lapple, and Ruby'd heard that was an Aladdin's cave; all plate and jugs and lanthorns fished out from the bottom of the Cut. Ruby heard that there were dredged bones, too, flesh stripped off by the Cut-eels, locked up in a chest. The Blackbird leaned back on her tiller, one hand raised to shield her eyes against the sun, and Ruby wondered how she kept her balance; how she dared to lean back, unsecured, above the water. The Blackbird glanced up at Wytepole Bridge—you had to pass under dead-center or you'd scrape the sides—but Isa must have caught her eye because the Blackbird's gaze was now fixed on her and Ruby could see why: Isa, stood there on the apex of the bridge, stone-still, eyes closed against the sun and her hands gripping the iron trellis, focused and intent as if she were trying to command the waters.

Isa turned and walked down toward Ruby and together they headed for Horn Lane. A warning shout behind them by the Cut; the grind and scrape of wood and iron on stone. Ruby glanced back over her shoulder, but could no longer see down to the water. She only found out later that the Blackbird, ruffled, had mis-steered and veered into the side.

Hungry, not talking, Isa Fly and Ruby turned the corner and found Horn Lane filled with music of a kind that Ruby'd never heard before: great loops and swags of strings, and above them a rounded barrel of a sound that rolled back and forth between the walls. Full-throated and fat-bellied, this music threw its arms so wide that Ruby felt that it would knock her to the cobbles with the force of its embrace. Her face grew hot. She looked quickly to Isa: Isa leaned back, eyes closed, face tilted up, against the long wall where the sun now warmed the brick. Silenced, stilled, she looked as if she might stand there all day and through the night, till someone stopped the music. Tears started up in Ruby, and with them, indignation, but Ruby knew a hundred ways to stop up tears, all learned from her Nan Annie. The best one Ruby used now—pinching at the flesh inside her elbow till her nails left two half-moons indented on her skin.

Down at the dead end of Horn Lane, a woman leaned out from an open window, high above the gate to Blick's. One arm dangled languid from the sill and ash floated from a half-cocked cigarette. Ruby knew her, just by sight and name and reputation. Perilously far she leaned, and Ruby (stomach clenched) wondered if you could survive a fall from there. She tugged at Isa, as if they should alert the leaning woman to the danger she was in. But Isa didn't seem at all alarmed; she crooked her arm for Ruby and, her eyes on the high window, murmured something about buttered bread and tea, and as they walked towards the Fried Fish Shop, the woman threw her cigarette down to the cobbles and drew her head inside. She slammed the casement shut and, with it, dulled the music.

Ruby crouched to work the lock at Captin's.

"Who's that?" Isa walked over to the half-done cigarette, caught up in a well between two cobbles, smoke rising. She took it up between her fingertips and held it up before her, as if thinking she might take a drag, then instead pressed the lit tip softly on the bricks of Captin's shop until it was extinguished.

Ruby turned and glanced up at the window. Saw the woman standing back a little, but clear enough, and watching Isa Fly.

"Truda Cole Blick; the one as I was telling yo about. Her's just inherited the factory. Her uncle died—last week, the week before?" Now that she was no longer worried for the reckless Miss Cole Blick, Ruby's indignation flared in her again. "This *music*! Have a nerve, her must."

Isa didn't seem to share her indignation and, holding up a finger to the corner of her eye, she looked with speculation at the window. "She will have a telephone in there."

Ruby stood up, quick. The key chinked on the cobbles. Panic rose up bitter in her gullet: Ruby knew you didn't go in Blickses Button Factory. All the children in the Cradles knew you shouldn't go beyond the Blickses gate. If you went in there, they'd put you on a huge spade in the furnace and they'd burn the fat off you until you'd melted down to nothing but your bones. Then they would take the whetted saw and slice your bones in rounds and cut them into blanks. (Ruby had a box of her mother's buttons that she'd added to over the years; odd ones, and all tiny. She could never bring herself to use one on a shirt cuff or to finish off a nightdress, lest she sew a trim and polished slip of some child's little finger to the cloth.) And those who were no good for buttons would be grinded up, not for making bread, but shoveled into neat, plump sacks of fertilizer that sat patient on the barges waiting to be shook out on the fields.

And if playground lore were not enough to keep you from so much as peering through the keyhole of the high, green gate, you looked to all the fumbling men in Cradle Cross who wore their jackets loose, unbuttoned—all horn cutters from Blick's. You can't do buttons up without your thumbs, and all the Cradles knew the Blick's fortune was paid out in lost thumbs on the factory floor. And if thumbs were not enough, *this* thought would hold you back: the sacks of horn, sat too long in the sun. When they came to slit the sack and peel it back, the horn inside was jumping fresh with maddocks—fat white grubs, agitating for a bit of room, some flesh. They had bets, the boys did, to see who could get in Blickses and come out with a wriggly handful without fetching up their dinner in the Cut. And Blickses *said* that those stinking wrinkled stubs laid out on that fenced-in bit of grass were pork trotters, but no one knew for sure. And if all this couldn't hold you back, come roasting day the smell of burning horn would make your insides twist and wriggle like a salted slug. You didn't go in Blickses!

Ruby said nothing of this to Isa, but with her hand clapped to her mouth pointed to a notice nailed up to the gate forbidding entry: No Persons Under 14 Years of Age Shall Be Admitted.

"When do you turn fourteen?" Isa asked her, sharp.

"Not till next month." All Ruby's spit dried up.

Isa laughed—"Let's not split hairs!"—and made straight for the smaller door set into the gate. "Are you coming with me?"

"But Captin's dinner!" A feeble protestation, Ruby knew, and as Isa waited with her hand flat on the small door set within the gate, she said nothing, only looked at Ruby with calm, unstaring eyes and for the first time Ruby saw that there was something childish, something shaming in these things, so careful, so devout, she did for Captin. Saw for the first time Captin was well old enough to see to his own dinner. A man who gutted fish as easy as she buttered bread, he didn't need her spooning stew out of the bowl and bread cut into pieces like he was a baby. (And when Ruby looked back, only two weeks from now, at how unmoored she had become from all she'd known in Cradle Cross, she looked back and saw Isa stood with her hand on the gate. Another knot—the one that kept her tied to Captin—undone and slipped free of its mooring.)

The door swung in, slapped back against the gate, and they stepped through. The yard was swept and ordered, upturned barrows and wide shovels standing to attention by the wall. Beneath the surge and swell of Miss Blick's music, their heels snapped, echoed on the stone. Ruby walked into the center of the courtyard. To the right, an imposing barrel-vaulted shed, open to the yard on two sides and with high iron gates to the canal basin; within it, stacked packed-up crates for shipping and, fresh in off the Friday boats, clumsy hessian bags of cow horn that shifted, muscular and bony like a sleeping cat, when one was pulled clear of the pile. Directly opposite, the arches of the furnaces, set deep, fat-blackened, where the horn was burned in neatly hand-sewn sacks. Tall mullioned windows on the first floor; nailed below them, bright enamel placards: BLICK'S-FED FIELDS GROW BETTER FOR OUR BOYS, BLICK'S PROUDLY SERVE THE NATIONAL KITCHEN, KEEPING ENGLAND FED AND STRONG.

Ruby turned in time to see Isa slipping through a paneled door set off to the left, and she ran to follow her, in part because she did not want to be alone beneath expectant, watchful windows, in part because she felt her grumbling unease brushed sideways by a new fomenting curiosity. Something heady, too, in trespassing and in not being ground for field-food or burned for buttons. A green painted board hung from two pegs on the door; a list of names in a restrained cursive hand and worked in gold. (If Ruby'd stopped to read it, she'd have seen the Blick line of proprietors laid out, from the founder, *S. J. Blick, Manager 1759–1804,* through the generations to the last *Blick,* Hector, *H. T. Blick, Manager 1914– .)* The door opened directly onto the foot of a staircase and the wooden treads were worn and slippery.

"Where am we *goin?*" Ruby tugged at Isa, two stairs up.

Isa turned to Ruby and acknowledged her with eyebrows raised, but no smiles. Ruby recalled that it was necessity that brought Isa here, not nerve or curiosity. She had to find a telephone and find out if Moonie Fly lived still; if he was as yet (and Ruby thought it was a strange word Isa'd used) *intact.*

The staircase opened on a large square office with windows on three sides and an L-shaped desk set in the center, looking out on Horn Lane and the yard. The walls may once have been a delicate powder blue, perhaps back in the time of S. J. Blick, but now were dirty, overcrowded; hung with photographs, posed portraits nudging frames of family groups askew.

In the middle of the room stood Truda Cole Blick, head cocked like a showy bird and frowning at a plume of papers fanned out in one hand. Splayed out on the desk before her, an ink-stained, bulky ledger; little double-entry notebooks weighted open with apples; a pile of chitties skewered on a spike. Her strong plain features were marked out with crisp dark lines at the eyes and sharp-edged cherry at the lips; black hair sliced in a swinging cut that sat lightly on the jaw and made a heavy line. The music was so loud it pressed against them. She hadn't heard them come.

For all the times she'd watched Miss Blick, this was the first occasion Ruby had been in a room with her. (So many new things in these few, stretched hours since Isa Fly had stepped ashore.) She had never quite believed in Truda Cole Blick; her skin too smooth and painted, her dark hair varnished, fitted, with that curl over the brow. Close up in the Blick's office, Ruby wondered, if she reached up and pulled at Truda's hair, would it slip off in one piece, leaving stubble underneath?

When at last she looked up at the strangers in the room and dropped the papers from her hand, it was Ruby, strangely, that Truda set upon. She twisted up the doll-curl on her forehead and for a moment stared at her. Ruby couldn't hear what Truda said, but her lips curled back from her teeth as if the very words were sour. She stamped on papers as she crossed the room to lift the needle from the gramophone that squatted on a stack of thick and yellowed books. Facing the wall, she let her head drop forward. Muttered, "Spare me!" Swiveled on her heels and crossed the room till she stood a foot away from Ruby. "Who the devil said you could come up here?"

Ruby felt her cheeks flush russet.

"Look what you made me do." She picked up a rowdy fist of papers and slammed their edges square against the table. "As if I weren't in disarray enough, without stray children adding to the chaos. I should drop you in the well and drown you like a kitten." Her voice was deep and rich, a swollen plum. A voice, thought Ruby, quite unlike her own. *Her* tongue lapped and clicked and battered around words: *"Ova theya. Dowan the towan. When um yo a-comin owum?"* A slow Cradle lilt, had Ruby, carrying the extra vowels, and against its troughs and peaks, Truda's voice was strict and sleek.

"So which one is it? We owe you, or you owe us? Although I can't believe I am indebted to one quite so young."

Ruby, in confusion, shook her head and bit her lip and dropped down to her knees to pick up the rest of Truda's scattered papers, but Truda swept them clear of Ruby with her feet.

"Don't tamper, for God's sake!"

For an instant, on all fours, Ruby wondered if she would be shoveled in the oven after all. But then she saw that Truda had no shoes on, stockings darkened, rimmed with salty tidemarks around the toes, and this made roasting somehow seem unlikely, and, while Ruby couldn't say precisely how she did it or what words she used, Isa Fly stepped forward now. Spoke softly in her rounded voice, smooth as a beach pebble, soothing Truda, weighting Truda down, asking her about a 'phone call home to see about her father, who was dying. (One head of white hair, one gloss-black, bowed together.) Now Truda, troubled, twisted up the dark curl on her brow and stared dumb at Isa (not like the bread-queue women who had watched her as if Isa was a strange fish flapping on a plate. Truda looked keen and anxious like the young men in their Sunday shirts up in the chapel gallery, seeking out their sweethearts on the other side); now Truda, soothed, led Isa to the anteroom where they kept the telephone ("My uncle couldn't bear to hear it ring.") and when she came back in alone, she gestured Ruby toward the bald-cornered wing chair before the fireplace, where paper, logs and kindling were laid out in readiness for lighting. On the chair, two pillows; a blanket, roughly folded. "Shift that lot and take a seat." Then "Ruby," Truda said, as if to try the name out. "Ruby what?"

"Ruby Abel Tailor."

"Do your parents work at Blick's?" She thrust her feet back in her boots and yanked the laces hard.

"No. My dad does boats."

"I was rude to you, before. I'm making coffee. It came in with the last horn. Have some, do." She bent to pick a speck of lint free from her trousers, peacock blue. "I prefer it Turkish. Thick as treacle and as sweet." (Later, Ruby swore that she'd declined, but she remembered Isa handing her a tiny gilt-edged cup in blue and gold, rattling on its saucer, sipping at it, tentative—too much sweetness, too much bitterness, mixed up in one cup. Remembered how Nan Annie spoke out against the trifle at the Sunday School Treat—she said it would encourage children to think fancy: too many good things in one bowl.)

"Who is she? Do you know her?" Truda said, jerking her head toward the anteroom. "She doesn't bear the taint of Cradle Cross."

Ruby shunted, awkward, in her chair and pressed her hands between her knees. "She's Isa Fly. She's come from Severnsea."

"But if her father's dying, what's she doing here?"

Ruby sat up straighter and, proud of her knowledge, told Miss Blick what she knew about the quest for Lily Fly and how finding her would bring Moonie peace and might just save his life.

"They couldn't write?" Miss Blick's hands were planted on her hips. "They couldn't send someone else to track her down?"

"Her said her had no choice: her had to come."

Truda shrugged and spoke more to herself than to Ruby. "If I could have been with Hec when he was dying . . ." She breathed in deep then said firmly to herself, "Come on, Truda: coffee." She opened up two doors. Behind them, in a deep, neat closet, all the makings of a kitchen: shelves of tins and cups on hooks; a single gas ring; a plumbed sink. "Yo could live up here, yo could!" Ruby stood up and, uncertain whether Miss Blick would approve, sat down quickly again.

"Hector well-nigh did. The factory was his all." Truda unhooked a copper pan and filled it from the tap and called over her shoulder. "Do feel free to roam but please resist the urge to *tidy*. We are in utter chaos, as you see."

Ruby stood to take a close look at the photographs cramped around the walls. A hundred and more women stood in smiling lines in aprons; a dozen men, slick hair, stiff collars, stood wary at the edges of the group, assembled in what looked like the Blick's yard. A charabanc, full to spilling, and women waving in wide and billowed sleeves: "Sam^uel. Blick and Sons Fine Horn Button Manufactory, Works Outing 1903." Single portraits of young men in uniform, all in white; one leaning, primly nonchalant, on a chair-back before a wild Saharan landscape painted on a sheet; one with his fist resting on a covered table; another with a child; one holding a small, reluctant dog with bulbous eyes; all looking somewhere to the right, but never straight at Ruby.

(Up home there was a photograph of Jamie Abel in his khaki, standing easy out the back before he had his War; cap tilted on his head, hands behind his back, and smiling, something Ruby rarely saw him do. It was her mother's photograph. Nan Annie made her keep it in a drawer, in case she upset Dinah when she called, because Dinah only had the picture left of her boy, Horace, and she kept that turned to face the wall.) She'd never thought, those times she spied on Truda, that photographs of dead men were watching Miss Cole Blick.

"Water's on." Truda folded out some low carved legs; put on a bronze tray to make it up into a table.

"I'm sorry about Mr. Blick," said Ruby.

As soon as the words were out, something shifted inside Truda, something Ruby couldn't see, but her shoulders sagged and her head dropped as she crouched over the table. She stayed that way a moment, and Ruby watched her back expand, collapse with each great slow-blown breath. But then she raised herself, and Ruby, watching Truda with a sort of nervous disappointment, knew she'd angered her, and knew just as clearly it was Isa, only Isa, who could calm her, as if she were a tamed horse that had bolted.

"*Which* Mr. Blick?" Truda marched up to stand beside her. "This one? Lysander?" She poked the picture frame so hard that it swung a little and knocked against its neighbor. "Let's see, Lysander, my big brother, died in 1914. Or was it Uncle Archie? 1914, too. Not the best year for the Blicks. Or was it Philemon, my other brother, that you meant? Not till 1918, Philemon. We thought he'd pulled it off—"

Ruby jumped in, quick. "Mr. Blick, the Hector one, I'm sorry about. Well, and the others, but Hector Blick I meant."

Truda headed for the kitchen and Ruby stood behind her, afraid to offer help, and shifting her weight from one foot to the other.

"And what precisely is it that you're sorry about?" Truda, gruff, upturned a canister of coffee beans above the grinder's funnel. "Sorry you believed the guff about him like all the others in this mud slick of a town?" She pumped the grinding handle. "How Hector Blick the Button Man shirked his duty and stayed home in wartime? How he made the buttons, not only for his braver brothers' battledress, but also for the Hun, for those who sliced and gutted them like pigs on hooks?"

Ruby knew these stories about Blick's. Ruby had heard Dinah more than once say there was blood on Hector's hands and that of all the Blicks. Yet she wasn't sure she wanted to be herded up with Dinah, so while Truda ground the coffee, Ruby pressed her sympathy on Truda with some irritation. "*Sorry,* I am, about you *losing* him."

"*Losing?*" Truda pulled a little drawer out from beneath the grinding handle, scooped out the ground-up coffee and stirred it with the water on the stove so vigorously that she splashed the scalding water on her hand. "It's loathsome, all this talk of losing. Don't *you* start. If you *lose* someone there's hope of finding them again." She sucked the skin around her thumb. Took down another canister and twisted off the lid. She stood there with the canister in one hand and a large spoon in the other. "I've always thought it abhorrent, all this *losing,* since I was a girl. All those strangers nosing around the house when Ma died. She didn't *pass away.* I didn't *lose* her. She coughed herself to death. I didn't misplace her, like a good hat on an outing."

Ruby felt a clawing in her stomach. She wished she hadn't offered her condolence. Truda Cole Blick grabbed it from her, ripped it into pieces. (Ruby's mother Beth had been snatched up, burned down by the same rampaging influenza before Ruby was two, but Ruby had no memory of how she'd spent the days that followed, lumbering to each corner of each room and to the bottom of the stairs and looking under tables, asking, palms up, for her mother.)

Truda held the sugar high above the pan. "And I didn't *lose* my Hector. He had tried too hard. His heart burst in his chest." She let the sugar drop and stirred it with a sluggish spoon.

Ruby chewed her lip and looked out of the window and they remained silent while the coffee churned and boiled. *I am here with Isa Fly,* said Ruby to herself, *and if I help her, she will take me to the sea.* Then, at last, the door squealed on its hinges and Isa came back in, with a tight smile and a dark glow in her seeing eye. (And that was how it was with Isa Fly at first—when she came in, there was a lightness in the room, an absence like a slackening, like easy breathing after all-night pain.) It was Isa Fly who made it right between them; Isa Fly who laid a hand on Truda's forearm and eased Truda's fingers from the coffee pan and urged her to sit down (Truda wilted back into the wing chair as if she'd been on a forced march through the nights and days with no relief); and it was Isa Fly who put a hand to Ruby's cheek and told her quietly how Truda's grief was bloody, raw, uncured.

Ruby, who found disorder impossible to bear, glanced, tentative, at Truda for permission to pick up papers from the floor. Truda raised her eyebrows, nodded her head in consent.

"What news of your father?" Truda, with her legs flung sideways in the chair, sipped the coffee Isa brought for her. (Astonishing, to Ruby, how Truda had lain back in Isa's company so readily. But then Ruby knew that she herself would sit at Isa's feet and have her braid her hair if Isa Fly would only ask.)

"He's rallied, now I've left," Isa said. "He's rallied at the hope of absolution. But he is ranting again."

"Absolution? Oh, Isa Fly, you *must* explain!"

Distasteful, Ruby thought, this glint, this glee in Truda, although Isa didn't seem to catch it. Ruby wanted to protest that she'd told Miss Blick this already—*Ay yo been listening to me?*—but Ruby was unseated by the ease between the women and stood to take the coffee Isa offered and, seeking to distract her friend from Miss Blick, asked her what Moonie was saying now. "Is he still shouting at the sea?"

"He sent word with the doctor that he would fling himself down from the cliffs if I dare go home—"

"What?" Ruby interrupted. "If you dare go home without finding the lost daughter?"

"He's threatened you?" said Truda, swinging her legs around and leaning forward in her chair. "He threatened you like that?"

"Brammeier says he's in a desperate state." A new tone in Isa's voice, almost like trapped laughter. A question lit on Ruby like a moth: how could Isa tame a wild, arresting creature like Miss Blick yet be at Moonie Fly's command, this babbling man who shouted at the ocean? But no sooner had it landed—this awkward, ticklish idea of Isa Fly in thrall to her father—than it left her. Such questions about Isa, Ruby came to find, would never rest for long. There was always some distraction that made them flit away. This time, it was Truda leaping from her chair. "I'm starving. Let's have lunch."

It was a meal like Ruby'd never had before. No knives, no proper plates, no sitting at a table. Nothing warm except an end of old bread, softened for ten minutes in a cloth above the grate. Truda took a short knife from the desk and took shavings from a hard, curved rind of cheese (up home, thought Ruby, cheese like this would go for pigs, not for the table). The rest came from the jars and tins in Hector's cupboard, slipped in with the horn shipments by suppliers, Truda said. Each foreign label Truda translated with long-fingered flourishes as she twisted off the lids or jacked them open with her knife—goose fat stirred through lentils, artichokes in oil, a flat tin of black roe marked in Cyrillic script.

Truda talked and Isa listened; Ruby was suspicious of the food. "Enjoy it. This is it," said Truda, sweeping her fork over the low table in an arc. "The people who provided lunch, they telephoned me yesterday. I see why Hector distrusted those contraptions." She pulled a handkerchief, yolk-yellow, from the pocket of her jacket and dabbed it at the corner of her mouth. "Now that Hector's dead they think that Blick's will, well, unravel. No more horn from *them,* they said, until I settle the account. Oh, I can't blame them—they don't know me. But we barely have the horn to make our orders."

"And you can't settle the account?" asked Isa.

Truda laughed. "There's nothing in the coffers, Isa Fly. Hector gave it all away. *Generosity,* that's the true affliction of the Blicks, no matter what Dinah Hatchett Harper and the like of her might say."

Ruby felt uneasy. Knew she had been silently complicit in the cake shop whenever Hector Blick was cited as the cause of Dinah's ills. She tried to bite the artichoke that had been so hard to skewer.

"Is there anything to sell?" said Isa. "Any way of scraping up enough to give your suppliers, just enough to buy a bit of trust in you?" (Ruby thought this was astute, and did not see it as the first hint that under Isa's aegis, Blick's Button Factory would be thoroughly unpicked.)

"The horn down in the shed, I suppose—but it's worth more in buttons than sitting there in sacks, so there's no point selling it until we've made them up." Truda leaned back and let a sigh out at the ceiling.

Isa tugged, discreet, at the collar of her blouse, and before Ruby could say *Am yo too hot here? Shall we go outside and get some air?* Truda said "Be a *dear,* will you, Ruby, and open up the window that I slammed so impolitely. Isa's *baking* here."

Ruby didn't want to be a dear; she didn't like the way that Truda threw out these little marker buoys to ring herself with Isa Fly. She did as Truda said, but did it slowly: lingered at the window with her fingers around the handle and, for a moment, watched Horn Lane. Never seen it from up here, of course. Never seen how the slates overlapped like scales, sheen dulled like the fish on Captin's slab. And oddly, never noticed the vacant sign bracket that hung, curling from the wall, next door to Captin's. The button shop. Closed now, the windows pasted, still, with parcel paper. Mind, Ruby could remember back when Old Mrs. Cole was still alive, the paper stuck there. To keep the stock from fading, Nan Annie said, but they all knew it was to keep the children from the windows. And if children *tried* to come in, hopping at the door with their penny bag-of-bits from the fish shop, Old Mrs. Cole would shout that they were greasing up the panes with chippy fingers; she'd come out on the step and flick her broom at their feet as if they were crumbs that might bring mice.

She'd had no time for children, Old Mrs. Cole. But Ruby knew that if you stood still, just to one side of the door, you could peek in while she was busy with a customer. Old Mrs. Cole was chapel, Ruby knew, and some in chapel didn't hold with buttons. Disagreed with all things fancy and only sewed with hooks and eyes, because buttons were too showy. Ruby thought it fitted, then, that in *her* button shop, Old Mrs. Cole had shelves stacked high with long brown boxes, dull and soft with dust. If you went in for a button, Ruby knew, and started telling Mrs. Cole what you were looking for, she'd stand there, tapping silver scissors on her counter (she kept them hanging from a chain around her neck), and before you'd finished talking she would turn around and pull a box from somewhere near the middle so she didn't have to stretch too high or low, and before you knew it, she'd have snipped a button from a little piece of card and dropped it in a paper bag, avoiding your eye as if it were an illicit pill, her hand stuck out for her pay before you even had a chance to check it was the button that you needed. *Wanting* buttons—frivolous. *Choosing* them, *deliberating*—beyond extravagant.

With her elbows on the window sill, her chin cupped in her hands, Ruby watched the sign casing swing gently from its bracket. The button shop. For all she'd seen from the doorway, she'd never been inside.

"Could open it again, her could," she said, more to herself, to Horn Lane, than to Isa.

"Speak up, Ruby," Truda called. "Ar-tic-u-late."

This, thought Ruby, *is why her get stared at in the bread queue. Her's so elevated, her's all but levitated.* She turned and leaned against the window frame behind her, chin out, all but shouting out each word at Truda, as if she were an old crone with a hand cupped around her ear. "Open up the button shop, yo could, if there's buttons in there somebody could sell."

"An enterprising spirit," Truda said, "but I fear you have a business sense like Hector. That shop has never made him any money. Blick's profits come from buttons by the barrel, not selling mismatched horn blanks ten-a-penny. Now come sit with us, young Ruby. We have figs. From Persia. Just enough for three."

This push-and-pull made Ruby feel quite giddy, and she wished she had the spit to tell her no one liked her, no one trusted her—they all *hated* Blicks. But there was something nervy in the way that Truda preened and swanked, something clipped and fettered. Something Ruby knew, and understood. So she sat down on the arm of Isa's chair and talked with them about the button shop until the tins and cans were emptied but for oil and shards.

It wasn't eating Truda's food that bound up Ruby with the Blicks and with Isa. Time enough she'd eaten sloppy butter pie at the Mission with the Ruths and the Naomis, served with hacked-up onions and carrot, dropped from cold fingers into a stewing pan, a thin, curdled sauce of salad cream and water, slick and chewy. No magic, Ruby knew, in sharing the same table.

Truda pointed her knife at Isa. "So tell me, Isa Fly—where are you staying while you try to unearth this missing sister?"

Ruby spoke up before Isa could. "We was going to see about a room up at the Leopard, wasn't we, Isa?"

"God, no! Not the Leopard! You will not sleep, Miss Fly, with that landlord watching over you and all those jeering men below hawking into sawdust."

"You could stay at Captin's," Ruby said. "On Captin's couch, like last night."

"Now, Ruby, that's neither dignified nor decorous!" Truda held a hand over her mouth in mock disgust. "What will the women of the Ruth and Naomi Thursday Club have to say about *that*? Isa Fly, you cannot stay there. The Fried Fish Shop? I won't allow it. Apart from the impropriety, you'll stink of fish, of vinegar. I have a house on Tenter Lane. Vast. Many rooms. All empty."

Somewhere between the coffee and the figs that Isa sliced so thinly that they melted into sugar on the tongue, it was all fixed. Ruby pushed aside her reservations and all she knew of Blicks. Somewhere between the coffee and the figs, Isa had made Truda an offer—she and Ruby would set the button shop to rights (all Isa had to do was raise her eyebrows in a question and Ruby Abel Tailor acquiesced), as

Truda clearly had enough to do already (Isa swept a hand around the office) and they would spend a few days trying to sell enough to buy a bit of faith from the suppliers. "I'm skeptical," said Truda, "but I could be quite gracious if proved wrong." Isa would stay, not up at the Blicks house, but in the room above the shop. ("Just till you've found your sister," Ruby added.) And Ruby agreed to work as Truda's errand girl, and didn't give a thought to what might follow.

Chapter 3

Nail, *v.* 1. To fix or fasten (a person or thing) with nails on or to something else. 2. To fix or fasten (the eyes, mind, etc.) to or on the object of one's attention. 3. To secure; to succeed in catching; to steal.

SUNDAY MORNING AND, at the Hunting Tree, the cockerel woke Ruby with the light. She scrubbed her face with water from the jug (still icy, though the air was warm already), tore the pig-brush through her hair, and as she did her buttons up, watched Nan Annie in the garden with a basket on her arm, pacing down the rows, just wide enough to step along the worn, compacted paths, first one foot; then another. Canes leaning, straining. Nan Annie crouching, reaching. Beyond her, fruit bushes; beyond them, the orchard at the top end of the garden and a high wall crooked around it. A gate was set well back in the wall, forking hinges rusted, green paint flaking free; but for all that, Ruby knew it was quite solid, just unused. It would be the quickest way to slip through to St. Barbara's—the long grass of the priory lay just beyond the wall—but the handle was corroded and they always went the road-way, she and Annie, on their visits. Ruby's great-grandmother, Eliza, had stayed at St. Barbara's infirmary for more than thirty years. The wounds that took her there had healed up long ago, but, as Eliza said, "The sorors ud be lost without Eliza," so she wouldn't dream of leaving. Every Sunday Nan Annie went up from Hunting Tree, clean sheets for her mother folded up with lavender in one basket, and new pickings from the garden in another for the nuns.

One thought worried Ruby while she tugged her sheet and folded up her blanket and shook out the eiderdown bunched up at the bottom of her bed: *What if Isa comes to like Horn Lane so much she doesn't want to go back to the sea?* She traced the cobalt dolphins, looping nose to tail across the quilting, cherry red, and tugged her bedding straight. *What if her becomes so sunk in Blickses her forgets what her has come for?* She walked down to the low window with the whorly handle at the far end of the landing, past rooms with unused beds that never needed making (a house spread thin, this was, and meant for many children). She took up the white jug with the haughty lip, filled with camellia, and took it to the bathroom for fresh water. *What if we never find the missing daughter, and Isa Fly won't take me to the sea?* She set the filled jug squarely on the thinning rose-weave runner. Wormholes, tiny dark pinpricks, all along the edge. She eased the window open, but no breeze. She leaned out of the window as far as her shoulders (like Truda Cole Blick the day before). No sea, of course. No water. Their clumpy vegetable garden and, beyond it, fields planted up with larches sloping down toward the town. So much earth, heaped up here in the middle of the island. *What if I am never near seawater?* Ruby thought. She keened for it. She yearned to feel a salt-breeze on her face.

She ran downstairs to catch her nan before she left. On the table, tea was cooling in the pot; an end of bread and a plate of butter, clear at the edges where it had melted and set hard. She poured tea in a tin cup from the hooks beside the grate and took it outside. Nan Annie was plucking stringy beans and sweet peas for the sorors.

"Nan," she called. "Dun yo know anything about a man as left Cradle Cross when yo was young and left a little girl behind?"

"Who's asking?" Annie snapped and stopped her picking.

"This woman who just come to Cradle Cross." Ruby joined her nan down by the beans. "Someone must of took the daughter in: the mom died, I think, and the dad went away."

"Sounds like yo, Ruby."

She flinched at the comparison. "This ay me—it's years ago." She made the calculation in her head. "Somewhere either side of 1900. Lily Fly, the girl is, and her dad was called Moonie."

Nan Annie twisted off a bean and dropped it in her basket. "This Moonie did her in."

"What?"

"Sounds like he did her in. He hit his wife too hard one time. He killed her, then he ran away."

A woman killed, thought Ruby. *Moonie a fugitive?*

"Doe look so shocked. It happens."

"Yo heard of him then, Nan? Yo heard of Moonie Fly? And dun yo know what happened to the daughter?"

"No, Ruby. I'm speculating." She pushed past Ruby; walked toward the house. "I ay heard of him."

So she wasn't saying Moonie killed his wife?

"No, Ruby, I was making it up. I never heard of *him,* no more un *her,*" she called out, without turning round. "Yo heard of pigs that's wanting feeding?"

Ruby fed the pigs (the peal of crude indignant squeals at being left, unfed, since yesterday) then drank a little of her tea, but it was too strong and it dried her tongue. She tipped it on the bare ground by the pigsty, where it pooled and did not sink. (They had dug hard to work this clay, to make this garden thrive.)

Before she left, Nan Annie pressed a coin in Ruby's hands: "Put this on the plate at chapel for me," and then she marched off, leaning forward from the waist, the basket on her arm. She called over her shoulder, as she did every Sunday, "Dinah ull tell me if yo doe put it on, so doe think as yo can spend it all on sherbet."

Truda Cole Blick had paid Ruby to be Blick's errand girl with the loaning of a bicycle; she hadn't asked her to do anything too sinister, so far—just slap up a big bill poster with thick paste at the Breach end of Horn Lane and push a few hand-copies through some designated doors last night. Now Ruby settled Jamie Abel's dinner in the basket on the front and, from the handlebars, hung two net bags with provisions for Isa. She eased three eggs down deep into the pockets of her gray serge coat (she could have done without the heat, but it was sturdy and it would protect the eggs), then kicked the stand clear of the ground and, hitching her skirt up high, she straddled the new bike, edging forward on her toes until she reached the road. Downhill, then, past woods and hardwood hedges, bumping, rattling down the dirt track till she got down to the Ludleye Road, tarred new that summer and still sticky in the hot. Past a batch of houses and a young boy with a cart; a woman with a basket. Legs out rigid and her fingers stretched out ready on the brakes, Ruby found she couldn't keep her thoughts on Isa, or the sea, or what Moonie (if Nan Annie was right) might have done to Lily's mother. She freewheeled past a field of broken horses, eyes narrowing against the early sun, and leaning back into a modest, following wind.

Hurtling down the Breach, she took the bend into Horn Lane just too quick and skittered on the cobbles. The weight of the net bags shifted. She could perhaps have held the steering steady if she hadn't been distracted by the swollen music spilling once more from the open window at the far end of Horn Lane: distracted into thinking about Truda; how the music meant that Truda must be working, not diverting Isa from her quest. Unless Isa Fly was up there, drinking coffee, bittersweet, with Truda lolling on her wing-backed chair . . . She swerved too late, her backbone jarring, and the handlebars wrenched free from her grip. She was too close to the gutter. The rubber of the front wheel yelped against the high curb and she fell sideways, half-astride, onto the pavement outside the button shop. She couldn't right herself—the bicycle fell with her, her skirt hem caught on the saddle, her left leg hoisted high above the crossbar.

She extricated herself gingerly, looking around and hoping no one saw. Her cheeks pinked. It was not a bad fall, Ruby told herself. The fruit would be bruised, but Jamie Abel's bowl was unbroken, his dinner saved, all but a dark patch where the gravy'd swilled up against the top-cloth when she fell. She set the bowl down on the pavement and tried to make the bike lean on its kick-stand, but it wouldn't, not on cobbles, falling three times over before she heaved it up onto the pavement and leaned it instead against the wall. She yanked her skirt straight—not torn, thank goodness. Smut-flakes had settled on it and smudged to gray when she bent to rub them off. (Ash always settled on the streets of Cradle Cross, and twisted up in lithe play around the ankles in the slightest wind.) Her coat had no doubt saved her elbow from a skinning, but there was a patch above her left knee scraped pink and a long gash just inside her right knee where a protruding twist of metal had snagged the skin; from it, Ruby's blood welled, livid and effusive. She was glad no one saw.

Except, of course, they did. The door-within-the-gate was opening at the Blick's end, and Isa Fly was coming out, intent on Ruby, and it was only now that Ruby felt her eyes prickle with tears, wanting Isa Fly to tend to her, but at the same time longing to be brave and bold and, most of all, dry-eyed.

"All right, I am," she called, her stomach tightening as Isa came toward her. "I day fall very far, or very hard." Blood trickled down her shin.

"What is all this?" Isa gestured at the bags. "It's not safe, Ruby, cycling like that."

"Theym things for you," Ruby said, but what she had gathered up at home seemed immoderate. The jar of pickled cabbage had become uncorked and vinegar had seeped into the tablecloth she had brought down for Isa.

"Let's look at you." Isa bent to look at Ruby's left leg, then the right, and bent each leg back at the knee. The gash stung with the stretching. "Truda said you steered straight for the pavement." Isa gently probed the flesh around each foot to check for swelling: cautious, firm, as if Ruby were a strange, unstabled horse.

"I day!" said Ruby. Her belly fizzed and twitched. "And what was yo doing up there anyway?" She pulled her ankle free of Isa.

"Having breakfast." Isa Fly spoke lightly as she got up on her feet.

"But *I* got breakfast for you, see!" Ruby reached into her pocket. Her fingers came out yolky, stuck with bits of broken shell and skeins of white, and she turned away from Isa, biting hard down on her lip.

Isa pulled a hankie from her pocket and held it up for Ruby.

"Ay no need to dirty yours up." Ruby took a cloth from her own pocket; pulled each finger with it till it came clean. Picked each shard of shell off with a fingernail. Didn't look at Isa. Didn't cry. In this, Ruby was still firmly planted in her childhood—hadn't learned, yet, how to fold her anguish up and tuck it in a pocket and pretend it wasn't there. Instead she let it settle like a shawl on that droop-stoop of her neck, and whatever else they said of Isa Fly, she showed a gentleness with Ruby's injured pride. Shrewd enough to treat her brisk and not to catch her eye.

"I've got a good tincture for sharp grazes like this one. Come inside." Isa smiled and put her arm through Ruby's. For a moment Ruby tensed and looked up at Truda's window. Truda raised her cigarette in salutation—"Quite an entrance, Ruby!"—then drew back from the window.

Ruby broke free from Isa's arm and bent to pick up Jamie Abel's dinner, wincing as the skin stretched on her knee.

Isa said, "When I've seen to this leg, you can make me tea. To make up for missing breakfast."

There hadn't been time, yesterday, to clean the paper from the windows, so it was gloomy in the button shop, dust motes lazy in the crack of sun that eked in between the top edge of the paper and the window frame. Isa led her straight through the back door to the kitchen, the table set out with two cups and a squat green milk jug covered with a beaded cloth; a stone jar filled with tansies, lanky, bright. As if Isa'd always been here, Ruby thought, as if it should have always been this way.

Yesterday, she'd worked in the button shop all afternoon, after she (as her first errand for Blick's) had washed up all the cups and jars and tins and, as instructed, put the coffee grounds aside for fertilizing Hector's rhododendrons. More washing up to follow in the button shop, where she and Isa had stood at the cracked porcelain sink and swilled out bottles, jars and set them, mouths down, on a clean cloth on the window sill to drain. Isa had come and gone that afternoon: Ruby prompting her to slip out to the towpath with the scrape and clatter of each passing boat, in case the boatman knew anything of Moonie Fly or Lil. In between, they scrubbed the wood up with a hard brush, rubbed beeswax into the oak counter. They buffed up all the glass with muslin, and when it gleamed, all clear and green, Isa snipped the buttons from their cards and dropped them, clinking, into jars. She sat on the high stool, sorting buttons with a tiny spoon hung from a cord around her neck, laying like with like. It was only when

Isa sorted a little jar of neat, pale buttons, gently curving, thin as fingernails, that Ruby's reservations about Blick's Button Factory floated to the surface, but Isa stood the jar up on a high shelf and told Ruby just how glad she was that Ruby and her Captin had brought her in last night and Ruby thought, *Last night!* and how distended time had got since then, and how it felt that she'd known Isa for a lifetime, and how she wanted Isa's fingers twisting up her hair, and she forgot about the gently curving buttons.

Now, Sunday morning, her skinned knee smarted and she was uneasy. She insisted on making the tea first for Isa, but with hackles up and thinking how it wasn't fair that Truda had stolen her when Ruby had no good friends for herself. *Does her think as this is all I'm good for, making tea?* She almost said to Isa *I'm sorry I doe have any coffee for yo,* but she bit it back and she was glad she did. While the tea was brewing, Isa made her sit still, knelt down at her feet, and with a bowl of salty water and a cloth she blotted up the blood (frowning, saying how it flowed too freely for her liking) and washed the cut on Ruby's leg, and pressed a wadded rag to stem the bleeding.

Ruby bit her lip to stop the wincing.

Isa stood up, then, instructing Ruby to keep pressing on the wad. She took a small tin from the bag that never left her side. Her fingers flew up to the cord around her neck and from underneath her shirt she drew up the tiny spoon with the neat hole in its handle. She eased the lid off with the blunt end of the spoon; snipped a bit of muslin from a clean cloth hanging at the grate and, laying out the cloth in her cupped palm, used the handle of the spoon to scoop a little of the livid yellow paste out of the tin.

"Did you make it up yourself?" Ruby said, suspicious, because there was no name stamped on the tin, no BRADBURY'S PREPARATION like the tin Nan Annie kept for cuts. "Is it mustard?"

"Not mustard," Isa said. "Arnica and yarrow. Other things." She pressed the paste into the cloth and knelt to hold it firm against the cut on Ruby's leg. "Keep it on," said Isa, standing up to wash her hands, her little spoon, "until I say to take it off."

Ruby sat, obedient, bent to press the edges of the cloth against her leg. It burned a little, Isa's paste, but Ruby knew that sometimes mending hurt and so she watched as Isa took her fly-box from her bag. She flicked the catch up and from an indentation in the lid took out a needle and a reel of yarn so pale that it was almost invisible. "Filament, from Whalemouth," Isa snipped a piece off, "is not to be wasted. Mind you never use it idly." (Ruby felt a thrill at this, at Isa Fly instructing her, and it's so hard to be *wary* when you're thrilled.)

Isa slipped the needle from its sheath and held the line of filament up high to thread it through the eye. She missed it, several times, and Ruby wondered if it would be rude to offer help. "That looks tricky," she said.

"This blind eye," Isa tapped the corner of her right eye with the needle, "means I can't judge depth. Not at first glance, anyway. There's other ways of telling."

"Dun yo want me to do it?"

"What, my *threading*?" Isa said, incredulous.

It wasn't quite that Isa was offended by the offer, Ruby thought, or that she thought Ruby incapable, she felt sure. Maybe that she wasn't used to being helped.

"Ruby, I have threaded flies for Moonie ever since I could hold a needle."

"But when yo take me to the sea wi yo," said Ruby, testing Isa out, "will yo teach me how to sew flies? Will you teach me how to fish?"

Isa didn't answer and there was something in her briskness as she knelt down on the flagstones with the needle clamped between her lips that made Ruby wonder if Isa Fly had meant it when she'd agreed to take her to the sea.

Isa pulled a piece of flannel tight round Ruby's leg. She took the needle from her lips and sat back on her heels. "Moonie likes to think he taught me how to fish when I was tiny. Not that he ever caught a thing—he said there was a curse put on his rod. He taught by telling, not by doing, Moonie did." (Ruby didn't like the sound of Moonie Fly, who seemed content to sit back while another did the work.) "He'd anchor us a mile offshore, and when I'd hooked us supper, he would light his pipe and watch the waters while I dived and bucked and whooped. That's before he took against the sea and what was in it."

"And what *was* in it?" Ruby's eyes grew wide, but Isa dropped her gaze and leaned in close to Ruby's leg. Ruby pulled back sharp, thinking in that instant that Isa was about to plunge the needle in her skin, but Isa only pinched the flannel to a seam, and, glancing up at her, said, "Ruby Abel Tailor. What *do* you think of me?"

As if, thought Ruby, *I had spoken out my fear of being all sewn up.*

Quicker than a Ruth or a Naomi, Isa sewed the cloth around her leg so it stayed up, tight but not constricting. Isa stood. She sank the needle, swift, into its sheath, and placed it back into the box. She pushed it back into her bag and walked away from Ruby, and leaned against the wall just by the window.

She doesn't want me here, thought Ruby. *I am no use to her.* She had yet to prove her worth to Isa—they were no further on than yesterday in finding Lil, no closer now to going to the sea. She looked at Isa staring at the Cut. "I've written down a list of all the Lils as I know of in Cradle Cross. I'll ask about today. We ull find her, Isa." She stood and flexed her knee to test out Isa's dressing: it stayed tight. "I gi yo my word."

"Don't say that, Ruby." Isa kept her eyes fixed on the Cut. "Don't make me a promise you can't keep."

" 'Seek and ye will find': that ay my promise, Isa. That is Bible."

"You sound so very certain."

"And yo ay?"

"I am sure of nothing, these past days."

She thought of Nan Annie; her speculation. She crossed the room to stand close behind Isa. "If Lily's here to find, then we ull find her."

Isa turned; squeezed Ruby's arm and told her to sit down. "Rest that leg until the bleeding stops." She became brisk; poured the tea and sorted through her bag set on the table. "I heard trains this morning. The railway station: is it that way, up the Cut?"

"Why?"

"How long does it take to reach Muckeleye?"

"Yo want to get a train?"

"I want to know where I *could* catch a train."

"Am yo leaving?"

Isa took her fly-box from her bag again.

"Why dun yo want to get a train?"

"I'm simply asking where the station is." She flicked the catch and looked inside the box.

Ruby explained about the Junction on the other side of Rudge's; not for passengers, just for freight from off the Cut.

"Buses, then." Isa picked out a hook and a little cloth. "The bus to Muckeleye."

"Yo think as yo'll find your sister there?"

"No, Ruby, I don't." Isa polished up the hook.

"Yo will find her, Isa!"

"So you keep insisting."

"Yo ay been here two days yet and already yoom fit to gi it up? Yo cor gi up so easy! We just need to know more about um: him and Lil; her mom. Something to nudge a memory out the back of people's heads. Have yo got a photograph of Moonie stowed in here?" Ruby reached for Isa's bag, but Isa pulled it out of Ruby's reach.

"No."

"Well, could he send one in the post?"

"He isn't fit for such things, Ruby."

Maybe they could write a list of questions, then, said Ruby, and read it to the doctor on the 'phone: where Moonie lived in Cradle Cross, or who he worked with; what Lily's mother looked like; her family name before she took the Fly; or, if Isa wanted, she could come up to the Club that afternoon—the Ruth and Naomi Thursday Club (it met, Ruby explained, on Sundays, too).

"They know all the people round about, and some of um are so old as they ud of known Moonie for definite. Trembly Em is in her middle sixties: her is even older than my nan. If Moonie went to chapel, her'd of knowed him."

He wasn't one for chapel, Isa said, nor Roman church, nor God by any light. So Ruby asked if he was one for drinking. Isa nodded.

"Well, in the Leopard, maybe. Captin could ask about. Is he a man for friends? What kind of man is he?" (*The kind*, she thought, *who'd leave a child behind, with cause enough to think the mother dead.*)

Isa set the hook down on the table. She pressed a finger to her gauzy eye.

"Could the doctor ask him just *one* question? A name for Lily's mother. He woe have forgot that."

"He had plenty of names for her, Ruby."

Ruby said she didn't understand.

"Crude names." Isa put the hook back in it place. "Coarse names. Curses."

"Maybe he just meant um for a nickname."

"No, Ruby, he didn't."

"Maybe there was clues in what he said."

"Clues?" She shook her head. "He can't be questioned this way, Ruby."

"Isa, if yoom worried about what made Moonie leave—"

Isa slammed the lid down on the fly-box. " 'A ripe plum wanting picking,' Moonie said."

Ruby bit her lip.

" 'Her turned sour in the eating: made me sick.' Do you find a clue hidden in that?"

Ruby flushed and hot tears started up. She bent forward; made a show of looking at her knee. She pressed her tongue up hard against her teeth.

Isa walked over to the window, and when she turned around her tone was more gentle. "Fishing, Ruby." Isa pressed her eye. "To my knowledge he never caught a fish, but he liked to go fishing."

Ruby looked up, tentative. "So yo could ask the fishermen; the ones as fish that stretch after the Locks and after Lapple. If Moonie liked to fish they might have knowed him. Tell yo where he lived, they might, or who he was married to."

"I will. Len said he'll take me. I am expecting him."

"Oh." Despondent, Ruby fiddled with the edges of the cloth around her knee, but Isa asked her what she knew about these blind men by the Cut.

They drank their tea and Ruby told Isa that these men were half blinded from working chain—white hot—too long and sat hunched up on the Cut and tried to catch a bit of something for their supper. Told her there were some in Cradle Cross who thought them twice-blessed, these blinded men, because they were twice-protected. First, because the able men who struck on chain were kept at *home* for War Work while others from down Blickses took up wide-legged poses in their khaki. A second time protected, because if they'd finished with the chain and weren't yet forty (still young enough to be called up to the fight), it was broken backs or burned-out eyes that kept them home, unfit for war. Ruby said that Dinah Hatchett Harper got to wishing she had built a little furnace out the back for her boy Horace and got him striking on a chain instead of getting him apprenticed down at Blickses: a blinded son, a broken son, would be better than no son at all.

A knock at the back door: Captin, in his Sunday coat, hair slicked, forehead glowing from the sun. He kicked the dry dust off his boots and waited to be asked in. This neatened Captin; strange. All those times he'd lain down like a tamed bear on the floor, roaring, cuffing softly at her while she clambered on his chest, and here he was all done up to go fishing!

"Len! Come in!" Isa smiled—a broad, enticing smile.

"How am yo, Miss Fly?" He glanced about the room and peered through to the shop. "Yo made it look nice."

"We did it yesterday," said Ruby. "I told yo last night. In the fish shop."

Captin tossed her a light, "Oh?" but his eyes were fixed on Isa. "Ready, then, Miss Fly?"

He hasn't even noticed this patch on my knee.

Isa glanced at Ruby. "Would you like to come with us, Ruby? Or is your leg too sore for all that walking?"

Before Ruby could answer, Captin said, "Her cor. Yo cor fish, can yo, Rube? Her nan doe like her to go near the water. Annie ud have a fit if her knew as I'd took Ruby by the Cut!" He was halfway out the door already, calling that they'd better get up there quick before the sun had sucked up all the water.

Isa pushed her fly-box back into her bag. "I'm sorry, Ruby."

Ruby pinched the skin beneath her chin. She'd felt, for a moment, that she owned Isa; not like—*finders, keepers*—she might own a treasure washed up from a wrecked ship; she owned Isa like an article of faith. She sucked hard on her tongue. She felt a scalding knot of tears scratch once more at the corners of her eyes. Ruby could not look at Isa, yet she wanted Isa close, to have Isa plait her clumsy hair and rock her still and sing close and sweet and calming in her ear. Ruby stared down at the flowers on Isa's table: she traced the shape of them, following the stems down to the jar.

But Isa was speaking to her and something in her tone commanded Ruby and she lifted her eyes to meet Isa's.

She had taken her book from her bag. *"This,"* she said, and gave the book to Ruby, "is how I learned to fish. Read it." She squeezed Ruby's shoulder. "Truda's making lunch at noon. Come up and tell me if you've made any sense of it."

She took the book to be a promise, Ruby did, that one clear morning she and Isa would stride out toward the sea, into the shallows with their rods over their shoulders; one evening they would build a bake-hole on the shaley beach and burn their fingers breaking up the fish. She played this out like a story as she took her dad his bowl (and didn't stop to talk to him today) then sank down on the ashy curb outside the button shop and settled the book on her lap. A thick volume, bound in hide the color of dried blood. Several books, in fact, bound up together, collected by Juliana Berners, Abbess of St. Albans.

The book needed two hands to hold it open, and all her concentration. A blocky type—even when she could decipher it, the words were unfamiliar. Distracted, too—the gut-pull of that music out of Blickses! A panicked flutter in her belly—she would *never* learn to fish this way, she didn't know the things that Isa knew. But as her eye began to flicker back and forth across a sentence, resting lightly on the words, she found she grew accustomed to them; the edges, then the substance, then the sense emerging like familiar shapes in a darkened room.

She decided she would save the fishing part, the *Treatise on Fishing with an Angle,* until she felt she could read the letters with full confidence. Practiced, first of all, on *The Book of Secrets.* These pages opened readily and wide—the spine was broken, here, from frequent reading—and Ruby soon saw why they had been favored. It was rich in detail and practical instruction, and she found this calming and absorbing: a recipe for book glue; instructions on mending torn pages; advice on lace making; planting patterns for herbs; how to restore a dovecote; the dimensions of a man's shirt. She let the cover fall from time to time, then opened up the book at random: names of wines; properties of a good horse; four things to dread. There was something soothing in the rhythm of this book and all its certainty: "A hare is coursed; a boar is vexed; a wolf is trapped, a hind is chased."

So lost was Ruby, so utterly absorbed in Isa's book that for the first time in all the years she could remember, she missed Sunday chapel and did not remember it until she chanced to glance toward the top end of Horn Lane. Saw Glenda, Dinah's daughter, standing, staring from the Breach, carrying a wide wooden tray covered with a towel. She was younger than the other Ruths—not much older than Miss Blick—but Glenda Hatchett Harper wielded the authority of age. There was compulsion in her stance, and Ruby (with the sense of being woken suddenly) pushed the book into her pinny pocket and stumbled up to meet her. She pulled Nan Annie's coin out from her coat and tried to wipe it, still sticky from the broken eggs.

"Trying to deafen us, is her?" Glenda shouted down Horn Lane to Ruby. Eyes like flies in whey, Glenda was a sticky woman; viscous where her mother was all acid. "Missed yo was this morning, Ruby." Black treacle in her voice and in her eyes. "And that, Ruby, was such a shame because it ud of been your turn to take the giving plate around, and yoom so careful and so quick. Mrs. Fine-knee Bacon stepped in, which was kind of her. Her shaking wor too bad. Her day drop the plate." (Em Fine-knee Bacon: known, not to her face of course, as Trembly Em, because in times of agitation she was over-taken by a shiver springing from her fingertips. When the shiver started, she would hold her head between her braced and quivering fingertips until it ran its course, right through her.) Glenda shifted so her other hip could take the weight of all the custards on the tray. "But sure, I am, as Ruby had a sound excuse. Sure, I am, as Ruby day spend *all* the morning with her nose pushed in a book while we was all at chapel singing out our praises to the Lord."

Ruby shifted from one foot to another, not thinking about chapel and the giving plate, because something Glenda said had sparked a flint in her. Trembly Em was keeper of the chapel register of births and deaths. There might be record of a Lily Fly in there, or at least of Moonie and of who he married; where they lived.

Glenda waited, eyebrows raised, expectant, hoisting up her smile.

Ruby scuffed the ash up with one shoe then ground it back down with the other, because she knew that if she looked up, Glenda would see she didn't feel ashamed of missing chapel. "I was taking breakfast down to Isa Fly."

"Isa Fly?" A new glint in Glenda's dark eyes, and a sharp tilt of the head. "Is that that one who got yo asking all her questions, yesterday? That one who's squatting in the button shop?"

Now Dinah's Glenda was more diligent than any of the Ruths and the Naomis when it came to teasing truth from tattle. She was agile as a spider and tenacious, working, weaving, and before you knew it she had leaped with what seemed loose and inconclusive and, spinning out a fine and filmy thread behind her, anchored it to what she knew already, creating something orderly and treacherous. So Ruby, guarded, sank inside herself a little, reluctant to have Glenda steal from her what she had so far gleaned of Isa-from-the-sea and try to spin with it.

But Glenda shoved her cake tray into Ruby's arms and, Dinah-style, planted her hands firmly on her hips. "Look here! A nerve, her's got!" She was glaring at the bill that Ruby pasted up just yesterday for Truda. " 'Notice is hereby given that pay is to be *docked* for every button *scuffed, chipped* or incorrectly *drilled*.' " She poked the poster with each word, then tried to prize the corners from the board to tear it down, but Ruby'd stuck it well and Glenda soon gave up.

Ruby felt it would be prudent to divert Glenda's course away from Blick's and saw fit not to mention that it was she who'd pasted this bill up yesterday for Truda. "Yo know everyone about the Cradles, doe yo, more or less?"

"What?" Glenda's nose was wrinkled as if a gnat was at her.

"When yo was growing up, did yo know a girl named Lily Fly?"

"What's that to do wi Blickses?"

"Nothing. It's just that everyone comes into Maison Hester's for their bread. They always have. I thought yo might of knowed her."

"What am yo on about? Her doe work at Blickses, does her?"

"No, I doe think so . . ."

"Well, then. I cor press her to help us sort this lot out, can I? How her has *spit* for this I do not know. Scuffed? I'll give her scuffed."

Glenda peeled back a bandage to show Ruby where the flesh was pur-pling on her thumb-heel around three oozy V-shaped nicks. "*That's* scuffed." She thrust her other hand at Ruby (*like that picture in the* Illustrated Gospel, Ruby thought, *where the Risen Lord holds out his hands to Doubting Thomas and looks indignant*) and spread it palm-up under Ruby's nose, so close, so sudden that Ruby reared and took a step down backward from the pavement, toppling on the road so that she nearly dropped the cake tray. "What does her think? I prick me fingers for the joy of it? Blickses doe pay *me* extra for me in-juries."

The custards had all lurched to one side with her fall. Ruby tried to shake the tray to nudge them flat again, but one fell face down on the ground.

"Oh, gi it here." Glenda snatched the cake tray back from Ruby. "Yo can have that custard free. A bit of dirt woe hurt. Yo see, our Ruby? *That* is generosity. *That* is understonding. Accidents can hap-pen. Did I say as yo ud have to pay for damaging me goods? No, I day. And *that* is what the Blicks doe understond. Pay docked? Dock *her,* I will, and I woe be the only one . . . Now look! There's sommat of the specter about *her.*"

Ruby followed Glenda's gaze along Horn Lane. Isa was outside the button shop and looking up toward them, the full sun dancing in the mirrors of her skirt.

"I got to go!" Ruby brushed the flour where it had settled on her clothes. She began to run down Horn Lane, but her knee was sting-ing. She slowed down, but kept walking, and she did not look back.

When Truda saw that Isa had brought Ruby up for dinner (Truda called it lunch), she sighed and raised her eyebrows and Ruby shifted from one foot to the other. "Is the gallant Captin also joining us today?" But Captin had taken fish up to Nan Annie. "A guilty fish, that is, Ruby, because he's been with Isa," Truda said. "When your grandma slaps it on the plate tonight, don't eat it. Mark my words: guilty fish tastes bitter."

They ate sardines on toast; then, while Isa telephoned the doctor, Miss Blick taught Ruby how she should make coffee. "So you don't fish, Ruby? (No, wait for the water to cool down just a little!) Or perhaps you didn't want to play at *chaperone*."

Ruby shook her head. "It wor that."

"I could be offended! Isa's virtue is in danger from the ancient
Leonard Salt, but you see a need to escort her up here?"

"Isa asked me to come up. I day invite myself."

"Or was it that they wouldn't let you join them? Captin wanted Isa
to himself and Isa humored him—"

"Isa *wanted* me to go. Her *asked* if I'd go fishing." She remembered
Captin, quick to remind her of Nan Annie's prohibition.

Truda raised her eyebrows. "Yes?"

"It's just I ay supposed—" Ruby stopped short: what would she tell
Truda? That Nan Annie wouldn't let her walk beside the water? *I will
look saft-headed; like a bab!*

But if she wouldn't tell Miss Blick, she wanted Isa Fly to understand. Nan Annie had her reasons, Ruby knew, even if *she* didn't fully
understand them. She had heard someone say that in the bread queue,
and she saw these reasons hung up, solid, gently swinging like the
haunches in the meat shop. She resolved to show the Almanac to Isa
when they were alone; the yellowed cutting, pasted in. (The facing
page: THE MAN WHO SLEPT THREE DAYS INSIDE A WHALE AND LIVED
TO TELL THE TALE.) The photograph was blurred, but clear enough to
see the sea, all squirls; an upturned, fractured hull; women, mouths
like Os in huddles on the quay. A caption, underneath: "The Sinking
of the *Lickey Bell*: Severnsea Bore takes Sixty Souls." *We lost my
Grandad Jonah in that boat,* she'd say to Isa. *And our baby, Grace.
Her ud of been my auntie, if her'd lived.*

She wouldn't trust this story to Miss Blick, so instead told her that
it was a Sunday morning; time for chapel, not for fishing.

"Yes, but the ungodly Ruby didn't go to chapel. I saw you," she
pointed a coffee spoon at Ruby, "sitting on the curb. A child sunk in
a book in Cradle Cross—it catches one's attention."

Exclusion wasn't new to Ruby: each term school-yard circles
formed, re-formed in new configurations, with Ruby always stood a
pace outside. She'd told herself, till now, that friends brought with
them ties and obligations that—*I am saving up to buy myself a passage to the sea*—she would be unable to fulfill. Besides, there were

places where she was always welcome: the Fried Fish Shop, for one; St. Barbara's Priory.

But now Isa was here, and Ruby found she didn't want to be left out. Nor, it seemed, did Truda, for when Isa came back in, they each clamored to be first to ask her how her father was. Ruby offered coffee, but before she could carry it to Isa, Truda strode up and took the cup from her; announcing that it wasn't *coffee* Isa needed, but distraction: a drive into the hills; a walk over to the inn at Parry Lean. She emptied Ruby's coffee in the sink; told Isa she would buy her ginger beer.

Ruby pressed on, loud, persistent. "I thought as we could go up to the Mission, to the Ruth and Naomis." They could ask them about Moonie, or if anyone knew who took Lily in.

Truda laughed. "God, Ruby. That will drive her into deeper misery! What if one of *them* is Lily Fly? Surely it is better *not* to know! Imagine finding out that Dinah, of all people, took her in; that Glenda Hatchett Harper is your kin . . ." She put her hand on Isa's shoulder. "Come for my sake, then, if not for your own. I need to get away from this"—Truda looked around the room—"an hour. Two, at most. Think of it: clean air, and a cool drink in the shade."

And to Ruby's cold dismay, Isa consented. Ruby flushed. She busied herself collecting up the plates, stacking them in the sink. She looked behind the little curtain underneath for soap flakes and a brush, but Truda took them from her. "You're not my kitchen maid. If you insist on making yourself useful, go!" She pointed the dishbrush toward the stairs. "Interrogate your Ruths and their Naomis."

Such triumph was there in Miss Blick that Ruby could not hold her protest in and spoke in a fierce whisper: How would she help Isa to find her sister, up the Leans, when there was nothing there but sorors and folk courting! Ruby frowned and folded her arms as she'd seen Dinah do, but Truda laughed and said they'd call in at St. Barbara's if it would bring Ruby some satisfaction. The sorors ran a girls' home around the back of Parry Lean; abandoned infants; wayward girls. "All coal-tar soap; redemption," Truda said. "We'll ask if *they* took in this forsaken Lily." And before Ruby could find a way to step into their circle, Truda ushered Ruby down the stairs.

Chapter 4

Stitch, *n.* 1. A thrust, stab. 2. A sharp sudden local pain. 3. A grudge, dislike, spite.

THE RUTH and Naomi Thursday Club was not founded to burn witches. It was founded back in 1918, in the dulled wake of the War, so that women could, in silence, share their grief; unfold it for the others, hold it up, compare the warp and weft, the size, the stitching.

"My daughter drowned before her had a birthday. My grief is here; this handkerchief. I've worked her letters here, fine stitches in the corner, but look at all the rest of it, this empty space, that says what might have been."

"Yes, yo were blessed with grief so small that yo can keep it in your pocket. My son was fully grown when I lost him to the War. My grief is larger than a sail."

"Ah, but I also lost the shelter of my husband. I had the time to know him and to love him and he kept me warm and dry. So I have draped my grief about me for a cloak to keep the wind away."

On and on. These women, sitting in a circle, tending to their grief and mending where the years had worn it thin. This was their tradition: those who had no grave to trim and tend, nowhere to kneel and weep and feel the warm earth easing damp into their knees, worked up handkerchiefs as tokens of remembrance to fold away in scented drawers or keep under their pillows. A new handkerchief, each year. The birthday of the lost one picked in silks; sometimes the day they'd died. Devices more elaborate, each year. A simple ox-eye daisy chain at first, around the hem, that twined the next year with green ivy, and the next with rosemary. Among themselves they called it "losslinen."

Nan Annie hung hers from a sheltered, secret tree. Ruby knew because she'd followed her one autumn morning when the sun was low. Something furtive and determined in her nan had caught Ruby's eye and Ruby had shadowed her, crouching low in the deep ditch that ran along the Lean High Road; around the outside of the west wall of the priory; underneath the wooden lich-gate and along the hatched clay path; past leaning graves that strained against the incline of the hill. She'd been disappointed, then—Ruby'd been there every other week with clippers to trim her mother's grave—as Nan Annie's fingers only trailed against Beth's gravestone as she passed (almost absentmindedly, like someone in the draper's stroking the loose edge of a bolt of fabric but with eyes trained on another altogether). Toward St. Barbara's Common Chapel with its high red side, Ruby'd followed her, toward a wall of aging thickened larches, where Nan Annie paused and looked around her (not seeing Ruby, who was squatting in the long grass of an unloved grave). And then, Nan Annie wasn't there.

Before that autumn morning, Ruby'd thought this line of larches marked the boundary of the graveyard, set out trim and careful on three sides of the church. As lightly as she could, she ran toward them. There were two lines of larches, one set back behind the other, offset to form an opening. Beyond this hidden entrance, the narrow clay path dipped quite suddenly and she'd watched Nan Annie slowing, stepping down sideways. Ruby had stooped and waited in between the larches, watching through their legs, but the hollow, scooped out deep in the soft clay and shaded by the chapel, was rich and green—so thick with wych-elms that Ruby couldn't see what Nan Annie was doing. Ruby'd drawn back further, waited deep beneath the wide arms of a cedar near the lich-gate so that she'd not miss Nan Annie when she left. She'd leaned against the trunk (angled hearts and dates scratched in the bark, and squashed ciggy butts in the dips between the roots), taken out her Almanac and looked over her lists while she was waiting. She had many lists of things she wanted; she'd always wanted sleek hair, just like Truda Cole Blick, so she'd written, "Hair, 100 strokes each night." But then, with just one brushing, it bushed out like a frightened animal, coarse and dense and dull. She thought that she was being punished for her vanity, so wrote down, "Nine Ways to be Holy," but then she failed to learn her Scripture, and was weighed down by a heavy lump of disappointment, leaden in her belly. This lump could be shifted only by another list of ways to change. The weight of all this unfinished business, all these uncrossed items on her lists, pressed down on Ruby like the knowledge of a curse. The trouble with this curse was that she felt she'd put it on herself when she wasn't paying attention and had no idea of how to lift it.

So Ruby, underneath the cedar, had been glad when Nan Annie emerged, but stayed put until she'd gone beyond the lich-gate, out onto the lane. Nan Annie must have spent a while behind the larch wall—coming out from beneath the canopy, Ruby was in full sunshine.

Ruby hadn't followed anymore, but had slipped past the larches and taken the steep path down into the little gorge behind the chapel where sunlight guttered with each movement of the trees. Hot days in this hollow would be fetid. At the far end a steep earth wall rose up higher than the trees, and in its lee there was a pool. (She found out later it was called St. Barbara's Spring.) The pool, the clay around it, overhung with twisted branches; dancing from them, strips knotted closely to the branches, moving freely in the breeze. Ruby'd crossed the hollow (no laid path here, just a thread of footprints through the grass) and stood beneath the branches and looked up. Ribbons: thin for bonnets or bootees, broad for bridal flowers; a stocking and a neckerchief; a tie. They'd flickered on her head and stroked her shoulders. And on the low branches that dipped toward the water, embroidered handkerchiefs hung out, waiting there forever to get dry.

Some were elaborately worked. She'd grabbed the nearest—held it by the untied corners. *10 August 1901*—the day the *Lickey Bell* went down; the day of Grace's death—was worked in gold; a cursive monogram, all quirk and coil, so tangled that at first she couldn't tell the letters. Snowdrops bowing large and full in clusters and with tiny azure flowers winding around the stems. Some were plainer—

scalloped round with black and *J* and *N* and *T* (for Jonah Nailer Tailor, Ruby'd guessed) set fine and clear. She'd checked enough of them to see that these linens were *all* sewn and hung up for her grandad and her aunt, lost in the waters of the Severn with the sinking of the *Lickey Bell*. She'd begun to count them for some reason (respect for her Nan Annie and her stitching?) but by then the sun had risen high and she hadn't been quite sure if she was counting linens on the branches or reflected linens bobbing in the pool.

They never spoke of it, and if Nan Annie *had* seen Ruby following, she'd never said. But when Ruby handed around the teas each Thursday and each Sunday afternoon for all the Ruths and the Naomis, she gave a glancing thought to St. Barbara's Spring and all the other secret shady places through the Leans and through the Cradles, to all the years of grieving stitched and rippling from a tree.

Ruby did not look back up at Blick's, but went straight down to the Mission to Canal Folk. (She'd left the Blick's-loaned bicycle inside the main gate of the factory—her knee stung when she bent it, so she didn't fancy cycling. She didn't fancy answering the questions that the Ruths and the Naomis would ask her either. "Nice bicycle," they'd say, and she would have to tell them why she had it, that she was Truda's errand girl, and she was in no mood to defend Blicks.) Trembly Em was there already at the front doors; a pale-armed, red-cheeked jelly of a woman with a basket on her arm, panting as she bent to work the lock.

"Hello, Ruby love. Parched I am, this heat." Em asked after Nan Annie; was she coming, or was she with Eliza? "If I cor cope with all this heat, I doe know how Eliza's taking it. A good girl, our Annie is, to go and sit all Sunday wi her mother."

Ruby kicked one foot against the other. "Aunty" (Annie insisted Ruby call Em this, although they weren't in any way related), "wondering, I was, if yo could help me wi someone I'm looking for." If Em Fine-Knee Bacon had no recollection of a family called Fly, if the name hadn't lodged inside her head, she might let Ruby look for Lily in the records.

Trembly Em let Ruby go in first (Em was the kind who always

stepped down prompt into the gutter when others came toward her on the pavement), then pulled the door behind them and plumped down on the oak bench just inside (IN MEMORY OF FRANCIS BLICK etched on the silver plaque). It was dark in here and smelled of creosote. Smiling, panting, Em held a finger up to show Ruby that she would have to wait a minute while she caught her breath, and handed her the club keys to get started.

It took more than a minute. In the main hall, Ruby pulled the heavy crimson curtains from the windows and unhooked the besom from its high peg in the cupboard. When Blicks had built the Mission years before, they'd lined the walls with a light turkey-oak and the wood glowed golden in this light. She swept the floor with vigor—a slap down and a fierce drag on the broom. She dragged the chairs into the middle in a circle, then lifted down the Bible from the top shelf of the cupboard and opened it out where the ribbon marked the place—the same place, every week. A testament to choosing who you're bound to, holding firm to one lithe supple rope when you've woven it together:

> Entreat me not to leave thee, or to return from following after
> thee: for whither thou goest, I will go; and where thou lodgest, I
> will lodge; thy people shall be my people, and thy God my God.

She paused for a moment as she set the Bible open on a chair. The Ruths and the Naomis, this coalition of bereft women, pledged this to each other, but Ruby never said it, not being old enough to be a Ruth or a Naomi. A further line they never said on Thursdays: "Where thou diest, will I die, and there will I be buried: the LORD do so to me, and more also, if aught but death part thee and me." It thrilled her, this commitment-to-the-death. She herself felt no such loyalties (except to Captin, perhaps, and a tentative regard for her Nan Annie). But now Isa was here. She said the vow in a low whisper, just to test it.

"Blessèd cool in here." A voice made Ruby start—she slammed the Bible shut as if she'd been caught out. Trembly Em was standing in the doorway. She made her slow way to the chairs and lowered herself sideways into one, setting down her basket on another. "So,

Ruby." She shunted in her seat. "Yo said as yo had someone yo am looking for." She patted the free seat beside her and Ruby sat down, hoping she had hidden her reluctance. Trembly Em repelled her, but she wasn't quite sure why. Maybe it was her eagerness to please that made Ruby squirm. She had seen her, in the bread queue, staring at Nan Annie with a raw yearning that made Ruby shudder. Not a *courting* stare—she shivered at the thought. Maybe—Ruby knew this was unkind—maybe it was the trembling she hated. (It began when, just a few months above Ruby's age, Em fell down from a tree. Nan Annie brandished Em's story as a warning: "Let it be a lesson about fiddling with boys. Yo doe want to be chucking yourself out of trees to try and finish what they started. If yo let um handle yo before yoom ready, yoom bruised fruit. Fit to rot. And other men woe want to pick a rotten pear." But Ruby never understood the lesson; felt sure *she* would have been more careful climbing trees.)

Ruby shifted in her seat. Em smelled talcy: rotten roses, like the stuff that, when she was younger, Ruby made by mixing fallen petals up with water in a jar. This close to Trembly Em, she saw fine particles of powder resting on the blonde hairs of her cheek; the clownish rouge that didn't blend; the mottling of flush and pallor. Ruby put a hand up to her own cheek, smooth, unwrinkled.

"Weem trying to find someone called Lily Fly. Her might go by another name, but when her was a bab her name was Fly."

Em frowned. "Is her from round here?"

"From Cradle Cross. Her ud be thirty odd."

Em breathed heavy: dabbed at pips of sweat lined on her forehead. "Lily Fly? I cor say as I remember that name, Ruby."

"Her dad then: yoom of an age wi him. Moonie, he was called. Yo heard of him?"

Em licked her lips in concentration. "Moonie."

Irritation surged and swelled in Ruby and she gripped the edges of her seat. "Moonie Fly. F. L.Y. *I fly. You fly. He flies.*"

"No. No, Ruby." Em shook her head, rapid and defiant as a child. Loose skin shuddered on her neck. "No, I never knew a man called Moonie Fly."

Ruby blew her breath out in frustration. She scuffed the floor beneath her chair. *I must find something useful to give Isa.* She watched her scuffed toes shuttle back and forth. *Truda gives her ginger beer, but I will give her something that she needs: the name of who took Lily in, or who her mother was.* "I was thinking as there might be something put down in the chapel book. Lily being born, or Moonie married. Maybe Lily's mother, when her died. So ud yo mind if I—"

Em pulled a folded hankie from her sleeve and patted at her brow. "There was a boy once I called Moonie."

Ruby stopped her scuffing; looked at Em. "You knew someone called Moonie?"

"He wor *called* it; it wor his gived name, just an ekename as *I* gid him." Em pressed her fingers to the locket at her neck, her hankie hanging limp against her chest. "He day care for it. Said as it was spiteful." Em's hankie fell onto her lap and her hand shook as she tried to pick it up.

"Your Moonie—"

"He wor never *my* Moonie."

"He day have a daughter, Lily, then?"

"No, Ruby, he day."

There was a grim conviction in Em's tone, but Ruby ignored it. "But when did he leave Cradle Cross?"

"He day *leave,* Rube. We lost him."

"Lost him? Lost him how?"

Em tried to pick her hankie up again, but her fingers had grown rigid and wouldn't close around the cotton.

"What happened to him, Aunty?"

Em's whole arm was trembling as she tried, once more, to pick the hankie up. Ruby, impatient, reached across and snatched at it and balled it in her fist. "Did he die, is that what yo mean? When yo say lost, yo mean he died?"

Em nodded.

"What happened?"

"God rose up." Em's nodding continued, and she wrapped her mouth, wide, slow, around the words. "Swallowed him."

"What do you mean, God swallowed him?"

Em pressed her fingers to her temples, as if by this effort she could still herself.

"So yoom certain as this Moonie of yours died?"

"He's dead." Em's stare was sharp, forbidding and she almost looked angry. "Now leave it, Rube, ud yo?"

"But yoom certain of it? Will it be in the records?"

"Yo cor go poking through the Register. A document, it is, and yo cor just browse through it." Em's nodding didn't stop and although Ruby knew what would come next, she pressed her questions.

"Yoom so certain he's dead as yo'd swear it on my head?"

"God slew him, Rube!"

Em tried to raise her arm but couldn't, so Ruby shoved Em's hankie in her pocket; grabbed Em's fingers. Kneeling down, she guided Em's hand, firm, onto her head. "On my life, yo swear your Moonie's dead?" Ruby felt Em's fingers flexing in her hair.

"He's dead, Rube; dead as dead. And now he cor torment us any more."

A chill disappointment flooded Ruby; nothing here to bring to Isa Fly. She released Em and tried to stand but Em's weight bore down on Ruby's head. "God is righteous, Rube, and God answers the prayers of His faithful."

Ruby ducked away and sat back on her heels. Em's face was raddled. Tears slid down her cheeks, dripped from her chin, and Em didn't seem to care. "I know he's dead because I prayed for it, yo see." Em leaned in toward Ruby. "I asked the Lord to bring his justice down on Moonie, and the Lord answered me." Em whispered, wet and noisy, on her ear. "I prayed for it, and He struck that man dead."

Ruby sat a little distance clear of Em until the fit abated. Em's arm had crashed against her basket as she fell, knocking it down from the chair and spilling losslinen. Ruby was grateful for the diversion and (glancing up at Trembly Em every few moments to see if she had stopped yet) picked up the linens one by one, folding them square and placing them with care inside the basket.

Em was rousing, tugging at Ruby's skirt and babbling—"Rube's a good girl, just like her mom, her is, our Ruby is just like a little Beth"—when the door swung wide and Dinah strode in, holding forth: "Dock us? I ull dock her, soon as look at her!" Her daughter, Glenda, followed behind and then women Ruby knew by given name

and ailment, from long waits in the bread queue: Nancy Lupus; Florrie Kidney; Joan Dyspepsia. They clustered around Trembly Em but
Dinah shooed them back and, easing herself down onto her knees,
sent Glenda to the kitchen for cold water.

Dinah laid her palm across Em's forehead, and Em smiled up at
her.

"What did yo do to her, Ruby?"

"We was only talking!" Ruby stood and backed away from Dinah.

"Yo must of stirred her up. Was yo tormenting her?"

"If I did, I day mean to!" *That word again,* thought Ruby. *How
can asking questions be tormenting?*

Em tried to sit, but couldn't do it. "It's fine, chick. Fine, I am."
Dinah moved behind to hoist her up.

"See," said Ruby, "Aunty says her's fine." Em was trying to catch
her eye, but Ruby looked away; felt Em had cheated her with the
wrong Moonie, and she had less than nothing to take Isa. She'd have
to find a way to check the chapel book, despite Em's prohibition.

"Yo got my hankie, chick?" said Em.

Ruby plunged her hand into her pocket and yanked the hankie out,
but when she'd passed it on to Em she slid her fingers in her pocket
once again and they closed round Em's keys.

As Ruby always did, she left the room before the meeting started with
the hymn, led by the tremulous and reedy Ada Snaith, and went
through to the kitchen. She stood against the closed door and spread
out the keys she'd had from Em on her left palm. She moved them
round the ring as she worked out what went where: *this* one for the
cupboard; *this* one for the hall; *this* one for the main door . . . until
she had identified them all except a key no longer than her little finger. By the third verse of "Will Your Anchor Hold?" she was certain
that she knew which key would work the wooden box in which the
Register was kept. She'd seen Em carrying the flat box over to the
chapel whenever there were babies born or some old man had died.
She knew from times she'd carried Trembly Em's basket that Em kept
the box locked up in the office in the Mission, on the top of the bureau beside the desk.

She didn't look just yet, but set to, filling the tall urn and firing it up, laying out the cups and saucers on a tray. Glenda had put her custards in a basket on the side, and Ruby (who would usually take her time to lay them in a pattern), tipped them, hasty, out onto a platter. She usually sank down on the low stool beside the gas stove and did her Almanac. Not today. She imagined herself later on that afternoon standing on the broad step to the button shop, knocking at the door and waiting there for Isa; Isa, curious when Ruby pressed into her hands a fold of paper; Isa's spreading smile as she opened it and found written there the information that would lead her closer in to Lil; and later still, Isa's arm protective around her shoulder as they watched the Cut retreat beyond their rudder.

The chapel office smelled shut-in, but then the windows looked out on the Cut so Ruby could see why they liked to keep them closed, even though the air inside was sour. She tried the casement window, but there was no give.

She left the door ajar so she would hear if someone crossed the entrance hall. The desk was clear (letters clipped in bundles hung from nails on the walls. Copies—Ruby knew because she'd done some of them herself—of letters written up for free for boatmen to the firms they leased their boats off). Ruby, careful, laid the box down. She crouched beside the desk to fit the key into the lock, her eyes flicking up toward the door with every cough and every scraping of a chair. A sticky little lock, it took some wiggling to work, but it clicked free and Ruby stood to open up the box. The book inside was not distinctive (not like the angling book that Isa had loaned Ruby just that morning); rough-bound in coarse dun leather with a matching fringy bookmark poking out. She peeled back the pages—so thick that they crinkled when she turned them—and out of curiosity, her finger running down the lines, she found her own birth written in green ink (like all births) on the top line of a page, and at the bottom of the facing page, in black, the death of her own mother. The pages that preceded looked a mess: some penciled words inked over, some left as they were and some crossed through. It made no sense until she read a line or two, and a name snagged her: "Horace Hatchett Harper. August 1917 ~~missing, presumed~~ dead."

There were five pages like this, and Ruby didn't have the time to read them all.

She found no record of a Lily Fly, but she could be industrious when so minded, and not wanting to go to Isa empty-handed, she added to her list of Lils another few born around 1900, and then, because the list looked short, other girls born around the right time (Truda Cole Blick, Glenda and her own mother Beth among two dozen on the list). She thought about what Trembly Em had said: *Moonie wor his gived name.* There might be another man in these lists born John or Alf or Jim who became known as Moonie. How old was Isa's father? Sixty-five? She moved back through the Register to 1868; began another list, discounting men she knew to be alive and men she knew had died (her pencil hovered for a moment over *Jonah Nailer Tailor* as if she ought to somehow let her grandad know she had called by). No boy with the surname Fly. She wrote down the thirty or so names, then moved forward through the Register, looking for black ink. Sixteen of her thirty boys were dead by 1870.

Part way through 1871 (and two more dead), she jumped; someone was knocking on the window. She straightened up and crossed the room; she stood to one side of the window and peered out. No one there, but she heard giggling, then children's voices singing out in shrill and mocking voices; some hymn they'd coarsened and bent out of shape. She stood at the window; bit her lip. The water was quiet, being Sunday, all the lock gates done up tight with chains. She watched the Cut, eyes up and down the towpath, but the children had run off now and she heard nothing but a growl, a diesel rumble: it had to be the dredge-boat, Ruby knew: the only one allowed to work on Sundays, and the dredger held the key to all the padlocks. Ruby watched as the boat drew closer, looking for the scrape along the side. The boat drew level and Ruby wasn't sure what she did to draw attention to herself—looping that curl back behind her ear?—but the Blackbird turned sharply and looked at her.

The Blackbird on her dredge-boat slunk from view just as the meeting in the hall was drawing to a close—the women's voices intoning together, *Entreat me not to leave thee, nor to return from following after thee,* prompted Ruby to shut the Register back up in its box and put it on the bureau. She slipped back to the kitchen where she filled the tin teapot from the urn and splashed a good half-inch of milk into each cup.

As she took the tray around they were talking about Blick's and what they'd taken to calling the Docking Bill. She was relieved that they weren't much used to asking *her* opinion. Although her well of Blicks-loathing was drying, she wasn't ready yet to declare to the Ruths and the Naomis she was running errands for a Blick. *They work for Truda, some on um,* Ruby thought, defiant: *Why can't I?* But her own reprimand came fleet in; she knew that in the eyes of all the Ruths, the two things were not equal. Right now she didn't *care* about scuffed buttons, docked or not.

It was Em's turn this week to wash the crocks with Ruby, but Dinah insisted on escorting her straight home, with Glenda taking her place in the kitchen. It didn't bother Ruby who was helping, as long as they were quick; she was itchy with anxiety for Isa and wanted to be finished at the Mission. She began slopping soapy water round the cups, but Glenda nudged her to one side and thrust a tea towel in her hand, muttering about more water on the floor than in the bowl. "Yo ay concentrating, Ruby, am yo! Yoom fretting about Mrs. Fine-knee Bacon."

"No, I ay." Ruby picked a wet plate from the rack and asked if she could leave the crocks to drain, but Glenda said that no, it needed drying, all of it. "Yoom too keen to get off, Ruby."

Ruby gave the plate a desultory wipe.

"Yo can get off as soon as this is done." Glenda filled the bowl with more hot water. "No one thinks as it was your fault, Ruby. It's just Em ay been *took* for a good while."

Ruby said nothing, thinking of the Blackbird and how she'd looked at Isa on the bridge. She wanted to be certain Isa Fly was safe.

"If yoom thinking, Ruby, as it was something as yo said . . ."

Ruby calculated that the dredger would be passing at the back of Horn Lane now.

"Yo know what Mrs. Fine-knee Bacon's like. Strung tight. Yo cor go blaming yourself for that."

"I ay," Ruby protested.

"So what *was* yo asking her then, Ruby?" Glenda waited for her answer, turning on the tap to rinse the teapot. She filled it, swilled it, emptied it, and then did it all again; too careful, Ruby thought, and painstakingly slow. Like when Glenda took her time to weigh the bread, or inspected each custard before she put it in a paper bag: Glenda's way of keeping you detained until you gave her what she wanted.

And as there was no cause to be evasive, and she wanted to get back to Isa Fly, Ruby said, "I asked if her knew Moonie Fly or Lily." She set aside the cup that she was drying. The sooner Glenda found out what she wanted, the sooner Ruby could get to Horn Lane. Ruby took out her Almanac. "I got a list in here of Lils who it might be. Lilys who was orphaned, or at least left without a father."

Glenda flicked the Almanac away. "This is them that white girl's looking for? That white girl outside the button shop today?" There was a shift in Glenda's stance; a sudden tension. "Yoom pestering the old folk for a stranger?"

I asked you *this morning about Lily Fly,* Ruby thought, *but* you *didn't get took up in a fit.* "I day think it was pestering to ask someone a question."

"Depends on what the question is and where it's coming from." She grabbed the Almanac, and Ruby hid a smile. Glenda Hatchett Harper never missed the chance to show off what she knew. "Lily Siviter? Her dad carried stretchers in the War. Too old to be a soldier, but he never come back. Lily Basterfield? Her dad's Jim. He lives up Tenter Lane."

She worked through Ruby's list till they were all accounted for: Lilian Shilvock's father Bill died in the accident at Rudge's when Glenda and Lil Shilvock were at school. Lily Bache's dad died last month. ("Yo should of knowed that, Ruby. We took a plate round chapel for her mother.") Lil Heath's dad worked at Blick's, packing barrels; Lily Billingham's had died of flu; Lily Rose's dad? Alive, but not so well. They'd had the doctor to him twice this week.

Ruby put a line through all the Lilys. Nothing to show Isa here. If there'd been time she might have felt defeated, but Glenda was demanding her attention. "What's your nan think of all this? Yo pestered *her* about this Lily Fly?"

She told Glenda about Nan Annie's speculation. "Her doe know the daughter, nor the father. Her said it sounded like he did the mother in and run off when he'd done it."

"And that's what yo been asking Em about? Men murdering their wives? No wonder her was took, Ruby! What was yo thinking of?"

Ruby blew her breath out; shook her head. "I day ask her nothing about *murder*! Her got upset about some boy as her called Moonie, but he ay the one I am looking for. Her Moonie died. Except her day like it when I said *her* Moonie. Her said as he wor hers."

"And that was it?"

"I only asked if her was sure about Moonie being dead, but that was all. I day ask any more."

Glenda shook her head: explained ("What wi yo being far too young to know yourself") how folk don't like to have their old anguish dug up; Em no doubt had a passion for this lad (and no, *she'd* never heard of any Moonie), but maybe he was promised to another girl. "Em ay too good wi strong emotion, Ruby, so doe torment the woman anymore."

And, disappointed that there was no scandal, just Mrs. Fine-knee Bacon being saft ("And I think your nan is playing wi yo, Ruby. I think we ud of heard about a woman murdered and her husband runned away. It ud be Cradle legend!"), Glenda said to Ruby she could go.

When Ruby got to Horn Lane, out of breath, she found Isa, anxious, in the shop. She started to tell Isa that she'd seen the Blackbird skulking down the Cut, but Isa interrupted and gripped Ruby by the elbow and led her through the shop into the back. "Do something for me, will you, Ruby?" A strangled tone in Isa's voice. On the table, a fish stared up from a thick stack of newspapers. Ruby shifted her gaze, quick. Despite her three years working in the fish shop, each time she met the liquor of a fish eye, she felt raw, accused. *We swam in wild waters,* all fish said to her. *We found our lie and we were steady there, waiting in the lee of our cool rock. And where did* Ruby *swim?* Her eyes flicked across Isa's fly-box, open, and a smooth-skinned wooden club.

"What's this?" Ruby took the little club and turned it in her hands.

"My priest." Isa took it, firm, and didn't put it back down on the table. Gripped it with what looked to Ruby like resolve and held it ready at her side.

"What's it for, your priest?"

"For swift dispatch of anything I catch and don't throw back." She kept her voice low and her dark eye on the window.

An odd name, Ruby thought, *for something lethal.*

"Will you go, please, to the window, and tell me what you see?"

She was uncertain which was more alarming: that Isa had composed herself, had primed herself for something, or that Isa had asked Ruby to investigate the threat. But to her surprise she found that being *thought* bold *made* her bolder, and—six steps, sharp and resolute—Ruby crossed the room. Isa followed her, but stood to one side of the window. "What do you see?"

Nothing but the slow and sullen shifting of the water, which habitually could work her up into a trance. The waterline was low because Ludleye Gutter, the main feed-river, was parched by the dry spring; below the towpath, dried-out arrowhead, browned and flattened to the sides, marked out the old high-water levels. She tried to heave the sash up so that she could get a better look, but it would not shift. She followed Isa's gesture and taking up a long key from the sill, she unlocked the back door. Though Ruby tried to ease it wide, the hinges groaned from being so long idle and ungreased. Ruby looked out, left, then right. She leaned out, anchored by her fingers around the doorframe.

No one on the towpath, but a slight splash drew her eye back up to Wytepole Bridge. A boy there, crossing, who'd no doubt stopped to pelt a stone for luck down in the Cut. She dropped her eyes down to the tunnel underneath. No one would lie in wait in there—it smelled of meat and piss and the ceilings were curved low for narrowboats, damp fleecy lichen eking from the brick. She even looked down at the water, but knew that there'd be no one in it, for there were signs forbidding swimming in canals; fines for those deranged enough to try it.

She sat down on the top step and with her palms laid flat against the stone, warmed through by the sun, she edged forward, lowered herself down another step, no further, all the while her stomach twisting as she thought what Nan Annie would do if she saw her perching so precarious and so close to the Cut. Wondered for a moment if this was all contrived by Isa to get her, Ruby, closer to the water. The Cut smelled dark and heavy; a purple diesel film on the skin of the water that gave off little rainbows when it caught the light; the towpath ripe with drying balls of horse dung, steaming flies. Unbidden, rising in her throat like bile, she thought of something tugging her beneath the murky water and holding her there till she bobbed and sagged below the surface like a swollen pig bladder. Set adrift on foul, swift-moving thoughts, she glanced up at the sun and looked around for something fixed, secure—and saw Captin's emptied gut-bucket with the broken handle on the steps next door. How he would chuckle at her, cuff her around the shoulders and polish up imaginary spectacles when she told him how she and Isa thought that the Blackbird was watching them, and waiting. She began to lever herself back up to the top step to tell Isa that there was nothing to see. Checked one more time, a quick glance left toward the kink round Blick's and right to Wytepole Bridge.

The fender of a dark boat was protruding. Ruby stared into the tunnel, but could see nothing. Nothing except, marching around the prow, the name that had caught her eye again a half-hour back, when she was watching from the Mission.

"It's the dredge-boat," she called back over her shoulder. "The *Cassandra*. What's it doing here?"

"*Cassandra?*"

"The Blackbird's boat, it is. What's her doing? Is her waiting in the tunnel?"

"The boat went past. It turned around at the basin. I thought it had gone."

"What's her *doing?*" Ruby cupped her hands around her eyes. "Is her watching the towpath?"

"Come back inside," said Isa. "Come in, and lock the door." Isa went through to the shop and laid the priest out on the counter. Ruby followed. "What do you know about this dredger?"

"Not much: only tattle about what her's pulled out of the Cut. Her's just the dredger. Her goes up and down the Cut to keep it flowing."

Isa held her palms against her eyes, and then, as if impatient with herself, she dropped her hands and walked around the counter. She took a box from the shelf and tipped its contents out onto a saucer, saying nothing, shuttling buttons from one side of the saucer to the other.

"Why?" Ruby pulled the stool up to the counter. "Do yo know her?"

Isa didn't answer: she picked the largest buttons out and laid them on the counter.

"Because I saw her looking at you yesterday, when yo was on the bridge."

Isa looked up. "And you didn't think to tell me?"

She spoke so sharp that Ruby flushed. "All her did was look at yo, and her woe be the first! Yo stand out, Isa. Yo doe look like women around here!" But Ruby did not speak entirely true, and she knew it: the Blackbird was not, like the other women, thrown by Isa's white hair and her blind eye and by the many mirrors on her skirt; the Blackbird had not been startled by the sight of Isa Fly. She was *shocked* to see her. She seemed to *know* her; and how could someone in landlocked Cradle Cross know Isa-from-the-sea? Ruby did not look at Isa—such a question was, she felt, disloyal and if she looked at Isa, her white eye would read it. "I day mention it cause we was busy, Isa," she protested. "We was wanting to find a telephone to ring about your dad."

But Isa didn't calm her, didn't lay a hand on Ruby's arm to reassure. She was taut with a fine, strong anger and Ruby felt tears starting up and dashed her sleeve, brisk, fierce, across her cheek. "Her was just looking, Isa! I day think as it mattered, someone looking!"

Isa's anger seemed to slacken. "Forgive me. You are right: I am not accustomed to the staring. At home when people look at me, it's not because I've caught their eye by looking different. They know who I am—they want something from me: a set of flies for grayling; a hook that's good for trout. But here . . ."

"Her just looked up at yo." Ruby reached out for a button and pressed her finger in its curve, pushing it round in a little circle. "Yo *has* to look up when yo take the bridge."

Isa reached behind her for a bottle of buttons like the ones that she had sorted. "Put it from your mind, Ruby." Isa uncorked the bottle and dropped the largest buttons into it.

"Yo ay worried, then, about the dredger?"

Isa held her palm out for the button under Ruby's finger. "I am not sleeping well."

"So yo doe know her, then?"

Isa dropped in the last button and eased the cork into the bottle. "She resembles somebody that I knew in St. Shirah . . . But this heat! Maybe I am seeing visions. Like parched men in the desert."

"St. Shirah?" Ruby said. "Is that where yoom from? Yo never said?"

"What does it matter?" Isa snapped.

She didn't want to tell me, Ruby thought.

Isa added, more gently, "I think I need to rest."

Ruby held the saucer up. "Dun yo want me to sort more buttons out?"

Isa shook her head and turned to put the bottle back onto the shelf. "I have been short with you and you have been so diligent; all these questions about this missing daughter!" There was so little vigor in her voice that Ruby could not tell if Isa thanked her; it could just as easily have been a mild reproach.

"*Diligent* ay brung yo Lily Fly! And the only Moonie as I found yet is a dead one."

Isa turned around. "You found a man called Moonie?"

"I ay found Lily, though."

"You found somebody here who knew my father?"

"No, Isa. *Not* your Moonie." So Ruby told her about Trembly Em, and how she'd been no use at all; she'd loved a boy and now the boy was dead.

Ruby did not want to leave Isa with the dredger watching her (for, despite Isa's attempt to dismiss talk of the dredger, Ruby was quite sure that the Blackbird *was* watching Isa Fly), but somehow Isa steered her from the room and out onto Horn Lane without making her feel she'd been evicted.

Later, in her bed, Ruby took her Almanac and found St. Shirah on the map between the villages of Gleed and of St. Stephen. She marked it with an ink dot and wrote in pencil, "Where Isa lives," and added, "R will stay here too." And with her nail she traced the coastline around Sawdy Point; up to the hook of Gleed, and down again.

Chapter 5

Angle, *v.* 1. To fish with a hook and bait. 2. *fig.* To use artful or wily
means to catch a person or thing.

RUBY COULD NOT get to Horn Lane till late on Monday morning.
Nan Annie had been up since first light working at the washing, and
she needed Ruby at the handle of the mangle; hanging sheets up on
the line. Nan Annie dispatched her, then, with Jamie Abel's dinner
and instructions not to dawdle: Captin needed her behind the fish
shop counter for the dinner rush, and he expected her before the
sounding of the Bull.

After yesterday and that humiliating tumble in Horn Lane, Ruby took
the Breach at a more moderate pace and leaned the bike against the
wall inside the gulley next to Maison Hester's. Through the folds and
entries to the Deadarm Ruby ran, quick as she could without slopping
Jamie Abel's dinner out the bowl. She wanted time to call at Isa's, to
go over the list of people from the chapel records who they could ask
about the Flys. The sooner they found Moonie's missing daughter, the
sooner they could go down to St. Shirah.

She skittered down the slope toward the Deadarm. Could hear her father hammering inside the boat, still in its cradle. He kept a steady rhythm, relentless and unyielding in each strike of iron on nail, and as she set his bowl down on the towpath's edge, something ruptured inside Ruby. Flooded, she was, by a pulsing swell of long-dammed indignation. *What will he do when I have gone?* (She told herself, defiant, that she would not yearn for *him.* How could she miss her father when she had not so much as touched his hand in seven years?) *What will he do without me? What will he do when I have gone to sea? Who will bring his dinner? Who will come and fetch his empty bowl? Who will bring his tea leaves and his bread? His tooth powder, his soap?*

A flimsy way of living, this, thought Ruby. Her father sheltering beneath a workbench on a bed of horn sacks filled with shavings from the oak; his evenings lit by paraffin in a black lamp hung high from a nail, and sleeping in a tarry dark, sticky from the years of cooking pitch and bitumen. Seven years, he'd camped here, emptying his cack and piss into the Cut, and from the start she'd told herself it was a temporary arrangement: one day he'd come home. How could *this* be anything but short-lived?

Jamie Abel hammered on. A lurching in her belly, and Ruby saw with piercing clarity, so sharp it snatched her breath, that *she* had shored this up; she had sustained his segregation. With every bowl that she had brought him and every twist of tea, she had lent this arrangement permanence and given her consent. As long as she continued, daily, laying down his dinners, he would never leave the Deadarm. Too easy for him to stay here, and she had made it so. She'd said as much to Isa: "Everything he needs, I bring it. He ay got cause to come back over here."

But when I go to sea with Isa Fly, thought Ruby, *he will* have *to leave his island, and that will not be fair.* All these years at Hunting Tree without him, and for him to come home only when she'd gone. She'd heard Nan Annie, on to Trembly Em: "*I* day send him into exile." And she was right. Jamie Abel didn't *need* to sleep here. Eat here. Cack here. He was sulking, that was all.

She wanted to kick free the props that she'd constructed. Decided she should test him. Decided that tomorrow, she would *not* bring him his dinner. Would he come looking for her, down Horn Lane? Come to Captin's shop to get some chips? Or would he try to stay here, hungry, on the Deadarm—fry bladderwort and Cut-eel for his dinner?

For today, she left his dinner bowl and shouted only once to tell her father it was there. Didn't wait, but scrambled up the slope. Was at the gully mouth when she heard him shouting.

"Rube! Doe go!"

She stopped, eyes shut, and banged her fist against the wall. Thought about pretending not to hear.

But he called after her, "No school today?"

She twisted around and shouted, angrily, "It is the holidays." Too low for him to hear, she added, "Doe yo know anything?"

He shrugged and pulled his tin out of his pocket, taking out a skinny paper-fag he had rolled earlier.

Another thing he'd go without, she thought, *unless I brought it for him.*

"I'm coming to the bottom of the packet."

"And?"

He struck a match and held it to the fag. "What's eating yo today?" Curious, he was, but unriled by Ruby trying to be firm and cross like Truda, and his composure only vexed her all the more. It looked like he was trying to hide a smile. "It's just as yo tode me, Rube, as I should say when I was running out of baccy."

"Is that it? Yo called me back to say about your baccy?"

He looked away and blew smoke at the sky. "Someone come round this morning."

Ruby waited.

"The dredger, it was."

"What's her want wi yo?"

"Her boat's got a bad scratch. Her's bashed the dredging spoon. Her wants me to take it in and look at it."

"Why am yo telling me? I ull be late for Captin's!" Ruby turned and started up the slope.

"Her was asking after you."

Ruby stood still on the slope and scuffed with her toe at a bald patch of ground.

"Asking, her was, if I know who your friends am."

She kicked at the clay and called over her shoulder. "What did yo say?" Then, quieter, "Did yo say to her as yo ay got a clue?" She kept on up the slope and did not look back, even when her father called after her that he'd said nothing, for he'd not known what to say.

She ran through the folds and out onto the Breach. A smaller girl—one of the Bastock lot from Stower Street—had got hold of the bicycle and with the help of her friends was straining to straddle it and stay upright. Ruby snatched the handlebars from her and the girl did not fight her for it, but as she jolted it down the cobbles to Horn Lane, the girl and the others sang out after her:

> *Ruby's made a new friend:*
> *Her name is Isa Fly.*
> *Her made her out of bits of horn*
> *And gid her one black eye.*

At the button shop, Isa Fly was scraping parcel paper from inside the front windows and washing it down as pulp. She turned and smiled at Ruby and asked her how she'd slept; had she had breakfast? How had she spent the morning? And, oh, what did they grow at Hunting Tree? Was the soil kind or did it take a lot of tilling? Ruby, who wanted for attention, responded like a dry plant given water. She told Isa that it was hard work cutting lime into the clay and trying to turn it; how they grew mainly string beans and onions and how the pigs kept her awake on summer evenings. Isa went on, working at the windows, but throwing another question out from time to time. Ruby decided not to spoil it by mentioning her father and what he'd said about the Blackbird. The air was close with steam from new water boiling on the stove. A jar of beeswax polish stood open on the counter: Ruby lifted it and breathed the turpentine. "I got a list to show yo."

Isa peeled off a long piece and let it drop into a bucket on the floor. "Oh yes? What sort of list?" A tightness in her voice; Isa, trying to be light.

"That list as I made yesterday. I took it from the chapel book.

Births and deaths and marriages. We never got a chance to talk about it. People who might of heard of Lil, or might of known your father."

Isa scratched the glass but didn't answer, working her nail over a nub of paper left behind.

"I could come wi yo if yo like," said Ruby, "when I finished helping Captin wi the dinners. Tell yo who people am and where they live."

Isa started scraping at the base of another strip of paper with a squat, flat blade. "You do not need to do this."

"It ay no bother. I want to help." *And when I've helped you find her*, she thought, *you will take me to the sea.* "I'll put the list down for yo." Ruby twisted the lid back onto the polish and felt in her pinny for a little scrap of paper. She pulled out a square of sugar packet. She flattened out the thick paper and transcribed the names of those she'd written in her Almanac. Wary, she glanced around at Isa Fly from time to time, but Isa looked straight on at the window, contained and resolute, working the scraper.

"Will yo be able to read it?" Ruby held the square up. She had pressed hard with her pencil and the names formed indentations on the paper. "My writing ay too clear."

"Leave it on the counter, would you, Ruby? My hands . . ." She held them up to Ruby, muddied water coursing down her arms.

"I can ask round for yo, if yo want. It's just yo ay made much of a start, yet, and yo been here two days already."

Isa paused, and Ruby tensed: she'd made it sound as if she were impatient and she didn't want to show it. But she *was* impatient and she was bemused: Isa had not been spurred by her anxieties for Moonie, Ruby knew, for when she ventured to ask Isa if she had news of him, Isa was impatient and dismissive as if she had forgotten him and did not want reminding. "Not worse, not better, not yet dead. Still petulant, says Brammeier. Still noisy. Still deluded."

"It ay as I think that yo been lax, or anything." She spoke quick and loud to silence all her doubts. For she found Isa's story strained and somehow grating—this notion that Isa Fly had left the sea to save a father whom she didn't seem to care for, to find a woman whom she'd showed no interest in . . . Something contrived in it, like the wooden sideshow that came round with the traveling fair: a witch-in-white inside a tipping boat, a lost girl, and a frowning moon-faced bully who slid, stilted, across a stage. Ruby felt that if she got too close and lifted up the curtain she would expose the cranks and cogs that moved them. "Busy, yo been. Yo ay had much time, what wi going fishing and then all as yo has done here in the shop and helping Truda."

Isa still said nothing and worked the scraper; slow strokes with a grim consistent force.

"It's just I'd like to help. I doe mean to pester."

"You'd like to help."

"But I cor until I finished wi the chips. I cor stay now—I got to get next door."

Isa turned, frowning, and it looked to Ruby that she was trying to work out what to say to her, and Ruby wanted to tell Isa that Jamie Abel was asking such strange questions (and how odd it was for him to ask her things at all), but then someone was calling Ruby and Isa said, "It sounds like you are wanted," and Ruby ran into the street.

Truda was leaning from the high window. "Might you stop yapping with Isa for a moment? I've been hollering! Did you not hear? I need you."

Ruby looked up, hands around her eyes to shield them from the sun. "I only got a minute! Captin needs me too!" She thumbed toward the fish shop, where she could see that Captin was bent low, adjusting the gas jet under the vats.

"Then you'd better hurry." Truda pulled back from the window.

The Bull sounded out as Ruby crossed the courtyard, and she was jostled by the stream of buttoners all going for their dinner. She tried to slip between them and through the door up to the office, but someone grabbed her wrist and yanked her to one side: Glenda Hatchett Harper, looking ruddy. "Tell me, Ruby." She grabbed Ruby's shoulder. "Yoom in the know. Is it true her's docking our wages" (she nodded up toward the offices) "so as her can pay that white girl as her's instated in the shop?"

Others slowed to listen, and Ruby tried to say that it wasn't like that, not at all, but Glenda looked at her with eyebrows raised and

Ruby stammered that she had no time to talk. Glenda almost pushed her as she took her hand away. "Miss Blick wants me, and then I got the chips."

Glenda called out after her and louder than she needed: "You got your priorities straightened out then, Ruby. Miss Blick first, and then, when you fancy getting round to it, the chips for all the workers."

She ran up the stairs to the Blick's office, but waited on the top step, poised to run down again. Truda was at the desk, head down, and writing with a fierce and jerky hand; her other hand spread wide across a ledger.

"Yo called for me, Miss Blick. Only, like I said, I should be down wi Captin doing chips."

"I'm certain Captin can dole out chips without you."

"I doe dole um. I wrap um."

"I don't give a hoot." She looked up at Ruby. "You can take two chips and make them do the cancan, if you like." Her fingers performed high-kicks on her desk.

"Your buttoners ull be queuing for their dinners. Slow, he'll be, without me."

"My buttoners?"

Ruby nodded.

"I suppose they are." Truda took up a bundle of folded papers in one hand and with the other reached down for a satchel by her chair. "Letters." She pointed them at Ruby. "Can you post them? Would you mind?"

"What, in the post box? Is that all?"

"Nope." Truda stuffed the letters deep into the bag. "They need to go by hand."

"What's in them?"

Truda tapped her nose. "They're not for your eyes, Ruby."

"Why can't you put them in the post box?"

"I need them delivered today. And I'm being mean about the stamps." She held out the satchel, but pulled it back before Ruby could take it. "Watch that you don't lose them: the clasp's broken. And I'll tell you this: these letters will not make you popular."

Ruby shrugged. She hadn't many friends she cared to keep.

"You don't have to do this." Truda held the satchel close now, indecisive. "There is no obligation."

Ruby reached out for the satchel. "You lend me a bike and I do jobs for you. That's what we agreed." She looped the strap over her shoulder and made for the stairs.

"How was Isa?" Truda called after her.

Ruby stopped on the top step. "Cleaning windows."

"Yes, I saw. How did she seem?"

"Het up."

"Did she mention this sister; her father? We spoke with that soror at the priory gate. She had no memory of a girl called Lily Fly. She promised that she'd check through the school records, but—"

"Miss Blick, I got to go."

She was at the bottom of the stairs when Truda called down after her, "The letters, Ruby: chuck 'em at the addressee, then run and don't look back. And please don't call me Miss Blick. So prim. And I am anything but prim."

Ruby pushed through the crowd lined up at Captin's and ducked behind the counter, where Captin looked harried and slightly pink. She stowed the satchel underneath the counter and, as she put her apron on, started to explain where she had been, but Captin silenced her with a nod toward the queue. "Glen's already come in. Her told me where yo was."

He didn't talk to Ruby while they worked, and even an hour later when the door was shut and Ruby was scrubbing the counter and Captin sifting bits out of the fat, she didn't feel that he'd forgiven her. But then it was time for tea and he offered to make it, although it was Ruby's job. She wasn't certain if this was a slight—*that Ruby, I cor trust her wi nothing*—or conciliation. And when he called her through into the back, he had cut up buttered bread and laid it neatly on a plate in the way that Ruby usually arranged it and he did it, she was sure, to show he didn't need her.

They ate their bread without talking—she only took one piece, and drank her tea in one quick scalding draft. "I cor stay." She wiped her chin dry on her sleeve and pushed her chair back from the table. "I got work to do for Truda." She spoke the words precisely—a pebble in his pond—and Captin all but snatched her cup up off the table and put it in the tin bowl with a clatter.

"I ud better do the clearing up myself then, doe yo reckon? Free yo up to do Miss Blick's bidding."

Ruby didn't go to Captin for their usual embrace; brief but tight, with Captin's raised chin scratchy on her forehead. She tried a light, indifferent leave-taking, a raising of the head and "See you later." Captin did not look round from the sink, but only gave a sullen grunt. She yanked the door shut between the shop and the back room.

She was crouched beneath the counter to retrieve the satchel when she heard the middle door open. She did not stand up, and Captin spoke at Ruby from the shop-side, out of sight: "Before yo go, I forgot to say: the Blackbird was on the Cut this morning, calling out to my back window, asking after yo. Now what yo been chucking in the Cut to get the Blackbird calling here, looking so vexed?"

When, in the coming days, the Ruths and the Naomis began to ask their questions about Isa Fly and how she'd hooked in Ruby, hooked in Captin, even hooked Miss Blick, Ruby would look back and try to see how she had done it. How, after only two days in the Cradles, Isa Fly had learned to read Ruby, and how, when Ruby stood outside the fish shop, fumbling with a satchel, trying to make it fit in the bicycle's front basket, Isa knew to leave her windows and come out to Ruby and ask her if she wanted, later on, to come to tea. How could Isa know quite how much Ruby longed for easy habits, like sharing meals with Isa, to wear grooves into her day? She wanted to sit close to Isa on the back step and eat fish with burned fingers out of paper. She wanted to lean in to her shoulder and have Isa pick a bit of stray crumb from her sleeve.

She could not say yes to Isa, though she longed to, because Captin would be coming up to Hunting Tree with a Monday fish, and they had a proper tea on Mondays, the three of them together. He'd fry it by the fire and they'd eat it at the table, because Nan Annie didn't like to eat food out of paper. With Captin there, Nan Annie moved more freely around Ruby—even reached out once or twice to flatten Ruby's hair or pinch her cheek with something like affection. But the Monday ritual that, till now, Ruby'd relished, felt like a stricture binding her that day.

So when Isa Fly nodded and held her lips tight in a line, Ruby grabbed at Isa with the hand that didn't hold the bicycle and said in a voice that Ruby recalled later as a crude childish complaint, "I want to eat wi yo! I doe want to eat wi Captin and Nan Annie!" And Isa Fly had smiled at Ruby with a momentary lightness in her clear-and-seeing eye and said simply, "I know."

While Ruby posted Truda's letters under doors and pressed them into hands around the town, she allowed herself to weave a sweet, obliging story: Ruby stands on Horn Lane outside the button shop; buttered light spills through the windows; within, poor sad Isa sits distracted with her fly-box on her lap and dashes quick tears from her cheeks; Ruby knocks gently at the door. The slow, unfolding joy as Ruby leads the missing sister in . . . *"We sought you and we did not cease. We sought in every corner."* (She didn't bother to weave Moonie Fly into her story: he held no interest for Ruby, except that it was his disease that brought her Isa Fly.) As Ruby's satchel lightened, she stretched her yarn and wove new strands: Captin standing on the towpath, Truda, sulky and magnificent beside him, their lanterns held aloft as Isa Fly and Ruby wave, buoyant, gracious, from the stern of a boat bound for Severnsea.

Ruby showed no interest in the letters that she posted, except to note that there were many, and from time to time a name she recognized. Mr. Eli Dodd, the chemist; Dinah Hatchett Harper; even one for Captin. A few people called after her, "What's this about?" but she pretended not to hear, aware (and with a quiver in her belly) that from now on there'd be no hiding the fact that she was doing dirty work for Truda Cole Blick. She didn't doubt that whatever Truda had put in these letters, it would rouse the rabble just as the Docking Bill had done. Just last week the weight of this opprobrium would have dragged on Ruby, kept her flushed and edgy; but now, with Isa Fly in mind, she felt fleet, sure-footed. As she went she spoke aloud the

Twelve Manner of Impediments which cause a Man to Make no Fish, which she had memorized last night by writing them out, line and line again, over several pages of her Almanac:

> *One, if your harnays is not mete nor fetly made;*
> *Two, if your baits be not good nor fine;*
> *Three, if you angle not in biting time.*

The letters had been tied up into batches to make posting easier. It wasn't worth the trouble to get on her bicycle while she took them around the central streets of Cradle Cross—she'd be hopping on and off every three feet. But the last batches were for houses on the outskirts, more dispersed, so Ruby stowed the satchel in the basket. Easy to forget how young Ruby was: one moment up on the pedals and pumping hard to overtake a group of boys, then slowing to a more sedate pace and sitting poker straight when she remembered to be elegant. (Tall Lane: a letter for Thom. Tolley.) As she passed the old church with its squat Norman tower, the Ludleye Road got steeper and she had to get off and push, pausing to turn and breathe heavily toward Cradle Cross. (The pair of white cottages by St. Kenelm's: a letter for Jim Foley, and next door, too, for Boz Clinker Bissell.) *"Four,"* said Ruby, *"if the fish be frayed at the sight of a man."* (Boz Clinker called out after her, "Did yo say sommat, Ruby Abel Tailor? Am yo cheeking me?")

Once she'd broken the hill, the ride was easier—short, hard climbs followed by the swooping hollows left by depleted mines. The seams weren't rich; Cradle coal had been a dig-and-scrape below the surface, except one clustering of shafts and tunnels, but they weren't working, flooded in the General Strike when the pumps were left unmanned. There were rumors that they'd poured the tarmac on the Ludleye Road a few weeks back to cover gaps and chasms; the road was shifting, sticky in the heat, and if you didn't pay attention it could cave in under you. So Ruby didn't stop until the Crux Coci, beyond the mines, where the road bent back. No cross there any more to mark the Halfshire boundary; it was moved and lost when they shifted the line to take in Hunting Tree Hundred, where Ruby lived. A gap in the hedge; from here you could see the Crux Manicata on the far side of the Cradles, laid out in the dip below. Behind her, woods spreading west across to Owley and up the lowest slope of the Lean Hills, and then the crested back of Parry Lean. The Lean Hills were well-named: steeply rising, toned flanks; a young horse on a poor farm.

Ruby's belly grumbled—she hadn't eaten much today and she was looking forward to her tea. One more batch left in the bag: Ruby walked her fingers through to count them. Five letters; the first for Em Fine-knee Bacon.

Trembly Em lived in a railway carriage at the bottom end of Kenelm's Field. Ruby turned off the road onto the high, worn track that ran along the east edge of the field. To the right, an abrupt drop of ten feet down into the Ludleye Gutter, wide and shallow underneath its canopy of beeches. She jolted over stones and into ruts and soon decided she should leave the bicycle and collect it on her way back to the road—she didn't want to end up being thrown into the Gutter. In other times, sent down there with a bag of chitterlings or a bony pie for Trembly Em, she would have stepped with caution on the field-edge of the track and kept as far from Ludleye Gutter as she could. But *this* day, she was doubly distracted: contemplating bread and salty butter, her mouth seared by a fresh-fried sprat; and still reciting the Twelve Impediments. *"Five,"* she chanted, *"if the water be very thick, white or red, of any flood late fallen."* And the water around here was *all* red: it ran bloody on the clay. The Leans were lush and full and fertile only where the land was worked over and over to get the water through the clag. No fat on this land; life and growth were coaxed from it. Remarkable—*startling* given this, the Fifth Impediment—that Isa had caught any fish at all on Sunday in the thick murk of the Cut. Had Ruby not been charmed, herself, by Isa Fly, she would have been unsettled by the memory of Isa on Horn Lane with three Cut-caught fishes flapping from her fist.

A movement caught her eye: a flare of red on green. She twisted; scanned the field. Nothing. Only Em, bent double at the pump on the far side, near that scrubby patch where she grew scorched and yellowed cabbages each year. This dry spring, this summer had already baked the soil to terra-cotta and Ruby knew Em wasn't built for breaking clay. She, Ruby, would be sent here soon to hack and slice the ground and work up water mixed with ash and gritty sand to grind the clay to something workable.

She let her bag fall to the ground and stood there for a moment watching Em. Ruby knew that when you pumped from Em's well, the handle squealed and yielded water rusty as the bucket. *Cradle water bleeds,* thought Ruby, *and I want a different water.* Isa's sea bleached wood; it burnished stone; around its reefs bred silver bass and pollack, rivet-cheeked; arching black bream teeming in the Sound. *All these fish I know! How pleased Isa will be with me,* thought Ruby, *when she hears what I am learning from her book.* She tried to think of something she could give to Isa in return—a pail of decent coal, an envelope of seeds—but nothing matched the promise she believed she'd wrested from her: casting flies out on saltwater, next to Isa, and safe with Isa there. She would find Isa a button. A bit of Whitby jet, or tawny agate. Something to say thank you for the promise of the fishing, and the sea.

Ruby waved, suddenly exuberant, to Em across the field. "I got a letter!" Ruby shouted, but Em neither heard nor saw, so Ruby walked around the scrubby field, and chanted to herself the Sixth Impediment. *"Keep you ever from the water from the sight of the Fish."* Em thanked her for the letter; she didn't open it but passed it from one hand to the other; turned it over; held it to the light. She was trying to press Ruby into staying for a bit of sop, maybe a cup of tea, her fingers pressing hard on Ruby's shoulder, when Em pointed back across the field and said, "Look, Ruby. Someone's trying to make off wi your bike."

Ruby spun around and felt a rush of heat into her cheeks, a plummet in her guts; a figure, all in black, was yanking her bicycle toward the far edge of the field. "What yo doing?" Ruby yelled, her voice resonating hard and clear. The figure seemed to struggle with the bicycle. She moved awkwardly across the ground—it was clear to Ruby, even from this distance, that it was a woman, for her dress was catching on the pedals. She couldn't see the woman's face; she didn't need to. Only one woman in the Cradles wore the black-plumed Cut-headdress: the Blackbird.

Ruby ran (as far as it was possible to run across this undulating clag), calling as she went: it looked as if the Blackbird was trying to throw the bicycle down into the Gutter; and now the bicycle was gone; and the Blackbird too had dipped out of sight into the little gorge.

Ruby stopped short of the Gutter at the place where she'd dropped Truda's bag. Her breath burned in her chest. She looked around, but the bag, too, was gone.

She stepped across the high mound of the track toward the Gutter. The ground fell sharp away somewhere among the nettle-sprays and bramble-snarls; beech trees stepped down the incline, their roots exposed and forming rungs. She grabbed a branch and pressed on it to test its strength. She peered into the gorge: there, out of her reach, jammed between branch and trunk, the front wheel cranked back like a broken limb, was Ruby's bicycle.

It was dark in the Gutter—the foliage was dense above her and frail straws of sunlight slipped in through the branches. She wrapped her arms around the nearest trunk and reached out with her foot to where a root was wide enough to take her. She wasn't scared by height. (She'd scaled the steepest slope of Parry Lean a hundred times and shunted sideways down again, steady, finding footholds lest she gather speed and run and fall and spin. Harder, coming down: the slopes of Parry Lean were clad in insubstantial War larches, all leaf and sinew, spindle-roots, planted to cover up the scarred and pitted hill when they cut the hardwood out for war.) The beech roots here in Kenelm's Field were stout and (she told herself again) *I ay scared of height.* Yet the Blackbird was waiting for her by the water, and fear coursed freely through Ruby. *"Look that you shadow not the water,"* she chanted to herself. The Seventh Impediment. *"Look that you shadow not the water."*

Ruby maneuvered, steady, down the slope and as she moved, a bristling curiosity caught on her like burrs. The Blackbird couldn't want the bike; why would she, when every week she could drag steel and tube and other costly things out of the Cut? So what did the Blackbird want with her? This question built in her and held her fear back like a dam, and Ruby climbed on down. *The water here is ankle deep,* she told herself. *No harm will come to me.*

She climbed down till she was level with the bicycle; inspected it. The front wheel wasn't buckled, just turned back on itself. She reached past the trunk and grabbed the frame with one hand (the other around a higher branch to keep her safe and balanced), but as she tried to work the frame, to ease it free, she glanced up at the way that she had come, back up to Kenelm's Field, and suddenly felt defeated. She didn't have the strength to pull the bicycle back up after her—the weight of it would drag her down the slope. She couldn't push it up ahead of her—she'd need at least one hand free to climb up. She looked down toward the water: it might only be shallow, but what if she slipped and the bicycle slipped with her?

She tugged on the frame: it was held secure. She'd leave it here, for now. It couldn't fall, and she'd need help to get it out of here. She started back toward the field: she'd find Captin. Who else would risk the bramble-snags to pull a Blick's bike from the Gutter?

"Am you forgetting something?" A hard shout from below: this voice shared Isa's modulation, but was tempered with the contractions and the stretched vowels of the Cradles, as if she'd snatched their way of talking and slapped it on her own. Ruby scanned the gorge below. Truda's bag! She'd have to go and get it. She felt for the next root-rung, moving down until she was a few feet from the bottom, with a clear view of the stream.

She reached the bottom of the gorge and twisted round to flatten herself close against the bank, each foot resting on a root. She looked downstream toward the culvert that ran under the Ludleye Road, but saw nothing; the Blackbird was upstream, on a jaggy outcrop with her legs tucked up and Truda's satchel close beside her. She leaned back on her hands, self-sure as a siren. Against her pitch-plumed bonnet she was white as bone; cheeks and forehead sculpted like the limb of salt-worn driftwood on Captin's shelf that Ruby coveted.

The Blackbird didn't speak, but stretched her legs toward the stream. Her feet were bare, bruised toes dangling in the water. She lowered her head and stared at Ruby, the black plumes on her bonnet fluttering. Her eyes shone dark and polished in her face, and Ruby didn't like her full attention. Her stomach tightened, but for a moment she was more indignant than afraid. She did not like the way the Blackbird appraised her, as if she turned her over like a penny in her palm.

"Why did yo nick my bike?" She tried to sound indignant and not fearful, but instead she sounded reedy, petulant. "It ay mine, even! It's Blickses!"

The air was sickly with honey-fungus; heavy with the stench of the cuckoo-pint she'd crushed on her descent, and she felt queasy.

"That woman," the Blackbird said. "One-eyed. All the color bled from her. What is she doing here?"

Ruby wrapped her fingers tighter around the root behind her back. *That's why she scuffed the dredge-boat on the bank. She knows Isa Fly.* "Her ay doing nothing."

"She is a stranger; you've made her your friend. What has she confided in you, Ruby?"

You are the stranger, Ruby thought. *You are not from the Cradles. You wear your robes like a disguise; you hide your auburn hair inside your bonnet. You barely step off the dredge-boat and when you do, you pick your way on land as if it shifts beneath you.* "I doe think as I should be talking to yo."

The Blackbird stood up on the rock and pulled down a limb of beech that spanned the stream. "She stood by you and took your arm." She hung Truda's satchel from the branch; it dangled, gaping open with the last few letters visible inside.

"Her day say nothing!" Ruby glanced behind her; anchored one arm around a trunk and leaned out to grab at Truda's bag, but it was too far. She'd have to step across the water to retrieve it.

The Blackbird slid down from the rock and crossed the flat stones of the stream bed. The hems of her skirts darkened and were lifted by the water. *How bold!* Ruby thought. *To wade out in the water with no thought about your skirt getting wet!* But then the Blackbird was swooping in on her and she had Ruby by the throat, against the bank. The Blackbird stared into her eyes, trying to locate something within them. Ruby grabbed the Blackbird's wrist, but she was pinioned; the Blackbird's breath a damp mist on her cheek. "Isa Fly said something in your ear."

"Her just said as we should get back to Horn Lane!" The Blackbird's fingers tightened, strong and cold against her skin, and Ruby plucked at them. "A telephone."

The Blackbird frowned. Her fingers loosened. "What for?"

"For calling home."

"To Severnsea?"

Ruby saw herself, distant and distorted, reflected in the Blackbird's shining eyes. Ruby squirmed and tried to wrest her head away. "To see if her dad was still alive."

The Blackbird's hand sprang open, starfish wide, and curled to point at Ruby. Nails like naked coral, ridged and grained like seashells. "He's *dying*? Then why is she in Cradle Cross?"

Ruby rubbed her throat. "Sent Isa here, he has, to put things right."

"What things?"

Ruby pressed her lips together: a daughter, left behind; a great price paid. *God's vengeance,* Isa'd said, *was brutal and sustained.*

The Blackbird raised her chin, eyes narrowed, and she waited. In Isa Fly, such taut, expectant poise made Ruby swell up with a childish pride, as if she'd just learned to do her buttons up and proffered her cuff, proud, to show what she could do. But Ruby shrank beneath the Blackbird's keen attention.

"Family things."

The Blackbird's frown deepened. "You are keeping her secrets?"

"Not secrets. *Family* things. Her day say it was secret."

The Blackbird pressed her finger hard on Ruby's breastbone. "Why is she here?"

She could crack me open, Ruby thought, *as easy as a shell beneath a beak.* "Moonie lived in Cradle Cross. He ran away to Severnsea. He left a daughter behind him. Have *yo* heard of Lily Fly?"

The Blackbird shrugged. "And she's supposed to be his long-lost daughter?"

"Putting things to rights wi her, it ull make Moonie better."

"Better?" The Blackbird spat the word out like a pip and wiped her hand across her mouth. "She has come to make him better?" The Blackbird tipped her head back in a hoarse and bitter laugh. "She hooks you in with *this*?"

"Hooks me in?"

"A daughter, left behind?"

"He is dying."

That dry tone, mocking, cynical. "Reconciliation will restore him?" The Blackbird turned away, shaking her head. "You've swallowed Isa's bait." The plumes of her headdress twitched. She began to wade downstream.

"Her dad is dying," Ruby called out after her.

The Blackbird stopped and span around. "She has hooked you in!" She waded toward Ruby, swift and splashing, and as she came she jabbed a pointed finger. "You think she'd tell the likes of you her true reason for coming here?"

Ruby tried to scramble higher up the bank—she could still feel the imprint of the Blackbird's fingers on her throat—but as she twisted round, her foot slid from its rung and almost dipped into the water. She found another footing. Isa had not *invented* this. Why would she? A father dying and a daughter left behind! Ruby had seen Isa's discomposure; she'd seen Isa trying not to cry . . . She held one hand up, protective, around her throat and shrank back against the bank.

"Look at you!" The Blackbird stopped a foot away and examined Ruby. "You hold the roots as if the water might just suck you in. Other children spend their summers flailing in the cooling pond behind the tubeworks. I see them, catching newts and trying not to sink. Not you: you worry about water and water worries you."

Ruby pinched the soft flesh underneath her chin and watched the Blackbird.

"The water worries at you like the sea against the stone, and one day the stone is worn to sand. So what has Isa used in your enchanting? What has Isa promised, to win instant devotion?"

She will teach me to fish with golden flies, thought Ruby. *Me and Isa, striding in the sea.*

The Blackbird stepped in closer. "When you discover what *family things* have brought her here, you come and tell me, Ruby. I'll help you not to be so worried by the water. I will teach you how to read the current with your fingers; I will teach you how to dive deep, straight and true, and how to spend your precious breath while you're descending."

She leaned in close and brought one finger to rest under Ruby's chin. She raised her finger, tilting Ruby's head back, and whispered in her ear. "But if you discover why she's come and you don't tell me, I will find you and I will drop you in the Cut. I will fling you hard against the side and I will tangle up your foot in nesting rust-wire. I will choke you on the frogbit and the cack. I will make you suck in water, wanting air."

And as the Blackbird moved off downstream, fleet-footed, rock to rock, her skirts trailing behind, she chanted a rhyme with a worn and assured edge.

> *Isa One-Eye, Isa Blind,*
> *Cut her eye out with a spoon.*
> *Isa steals and says she finds*
> *Isa No Fish, Isa Moon.*

Ruby watched the Blackbird go, down toward the culvert and the road, until she was a dark shape parting branches, and then Ruby couldn't see her anymore. *She folded herself up,* Ruby thought later; *she folded herself up and floated through the tunnel, down the Ludleye Gutter to the Cut.*

The lightly spoken threats had left a tart taste in her mouth and she sucked her tongue to clear it. Truda's bag swung lazily above her. The thought of the letters made her tired. She leaned back against the bank and blew her breath out. The branch that the bag hung from straddled the whole Gutter and Ruby discovered she could reach the end without stepping from the roots. One arm above her head, she grabbed the leaves bunched at its tip and pulled the branch down, sharp. The satchel shunted toward her, but the strap caught on a fork. She felt around the bank behind her, her hand closing on stiff spikes of bugle, then a stick. She poked the satchel with it—if it only would swing, if it would get up some momentum, she could grab it as it arced toward her head. A good plan, Ruby thought, but as she grabbed for the satchel and tugged it free, she toppled forward and half-fell, half-strode out into the stream. The Gutter ran shallow, so she didn't get a soaking, but her shoes and socks were wet, and Truda's satchel. She should have clambered up the bank right then and laid her shoes out in the sun, but with the Blackbird's threats still at her, she forgot to be afraid about the water.

Chapter 6

For the Almighty hath dealt very bitterly with me. I went out full,
and the Lord hath brought me home again empty.

RUTH, 1: 20–21.

THERE WAS, in Cradle Cross, a hierarchy of debt: the back-and-
forth that didn't count as debt—a spoon of jam, a fist of coal, a little
twist of paper filled with tea. Then Grocer Foley's strap book: an
ounce of salt, a jug of milk, a pumice for the step—"Shall I purrit
on the strap?" said loud, no disgrace in it. "Go on, then, purrit on
the strap." Grocer Foley would flick through his strap book with a
wetted thumb until he found your page (scraps of writing, all direc-
tions) and write in what you'd bought. No interest charged, no terms,
a little bit paid down each week. Nan Annie didn't have a page, to
Ruby's shame; never bought on tick, preferred to go without. Each
week, while Ruby flushed, head bent, to count the pennies in her
palm, Grocer Foley teased her: "Tell your nan as when her wants it,
I've saved a page for her!" Then there was Baitch's Hock Shop (Nan
Annie had never crossed the step): if you were short (maybe your dad
had drunk his wages in the Leopard) then Georgie Baitch would
give you cash at two percent until the next pay packet. (Baitch wasn't
fussy. In his window: shoes, a hammer; a set of yellowed teeth.) Ruby

didn't know of any other kind of debt, just knew that Nan Annie was living out an unbeholden life. She would not pay on tick. She would not pay on promise. Determined she should be in no one's thrall. Ruby knew this of Nan Annie like she knew the scar inside her wrist.

As she walked home from Kenelm's Field, up past the oak tree with the broken arm, up past the scorched earth where they lit the bonfires, Ruby considered what she'd read. She'd tried to scan the letters while Em wasn't looking. Em had pegged them up to dry with Ruby's socks before the furnace around the back and, shocked at Ruby, dripping—"What will your Nannie say?"—had gone to fetch a bit of towel for Ruby, and some tea. (Em didn't bash out nails any longer on her forge—a factory in Muckeleye made the fine-knees quicker by machine—but she still made those little trinkets for new babies as she'd always done: iron, worn close, warded off bad luck and greedy faeries.) But as it was, Ruby didn't have to strain to read the letters—Em had squinted at hers, taken it to the window, held it to the light and, shaking her head, said, "Go on, Ruby, love. My eyes ay too good today."

It was typed up on Blick's headed paper with a heavy finger (some letters blotchy, some crossed out with xs), except for certain portions inked in a fluent hand. (She found out later it was Truda who had typed them and Isa who had written in the names, the dates, the quantity and nature of the debt.)

Monday 23rd July, 1933

Dear Mrs. Bacon,

Our records show that on *August 1st, 1916,* Hector Blick, then proprietor of Blick's Fine Horn Button Manufactory, advanced to *Emily Bacon* the sum of *ten shillings* for the purpose of *purchasing iron ore.*

Blick's Fine Horn Button Manufy. demands neither full nor immediate repayment of this loan. However, I leave it to your judgment and discretion to

determine what token of repayment you deem to be
appropriate.

　　Yours sincerely,

T. C. Blick

Truda Cole Blick
Proprietor, Blick's Fine Horn Button
Manufactory

Every few words Ruby had glanced up at Trembly Em, but she nodded at her to continue and sat quiet till she finished. Em had dipped her head and cradled one hand in the other. Said the money came for her from Blick's not long after them brown envelopes saying that her sons—both Blick's furnace-men—had died out at the Somme. Mr. Blick thought that Em should buy her *own* ore for making up her fine-knees, instead of being forced to get it off the foggers. Ruby'd flinched at this—she'd always thought that "foggers" was a curse-word for a cheat or for a thief, the way she'd heard it thrown about by nailers in the fish shop, but Em explained that foggers were the middlemen who sold the ore to nailers and then bought the nails back from them. The foggers forged a profit without stripping off their shirts, stood at crooked scales and rubbed their hands by braziers in the open sheds up the top of Bundle Hill. They paid the nailers by the hundredweight (taking extra scoops of nails to account for any scrap) but not with cash: they paid with Nailer's Promise—little vouchers that bought scrawny meat and watery milk, but only from the shops owned by the foggers. (And this is how Ruby learned about a bleaker form of debt: being bound in an unhappy contract, obliged to trade with cheats who smirked and said as yo was lucky, as yo owed them your living.)

"Mr. Blick said it wor right," said Em. "He said I shor tell anyone, but he bought my nails off me direct so as I'd be paid in money stead of Promise." At this point she had passed her sleeve across her shining brow and said she'd thought the money was a kindness and she hadn't known that Blick's would want it back. Em had rubbed up Ruby's legs with a rough towel and sent her off with a slick, clumsy kiss. ("Doe worry, chick—this letter. I doe blame yo for it.")

With Kenelm's Field behind her, Ruby pulled herself up each little bit of hill by the landmarks that she used when she was most tired, when she couldn't face the thought of going home—*Just till the dark house with the firs that grow right up against the windows; just till the hairpin bend.* As she walked her toes squelched in her shoes. She tried to train her thoughts on Isa and on fishing at the sea. Too late to go back down there now to tell of her encounter with the Blackbird, and Captin would be round soon with their tea so, to moor herself to Isa, Ruby chanted the Impediments out loud, but could get no further than the Seventh, *"if the weather be hot,"* before she was yanked back to fretting once again about the letter, and what Nan Annie would say. She felt indignant, as if Truda Cole Blick *tricked* her into this. Everyone had seen her take the letters round: Dinah, Glenda, all of them. The last few dried-out letters, hastily delivered, were all in the same pattern, with the parts added in by hand: fifteen shillings owed by Florrie Rudge, a pig, 1927; two shillings, Phyllis Basterfield, in 1931, for a new pair of shoes. No reason to assume the first batches she'd delivered were any different. *I am a debt-fetcher,* Ruby thought. *I am collecting debts for Blickses.* She didn't care so much about the Ruths and the Naomis and what they thought of her. (Another measure of how Ruby'd changed in these three long days since Isa'd come in on the Cut.) *And anyway,* thought Ruby, *the Ruths am worked up against Truda, what with the Docking Bill—they woe waste spit on me.* But Nan Annie, owing money? And worse still, Ruby coming to collect it . . .

She turned off the Ludleye Road and up Lean Lane; walked on, reluctant, past the five-bar gate with its fourth strut missing; past the fingerpost to St. Barbara's; past St. Barbara's hedgerow sign in large print, words shouting, closely stacked:

BACON
MILK
CREAM
EGGS
HONEY

The last stretch was uphill through dappled shade beneath a canopy of beeches. Their house sat on the southeast slope of Parry

Lean at Hunting Tree Hundred, set back from the narrow road in a wide clearing. The path curved from the road to the back door (they never used the front)—she and Captin had made this path from broken brick, deep set in the clay. Now grass was tufting through the cracks. *Wants weeding*, Ruby thought. Her fingers, sweating, slipped against the letter. The door stood propped back in the latticed porch, but no sign of Nan Annie. She couldn't be too far—at one end of the table, all the rinds and makings of a stew: blebby pink potatoes in a colander, a mound of shredded cabbage with the heart fine diced, little rounds of carrot piled up high; a ham knuckle pimpled round with cloves, blood streaked on the blade of the knife. And a shabby chicken, half-plucked, belly up; its feet and neck were lolling off the board. She checked in the front room—Nan Annie sometimes went in there on hot days for a lie down. The curtains drawn to stop the sunlight getting at the rugs, air cloy with parlor-wax. No one there, and anyway, with these walls, double-thick, the kitchen was cool enough to rest in.

She checked her dress—not wet, except a bit of hem, and dark rings at her armpits—and stood the letter up on the mantelpiece. Poured water from a covered jug out in the larder; glugged it from a tin mug; poured out more. As she drank she noticed on the shelf a lardy cake that wasn't there this morning; three wedges of custard; a half-moon of onion pie. Glenda had been here, or Dinah Hatchett Harper, and the thought of this made Ruby's stomach tighten.

She wiped her mouth with the back of her hand and flattened down her hair. Unhooked her pinny. Got the bowl and water and a knife and set to on potatoes for their tea. Kept her head bowed as she sat peeling at the table, glancing, now and then, up at the back door and out into the garden. The house creaked, dry, marooned.

She had only peeled a couple—clumsy, today, and snicking out the flesh beneath the skins—when she started at the clicking of the high latch on the black door at the bottom of the stairs. The door slammed back, and through it came Nan Annie, dressed in her Monday frock under her apron, her hair still pinned in waves, and with a bloodied handkerchief wrapped around two fingers.

"Nicked my blessed finger. Good job as *yoom* back, finally. Take all night, it would, for me to chop, wi *this*." She waved her loosely bandaged hand at Ruby. "Do it tighter, for me, Ruby. At least then I can pluck." She sat down by the chicken while Ruby pulled the hankie tight and wrapped the ends up in a knot. Nan Annie seemed bright enough, but her moods were fragile and could shatter in a moment if she wasn't handled gently; if Ruby wasn't shrewd.

"Glenda brought this chicken. I thought as we could have it cold tomorrow." Nan Annie pinched out feathers, neat and swift.

Ruby sliced off a green edge of potato. You had to race ahead of Nan Annie, and guess where she was headed; try to read the road lest it was pitted and mined under. Better still, divert her to the safe and solid ground of your own choosing. Words tumbled out, fast and hard. "I saw as Dinah sent up custards. And a pie. Saw um, I did, in the larder. Day touch um, mind."

(In days to come, there'd be more visitors to Hunting Tree than there had been, well, since Beth died. Women bringing pies and jam and faggots, and wanting to press Annie about Isa Fly inveigling herself into Captin's broad affections. Saying they was not spreading tattle, but out of loyalty to Annie. And they thought as her should know that Ruby was in thick with Isa Fly and with Miss Blick, and did her know as it was Isa Fly had written all them debt-letters and that she was enchanting Truda Blick into unpicking, stitch by stitch, the business that the Blicks had built on shorn thumbs?)

"Her says her saw yo on a bicycle. I said her must be wrong cause I ay paying out for bicycles when Ruby's got two feet to fetch her round."

Ruby's tongue grew thick and dry. It battered, clumsy, at her teeth. "Dinah? I saw Dinah. Her's spitting, wi this business wi the buttons."

"No tattle, thank yo, Ruby. No, Glenda it was saw yo. *Dinah,* walking up here in this heat? No, *Glenda* come up special. Says as yo got yourself some new friends. Says as yo been all but living down Horn Lane, and now yoom gidding letters out from Blickses."

Ruby bit hard on her lip and stared down at her peelings. Wished she was chipping on the back step at the fish shop, with Captin shouting for his cup of tea.

"Glenda come to warn me. Her says as her thought I ud need preparing. *'Preparing?'* I says to Glenda. 'What am I—a bit of brisket, wanting boiling?' " She nipped a feather from her lap. "Her said as I shor be too hard on yo."

Ruby's knife slipped and she cut off more potato than she meant to. Didn't look up: felt Nan Annie's eyes on her.

"Yo think as we got food to spare? From what I hear I udn't be surprized if her come up and took the dinner off our plate."

Ruby peeled the next potato, slow and careful.

"Doe slacken, Ruby! Len ull be up soon and I've still got my pins in." Annie pressed the bird down with her wrapped hand and plucked, swift, with the other. Her forearms bone and skin and sinew. No fat on Nan Annie. "So I says to Glenda, 'Why ud I be hard on Ruby? All as Ruby's doing is her's showing her's determined. Her ay like me, our Ruby. Ruby wants a bicycle? Her'll get a bicycle, no matter what her has to do for it. And that,' I says to Glenda, 'that ay sommat as the likes of us should frown upon.' Is that how that Blick girl's paying yo, for debt-fetching? Wi a bicycle? What, so as yo can make a fast get-away when folk follows yo out wi a poker?"

Ruby hadn't thought of that—for all she was unsure of Truda, she didn't like to think of her as scheming. She used the sharp end of the knife to ease the eyes out, dropped them with the peelings in the pig bucket, and stood up. "I'll take these for the pigs."

"Not yet, yo woe. This letter. Where is it? All the Cradles got one. All the Cradles know as yoom the one who's gid um out. So, where's mine?"

Ruby pointed at the mantel with her knife. Nan Annie wiped her hands clean on her apron. "I says to Glenda, 'Her's little, but her ay a runty pig.' " She opened up the letter. Held it loosely at her side—didn't read it, not yet. " 'Her doe snuffle at the back and dawdle at the hind legs of the scrum. Her doe raise her eyes up, time to time, and hope the sow ull waddle up and gid her a good go at milk. Not Ruby. Her wants sommat, her gets it. No matter what.' "

Ruby looked up while Nan Annie read beside the grate, her palm flat on the wall to lean against. She said nothing, only nodded, lips pressed in a line. Ruby knew just what was in there. Three hundred pounds to Annie Nailer Tailor, in 1902. Nan Annie crossed to a clean patch of the table near to Ruby and laid the letter on it. Found the folds and pressed on them to sharpen up the creases.

"*Impediments which cause a man to make no fish,*" said Ruby, in her head. "*Eight, if it rains. Nine, if it hails, or snow falls. Ten, if it be a tempest.*"

Annie took the letter; propped it back up on the mantel, but when she turned she looked down at the flagstones where Ruby tapped her feet in agitation. Nan Annie's eyes flicked down to Ruby's toes. It took Ruby a moment to see what Nan Annie saw, but when she did, she thrust her feet under the table.

"Socks, Ruby?"

"What?"

"Where am your socks, Ruby?"

"I got hot."

"*Hot,* yo got? What, did yo take um off just now, when yo come in, and put your shoes back on? Where am they, then, these socks? Yo ay been upstairs."

Ruby pinched the inside of her elbow. "Theym at Trembly Em's."

"Trembly Em's? Doe call her that. It's Aunty, or it's Mrs. Fine-knee Bacon! Trembly Em! Doe gi me cheek, on top of all this else. How come Emily's got your socks? Her feet cold, were they?"

Ruby's head hung low and Annie craned down to look full at her. "Were they? Is that it? Did Em get chilly feet?" She yanked Ruby's chair clear of the table, and Ruby tumbled to the floor. Nan Annie's dark eyes glinted like cut coal. "Take um off!"

"What?"

"Shoes, our Ruby. Off!"

"No, I'm fine. My feet am fine." She jerked her feet in under her, her toes bent up tight.

"I said, take your shoes off!" rasped Annie. She snatched up Ruby's ankle and tugged her leg out straight. Left white indentations behind on Ruby's skin. Wrested Ruby's shoe, still fastened, from her foot. Pushed her fingers inside to the toe.

"One shoe wet's a puddle, Ruby, surely. Ay many puddles around here, mind, this heat." She yanked the other shoe off; felt inside. She let one shoe drop to the floor; slammed the other on the table. "Stand up!" Her voice split the afternoon to splinters.

Ruby *tried* to stand up, but she hadn't got her footing and she stumbled backward. Chair legs clattered on the flagstones. Annie leaned down, grasping Ruby's wrist, and wrenched her from the floor. Ruby stood there, limp, hands bent up around her chest. *Isa is retreating down the Cut just as she came, and I am left here, stranded on the towpath.*

"Arms down!"

Ruby tried to straighten her arms and move them to her sides, but couldn't make them do what she was asking. It didn't matter anyway—Nan Annie forced Ruby's head forward and thrust her hands in Ruby's hair, pressing down and pulling around the crown and around the ears and around the nape as if she were checking for nits, but Ruby knew she wasn't wheedling for eggs or lice. On a dry day, she was checking Ruby's hair for damp.

She pressed around the edge of Ruby's sleeves, and tugged the skirt up, feeling along the seams. Nan Annie smelled of bergamot—her Monday rinse in that oil with alkanet that gave her hair a hint of its old red. When she was done she marched across the room away from Ruby, one hand on her hip and one on her own head, pressing hard down on the crown as if she tried to keep her head from splitting open.

Ruby usually kept quiet when Nan Annie's anger flared, but she held her fingers to her throat. She had been threatened by the Blackbird, but the encounter in the Gutter made her bolder. "An accident it was, Nan Annie, honestly it was. I day mean to go in water, but when them letters had fell in I had to get um out again else . . ."

"Else what?" Nan Annie creaked as if her anger had all dried out.

Ruby knew it hadn't and she held her breath in, tight. She'd only made it worse. Going in the water for a Blick?

"It ay as if yo ay been tode, time and time again, by me, by Captin: doe play down the Cut."

"It wor the Cut, it was the Gutter." Ruby edged around the table till it stood in between them.

" 'It wor the Cut, it was the Gutter!' " Annie parroted, and petitioning for strength, looked to the ceiling. "Think that is better, dun yo?" She strode across the room and planted one hand firm upon the table. "Dun yo remember last year, with the dredger?" She leaned across and grabbed Ruby's chin. There was spittle on her lip and mustard-markings on her teeth; curls springing from their pins. "Is that what yo want, is it? For the dredge-boat to fetch you out like that little lad?"

Ruby knew the story—old enough to crawl, but not to swim, a boat-boy must have slipped in off a barge and got caught below the fender, because they were poking poles down for him to catch on to every side, but still they couldn't find him.

"The *state* of him. They hardly knowed he *was* a baby, is what they said, when they found him two weeks later in that tunnel up at Lapple." She came around the table and the words spilled thick, glowing with her anger. One hand closed round the damp shoe on the table; the finger on the other hand pressed into Ruby like Annie was trying to pierce her. "Is that what yoom a-wanting? For me to find yo, maddocky and puffed up like a bladder?"

"I day drown, though, did I?" Ruby remembered how the Blackbird threatened her. "Nothing bad has happened to me, Nannie."

She knew as soon as she had said it: she should have sewn her mouth shut.

"*Something* has happened to yo, Ruby," Nan Annie said, and with each word, she slapped the sole of Ruby's shoe against her skull. "And. I. Woe. HAVE. It!"

Not for the first time, it was Captin who saved Ruby, rapping loudly at the open door and walking in before Annie was too sunk down in her anger. He dropped his fish-in-paper on a chair and Annie let the shoe fall to the ground and turned away to nip the pins out of her hair and drop them in her apron. Ruby ran at Captin and he wrapped her in a hug and kissed her on the crown, and let his head rest there. She breathed in cottonseed and kelp and pipe smoke, toffee-sweet, and leaned into his chest to hear his heart go; ran a finger up the bristles on his cheek, against the grain.

Yo, it is, she thought, *as I will miss most when I am gone, with Isa.*

Chapter 7

Tick, *n.* 1. A light but distinct touch. 2. A beat of the heart or of the pulse. 3. On credit, on trust.

EARLY TUESDAY MORNING, Ruby found Nan Annie kneeling on the flags before the dresser, pulling out the linen by the handful, throwing it behind, as if she were bailing out a sinking boat. She asked what she was looking for, but Nan Annie wouldn't say. She prized open the Squirrels Cherry Lips tin (the one that smelled of crumbs and hair) and shook it out: nubs of silk and yellowed scraps of paper; suspender snaps and curtain rings; flat brass buttons, rusted screws. Tipped up the baskets—shirts, frocks, waiting to be pressed. Turned out drawers; shook them out onto the table. Two piles emerging as Nan Annie sorted through them, nimble, reckless. In one pile: serviettes they'd never used; antimacassars with the broderie anglaise eyelets, the ones too good to put out; the souvenir book that Captin got them with his tokens from the paper, printed up with photographs of royalty and the War; the button box—an old, blue baccy tin with scrolls in silver on the lid. The other pile: cotton reels, empty but for three last winds; shriveled conkers; a pearl-head pin; a broken pencil end. Draped over a chair, Grandad Jonah's good suit with the stripe in. Ruby knew Nan Annie'd always been reluctant to be rid of Jonah's suit, even though she knew that there were living men who'd get good wear out of it. Ruby had heard her telling Trembly Em she didn't want the shock of seeing Jonah's good suit walking round with the wrong feet at the bottom, the wrong head poking out the top.

When Nan Annie was like this—fierce, combustible—Ruby stayed well clear. That is, before Isa. Today, Ruby offered help, but Nan Annie was absorbed and didn't raise her eyes. She would not be beholden to the Blicks, she said, to anyone, so she was taking their best things to Baitch's. He could put them in the window of the hock shop; he could keep them there beyond her year-and-seven-days and she would not redeem them, and no, she didn't care that he would give her a poor price. How else would she get this money for the Blicks?

Five days ago, before Isa came, Ruby would have voiced some cautious protest; would have *cared* about Nan Annie pillaging and laying waste, so cavalier, to all the casually assembled fragments of their home. But now she felt that Isa and the promise of the sea had set her drifting free of this dry and hollowed house at Hunting Tree.

She was not sentimental, but still, she didn't want the button box to go. Nan Annie had once thrust the tin on Ruby on a wet day when she'd grown fidgety and cross—had said that Beth spent hours sorting the buttons by shape and size and color. Ruby was lightly curious about her own dead mother, and Annie rarely spoke of her. If Ruby thought of Beth at all, it was not as Beth-her-mother but as another child who'd lived at Hunting Tree. And thinking of Beth-as-a-girl, she'd sit before the dresser with the tin and let the buttons sink down through her fingers.

So, while Nan Annie had her back turned, Ruby lifted the tin, slow, to stop the rattle and stowed it deep in Truda's satchel, the leather stiff from being dried beside the grate.

Nan Annie dispatched Ruby—"This rate, yo'll be late!"—without a mention of what had happened yesterday except to say, as Ruby left, that she'd have her on the pig hook and Ruby knew what-else, if she come home wet again. (Down in the cellar, two huge, fierce hooks protruded from a low beam—the place where Annie cured the hams. When Ruby was in trouble, Annie'd take her down: *Yoom going to face the pig!* The threat had long grown palsied—no point hanging Ruby by the collar when her feet could touch the floor.) No gall, she felt, at this. A minor daily cruelty that bound up Ruby with Nan

Annie in a skein. She slipped away gladly, with dinner bowls for her and Jamie Abel set firm in her basket, but as she left she checked she had her Almanac and Isa's fishing book tucked in Truda's satchel—didn't want Nan Annie thinking they might fetch a ha'penny for the leather.

She'd envisaged Cradle Cross tipped out since the letters—people pulling hand-carts piled with mantel-clocks and candlesticks and parlor rugs to repay loans to Blick's, joining an awkward queue at Georgie Baitch's door. Instead, as she careened around the corner to the Breach, the tin of buttons rattling in her bag, she saw Glenda moving up and down the bread queue outside Maison Hester's, pressing handbills into palms. Ruby stared on past and tried to look absorbed in thought. Knowing how she could be caught up by Glenda and pressed to tell how Nan Annie took the letter, she focused on the pillar box beyond her on the corner of the Breach and Stower Street. She was intent on reaching Horn Lane without incident or interruption—she wanted to tell Isa about yesterday, the Blackbird in the Gutter and how she and Captin had to rescue the Blick's bicycle together. But before she'd cleared the queue, Glenda stepped out in the road and stopped her with a raised palm (and, Ruby felt quite sure, a ready kick aimed at the wheel if the hand was not enough to make her stop). Glenda tucked a paper into Ruby's pocket. "For Mrs. Nailer Tailor. Tek it home for her."

The papers waved as talk of Blick's weaved through the queue—they'd heard it *wor* the Blick girl who'd written all the letters; that new one with the white eye, her who'd got herself ensconced at Gertrude's button shop, *her* had wrote the lion's share, and what was Blickses to her? They held up Truda, pointing out her flaws and cracks (*Her's gullible. Her has been taken in. Her doe care one bit for us, or for the legacy of Blickses . . .*) but something more surprising, Ruby thought: they were polishing up Hector—rubbing at the smears they'd marked him with themselves: *Say what yo like about his niece, but Mr. Blick was generous—generous to a fault.* They reminisced about his Friday habit, how when the Bull had sounded he would wait inside the gate and with a sly hand pass out those queer stock-gifts: peaches; salt-fish; licorice. And their refrain? *He gid it out, did Mr. Blick, and he day want it back.*

Glenda didn't linger in the road, but moved back over to the shop to give out papers to those who'd joined the queue, and while Ruby pushed her bicycle, she read the paper, printed in a heavy, angry hand:

BLICKS OWES US
FOR ALL AS WE HAVE LOST.
WE WILL NOT BE PAYING.

It had been Ruby's morning habit, when there was no bell to beat, no lessons, to have a cup of tea with Captin and to scan last night's *Muckeleye Gazette* for anything that should go in her Almanac, before she took the bowl for Jamie Abel. At least, this *had* been her habit, before Isa. This morning it was Isa that she wanted, but the button shop was empty when she got there, *and* the kitchen out the back, and when she shouted up the stairs, there was no answer.

She had all but closed the middle door when she saw Isa's bag squatting on the floor beside the grate. It must mean that Isa wasn't far away, because she'd never seen her go without it, not even up to Blick's or round to Captin's. She should find Isa and take her the bag; she wanted Isa Fly to think her helpful. Besides, only yesterday, the dredger had stolen Truda's satchel as a lure: what would she do if she looked through the window and saw Isa's bag left here, alone, unguarded?

Ruby put down Truda's satchel and lifted up the bag. She bit her lip. She should take it straight round to Isa, but she told herself there might be something in there that Isa'd overlooked, something that looked ordinary to Isa's eyes but might just be the key to finding Lily. A prickling at her neck; Isa had plainly pulled her bag away when Ruby asked her if she had a photograph of Moonie, *but maybe,* Ruby thought (knowing that this was a fabrication), *she was worried I would fiddle with her hooks; maybe she thought I could of cut my finger.* Isa had plainly said she had no photo of her father, but perhaps she was mistaken—she'd said that she was sure of nothing—and what harm could there be in checking for her?

Ruby set the bag down on the table. She ran over to the back window and glanced along the towpath; no one there. She stood once more at the bottom of the stairs and sung out "Isa," but more quietly this time, then checked that there was no one loitering outside the button shop. She left the middle door an inch or two ajar and, with her tongue between her teeth, she undid the buckle on the bag and flicked back the leather strap.

Isa's scarlet cape was rolled inside, too hot to be worn by day. She tried to feel around, below it, but the cape was bulky; she'd never find a thing in here this way. Ruby checked the towpath and the shop front once again, then eased the cape out of the bag and laid it on the table; beside it she set down the fly-box, Isa's priest, a fox-red writing case with tiny bronzy stitching around the edge. There were envelopes tucked under the deep flap on the left, a pad of creamy paper on the right with "Brammeier" written on it and a number alongside; on the flap, a calendar for 1895 in a stitched-on frame and, held firm by a narrow strap, a tiny book no bigger than her palm. She slipped it out. The book was set out for addresses with an index down the edge; on the inside, in a fluid hand, *"To Florence, on her tenth birthday."* Isa had written her own name underneath—passed from one hand to another, Ruby thought, just like her Almanac. She peeled the pages back. There were no addresses, but on the A page, in a childish hand, *"Anselm, 14th Jul. 1902."* Nothing on the B page, but in a different hand, someone had written *"Clement"* on the C; beside it, *"4th March 1890."* They'd used it as a birthday book, she thought: *"Florence"* came later, and on the G page, *"Gladys,"* all in the same fluid hand. No more than a dozen entries; Ruby copied the names and dates into her Almanac and wrote beside them, "Who are they? Ask Isa?" But then, remembering that she hadn't asked permission to go hunting through the bag, she scored the questions out. She checked at the door and window once again, then went back to the table; pulled out the envelopes and checked through them, but there was no photograph of Moonie tucked inside. She took out a hairbrush in a case, a cotton undershirt. The bag was almost empty now, except something rolled up at the bottom, but as she lifted it the fabric unrolled— a nightdress, Ruby thought—and something fell from it, something long and wooden. *Perhaps,* she thought, *a second priest for fish?* She bent to grab it, but it spun across the floor and underneath the couch. She knelt on the floor and reached out but, before she could retrieve it, the bell above the front door sounded and Ruby scrambled to her feet. She shoved Isa's possessions into the bag and was fastening the clasp when Truda peered around the middle door, nodding at the stairs. "Isa up there?"

Ruby shook her head, and started to explain that she'd just come for Isa's bag and that she thought it wasn't safe to leave it here alone, but Truda shrugged and muttered about coffee on the stove, and in no time she'd left the room and closed the door behind her.

Ruby let herself into the chip shop to ask Captin if he'd seen Isa. (She'd tell him they could have their morning cup of tea a little later.) There were voices, laughter, out the back, and Ruby, hearing her name spoken, stopped short of the middle door and listened.

"I've seen how you treasure Ruby." It was Isa, and Ruby smiled; felt warmed by Isa speaking well of her.

"Well, her's precious." Captin, a bit gruff. "And her's such a devoted creature, Ruby is. So keen, her is, and so affectionate. But . . ."

Ruby shifted her weight. *He talks like I'm a puppy.*

"But what, Len?" Gentle, Isa, and persistent.

"O, I doe know . . . I *think* I love her like an uncle would, or a grandad, even. But . . ." Ruby strained toward the door, but Captin didn't finish.

Ruby knew Isa could tease thoughts from you that you didn't want to shape and say out loud. She pressed her lips together. "But I cor be sure of that," Captin was saying, "because her ay mine, yo know. Because her ay . . ."

"Kin, is that it? Because she isn't kin."

Ruby raised her eyebrows. Isa did not speak this like a question but a stand-up fact, and she waited for Captin to knock it down. *O, no Isa!* he'd say, *Yo got that wrong. Her ay kin but her might as well be.* A gnawing dread, like hunger, in her belly. She waited, urging him to say it, but he didn't. Instead, he was saying how he'd missed his chance to have his own, with Annie. That they were barely more than kids themselves. That he was all set to ask her dad for her hand; he was waiting for the day her came of age. But Jonah, Ruby's grandad, jumped in first and that was that.

"But when he drowned, when Jonah drowned," Isa was saying, "you stepped in and took care of them?"

"I had to. I was there, yo know."

"You were on the boat with him and Annie?"

"No, but I'd put Annie on it; her and baby Grace."

And now he was telling Isa about Grace—a sickly baby with weak, sticky lungs—and some salt-cure Annie'd read about, and how Jonah was up and down to Whalemouth; how Jonah was thriving on his trips.

"Annie says to Jonah as her wants to go down wi him to Whalemouth, wi Grace, while it's still warm. Her thought it was the one thing as could save that precious bit. Jonah says as her was saft to even think it; he says as going to the sea would like as kill the child as save her. But Annie Nailer Tailor, her is stubborn! Her talked *me* into taking um down there. We followed Jonah down to Ludleye Port and I put um on the same packet as him. Her said as her'd surprise him on the boat, that he ud have no choice but to take um down to Whalemouth wi him."

"So what happened? Was Jonah very angry?"

A scraping; Captin, shifting in his chair. "I day stay on the dock to watch what happened. If Jonah saw as it was *me* put Grace and Annie on that boat . . ." A sharp, brief sniff. "No, I day stay around. I went off to the big inn on the quay. I was asleep when all the shouting started. Had too much bitter, too quick; passed out, I was, in a warm corner by the fire. I roused up quick enough."

Many times, Ruby had worked this scene over in her mind till it spooled out, slick and smooth, before her with no effort, like the Pictures at the Limelight she had seen on birthday trips with Captin: men leaping from moored boats in oilskin coats, spearing peat slabs to set them burning on the quayside, and by this light trawling the edges of the Severnsea Shoulder with wide-mouthed nets. But Captin's story jarred; he didn't tell the tale as she'd imagined it; Captin didn't talk about the light.

"I went down to the water and I found her wading to her waist and calling out for Jonah and the baby. Annie was one of them as made it to the shore. White, her fingers was. Wrinkled up like a skinned bit of cod. Her stayed out there hours. Tried, I did, to get her in the warm and get the blood flowing back into her fingers, but her fought me off and all as I could do was stand by her and we combed the water with our arms, our fingers. The things as we snagged in that water . . ."

He paused, and Ruby heard a sympathetic noise from Isa, a pained expressive sigh and, for some reason Ruby didn't try to understand, this sigh enraged her: Isa had been taken in! This was not Captin's story, it was Annie's. He was making himself out to be sorrowful, heroic, when all he did was hold Nan Annie's hand! It was Annie, not Captin, who lived-to-tell-the-tale; it was *hers* to tell. Yet Annie never told it. Ruby had gleaned scraps about the baby and her grandad while listening at doors; collecting up the cups on Thursdays for the Ruths and the Naomis; crouching in the herb bed underneath the window, cutting seed heads from the chives and the angelica; lying flat and still upstairs at home, one cold ear pressed against the floorboards, while Nan Annie laid her head down on the kitchen table, weeping into folded arms and plucking at the wet hair on her cheeks. But if Annie didn't want to tell her story then, Ruby felt, it passed to her.

And now Captin was using it to pick up sympathy from Isa.

"I stood wi her and found his name—Jonah's—on the list of them still missing from the wreck. Him and the baby. I sat wi Annie when her come back home without um." A guttural, dismissive noise. "So, I tried to do my bit. I cherished all on um. Annie, Beth—that's Ruby's mom as died when her was twenty-two—and now our Rube. I try, Isa. I try to do my bit."

"And in all these years, you've never thought to marry Annie?"

"How could I? Even if I'd asked, her ud of turned me down because her was still married; her udn't say as her was widowed when they could never bring him home to bury. And I never wanted folk to say as Len Salt took advantage."

"And you consider it too late, Len?"

"For what?"

"To have your own."

"What, wi Annie? Annie's spry but her's past giving any man a child!"

Isa spoke low, a register that Ruby couldn't understand, a foreign tongue her ear could not make sense of. She was annoyed, and she leaned closer to the door. Isa had steered them with a sharp swoop and swing away from Captin's duty, from all his not-quite-kin, his proxy-fathering, from all the things that Captin didn't have; their talk had become light and giddy, and Ruby thought she heard them giggle.

Now Captin was laughing in a low, confidential way that Ruby'd never heard; the air was thick with not-yet-spoken possibility, and suddenly she did not want to hear them anymore. She moved to leave, but in her haste she did not account for Isa's bag: she knocked against the middle door and it swung open before she had a chance to turn and run. In the back room, Isa was sitting, legs up, coy on Captin's sofa, toying with the mirrors on her skirt. Captin was in the armed-chair with his back to the shop door; twisting round to Ruby—flushed, bright-eyed.

"Rube!" He tried to stand, but his limbs seemed heavy and reluctant.

Ruby felt a sinking in her stomach. She understood why Captin—*her* Captin—would want to sit with Isa, but didn't understand why the sight of Captin, rapt and flushed, would leave her curdled, wrung out, trying not to cry.

"Doe bother getting up," she said. "I woe be staying." There was no room for her at Captin's anymore, now Isa Fly was here. "And anyway, it looks like yo need help to get up out your chair."

She dropped Isa's bag and muttered that it wasn't safe to leave it in the shop. Isa threw Ruby an apologetic smile and Ruby knew she could not blame Isa for all this: for Captin, foolish, getting fat, and thinking he was younger than his years. *All the taters as I've chopped for him,* she thought, *and this is how he pays me.* She wanted to rush in, to drag Isa from the sofa by the hand and run shouting through the streets until they found the missing daughter, till they'd acquired for-giveness like a pill wrapped up in paper, and then she'd go with Isa to the sea.

"Rube!" Captin called, and there was something anxious in his tone. But before he'd got up from his chair, Ruby had run from the shop and down to Blick's. She snatched up Truda's satchel and ducked into the little gate too far to the left and grazed her shoulder on the wood but didn't care. Wanted to run at it again, to scrape the other one; dull herself; knock off her edges; distract herself from Captin, glowing, confidential. And there he was, looking up Horn Lane for her among the children who were rope-turning and jumping by the shed. (She'd heard the Blackbird chant this clap-song yesterday and wondered how it had spread round so quickly.) Captin was sorting through them, seeking her, and, seeing that Ruby wasn't in among them, he half-ran up toward the Breach, still looking. Ruby pulled the gate shut behind her with an abrupt, vicious click.

She found Truda at her desk, with one hand working at her curl, the other tracing down an inky line of figures in a ledger. Ruby stood still at the top of the stairs. "Prepare for fireworks, Ruby. I'm levying an hourly charge for room hire at the Mission."

"The Ruths woe like it."

"No, indeed."

"I posted all them letters for yo. I come to see if yo got other jobs."

Truda looked up but kept her finger on the page. "You dear. You have my undying thanks. You posted all of them?" Ruby nodded. "And how were they received? Did Dinah chase you with a hammer?"

Ruby laughed. "No, but Glenda's stirring folk up in the bread queue."

"*Plus ça change.*" There was a burst of laughter in the street, and Truda put a folded paper in the ledger as a bookmark and then slammed it shut. She crossed the room, stepping over paper-piles, the half-filled crates, the notebooks.

Ruby fidgeted with the buckle on the satchel: she still had it looped over her shoulder. "But there was this thing with the dredger, yesterday . . ."

Truda stood to one side of the window. She kept her eyes fixed on the street. "Did she get a letter? I don't remember writing one to her."

"No . . ." Ruby crossed the room, around the paper-piles, the ledgers, and stood beside Truda. "But her was getting worked up about Isa being here."

"She's not the only one."

The skipping game had moved outside the button shop, and they

could hear quite clearly what was being chanted in time with the turning of the rope:

> *Ruby's made a new friend:*
> *Her name is Isa Fly.*
> *Her made her out of bits of horn*
> *And gid her one black eye.*
>
> *The other eye's a fish eye*
> *Her nicked from Captin Len*
> *Now Captin's chasing Isa*
> *Cause he wants it back again.*

Ruby knew the faces and some of the names: that tall one was Lorna
Rudge; Vi Cope was the one tripping on the rope; Sal Bastock was the
other turner, and the small one from the Leopard was running in a circle around the skipping, taking in the button shop and rapping at the
door, then nipping round to hide behind the others.

"Friends of yours?"

"What, them?" Ruby shook her head.

"Well, good." Truda leaned out of the window and shouted, "Bug-
ger off, you scabrous creatures, before I drag you in and grind you up
for bonemeal." Ruby sniggered. The children did not disperse straight
away: they looked up to the high window and retreated backward up
Horn Lane in a sequence of loose flourishes and lavish, flailing curt-
sies. One of them—Sal Bastock, Ruby thought—began another chant:
"Truda Blick, her makes yo sick, her ay got tits, her's got a—" but
Truda slammed the window shut and said, with more bluster than
scorn, "Lord, where did they exhume *that* one from? I haven't heard
that exquisite verse in years. At least the Captin rhyme was more original." She swiveled on her heels, eyes narrowed. "You mustn't mind
it, Ruby, being sung about like that."

Ruby shrugged. "It ay the first time."

"It won't be the last." Truda threw her shoulders back. "Think of
it as an honor."

Ruby ran her finger round the buckle on the satchel, and Truda
gripped her shoulders. "You have been noticed, Ruby! You have been

enshrined in song!" But Ruby kept her eyes fixed on the satchel; did not want to look up, lest Truda see that it was not the song but her Captin enchanted, Ruby excluded, that had made her sad.

Truda took a cigarette and lit it. "So you'd like to be useful? You'd like an errand?"

Ruby nodded.

"These errands, Ruby, that I'm asking you to run . . . Should I require too much, then you must tell me. If you're harangued on my account . . ." She moved back to the table and picked up a batch of documents tied up with a ribbon.

"Fine, it is. I doe mind." Something piquant, she'd discovered, in provoking Cradle Cross.

"The blasted quaestor's coming to pick over the great carcass of Blick's."

"Quaestor?"

"Money man. Purser, bursar, treasurer . . . But quaestor sounds majestic, don't you think? No doubt he'll advise that if I want the factory to survive, I should sell my soul to raise a bit of cash. I suspect it is too sullied, now, to be of any worth . . ." Her words tailed off. "Someone needs to show him around the Mission to Canal Folk."

"Woe he want to talk to yo?"

"Not while he's walking around the place. He'll be checking for wood-worm; tapping walls. He'll come up here when you're done; he'll reckon up our assets, he'll do his inquisition . . . but these chaps don't listen to pecuniary half-wits like me. So, all you need to do is be polite and unlock all the doors and smile while you are doing it, but don't smile so much that you look simple." She checked her watch and tapped it, "He'll be at the gate on the hour. Give him those papers, would you?" She slapped them into Ruby's hand.

Ruby pushed the papers in her bag, but hesitated. "Truda, nobody's heard of Lily Fly."

"Of whom?"

"You know: this daughter of Moonie's. I been asking all about and no one's heard of her. But I was thinking: Moonie Fly is raving. Maybe Isa got the wrong end of the stick. Maybe there ay no missing daughter."

"Ruby." Truda held up a hand to stop her. "Do you like her?"

"Who?"

"Do you like Isa Fly?"

Ruby frowned, nodding. "Her's kind to me. Her listens when I talk." She bit her lip, thinking of Isa on the sofa, and Captin's low laughter.

"And you want her to stay a little while?"

She nodded once again.

Truda pulled open a drawer and took out a bunch of keys. "If Isa says she's here to find this missing sister, so be it." She dropped the keys in Ruby's hand. "Now, go. Quick." She twisted Ruby round to face the stairs. "Be off, before I drop my fag on all this paper and set the place alight and call in the underwriters." But before Ruby had reached the lower door, Truda was at the top and calling down, "Isa says her father mended boats when he lived here. That's your family's business, yes?"

"I asked my dad already. He day know anything."

"If it's anything like Blick's, there will be records of transactions; ledgers; letters. Maybe your family had dealings with the elusive Moonie Fly. It won't locate the daughter, but it might yield an address, a place to start."

Ruby's morning lumbered by. She was anxious to retrieve Isa's bit of wood from underneath the couch, but Isa had been working in the shop as Ruby passed, so she went on, met the quaestor and showed him around the Mission; and while he measured and wrote notes she moved from room to room. Empty for now, but at ten o'clock the Ruths and the Naomis would be in to fire the geysers up and fill tubs with hot water: Tuesday at the Mission was the day they helped boat families with their washing. (Less call for this now that so many hauliers had switched to running freight on diesel: the Cut was emptier, these days; men could get home between trips, and there were fewer families subsisting on the water.)

She unlocked the office; the washroom, with its stove, tubs hung on nails around the wall; the meeting hall; the kitchen. She unlocked the storeroom where they kept the mops and buckets and clean towels and paper-cabinets; she'd spent whole afternoons in here, filing copies of letters she'd written for boatmen, but now her eye was drawn down to the series of deep boxes made of tin, and stenciled on the lid: PROPERTY OF TRENT NAILER TAILOR and the year that they pertained to. She kept the storeroom door ajar and bent beside the boxes, listening in case the quaestor called to her. She needed to work back from 1900—the year before Isa was born, and therefore the latest, by Isa's reckoning, that Moonie Fly could have left Cradle Cross. She levered up the lid and as it slid off Ruby smelled the Deadarm: pitch and oakum; seasoned ash; paraffin and caulk. She lifted out a sheaf of papers, then bills and chitties clipped together with a dolly peg; then a book of orders, the pages edged in pink, a record of all work done on each boat, and by each piece of work, the name of he who'd done it.

When the quaestor called to say he'd finished, she put the papers back into the box—she'd have to come back later to look properly— and escorted him to Blick's.

As Ruby wound her way with her father's dinner through the Stower folds, she wished it was her Grandad Jonah waiting at the Deadarm and not Jamie Abel; that she could ask her grandad if he had known Moonie Fly, for the quicker she located his lost daughter, the quicker she could step outside the circle she had drawn around herself and, her arm crooked safe through Isa's, go to Severnsea. Her Grandad Jonah might have known him; might have known the daughter, or the wife. Jonah had worked at the Deadarm thirty years ago; that's how he'd met Annie—he'd been apprenticed to her father, Thomas Trent. He'd taken on the business when Tom died—she knew that much.

Ruby had no sense of her grandfather, except what she'd elicited from the study of a photograph up home, found somewhere in the bowels of the dresser: his wide, flat face; his smile like a slash in a wheel of cheese; sleeves rolled back and his arm hanging loose over the shoulder of a woman who barely came up to his shoulder: Nan Annie. Her face was turned to him, as if to catch the light, the beginnings of a smile around her lips; clear-skinned, eyes like beads of Whitby jet, buoyed and dark and lit, as if this carefree man had lifted something heavy from her and she was grateful to him. But he looked directly at the camera, not at her, with a swagger that made his pale eyes start and glow.

No swagger in her father: Jamie Abel was bent over, stirring at a pot of pitch. She signaled to him with a listless wave and said she'd left his dinner on the path, but he called to her, "Doe go, Rube! There's sommat I want to talk to yo about. Miss Severn come down here."

"Miss Severn?" Ruby wrinkled up her nose. "Who the fogg's Miss Severn?" She wanted him to shout, to snap back, "RUBY!" To be shocked enough to march over here and shake her as Nan Annie would have done, but to her irritation Jamie Abel spoke light and careful, casual. (She should have paid attention to this new color in his voice, but she was still too cross with him to care.)

"The dredger: Belle Severn. And doe be crude. It doe suit yo. Her wor christened Blackbird."

"Again? Her come round yesterday!"

"The spoon ay turning like it should. Checking it, I am." He unhooked the rope that kept the drawbridge lifted, paying it out slow to keep the descent smooth. Nothing strange in this: he did this every day to fetch his dinner from the towpath. But Ruby hadn't been here when he did it, not for seven years, and she felt a shiver quickening her limbs as Jamie Abel crossed the plank toward her. He stopped short of the towpath. "Get my dinner, will yo, Rube?"

Obedient, she picked the bowl up by the knot and stepped closer to the plank.

She hadn't thought about reunion, all these years, because that would confirm that they'd been parted. It wasn't like those photos in that souvenir book Captin got with tokens: fathers coming home safe from the War. He didn't pull her to him in a protective embrace. She didn't leap into his arms. It was not as if they touched. He did not look at Ruby, not straight in the eyes. She held the bowl and stood firm on the land; he stood on the bridge, pulling at the collar at his neck.

"Her knows this woman from before, her says. Her knows this Isa Fly. Her says her's cruel and I ay got no reason to doubt her. Her's worried for yo, Rube. Her's worried as yo ull get pulled into something."

"What?" Ruby folded her arms and whispered at her father. "What am I getting pulled into?"

"I doe know."

"*Yo* doe know cause *her* cor say. Her's making spit up about Isa."

"Yoom young, Ruby. Yoom kind. Yoom the type it's easy to take in."

She played with the knotted cloth around the bowl. "*Yoom* the one deluded."

"Ruby, listen!" Even when he simmered, his voice was low and even. "Her doe want to see yo getting used. Folk can take advantage."

And you would know, thought Ruby. She leaned out toward her father. "Here's your dinner."

He took the bowl; retreated, bleak-eyed, to the Deadarm. But Ruby was assaulted by the smell of him—coal-tar, pitch, cut wood—and felt, somehow, defeated as he climbed inside the dark shell of the dredge-boat.

Ruby had cradled all the blame since his departure, seven years back. She could not remember much about the trip that sparked it all—she was only seven years old—just that Nan Annie had begged them not to go. Some trip that the War Office had put on—Ruby never understood that part. Nan Annie saying: *Yo doe have to go. They cor force yo. The War was won, and yo ay still enlisted.* But, for once, Jamie Abel had insisted. Remembered hopping up and down, she did, and pumping on her father's arm, as their boat, majestic and sedate, came in at Dover docks; the gap between the gangplank and the quay; salt-cold on her cheeks; salt-spray in her mouth and eyes and hair; the English Channel gray, like pigeon soup. Later, being sick on her shoes and someone lending her a shawl. And then, her father trying to blunt the keen edge of her disappointment when the seas became too rough to carry on; telling her it was exciting, going half-the-way to France! And Ruby winching her own face tight into a smile, wanting *something*—bobbing flags, a finish line—to show they'd reached Halfway. But then the boat wheeled slowly round and as they headed back for shore, the chalk cliffs reared and waves thrashed at their feet and as they docked she felt a thrill she'd never known before—a thrill at being *here,* where sea clashed with the shore, right at the limit of the

land. Wanted to stay here, being sucked in, spat out, by the slick lip of
the sea.

It had taken all day and half the night again to get back home.
Three trains—her throat drying as they moved further inland—and
then a walk from Muckeleye in the dark, jolted to a drowse on her
dad's back. The evening paper beat them home; Nan Annie'd waited
up and slapped it on the table: STORM IN ENGLISH CHANNEL: MUCK-
ELEYE'S SOMME HEROES IMPERILED. (Ruby'd saved this: cut it out
when Nan Annie wasn't looking and pressed it in her Bible. Later still,
she pasted it into the Almanac.) Ruby had said too much, as ever, and
that's what did the damage. Woke creased and grizzly from her half-
snooze, not alert enough to read the cold set of Nan Annie's face, nor
to hear the coded warning when her dad maintained they hadn't been
in any danger, Ruby (sleepy, gleeful) told Nan Annie proudly how
they'd nearly drowned.

He'd tucked her up in bed that night, like every night, pulled the
covers straight and told her not to worry, he'd just be sleeping at the
Deadarm for a bit, just till Nan Annie calmed down. That was the last
time he had tucked her in. And Nan Annie was still seething, even
now.

She left her bicycle inside the gate at Blick's, then went to Captin's to
help with the dinner rush (*"Isa ay here, Rube. Her's helping that Miss
Blick."*) and he was awkwardly attentive, almost pleading (*"Yo knows
yoom precious, doe yo, Rube?"*) and when the clearing up was done
he tried to gather her, to kiss her head, but Ruby shook him off and
shrank away. There were ledgers waiting for her in the storeroom at
the Mission, and she felt a flicker warm her spine.

No one stopped her at the Mission—the Ruths were still there,
hanging washing in the little courtyard at the side. Trembly Em, she
saw; one of the Joans, and Ruby said that she was there on boatyard
business, to get something from the papers for her nan. (Once a
month, Ruby would fetch the bills and order sheets and cash box
from the Deadarm; at home, Nan Annie would sort them into neat
piles on the table; write numbers into columns—in pencil, first, then
inked, careful, on top; Ruby would fold the flimsy chits and slip them

into envelopes to post.) They nodded and said that she was a good girl, helping her dad, her Nan Annie.

She closed the storeroom door behind her. There was a window, but high up and nailed shut. The air was dry and heavy, and the light was meager; barely good enough to read by. She took out a sheaf of papers and her Almanac and sorted through the boat books and the bills, the Record of Work Completed and the letters. A glancing mention of a Fly, but when Ruby looked a little closer it was just a timetable for flyboats, and she was disappointed. There were a few flyboats still working the Cut; "fly" because these boats were quick; the horses changed every few miles to keep them fresh and fast.

She persisted in her search, but every now and then her eye would fix on something jarring: an unpaid bill for rivets; work not done, but paid for up front. Debts, scattered through the papers like the fragments of a wreck: the beer ticket at the Leopard, a bill from Dodd's the chemist, four months' worth of coal, two new suits, three shirts (and who had *two* suits in the Cradles?), a pair of shoes . . . She was soon diverted from the search for Moonie Fly and began to pile the debt papers up to one side: bills for oakum, clinkers, roves; doctor's fees; more medicine bills. She noted them in pencil in her Almanac. Demands from the haulage firms and writs from the courts . . . So *this* was why Nan Annie was in such great debt to Blick's. Jonah, Ruby's grandfather, had left these dues and unmet obligations bobbing in his wake.

In Cradle Cross, stories were passed round, from hand to hand, like teacups, and the stories that got told were mostly temperate, diverting things: how Tom Home's football broke the pastor's window; how Dora Snaith got water on her kidneys; how Mr. Dodd ran out of pills and made some up with sherbet for a bet. But each tale-bearer nursed a more costly secret in her arms; each believed she was the only one to hold this thing that bucked and kicked and struggled to break free. Ruby felt that she had wrested such a secret from the boat books and she had turned it loose and it would come for *her*.

Ever since she'd found out about the shipwreck, she'd been grateful to her grandfather: when children traded tales like ciggie cards, gaudy and high colored, of how the fathers they had never met had been killed in the War—"Three miles behind the enemy line! Three Jerries stuck through on his bayonet!"—Ruby had no story of her own father to slap down on the pile (Jamie Abel disappointed her in so many different ways), but Jonah had bequeathed her a distinctive tale to trade: the Tragedy of Shipwrecked Jonah and the Baby. She'd sketched it out for her friends in wild strokes: the unexpected rising of the Severnsea Bore; this vast wave forcing itself down the narrow throat of the estuary, the *Lickey Bell* all splintered into sticks, spearing boats and men and babies. It scored higher than another Tommy with a bayonet. And this was how she liked her Jonah: distant and distinct. These unpaid bills on shiny paper—they stripped the color from her Tragedy and made her Jonah dreary, commonplace, his currency diminished.

Her eyes were tired. She gathered up the last papers and notebooks and looped the satchel over her shoulder, peering down at it and wondering if it looked suspicious, if Trembly Em would guess what she was up to and report her to Nan Annie.

The evening Bull at Blick's had not yet sounded, and at this time Horn Lane was quiet, usually, except for the odd man with a barrow taking sacks up to the sheds. But today it was alive with children, gathering before the button shop, the small ones jumping up onto the curb and off again, the others crowding up against the windows. Sal Bastock, Lorna Rudge and Vi were set apart and working at their rope.

Something had altered in the few hours since she left. Ruby wasn't sure precisely what had changed and stood still for a moment at the mouth of Horn Lane. Sal Bastock saw her and she and Vi and Lorna started a new chant.

> *Ruby Abel Tailor*
> *Was hooked by Isa Fly . . .*

The fattened satchel dug into her shoulder. *I am helping Isa Fly to find her sister,* she told herself. *And then Isa Fly will take me to the sea.* She strode down the lane toward the button shop.

> *Then Isa Fly and Truda*
> *Cooked Ruby in a pie.*

She kept her head up, her eyes fixed on a faded sign, BLICK'S UNUSUAL BUTTONS. HORN MISCELLANY, done up in gold on green and swinging from the bracket fixed high on the wall.

> They ate her up for dinner
> But then spewed her right out
> Cause Ruby was too chewy
> And her stank of rotted sprouts.

The little ones were jumping at the window, pressing their fingers and noses to the glass until the shine was smudged away. Some even bobbed their tongues out and smeared the glass. She stood behind and looked in over them. The three shelves in the window were laid out with scalloped paper. Lined up on the highest shelf, slim-necked bottles for medicine wine, their yellowed labels marked "Cyclops" underneath an inky, wide Egyptian stare, the iris like a cartwheel, spoked. On the lowest shelf, clawed pop bottles ("Blick's Three-Hole Special—Limited Edition"); wide-shouldered flour jars labeled "Blick's Ornamental Two-Hole"; curving Dimple's bottles, full up to the ounce line with "Good Luck Fours"; on the middle shelf, a drafts board set with horn blanks (solid, plain—you'd want to keep them, turn them, in your palm) and a little tent card to the side: "Not for sale." In turn, children were hopping on the step—the door was weighted open with a wooden block—and some, grinning back over their shoulders, were even going in. Ruby stood and watched them from the window. One boy with a glass jar, held between rounded palms, shook it to make the buttons click and dance and tut. A girl climbed on the step stool, teetered to lift down a big-shouldered jar and pulled out the cork to hear it cloop. Another, sitting bent up underneath the counter, was trying to fish out something settled between floorboards. And in the middle of them, Isa, who had conjured up this shop as if from nothing, sitting on the high stool at the counter, sorting buttons into little saucers laid out in front of her.

This mobbing wouldn't last long—once they'd had a good look and gathered enough kindling to spark rumors, they would scare themselves away: their tattle spreading through the streets like horn smoke in the days and nights to come. *Those drafts from horn blanks in the window? Theym in new positions, every morning.* They'd swear that each piece had a name writ on in pencil, underneath, and Isa and the Devil played for souls.

Ruby was still watching through the window, wondering if *all* these children wanted to be taken to the sea, and willing them to drown in flooding caves like Hamelin's rats, when she jumped back from the glass at Dinah Hatchett Harper booming on the step, "Doe yo lot have homes, and taters wanting peeling?" The children yelped and scattered, ducking underneath her great arms, thick as anchor chain, before she could reach down to pinch them. Ruby stood her ground and, her hand resting on the satchel, waited silent at the window. But even if she hadn't, Ruby guessed that Dinah would have grabbed her by the collar, because Dinah swiveled to face her. "Not yo, Ruby Abel Tailor."

She waited till the children had dispersed and then pulled Ruby off the curb down after her, just into the gulley that ran alongside Captin's shop and out onto the towpath. She pressed two folds of paper into Ruby's hand. Ruby made to open them, but Dinah clamped Ruby's fingers shut around the papers. "Gi this to the Blick girl, now as yoom indentured to her. The other's for the white girl sat in there." She jerked her head in the direction of the button shop.

"Her's opened it up, like yo saw," said Ruby. "Yo can go in if yo want and gi it her yourself."

Dinah snorted. "What, me, go in wi her? That one as writ them letters out for Blickses? Never crossed that step, I day, when it was Gertrude Cole who had the lease of it. There ay *nothing* as ud make me cross it now. There's two words as I'll gi yo, Ruby. Hooks is one." She bent her finger up and held it close to Ruby. "The other one is Eyes." She hooked her finger over a crooked thumb, and Ruby flinched—imagined one of Isa's gleaming hooks sunk through flesh into the orbit of a fish. Dinah must have read perplexity in Ruby. "Hooks, Ruby, and Eyes! I'll gi um hooks and eyes! All them boys, there is, 1914—" She pointed down the gulley toward the factories along the Cut. "Them boys who gets their blue-and-yeller badge to show as theym on War Work: making tube; striking chain; stoking furnaces. So I goes to Hector Blick and says to him, why cor he say as all the Blickses boys is on War Work sose *they* ud get a blue-and-yeller?" She addressed her question out and up, to the high walls of Blick's, as if they might just answer her, then twisted back to Ruby. "Not just my Horace, mind, I asked for—I asked for *all* on um. And remember, Ruby, as this is the same Hector Blick who been gid enough white feathers he could stuff a pillow! But Hector Blick says as he woe so much as *ask* the War Office; he says as he knowed button-making wor (what was it he said?) *critical*. So I says, 'Critical? Buttons ay critical? What dun the War Office expect, as we ull all go round wi our clothes flapping open? Ay that a victory for the Hun, if we all lose our dignity?' And Hector Blick, he laughed—laughed, mind yo—and said as we could all use hooks and eyes if we runned out of buttons. And that's what my lad died for. Hooks and eyes. I ull gi um hooks and eyes." She breathed in, sharp, jaw set firm, biting on her lip, and looked away. "See to it, Ruby, as they gets them papers. Both on um."

Ruby was watching Dinah go, striding up the Breach, when Truda joined her at her elbow with a stack of ledgers and tipped the top half into Ruby's arms. "Help me carry these to Isa's, will you? And while you do, tell me what Hatchet Harpy wanted in the alley. She's been up and down a dozen times today, hurling missiles at my window with those piggy little eyes. 'Any moment now,' I thought, 'the glass will shatter and I'll find a pinless hand grenade tick-tocking on my floor.' But it would seem that Hatchet Harpy was waiting round for *you.*"

"No, not really. Yo it is her's after. Her gid me a paper—under these, it is, somewhere—one for Isa, one for yo," said Ruby, shifting the ledgers straight in her locked arms. "What am these, anyway? Weigh enough, they do."

"Records of employment. I thought Isa might find evidence in here of her elusive Moonie, or her sister. Or at least another Fly."

Ruby glanced at Truda—reluctance ran through Truda's words like veins in marbled stone. *Her doe want her to find them. Her wants Isa to stay here*, thought Ruby. *Her wants Isa all for herself.* She thought of Isa curled on Captin's couch that morning and felt a spike of cruel joy. *Well, Truda, yo cor have her.*

"Besides which, I have spent hours with that quaestor and there are little figures floating in front of my eyes like midges." Truda seemed shabbier to Ruby and, for all she wanted to keep Isa to herself, Ruby felt unnerved: the sleek and cocky Truda *could not* lose the townish swagger that always walked beside her like a shadow. Ruby felt like Wendy with her Peter Pan, wanting to kneel down and sew the shadow back.

"I did suggest to Isa that she go across to Rudge's—there might have been a Fly there, or somebody who knew her Moonie, but she insisted on getting the shop open. But most families have had a thumb in Blick's, so to speak, although I never heard Hec mention any Fly."

"*No one's* heard a mention of a Fly."

Isa must have heard them coming. She was leaning up against the doorframe, arms folded, head tilted.

"Miss Fly!" Truda span out a flourished bow. Isa flashed a brief, in-dulgent smile at her but kept her dark eye—quizzical and narrowed—fixed on Ruby, as if she knew something that Ruby kept from her. Isa stepped aside to let them in, rubbing Ruby's shoulder as she passed. "You left so quick, this morning. I've been worrying about you."

Ruby winced—the skin was still chafed where she had grazed it in her hurry into Blick's—and glanced quickly back at Isa in case she was offended. "Fine, I am. It's just I banged it on a gate."

"When you found my bag this morning, when you brought my bag to me—"

Ruby flushed: that bit of wood, that second priest that rolled under the couch—she hadn't had a chance yet to retrieve it.

"—was it already open when you found it?"

Up until this moment, Ruby had intended to get the wood and, when it was rolled up safe inside the nightdress, to confess to Isa that she'd had a little look inside her bag. She'd say sorry for her curiosity, of course, and tell Isa that, like all children, she tended to be nosy; Captin would confirm that Ruby was always asking to sort his pock-ets out, and she'd sort through the bits spilled on the table. It wasn't out of wickedness, she'd say, and that would be an end to her confes-sion.

But Isa frowned and studied her with such intent that Ruby with-drew all thought of confessing. Her mouth was dry. "Why, is sommat missing?"

Isa didn't answer, and Ruby was relieved when Truda spoke.

"We bring you ledgers . . ." Truda slapped them, one by one, down in a high pile on the counter. "We hope that these may aid you in your quest." She took Dinah's notes from Ruby. "So now let's see what Hatchet Harpy's got to say."

Ruby stood on tiptoe and tried to read the note over her shoulder, but Truda read it out loud, becoming more indignant with each word. *"Blicks owes us for all as we have lost! We will not be paying?"*

Truda screwed the paper into balls and with a howl she tossed them, in high arcing throws, towards the grate, but they bounced off the wall above the fireplace and she kicked them back toward the wall. *"Blicks owes us for all as we have lost . . .* Not *this* tosh again!" Isa gently moved the block and eased the shop door to, while Truda flicked her head back as if her neck were hinged and spat curses at the ceiling. "Does Hatchet Harpy think that Hector *relished* sending all those boys to war? Does she think he was untouched when he found he couldn't save them? Does she think she is the only one who *lost*?" She brandished six fingers at Isa and at Ruby, twisting up her face into a scowl. "Six times in twenty months he wore his black suit. Six times, Isa. And that's just family! God, I remember *that*. Sitting cross-legged while the teacher read the names out from those bloody lists. Fiddling with the buckles on my shoes and praying that my surname wasn't read. Didn't work, mind: Blick, Blick, Blick, Cole, Blick." (That's five, thought Ruby, then remembered Truda's mother was the sixth; had died of influenza, like her own.) "That's not *counting* all the times we went to chapel for Blick's button boys."

Ruby remembered Hector, just by sight: tall, like Truda, but un-tucked, with an untrimmed dappled beard; a habit of forgetting to duck down under low lintels.

Truda reached into her pocket and pulled out a tin. Her hands shook as she tried to pry it open, and she threw it on the counter. "And all that *rot* about how we made the buttons for the Hun. We put a stop to shipping out the German stock as soon as Russia mobi-lized for Belgium! If anyone had asked him, he'd have told them."

Isa took the tin and pried off the lid. "Come on. Through the back. Sit down for a minute." She took out a cigarette and held it up to Truda's lips.

"I don't feel like sitting down." The cigarette bobbed, lodged between her teeth. As near to whispering, thought Ruby, as Truda ever came.

"I have cake." Isa struck a match and held it shielded by her hand, the flame dipped to the end of Truda's cigarette.

"From Maison Hester's? No, thank you. I don't think I could stomach it today." She sucked in deeply and as she plucked the cigarette from her mouth her fingers shook. Crimson markings round the end.

"Do you think," said Isa, "you would let Ruby make you tea?"

Her truculence was fading. "I could try."

They all had tea together in the back—Isa insisted Ruby stay. And while they drank, Isa worked up fish hooks—heating them in the fire, bending them, then plunging them in water, as laid out in the Treatise—and Truda told how Hector Blick had saved Maison Hester's in the War. That long winter when torpedoes got the sugar boats, when the price of sweetness tripled overnight . . . A bitter winter; tart. But she conceded that Dinah Hatchett Harper had done her best with malt cake and with fruit bread, everyone said so. That is, until she got the envelopes, one after the other: son missing, husband missing, Glenda's young man dead. Dinah got thin, went to bed, and Glenda couldn't shake her into wakefulness or baking.

(Ruby had never been in Maison Hester's without full shelves, first thing in a morning, without rice pudding cut to wedges and a tray of custards in white paper cases and a queue of women waiting, ready baskets on hooked arms. Could not imagine Dinah dwindling. They made ends meet, the Harpers. More than that, they tied them round their doughy middles in a bow.)

Hot-handed Glenda, who was slow to learn her mother's trade, had tried to keep the shop door open, but her custards were more burned than seared and her bread was leaden. The flour man from Muckeleye came knocking at the door, and seeing the shelves lined with curling paper and a scattering of crumbs, wouldn't put another sack on tick, and that's when Truda found Glenda, damp-cheeked, folded on the steps down to the bread shop. ("Ruby's age, I was.") Truda went straight home and told her uncle Hec, and next morning, and every Friday morning till the War juddered to an end, Glenda found a sack of flour and a small bag of sugar (taken out of Hector's larder)—on her doorstep. And every Friday Truda found a bloody knot of bandages on theirs.

Truda stared down at the tea cup on her knees. "He kept the Cradles sweet, you see." She looked to Isa Fly and Ruby saw entreaty in her face. "And this is how they paid him."

Two days from now, Ruby would remember how Isa Fly had set her small curved hook down on the stove and turned to look at Truda. Ruby would remember this when she heard Dinah, two days from now, bellowing her rage and grief out to the Breach.

Chapter 8

Mermaids have been sighted all along the Shoulder of the Severn and as far inland as Ludleye Port, but the most notorious sightings have occurred around the treacherous kinks and outcrops off the coast at Lee and at St. Shirah.

"ANCIENT ADVICE TO SEAFARERS, DERIVED FROM LORE AND LEGEND,"
THE COASTAL COMPANION, SEVERNSEA, ALMANAC FOR 1899

THE BLOODIED BANDAGES laid on the doorstep to indict Hector Blick were most likely pilfered from the Floating Hospital, a fleet of requisitioned boats moored for the duration of the War in a quiet green arm of the Cut up beyond the Five Locks. Truda did not know this, but, as chance would have it, Horace Hatchett Harper was conveyed there, just two miles from home, in the summer of 1915. It may well be that those bandages that Truda hid from Hector every Friday were the very dressings that blotted up the blood and clots from Horace Hatchett Harper's shrapnel-shredded leg. (Not that knowledge of their provenance would have lessened her distress at their discovery.)

Dinah did not know at first that her son was laid out, seeping, sticky, on a lush stretch of the Cut. Did not know that, when his fever had abated and his skin was meshing, gummed, across his wounds, Horace spent his evenings sitting on the deck among the sedge flies, sketching the humped back of Parry Lean across the valley. Dinah might never have discovered his proximity (he was not allowed to put it in his letters) had it not been for a young orderly who told Horace she was *miles* from home herself. Couldn't bear the thought of Horace being so close to his mother and yet unable to tell her he was there. She took it on herself to carry notes and sketches down the towpath on her day off ("For my mother, Dinah." "For my little sister, Glen."), past the Five Locks, down through Nether Cradle and on to Cradle Cross. Dinah sent her back with custards and gooey wedges of sweet onion pie; Glenda sent his set of brushes with HHH carved in the fine horn handles.

When his wounds were healed and needed gentle stretching to get him fit for fighting, Horace was sent back home to convalesce. The orderly came down to visit him on her days off; said little, and leaned back against the counter in Maison Hester's watching Horace sketching outlines of a mural on the back wall for his mother—an Alpine scene: a haughty cow, a mountain range, a boy in green knee-britches. Glenda, who was fascinated by this girl's hair springing out in gold-red coils and twisting to her waist, brought fresh tea in good cups and hoped her brother would have sense enough to make this girl his own.

Horace was sent back to France before he finished painting in the cow—just the rear end done, the front end penciled in. A half-cow. Dinah didn't have the heart to paint it over.

He never got the chance to walk out with the orderly, but when the War was finished, she stayed around the Cradles, worked the Cut. And every Friday until the Horn Lane fire, Glenda walked down to the Cut to take her lardy cake and custards. And if Glenda could not find her, she would leave the basket on the foredeck of the dredge-boat, the *Cassandra,* with the same note every week: "For Belle, from Glen, with thanks for helping Horace."

Truda talked no more of Hector or of Dinah Hatchett Harper that day. As Ruby finished clearing up the tea things, Truda seized the top Blick's ledger from the pile and tossed another one at Isa and threw herself beside her on the couch. Like a swollen river that has burst its banks, Truda rushed through the pages of the ledger, spilling out the names.

"Bissell, Coley, Rudge, Rudge, Rudge, Coley, Foley, Harper . . . God, I can't decipher this . . . Could it be Hipkiss?"

"Slow down, Truda!" Ruby hung the cups back on their hooks. "Never find a Fly, we woe, that quick!"

Truda didn't look up but her finger paused, halfway down a page. "No? Bacon, Adams, Bacon, Baitch . . ." She sucked at air and blew it out again. "No. Indeed we won't. The elusive Family Fly." She slapped the ledger shut. "How is your father, Isa? Any news today?"

Now Ruby had been taught to wrap up her concerns and put them on a high shelf out of reach: the strain of reaching up should keep you from picking over them too often. But Isa had a different way entirely. Ruby had noticed how Isa only talked of Moonie when directly asked, but her answers were precise, meticulous, as if she unwrapped *her* parcel and held up each item within it to the light, weighing it and testing out its substance.

Isa closed the ledger in her lap and traced its edges with a finger. "Brammeier says that Moonie has grown thinner. More papery . . ." She glanced sharply at the window as if she saw something out there, but when Ruby looked out she saw nothing strange. "No *flesh* on him, he says. He spends much of his day nodding in the chair before the window, but he's wakeful in the dark hours."

"He's old," said Truda, throwing her book down and going to fetch another. "They get like infants, people do, when they grow old." She stopped and looked at Isa, who had her fingers pressing to her white eye. "God, listen to me! What do I know? All my kin keeled over well short of three score years and ten. Pay me no attention whatsoever. Did the good Doctor Brammeier have any words of consolation?"

"*Consolation?* No. He has heard complaints. My father has been screaming out at night, the same words every night, over and over, from the open window."

Truda leaned forward, elbows on her knees, resting her chin in her hands. "What has he been screaming?"

Trying, Ruby thought, *to look concerned, when her wishes Moonie Fly would hurry up and die so Isa doesn't have to meet her obligations . . .*

"Do you really want to know?"

"Oh yes. Anything to divert me from my pitifully introspective course."

Isa stood and cleared her throat. "He has been screaming *this* out at the coast, the bay, the sea . . ." She dropped the ledger on the table and went over to the window and heaved the sash up. She stuck her head out, and louder than they'd ever heard her speak, she screamed out, *"Fogg off now and leave me! Yo cacking FOGGER!"*

Truda fell back, hooting, whooping, hitting at the couch. But Ruby's smile was faltering; it seemed to Ruby that Isa wasn't acting out her father's words. She wasn't shrill or mocking. She was taking his words for herself and—no doubt in Ruby's mind—screaming them to somebody specific. Were Ruby to look out onto the towpath, to the Cut, she'd see somebody stood there, she was sure.

Isa pulled the sash back down. Looked at both of them with a brief smile that dried up before it reached her eyes. "Brammeier says he keeps repeating this: 'Her was never meant to live. Her was never meant to live.' "

"Who is 'her'?" Ruby asked. " 'Her who was never meant to live'?"

Isa's dark eye clouded and she was lost behind it. She didn't answer Ruby and Ruby was confused. Isa wasn't weighted down with anguish; she didn't pinch her arms to keep herself from crying. "Brammeier says that Moonie is delirious and he is right. And no one will believe a ranting fool."

If Ruby detected anything in Isa, it was briskness, and this should have been a warning, for what kind of woman is impatient with a dying man? She recalled what Belle Severn said to her; that she was duped, deluded.

"Isa," she began. "I meant to tell you. When I took them letters round for Truda yesterday, the dredger nicked the bike and Truda's bag to make me follow her. And then today, down at the Deadarm—"

Truda interrupted, sitting forward, looking at Ruby and then at Isa. "She nicked the bag to make you follow her?"

She was interrupted by a loud rap; Captin at the back door, wearing his good jacket again and holding up a paper parcel. He cast a wary eye on Truda and lingered on the back step, reddening through the dappling of his beard. Nodded, curt. "Miss Blick." He held the parcel out to Isa. "I woe intrude, I oney bought yo these. First-fat chips. I doe know as there's enough in there, but I day know as yo had . . . company."

Ruby wanted to reach out and grab his hand and say, "I ay *company*!" but she knew Captin didn't mean her when he said it. Captin didn't see her, and she kept so still she barely breathed because Ruby did not want to watch him trying to smile at her when she knew he really didn't care. Just as he turned to leave, despite Isa pressing him to stay, Truda called out, hospitable and cruel, "Oh, but Captin, don't go! I'm sure there'd be enough in here to share! But if we're going to dine *à trois* I must go and grab a claret from Hec's stash. To make it all more . . . palatable."

Truda dashed out through the front, and Ruby watched Isa lay a hand on Captin's arm; her broad, enticing smile. "Len, you don't mind, do you? Truda's been so kind, with letting me stay here . . ."

Captin raised his eyebrows. "I cor stay long. I cor leave the vats unwatched. Catch, the fat could, and then we ud all be fried." Yet he was kicking dry dust off his boots and shrugging off his jacket and saying that he would sit just for a minute. He did not look at Ruby. She slumped down at the table, pulled out a wedge of boat-yard ledgers from the satchel and thumbed fiercely through the top one on the pile. She didn't want his chips. She didn't want to be here, taking up a chair, while Truda and Captin cast out their hungry nets to pull in Isa, but neither did she want them thinking they had driven her away. But now Isa's arm was around her shoulder and Ruby could not help but look up and lean back a little into her, while Isa tucked a curl behind her ear. "Now, Ruby, shall we set a table? We won't all fit on the back step tonight."

They all set to: Ruby gathered cutlery and plates and Isa found thick tumblers that would have to do for wine, and Captin shifted the Blick's books from the sofa and cleared the table. "What should I do with these?" he said, holding up a boat-yard book. Isa said he should ask Ruby, she'd brought them. And Captin must have looked a little closer and seen Trent Nailer Tailor embossed on the front, because suddenly he was too close to Ruby and holding the book right up to her face. Ruby smelled a cidery pomade. "How come yo got these, Rube? What cause *yo* got to have um?"

She stepped back from him, around him and moved toward the table, and before she could think of what to say, Isa took the plates from her and set them on the table. "She's trying to help me find this missing daughter, Len. I told you."

"Yo woe find her in there."

"No, but Ruby thought there might be a mention of a Moonie Fly."

Ruby nodded, looking up at Isa. "He could of done a bit of casual or something, when things was too busy."

Captin shook his head. "I *told* you this already, Rube. I worked down at the Deadarm till the War. I never knew a man named Moonie Fly."

"Ruby was being helpful, Len. She thought there might be something; an address, another firm."

"Your nan woe be happy, Rube, wi yo sharing this wi all and sundry."

Ruby felt a flush of anger. "Isa ay all and sundry." She took up a knife and started sawing at a loaf of bread.

Captin glanced at Isa; back at Ruby. "Yo know as that ay what I meant. Annie udn't like it and yo know it."

Ruby felt a flush of anger. "*Yo* cor tell me what I can and cor look at! Yo ay kin to me." A fleeting spiteful glee; she'd wounded him, and, feeling mean and cheap, she grew defensive. "Why shouldn't I be looking at this stuff? Is Nan ashamed of it? I ay found a Moonie Fly in them books but I did find out as my grandad wor too good at this, was he?"

Taut, Captin was, restraining something, and it pulled him like a wild dog on a leash, but he glared at Ruby and said nothing.

"Is that why Nan owes Blickses so much? Did Hector bail her out when her was sinking?" An image, unbidden, of Hector scooping water from a boat.

Captin shook his head; went over to the door. "I got to check the fat."

"Oh, come on, Len," said Isa. "Don't be cross with Ruby. Would Annie really mind? Jonah wouldn't be the first to fail in business."

Captin nodded at the table. "Them chips ull be chilling."

"Sit with us, Len."

Grudging, Captin pulled a chair out. Isa undid one end of the parcel and tipped a few chips onto Ruby's plate, then wrapped the paper up again.

"You're looking pale, Ruby. You need to eat. There's butter for that bread." Isa took her fly-box from her bag and sat it on her lap.

"Yo ay going to eat?" said Ruby.

Isa shook her head. "I will wait for Truda."

Ruby ate, reluctantly at first, but the first-fat chips were crisp and neatly browned. She watched Isa weighing a gold feather in her palm, and Isa looked up; saw her watching. "I'll teach you tomorrow. If you like."

A stillness in the room, and Ruby thrilled at this: *Isa will teach me to tie a fly.* She glanced at Captin. *I will sit with Isa,* Ruby thought, defiant. *The two of us sat on the anvil rock across from Sawdy Point. The rock will still be warm from resting all day in the sun, and Isa will take out a wide-toothed comb and work loose all my knots and twist up all my hair in little plaits. Those tugs along the scalp; prickles on the neck like unexpected winkles underfoot. And we will cast our flies onto the water.*

Isa dabbed the cotton at the eye of her needle. "Sometimes I swear this needle winks to keep thread out. I feel I have to steal up on it; surprise the eye, somehow."

"I ay ashamed of him." Ruby spread butter on a tapered wedge of bread and glanced up at Captin, but he was wiping a cloth round his pipe and would not meet her eyes.

"Ashamed of your grandfather?" said Isa.

Ruby nodded. "I ay ashamed. I'm curious."

"Sometimes," Isa rolled a small bead in her palm, "sometimes in our cottage at St. Shirah, we were flooded—"

"I thought as yo lived high up on the cliffs."

"We did. I mean that we were knocked down, flat, by my father's exuberance. Rushing, pulling. Spinning us in his lank windmill arms.

Scooping us up, filling us with frothy tales of what he would do next. New ventures. 'This, my dears, will make me!' Then, just as suddenly he would withdraw and shut the door into the Sunday room and we would see his pipe smoke weaving through the keyhole. Leaving us to gather all the pieces of his enterprise, left high and dry, like jetsam on the sand."

Ruby knew why Isa told her this, to show she understood her disappointment in her grandad. Yet Ruby wasn't *disappointed*. She was angry with Captin, and she was newly curious about her grandfather and wanted to know how Nan Annie came to marry someone feckless and imprudent when Annie knew the number of sultanas in a jar. But she was snagged by something Isa said. "Said 'we' was knocked down, yo did. Who was 'we'? You and your mother?"

"No. My mother died when I was very young." Isa took up a new reel of filament and pulled at the loose end.

"Yoom like me, then: we both got no mother!" Ruby sang out, almost joyful. "Mine died of the flu. What happened to yours?"

Captin clicked his tongue in disapproval; complained that Ruby was too full of questions. But Isa said she didn't mind at all. "My mother was called Florence," she said, "but Moonie called her Flo." She held her thread up to the light.

"Is that the Florence—" Ruby pressed her lips tight shut to stop herself: she was not supposed to know about a Florence in a little birthday book, about a rolled-up nightdress, about a second priest. Isa frowned and put her needle down, so Ruby went on quickly, "I mean, what was her like, your mom? Was her like yo at all?"

"I have no memory of her."

"How old was yo when her went?"

"When she went?"

"When yo lost her. When her died, I mean."

"Not quite one year old. She delivered my brother, and then she got her fever. She saw him through his third day, then she died."

"Yo never said yo had a brother!"

Ruby felt dislodged by this new idea of Isa with a brother: it broke that common bond between them: both motherless, and lone. It showed how little Ruby'd learned of Isa in the four days since she'd come to Cradle Cross. It showed that there was more to Isa Fly than

Ruby knew, and things she'd never know unless she asked her the right questions, and how could you ever know you'd asked them all?

"Did he die an all?"

Isa shook her head. "Anselm was a sturdy little lad." She smiled. "Or *not* so little."

A for Anselm, in Isa's address book.

"When we were children, everybody thought he was the elder. He took after Moonie in his build: long and lean."

"And yo take after Flo?"

"I hope so."

"Her was smaller, then, built like yo?"

Isa shrugged. "Perhaps. My father said that she was made of china: fine, but too fragile. We were too much for her. Having two children within the year—it broke her into pieces. She wasn't strong enough, he said, to ride the fever."

"He put the blame on *you* for your mom dying?"

Isa said nothing. She snipped a piece of filament and laid it on the table.

Ruby's stomach tightened, remembering her nan's casual conjecture: *He hit his wife too hard one time.* "And yoom sure as your mom died of a fever?"

Captin looked up, sharp. "Rube, what kind of question's that?"

Isa shook her head and said she didn't mind. Captin took a pinch out of his baccy pouch and pressed it in his pipe.

"Childbed fever is too common," Isa said.

"So that ay fair, him blaming it on yo! Other people must of put yo right."

"There were no other people."

"Your mom—her day have kin?"

"I never met them."

Flo's family, Isa explained, had been unhappy with the match. Flo was from old merchant stock, and they thought Moonie far beneath them. But she was stubborn, Moonie'd said, and ran away to be with him. (In Ruby's mind: a ladder in a garden leaning up against a wall.)

"So there wor no one else? Not even someone like my Captin?"

Captin glanced at Ruby, and Isa smiled at him. "We weren't so fortunate."

"So is your brother back there with your dad?"

"No." Isa took up the loose end of her thread and pulled it taut through a small notch on the reel. "My brother's dead."

Ruby felt a rushing of relief, and then she colored with her shame. *How could I be* glad *about his death?* "But yo said as he lived. Did he die in the War?" she asked, as if showing interest in Anselm could make amends for being glad he'd died.

"He was too young to fight. He was fifteen when he died. It was in the bombing raids at Whalemouth."

Something struck at Ruby. "So all yo know of Moonie's what he tells yo." No one else to vouch for him or verify his stories.

Isa nodded and pressed a finger to her white eye. "Brammeier says he's prey to these *delusions*. I tried to tell Brammeier that it's nothing new with Moonie. There's a kink in Moonie's mind. His moods wax with the tides. You were right about the voices when you asked me, that first night, if not about red demons. He hears the voices calling from the rocks at Sawdy Point." Isa blinked repeatedly and held her white eye shut.

Ruby knew such voices: voices muttering that she was rotten to the core. She said nothing of this, though, not to anyone. "Did the voices get him into debt?"

Isa smiled. "No, they didn't. It wasn't debt that sank my father's businesses. He said that there were mermaids. 'Merymaids' was the word he used for them. They were persecuting him, Moonie said. They were holing his new hulls. They were cutting up his nets. Every time he lost a customer he'd say it was *them merymaids* who'd done it and never took the blame on himself. Even when our Anselm died, he said that it was merymaids who lured him down to the harbor when the zeppelins came. Everything that went wrong, it wasn't Moonie's fault: it was the merymaids . . . They've been persecuting him ever since I can remember."

"Isa," Ruby began. "The dredger, her's been saying things about yo—"

But Captin cut in. "Mermaids?" He frowned, incredulous. "Mermaids persecuted him?"

Isa looked at Ruby, mouthing, "Later."

"Oh, Isa, doe put *more* stories in her head. Always being snatched away, our Ruby is, by some saft notion. Like our Beth, her is, and like Annie used to be. Rube says as Blickses make buttons out of *these*." He held up his little finger; wiggled it. He leaned across to take a chip off Ruby's plate. "Her says the sorors let themselves through the gate into her garden and prune the apple trees at night. Her says as her is being called by the seashore. Too busy up here, Ruby is." He tapped on his temple. "I hears it all the time from her. Doe I, Rube?" He sucked salt off his thumb and pointed at her with a chip. "So doe feed her wi mermaids!"

Ruby felt she'd been made to look a fool. More than that, he'd plundered her to purchase laughs from Isa Fly and Ruby felt depleted. She pushed away her plate and stood up. "Yoom saft, sometimes, Captin. *Mermaids* ay the point of what her's saying! Weem talking about old men, like her father, who make a mess but never take the blame. Men like my Grandad Jonah, and the mess *he* made for us he left behind." (This wasn't strictly true, she knew, but she wanted to jolt him from his joking, hard, unkind.)

Captin snapped his gaze away from Isa and studied Ruby. "I ay sure as that's your business, Ruby. It's all done wi, now. Dead, it is, and buried."

In truth, Ruby didn't care that Jonah was feckless and inept, but she was still burning with Captin's jocular betrayal, and Jonah made as good a pyre as any. She piled her fury on him like dry tinder. "Find out, I do, that my grandad was no better un a fogger. Cheating people by not doing work they'd paid for. Not giving them their money when they had gid him coal or coke or rivets." (Isa turned away and busied herself, neck bent, tidying up flies.) "And it *ay* dead and buried." Ruby was shouting now, her gestures arcing, fierce. "I carry up a let-ter to Nan Annie saying as her owes Blickses more than her can ever pay them back and *that* ay buried debt. And when Nan Annie dies, that debt ull hang round *my* neck. Ay no one else to bear it." She picked up her satchel and bent her head to thread herself through the strap. "So yo cor say as it's dead and done wi. Blickses has dug it up."

She had never spoken like this to her Captin. Nor to anyone.

He looked at her dismayed, like a man who reaches in the pocket where he always keeps his pipe and finds it isn't there. "Why ay yo shouting at Miss Blick then, Rube, instead of spitting this at me?"

"Miss Blick just wants what's owed her! Blickses paid for shoes and pigs and medicine and no one ever thought to pay it back. *That's* why I ay shouting this at her. It wor Truda who got two suits and never paid the bill!"

"No, Rube." His voice quiet, bewildered. "And it wor me or your nan as did it neither."

She wanted to climb up on his lap like she used to; twist up the stubborn tufts that sprang up on his crown, but she said she had to go; she didn't like his chips, and left him staring after her, bewildered, and Isa's hand was resting on his shoulder.

Sullen, she met Truda with her claret on Horn Lane.

"Yo took your time."

"Someone caught me on the telephone. You're going so soon? Past your bedtime, Ruby? It's getting close to seven . . ."

Ruby scowled. "I'm going to get my bike."

Truda headed for the button shop, but swiveled on the doorstep, calling out, "So tomorrow, Ruby: you'll come up to the office? There will be work to do." She saluted with the bottle. "Us against the Cradles, yes?"

Ruby didn't answer. She went to fetch her bicycle from Blick's but once inside the yard, she leaned against the green gates for a moment, pressing her tongue hard against the roof of her mouth; staring at the placards and tracing around the empty furnaces, but this time, with no one watching, she couldn't stop herself from crying. She sank down to the floor and took out her Almanac: this sadness; this anger; it rolled and swelled in her, threatening to break over her head. She took her pencil out and found one of the maps: she traced over the coastline heavily—down past Lee, around the bay, St. Shirah, Sawdy Point, but her hand trembled and when the gate clicked open her pencil jolted and she cursed. She looked round; Isa, stepping through. She shut the gate behind her and walked over to look out of the iron gates between the courtyard and the Cut, then came back to Ruby; crouched beside her. One cold hand (*so white,* she thought) cradled Ruby's cheek and with a thumb she gently smeared the one long tear-streak that ran curving to her chin.

"You have something to tell me, I think, Ruby."

The bag, she thought, *and Isa's second priest.* She bit hard on her lip.

"Something about the dredger, I believe?"

Ruby breathed out hard, relieved.

"You said that she was saying things about me." Isa spoke with quiet urgency.

Ruby dragged her sleeve across her face to dry it. "Her knows yo, Isa. Her says her knows yo from before. How come?"

Isa, dismissive, shook her head. "I need to know what she's been saying."

"That yoom not here to find a missing sister." *That you've enchanted me.*

"And what did you say? Did you contradict her? What did you tell the dredger in return?"

"Tell her?" Ruby shrugged. "What has I got to tell? Your dad's dying; weem trying to find Lily. That's all as I know, Isa, and that's all as I said."

Isa stood up. "But Len said just a minute back how much you like embellishing; you like telling stories." This was a new Isa; sharp and fierce. Ruby, alarmed, got to her feet, protesting that she hadn't sought the dredger out. Belle Severn had left messages with Captin, with her dad, and then she'd nicked the bike and Truda's satchel; Ruby had simply gone to get them back, and then Belle Severn threatened her and said she'd hold her underneath the water.

A shift, then, in Isa's tone, a softening, and she elicited from Ruby how Belle had let the letters fall into the water; how her wet socks had betrayed her to Nan Annie, and when she'd finished, Ruby pressed her lips to keep the crying in.

"Your nan won't countenance you going near the water?"

Not mocking, Ruby thought, but calm, tender.

"But, Ruby . . ." Isa hesitated. "You have these plans to get to sea, to *live* by sea, and yet you cannot approach water?" Unriled, she was, quite patient. Words weighed like she piled them on a scale. "If you can't defy Nan Annie by so much as standing near the Cut, what makes you think that you can face the ocean?"

Ruby pinched the skin beneath her chin and sucked hard on her tongue. She could not look at Isa, yet she wanted Isa close, to have her plait her clumsy hair and rock her still and sing close and sweet and soothing in her ear. But Isa Fly went on and something in her tone commanded Ruby and she lifted her eyes to meet Isa's.

"The sea, Ruby, and what's within it, it can whittle you into a stick and break you into pieces. Take Moonie. Take my father. He taught me how to love the sea, but now he says the sea has turned against him. He looks at it as if it is a mistress who has done him wrong. He waves his arms, he thrashes at the tide. He hawks into the wind then turns his back, as if the sea would be offended! And then I see him looking sideways at the ocean, as if he were afraid. He is afraid, with good reason. So if you are wise enough to be wary of the water, to be wary of *approaching* it, then put your agile mind to this: reconcile yourself to living here. Don't even try to leave."

But I ay scared of water, Ruby thought. *That ay it at all.* "Does this mean yo woe take me wi yo when yo go to Severnsea?"

"Take you with me?"

"When yo go back. Yo said as I could come back wi yo. When we've found your sister."

Isa said nothing. Ruby would have to prove to her that she was not afraid. "Nan Annie, it is, who is scared of water. Her thinks as I ull drown."

"Look, Ruby. I need you to do something for me. It won't be easy, and it won't always be safe."

Ruby nodded.

"Watch Belle Severn, will you? Find out what she's saying about me. You're very good at listening, I know." While she spoke her hands went to her neck and pulled at a scarlet cord. "I have something for you." She slipped the cord up over her head and down over the white hair lying heavy like a mantle on her shoulder. "Here, hold it." She spoke quietly, respectfully, and Ruby held her hand out for the spoon.

It was smaller than a teaspoon and quite rough, as if it had been bashed out on a backyard anvil. Spoons like this weren't shaped over in Hockleye by the silversmiths. Too raw for that, as if it had been hammered by a nailer in a hurry.

"I had wandered off," said Isa, "above the deepest rock pools, by myself. My father always warned me to stay close. Four years old I was, at most. I lost my footing where the kelp was glossed against the rock. Moonie waded in, but found he couldn't keep a hold on me; he says no sooner had he got a grip than something pried his fingers free, and whatever Moonie says about the cause, three of his fingers were broken in the saving." She held her hands up, with the fingers all bent down except the index finger on the right, the index and the middle on the left, to show which ones were broken. "The way I thrashed, he swore that I was fighting something underneath the water, something holding me."

"What was it?" Ruby said, mouth dry.

"I was too slippy—panicked, probably—but Moonie grabbed me by the cord around my neck and pulled me clear of whatever held me under. He scooped me up and laid me on the beach to dry out in the sun. It saved me once from drowning, did this spoon, and ever since he's always said that it was meant for me to have the spoon, that I was meant to live . . . Take it. It will keep you safe in water."

"I cor take this! What about yo? Doe yo need it to keep yo from being drownded?"

"Me? I can swim across Gleed Bay and back again."

Ruby smiled. "And all the way to Sawdy Point and back?"

"I'll take a chance on surviving without it. Take the spoon. Watch Belle Severn, but be careful." Isa slipped the cord over Ruby's head. "She's not kind. She's not safe." She tucked the spoon in so that it lay beneath Ruby's vest and blouse. "Now will you come and have some chips with us?"

"Truda doe want me there; nor does Captin."

"Captin's turned his vats off."

"Now? There'll be folk at the chip shop hammering for their tea!"

Isa shrugged. "He's bringing round more chips. He said it doesn't get busy till later."

"But he's still cross with me about them books."

"Then you'd better come back and take them away."

Ruby said she would come by tomorrow, when the others weren't there, but Isa smiled at Ruby. "You would abandon me, would you?" She tugged gently on the cord around her neck. "I give you my spoon and in return you leave me with those two glowering across the table at each other?" She hooked her arm through Ruby's and, smoothing her hair, led her through the gate and to the button shop.

We mustn't judge Ruby for taking Isa's spoon so readily. How was she to know that her delight at cold iron on her breastbone, this modest, private joy at holding close this thing of Isa Fly's, would evaporate so readily, so soon?

Wednesday, all day, Ruby was kept up at Hunting Tree. Nan Annie took down dinner to the Deadarm and left Ruby with a batch of slow, fatiguing tasks: a new trench dug; potatoes to be wheeled up to the sorors; peas that wanted shelling; beds to weed.

Chapter 9

List, *n.* 1. Pleasure, joy, delight. 2. Appetite, craving; desire; inclination. 3. One's desire or wish.

THURSDAY MORNING, Ruby woke up itchy and dry-eyed. She'd dreamed all night of Annie-on-the-photograph, young Annie in a summer dress; fresh-licked, supple, sly-backed as a cat; Annie scratching at the wounds that Jonah's debts scored in her; Captin trying to scoop up Annie and put her out of doors; Annie sharpening her nails on Ruby, shredding her like dry bark on a tree trunk; Captin nuzzling at Annie's neck; dropping Annie into a pool and Isa helping him to hold her below the surface; Captin crying out to Ruby, *It ay my fault, and Ruby ay my kin.*

This sang in her—this refrain, unrelenting—as she freewheeled down the Ludleye Road. She tried to block it out with something brash. Dinah Hatchett Harper: she would do. Dinah, *all* the Ruths—they would be spitting about Truda wanting them to pay out for their meetings in the Mission. As she turned off the Ludleye Road, jolting on the cobbles down the Breach, she expected to see Glenda out again, pressing protest bills into the hands of waiting women. No queue though, yet—with her early waking, Ruby had got down sooner than was usual, and the street was still, quiet enough for her to hear, as she approached Maison Hester's, a raw keening seeping out from under the closed door. She leaned the bike against Dodd's next door and, tentative, her fingers twisted in the cord of Isa's spoon, walked down the stone steps under the low lintel. Only the top two rows of dimpled window panes showed on the Breach, as if Maison Hester's were slowly sinking. A bell tapped as she pushed the door.

At the back end of the shop, before the old half-cow mural, her hair subdued under a patterned scarf, Dinah stood wrapped up and strapped in by a mannish dressing gown and wailing like a pig. She had a bucket in one hand, a greasy rag dangling from the other.

"Mrs. Harper? Am yo all right, Mrs. Harper?"

Dinah didn't turn. "Fetching off his paint, it is!" she squalled. "I cor shift it wi'out fetching off his paint!"

It was dark in Maison Hester's, being almost underground, and Ruby couldn't see what it was that troubled Dinah so, but something smelled rank, suety. Further in stepped Ruby, across the checkered floor, until she stood by Dinah and saw what Dinah saw.

The half-cow mural had been smeared all over with great lardy swipes of tallow-fat that slurred the colors of the cow, the boy, the mountain together in a dunnish blur, and where Dinah'd tried to clean the tallow off she'd lifted off the paint.

Her face was raddled, drizzly, her eyes retreating under swollen lids. Her sleeves were oily where they'd brushed against the wall. "Tried a knife, I have, to scrape the tallow off. Tried blotting it through muslin. I thought as maybe soapy water might dissolve it but it's oney worsened it . . ." She turned to look at Ruby. "Why ud a person do this to a mother? What did I do that brung this on?"

Ruby shook her head, thinking about all the people who shrunk back into the shadow of their entries when they saw Dinah approaching; about the children she had bruised about the shoulders with her cuffing; about Truda hiding in her office to avoid her.

"Yo day do nothing, Mother." Glenda marched in through the kitchen, grabbed her mother's shoulders and looked, close, into Dinah's eyes. "Get upstairs. Ten minutes and weem opening the shop. So yo ud better get some clothes on unless yoom wanting all the Cradles seeing what yoom made of."

Ruby moved back against the side wall. Did not want to be in Glenda's way this morning.

"But this . . . ?" said Dinah, waving the fatty cloth at the back wall.

"But nothing. Yo know there ay no mending this. We leave it as it is today and scour the faces of them in the queue to see who looks ashamed."

"As if someone ud dare to show their face in here when they dun this to me."

"Upstairs, Mother. Clothes." She eased the bucket handle out of Dinah's hand and dropped the cloth across the bucket's edge. And then, more gently, "Ruby ull have a go at this for yo."

Glenda steered Dinah through the back and Ruby heard the clicking of a latch and Glenda calling, "Doe forget to gi your face a proper wash!"

Ruby lingered, unsure what to do. Nose wrinkled, she picked the cloth up by an edge—it smelled like Blickses sheds where they stripped the cows before they burned them down. She dabbed at the daubed tallow, but, as Dinah said, it was impossible to wipe it off without erasing more of Horace Hatchett Harper's half-done picture. For some reason just out of reach, Ruby felt that she was implicated in the desecration and she flushed when Glenda came back and took the rag and bucket from her. "We both know as there ay no point in this. Take a message to Miss Blick for me, ud yo?"

And Ruby now remembered how, the other afternoon, Truda had petitioned Isa when she spoke about the bandages left bloody on her doorstep; how Isa had looked back at Truda with what Ruby now thought to be avenging eyes.

"Tell her as the Ruths and the Naomis woe be meeting in the Mission. Her woe get a farthing out of us! Rent? Weem meeting *here*." She jabbed a pointing finger down toward the floor. "And tell her as her wants to keep a tighter lid on Blickses tallow vats. And yo, yo want to watch yourself, Ruby, doing Miss Blick's dirty work. It *was* yo, wor it, as put up that Docking Bill for her?"

Ruby bit her lip; nodded.

"How has Annie took it, this demand about the loan?"

"Her wants to pay it back. Her doe like to be in debt."

Glenda shook her head. "None of us do! We day think as it *was* debt! Her's changed the terms, Ruby, and that ay fair! I want to know—and I ay the only one—what is it has made Miss Blick switch like this and go back on the promise of her family!" She dropped the rag, greasy with tallow, in the bucket. "Why is it, Ruby, since this woman come, this Isa Fly, this friend of yours, that we been assailed wi all this venom out of Blickses?"

Ruby twisted up her finger in the spoon cord; if it would make her brave and safe in water, it might make her bolder on dry land. "Why am folk so quick to blame Isa Fly when they doe know her?"

Glenda shook her head with a grim smile. "There's them in Cradle Cross who knows her, Ruby, even if yo doe."

"Who? You mean the Blackbird?"

"Ask *Belle* what her knows of Isa Fly before yo come to me all high and mighty."

Ruby shrank back; pretended to be cowed. (She had the spoon; she was on Isa's business.) "Ask her? Ask the Blackbird?"

"Why? Am yo scared of her?"

Ruby nodded. Feigning fear came readily enough.

"Well, I cor say as I blame yo. Intimidates, her does, and folk take her the wrong way. Her doe like to *mix*."

"Why not?" Ruby timid, deferential.

"Some folk cor trust easy when they had a tricky start in life."

She knew from standing in the bread queue that Glenda loved to spin out other people's stories, but you had to ask her right. "What happened to her, Glen? What was tricky?"

"Now Belle doe tell this story light or easy, so if I hear it spread about then I ull know as it was Ruby did the telling."

Ruby nodded, eyes wide.

"Her was a foundling. Left on a rock to drown, her was, and that ud of been the end of her, Belle says, if it wor for Cass."

"Who's Cass?" Ruby whispered.

"Cassandra. Her mom-all-but-the-birthing. Cass tracked the father down—doe ask me how—but he day have spit for Belle. The mother, well, there wor no trace of her, so Cass brung Belle up like a daughter by herself down Severnsea."

Ruby nodded, trying to look sage. "That is a tricky start . . . but why does Belle live here now? Why day her stay in Severnsea?"

"Her come up to do War Work."

"But her left Cass behind?" She tried to hide the awe she felt at leaving family and disguise it as disgust, incomprehension.

"Her day *leave* her behind! War Work, Ruby! That ay leaving, that is obligation."

"But when the War was finished, her could of gone home then." And she was not hiding anything, not now: why would you stay in landlocked Cradle Cross when you could taste the salt of Severnsea?

"The old dredge-man died and Belle took on his boat. Someone's got to dredge the Cut, ay they?"

Ruby persisted: there must have been others to do that job. And didn't she miss her mom; her mom-all-but?

"There's different kinds of obligation, Ruby, and different ways of showing as yo care. I'm always fetching letters from the post office up to Belle's boat, or taking them up to the post for her. Distance ay no bar to being close. Belle and Cass, theym always writing to each other."

"Well, if her doe mix, her's lucky her's got yo to be her friend."

"Ar, well, her was good to Horace in the war. Her waited wi us, after. To see if he'd come back. Her waited wi us and her never left. That is faithful, Ruby. That is loyalty." She stabbed a finger at the mural. "And *that* is cruelty."

Ruby pressed the spoon against her chest. "All as I'm saying is I cor see why as yo ud stay in Cradle Cross if yo had the chance to live down by the sea."

"Thank the Lord we doe all think weem better than the town that's bred us, Ruby."

As Ruby walked away from Maison Hester's, she felt prickly and uncomfortably warm. She could see why Dinah was upset—the mess and stink that tallow made! And *she* would miss the half-cow, too, when Dinah came to paint it over (as she'd surely have to, with it ruined). Whenever Ruby had stood in the bread queue she had tried in her mind to fill the picture in before her turn came and never understood why Dinah'd left it half-done all this time. She couldn't see why Dinah bawled about it. She'd heard Nan Annie say of Dinah that she was the kind who'd always find new pain to nurse. "If light was shone in Dinah's darkest corners, her ud just sew heavy curtains." And like all children, Ruby saw the time before her own birth as an emptied reel of cotton, all paid out, sewn off, finished, and with *her* life a new spool was unwinding, unattached to what had gone before. For Ruby, Horace Hatchett Harper, who was dead before her birth, was no more than a spent reel rattling somewhere in the back end of a drawer.

She stepped up to the Breach with some relief; could still hear Dinah's sobs and felt as if they might just shake the putty from the windows. The folds and cracks of Cradle Cross were crawling with those who would have *liked* to strike at Dinah for her pinches and her slaps, for her bellowed indiscretions on the Breach, but Ruby could think of no one from Cradle Cross who had the mettle or the will to wreak revenge on Dinah. Yet much as Ruby told herself that Dinah Hatchett Harper deserved to be distressed, she was troubled by the picture in her mind of Isa, calm, stood in the dark in front of Dinah's wall and spreading tallow, thick, like butter onto bread.

When faced with livid cruelties perpetrated against others, like Dinah's ruined wall, or against herself, like pig hooks in the cellar, Ruby had a habit that preserved her. She would sink below the surface of the day into her lists. Whole days could pass like this for Ruby. She submerged herself within her lists, and they were like a lie—a place where fishes rest, somewhere safe and cool, somewhere to hide, to linger. She waited steady there, in the lee of her cool rock, and let the current of the day wash over her, around her. So Ruby turned her thoughts away from Dinah and from tallow on the wall, and worked on the inventory of what she should take with her when she went to the sea, a list that Ruby had paid out so often that it spilled from her like cotton on a Singer. "What I Shall Take to Sea": a bit cut off the block of Fairy soap (to wash herself; her clothes); two spare vests; a small packet of tea. As she walked, she twisted and untwisted the spoon handle on its cord and with every fourth step she listed one more item that she'd need: her Almanac, of course; the warm and speckled jersey that Em knit up last winter; her leather writing case (she supposed she'd have to write and let Nan Annie and her father know that she was safe). She filtered through the entries and the folds toward the Deadarm; girls were playing "Catch me, Isa!" (one girl, with her right hand slapped across her eye, chasing children with her other arm outstretched) and "Blind the Witch," a test of nerve in which a small, hard rubber ball was aimed at someone's stationary head. Or "Flytrap." Or "Witch Hunt." Or any of the other games that had sprung up these last few days since Isa came to town.

Ruby stopped in the mouth of the high tunnel opposite the Deadarm. The *Cassandra* was moored there. She watched her father, stripped to the waist, bend to dunk his head in a bowl of water. She'd leave his dinner here, and he could come and fetch it for himself. She turned to leave, but felt the spoon against her skin. She needed to show Isa that she could be bold, so she shunted sideways down the slope and called over to the island, "Dad, yo seen Belle Severn?"

Jamie Abel stood up, coughing, and shook water from his hair. He scrubbed at his head with a scrap of towel and walked to the island's edge.

"Whym yo asking?"

She gestured over to the boat. "Why'd yo think?"

"Her's mooring it at nights, Ruby. I can only work late on it, when her's done wi dredging for the day."

"It ay nighttime now, is it?"

"I tode yo, her ay here. Her doe *sleep* on the dredge-boat, Ruby."

"But ull yo see her later?"

Jamie Abel disappeared into his shed, muttering that she should wait a sec. Ruby twisted up her finger in the cord around her neck and held her shoulders back. Her father returned with a shirt over his shoulder, lighting up his fag. "Her's coming any minute to fetch the boat. Wait for her if yo want."

Ruby shook her head. "I got things to do. Tell her Glenda says as I should ask why her doe like Isa Fly."

"Why Glen doe like Isa Fly?" He set his lit fag on a tin dish on the shed sill.

"Doe be saft. Why the *Blackbird* doe like her. Tell her I wants to know her reasons."

She threaded through the folds of Stower Street; past the queues outside the shops along the Breach, and down into Horn Lane, where huddles formed around the breaking news like cold hands round a brazier: someone had wreaked a stinking, smeary havoc at Maison Hester's. One of the Bastock girls stopped Ruby and said that she had heard it from their mom who heard it straight from Glenda when they got their bread just now that it was Isa Fly who'd done it, and the children's fear of Isa was shot through with a glinting admiration. Ruby shrugged her off and walked on past. She still had Truda's spare keys and needed to return them, but first, with a quick glance up at the Blick's window, she tried the handle of the button shop and found it locked. She looked over her shoulder, but the Bastock girl was heading for the gulley, to the Cut. Ruby stepped into the doorway and sorted through the keys on Truda's ring until she found one with a tag marked simply "Shop."

After checking Isa wasn't there, she locked herself in and closed the middle door. Lying flat, her cheek cold on the flagstones, she looked under the couch. The wooden shaft had come to rest against the wall; she had to shunt right underneath the couch to reach it, dislodging clots of dust and horsehair from the webbing. She eased herself out and stood up, brushing herself roughly with her hands. She chastised herself: she should have tried to move the couch instead; her pinny was gray and mucky now, for this, a bit of wood? If it *was* a fish-priest, it was second-best, and she could see why Isa had to wrap it: it was rounded at one end but splintered and serrated at the other. She couldn't just slip this in Isa's bag: she'd have to find a way of rolling it back up inside the nightdress. For now it fitted, just about, in Truda's satchel. She threaded her arm through the strap and left the button shop locked up, just as she'd found it. *A square of towel; a pair of pants; some sugar lumps; a blanket.*

She hoped that Truda might offer her coffee; she was getting accustomed to the taste.

There was a record playing on the gramophone—a sad song about happy plots and marriage knots—and they hadn't heard her coming up the stairs. Isa, in a cotton shift, stood barefoot at the little kitchen sink, with Truda standing right up close beside her. Truda held the weight of Isa's hair clear of her neck, and Ruby was puzzled by her rapt study of Isa's nape, her shoulders. She twisted her spoon on its cord; she was possessed by a need, urgent but inexplicable, to let them know that she was in the room. She stole backward down five or six stairs and, this time, bounded up, shouting a greeting.

Truda stepped sharply away from Isa and, crossing to the couch, snatched up a blanket and started to fold. "Were you never taught, Ruby, to announce your coming in advance?" She was, thought Ruby, unreasonably gruff and irritable. "And how the devil did you get in anyway? I swear I double-locked the doors last night."

Ruby held the keys up high; shook them. "I was just bringing um back."

Though Ruby didn't ask her to account for Isa's presence, Truda seemed determined to explain. Someone had been playing the fool on the Cut last night, Truda said. Singing obnoxious songs. No, not someone sopped-up from the Leopard. A grown woman; sober, lucid in her taunting. And this, just two days after someone had the nerve to sneak into the button shop and take something from Isa's bag. "And naturally, she won't let me report it as a theft. Isa insists that it would have no market value."

Ruby glanced, nervous, at Isa, but she stayed at the sink, washing her face. Ruby fiddled with the broken clasp, then held the satchel shut. Why would Isa bother telling Truda that somebody had nicked a bit of wood? Or was it less the stolen object in itself that upset Isa than the notion of someone—the dredger, maybe—in her room and looking through her things?

"All in all," Truda was saying, "it became quite clear that Isa couldn't sleep down *there* with all that racket, so I said that she was welcome *here;* that she could take the couch . . . But do be civilized and knock the door, Ruby, next time you come up uninvited."

Ruby set the keys down on the desk and waited to be offered coffee or a seat or at least a list of errands needing running, but Truda dropped the blankets on the chair. "Did you want something?"

She told them about the mural and the tallow. "Theym saying Isa did it. As her got the tallow from Blickses vats."

"Partners in crime, eh, Isa?" Truda glanced across to Isa at the sink and raised an eyebrow. "What next? Shall we lace the widows' Thursday tea with brandy and see what secrets they spill out when they are not so temperate? What would Dinah do, inebriated? Would she climb up on the counter, do you think, and dance for us?"

Ruby twisted up her finger in the cord.

"Do you hear this, Isa Fly?" Truda called. "You stand accused."

"Doe make a joke of it!"

But Isa didn't laugh along with Truda. She asked for a towel; said nothing more as Truda pulled out drawers in a linen press. "Napkins . . . clean shirts . . . handkerchiefs! Hec may have had no nose for profit but he did at least have linen."

While Truda was searching, Ruby walked over to Isa and stood close. "If yo want, I ull take over in the button shop until the dinner Bull, so yo can look about for Lily."

Truda frowned and glanced across at them. "I've already suggested she try the records office up at Muckeleye," Truda eased a small towel from a pile and threw it over, "but she doesn't see the point." She slammed the drawer shut.

Isa dried her face. "You misrepresent me, Miss Cole Blick. Ruby's already checked the records, haven't you?" She smiled at Ruby and twisted up her finger in the cord round Ruby's neck. "You've got it on?" She leaned in close and whispered, "Good girl. *You* ask about for me; you're doing it so well. You do that and I'll stay in the shop."

"Ruby's only checked the local chapel records!" Truda sat down heavily behind her desk and reached down to lace her boots. "They're just for parishioners. The ledgers from Trent Nailer Tailor told you nothing; nor did the Blick's employment records. Your Moonie; this daughter—they must have been *born* beyond the Cruxes, even if they *lived* in Cradle Cross."

"What about the Barby Fair on Saturday?" said Ruby. "There'll be people there from all over the Cradles—Nether Cradle, Cradle Heath . . ."

"And what would you have her do?" said Truda. "Herd up all the women at the fair and sort them out by age and then round up those deserted by their father?" She turned to Isa. "Are you *certain* it was Cradle Cross he lived in? What kind of life must he have led to leave no mark, no indentation on the lives of all the people who live here?

We all leave *some* impression . . . And how careless: to leave a daughter, as if she were a set of cufflinks in a drawer!"

Isa stiffened. Ruby, until now, had thought of Isa as held-in, well-defended, and Ruby didn't like to see her get upset. "If yo was old, Miss Blick, and yo was ill, yo ud want Isa to be close, to bring yo tea and sop and everything yo needed, udn't yo?"

Truda barely moved her mouth. "Yes, Ruby. I would like Isa close."

"The last thing as yo'd want is being left alone." Ruby paused, but Truda didn't seem to understand. "Yo wouldn't send Isa away unless yo had good reason."

Truda yanked hard on her laces. "You don't need to speak so slowly, Ruby. I'm not completely dim. Your point is this: Moonie pays a high price—loneliness, no one to meet his needs—for sending Isa to unearth his long-abandoned daughter. Hardly something he'd do on a whim. He must be utterly convinced of the value of the quest—"

"Else why ud he send her?"

Truda raised her eyebrows. "Why indeed?"

There was an uneasy pause. Ruby filled it with a question about Moonie's health, but Isa was dismissive as if he was a duty she'd forgotten, and did not want reminding.

At the fish shop, when the dinner rush abated, Captin passed Ruby a thick waxy packet. "Sorry, I am, as I day gi this to yo sooner. Bits, it is, from the girls at Whalemouth. Things as they thought ud tittle yo. It come in yesterday."

She eased open the flap: cuttings, inside, from the *Whalemouth Post*. She gave a slight nod as a thanks and put the packet back up on the mantel.

"Doe yo want to open it up now? I doe mind, Ruby, if yo want to sit down on the step and do your Almanac. Finish off the jobs, I can, myself."

"No. I ud rather do it on my own, thank yo." *I doe want yo looking over my shoulder and mocking all the stories as I choose.*

Captin fidgeted about the room. *Inventing jobs,* she thought, *that doe really need doing:* straightening the fish papers, shining up his gut knife although it already gleamed, while Ruby did the necessary work like scrubbing down the table.

He lifted the limb of driftwood down and wiped along the shelf where it had sat. "Yo ay said nothing to your nan, Ruby, have yo?"

"About what?"

"About the other day."

"What, the other day?" She'd stowed the boatyard ledgers underneath her bed but would never have thought to mention them to Annie.

"*Friends,* I am, wi Isa Fly," said Captin. "Her talks to me, that's all. Her tells me about Severnsea."

Ruby waited.

"It brings me a bit closer to our Dil and all her girls."

Ruby took a cloth to rub the table dry. "Why ud I want to talk to my nan about that?" She did not look at him. A piquant thrill in this; Captin at her mercy. "Why ud her be interested in you and Isa being friends, in you and Isa talking about the sea?"

"A man can have more un one friend in life, Ruby. Being friends wi Isa Fly doe mean as I'm forsaking other folk. But people like your nan doe always stretch to seeing things that way. So best if yo doe mention me and Isa being friends."

Ruby stopped her wiping. *Just how saft dun yo think I am?* "It ay easy, Captin. I doe know what it is I'm supposed to say or when I am supposed to keep my trap shut up. I wor supposed to know as Blickses made my family a loan, but I learned about it, day I? Only trying, I am, to help Isa, to find sommat out about this Moonie Fly so as I can track down where his family lived."

"What's that to do wi Annie?"

"Well yo woe tell me about the boatyard when yo worked there. Yo woe help me find a soul who knew of Moonie Fly. I doe *want* to upset Nan Annie, asking her about my Grandad Jonah and all the mess he left behind, but if Jonah carried so much debt, he could of been in debt to Moonie Fly." She worked the cloth around the edges of the table. "So I ull have to talk to Nan again and see if her remembers paying off a debt to Moonie. I ull tell her yo was occupied wi Isa.

Telling stories, talking all about the sea, so I had to come and talk to her instead."

Captin stretched up and put the driftwood back in place. "No need for that, Ruby. I can tell yo about that easy enough. And then yo woe need to mention this to Annie. None of it."

Captin was ardent, and Ruby, like a teacher with a tapping foot, waiting for a late pupil's defense, said, "Go on," trying to sound more bored than expectant.

She learned that afternoon that Captin, when apprenticed at the Deadarm, had wanted more than anything to follow Dil, his sister, down to Whalemouth. Dil had been in service, a between-maid to a merchant family up in Muckeleye who'd moved down to the seaport and taken her down with them. "Forty years ago, her went, but I can see it like it was this morning. The first Friday of March, Rube. 1893." Dil had met Striper; settled there; had his children. It was the children of those children who sent Ruby offerings from the sea and fueled her longing for it.

Dil had said that Captin would be welcome, but what with her four babies under five, all steps and stairs, and Striper hardly bringing any money in, he'd have to pay his way, and that was fair enough.

Striper would sit from first light at the fish docks with his past night's catch squirming in a basket. Still there later in the high sun, with the basket skank and full. Folk wanted fish, but not from little one-boat men like Striper . . . Striper caught up plenty of fish, good and local, but his prices were too high. It was 1899 and there were these new trawlers hunting in Icelandic waters (Ruby saw them, corpulent as whales, as Captin spoke, scooping fresh fish into hungry nets and carving their way through the seas to slap down their swollen barrels on Whalemouth quay). The buyers at the fish docks were all wooing the long-range fleets, Captin said, all dealing with importers. But Striper noticed they were having trouble shifting their stock to the wet markets inland.

"I had a notion to get the cheap fish in bulk up to the markets and buy up Striper's fish at the same time and drop um in the barrels with the others. My notion was that we could make a deal with one of them wide-gauge river hauliers that worked out of Whalemouth and all up the Severnsea Shoulder—one of them could fetch the fish from down the docks and bring um up to Ludleye Port. They cor of come no further—them boats had rounded bottoms and they wor built for the Cut. So *we* could meet the fish there wi a fleet of flyboats. Our boats was up there with the best, in them days."

Ruby was hooked in against her will, and stopped scrubbing the table. She could see how Captin's plan would have helped Striper and his sister, but not how it would have helped *him* get to Whalemouth. And what had this to do with Jonah and his debt?

"Ah. Now we come to it. I says to Jonah as I could try to broker us a deal with the wide-gauges. I had no wife, no children to keep me tied to Cradle Cross. Not like Jonah. He'd took Annie to the chapel, and her'd not long had your mom—our Beth—and Annie was already rounding out again with the next baby. *I* day have nobody, only Dil, so I was free to travel up and down to Ludleye Port, to Whalemouth, to manage dealings with the traders and to supervise the shipping of the fish. I was going to keep the business slick. Keep the flyboats fly."

Now Ruby had for seven years cherished her sea-dream and never once imagined that Captin shared her restlessness. More than that: his yearning to leave Cradle Cross was far older than *she* was, stretching back into the last century. This new knowledge enraged her: he'd laid claim to something that till now had been all hers, and Ruby felt usurped. "My grandad's boat firm—wor it good enough for yo?"

"Stretching out for sommat on another's man plate, yo mean? That's what Annie said, back then." He'd seen it as a chance to spend a bit more time with Dil: she'd lost her fat and had no appetite—no strength, even, to sit up in her bed. He'd thought that if his scheme worked, he could earn a bit to get her proper medicine.

"So yo spent my grandad's money on some medicine for your sister?" Cruel, she was: she knew it. These past days she'd discovered a rich, dense seam of malice in herself, and now she mined it.

But Captin said the bills for doctors, chemists, in the papers weren't for Dil: they were for Annie's new baby, for little Grace. She was born too early: her lungs were sticky and she didn't thrive, so Annie bought in every powder, every tincture she could find.

. Ruby shook her head (she didn't care about the baby) and chided Captin for his recklessness, for risking Jonah's money with his saft fly-boat scheme, but Captin slapped the table: *he'd* risked nothing—it was *his* idea, but it was Jonah who'd taken it up, Jonah who'd gone to Whalemouth, Jonah who insisted Captin stay behind (he wasn't long apprenticed; Jonah said he needed time to learn to steam the wood, to learn about the angle of a chisel. Ruby sucked her breath in, not thinking about Captin being caught up in Cradle Cross against his will, but how *she* would wither were *she* stranded here that long). It was Jonah who'd gone to meet up with an import agent at Whale-mouth and got so cozy with him that he was having dinners at his table; even staying with him as a guest. Three months of back and forth between the Cradles and the ocean, gone ten days in every thirty, and all the time Jonah insisting that Hind's was baying for his business, but progress was slowed by contracts, seals, credentials—business talk that Captin didn't understand. And Jonah took his eye off his main trade—building new boats, patching old—and Captin, left in charge, was floundering. The Cut was hectic, then, and Captin couldn't get the work done quick enough. He didn't know about the paper side of things: invoices, bills. He knew his letters well enough; he'd had a bit of schooling. He was slow, but he could make his way to understand them. He didn't even think to open envelopes that were written out to Jonah. "He hated it if he thought folks was prying."

His reticence—he could see this now—had good as holed the hulls and sank the firm that made them. Jonah tried to catch up on the odd week he was home, said Captin, but there were oversights. Things slipped, and Annie wanted Jonah up at home. The baby wasn't well. The doctors didn't think she'd see the other side of winter.

Captin cleared his throat. "But then Jonah gets a telegram from Whalemouth: DELIVERY IMMINENT. STOP. COME NOW. STOP. So he goes off one more time, but, unbeknown to Jonah, Annie follows him. Her leaves Beth wi Em Fine-knee Bacon and I takes Annie and Grace and we follow him and catches up wi him. But Annie, her doe show herself to him until theym on the boat when it's too late for him to send her and the baby back. Annie says he come the lunatic, saying her was spying on him, and why day her trust him; going on . . ."

He ran his thumb along the shelf. "Well, yo know what happened wi the *Lickey Bell* . . . When we got back I sat wi her while her went through Jonah's papers. Well, I went through them, truth be told. Her was too wrapped up in her grieving. One debt propping up another: I couldn't find a way to keep the firm afloat. Told Annie then, I did, as it was *my* notion about fish and flyboats that had sent Jonah off to Whalemouth."

Ruby didn't want him thinking this was noble. Captin had put ideas in Jonah's head: he had laid a trail for him, and Jonah had been readily misled.

"So it *was* all your fault, then. Why day yo run off down to Whale-mouth when he'd gone? Jonah cor of stopped yo when he was lying at the bottom of the Severn."

"Told Annie, I did, as I ud take care of her and Beth. For Jonah. And by then, there wor no point in going down to Whalemouth. When that boat went down—August, it was, of 1901—Dil was already six weeks dead."

She distrusted something in his story. Couldn't quite see Captin as a trickster-boy walking deep into a forest, paying out his stones behind him in a line. It's not that Ruby doubted Captin—she was sure that he spoke the truth as he knew it. But his story was abridged, and there was more to tell. Her grandad had left debts behind for shoes and suits and shirts—it said on the demands that they'd been made for Jonah Nailer Tailor, and, as Captin had already said, he could not take the blame for those.

"But there wor no Moonie in the papers, Rube. I went through um all. It was me as went to Mr. Blick and asked him if he ud bail Annie out. It was me as sorted out the paying of the debts. I day gid nothing to a Moonie Fly. A name that saft? I ud of remembered. Her wor in his debt. So yo ay got cause to upset Annie now."

She made for Dinah's to do teas for all the Ruths and the Naomis. *A bit of ham, a net of apples, and a paring knife.* Some kids from across Wytepole Bridge (Jim Bache; Herbert Tolley) had joined the Bastock gang outside the button shop; in the window, a new and disparate display. Laid out on the middle shelf, a silver pencil with a metal end; a rounded pebble with a date painted on; a man's comb in a cotton case. Beside them on a tent card, written in Isa's wrought-iron hand, *"What you thought lost might yet be found."* Ruby smirked and waved at Isa as she passed. *Her has to go and make herself seem even stranger.*

Decamped to Maison Hester's, the Ruth and Naomi Thursday Club sat cramped up on borrowed chairs beneath Dinah's oval mirror (a great gilded thing heavy with acorns, bulky leaves, big-bottomed pears: why did the vandal not smash that instead?) and aghast, cast glances and threw tuts against the wall.

In Ruby's head, resounding, unremitting questions came like storm waves pounding at a cobb: *Why did Captin bother working up this scheme? If he wanted to be gone that much, why day he just go? If Captin hadn't dreamed this up, Jonah ud of stayed and Grace might of lived and Nan Annie might of been so very different . . .* These questions threatened her defenses: whatever Captin said about her follies, she had till now refused to contemplate how consequences flooded from past actions, how they formed the very currents that she swam in, swam against. There were thoughts that pounded on the dam but never breached it. Until now. She sank into her lists, her Almanac.

The Ruths and the Naomis talked about the coursing of a mother's grief, deep and strong and wide, and how when you lose a son you snatch at fragments of the lost life as it passes swiftly on the banks, trying to find an anchor, to keep from being swept from him forever. These fragments: a scent of him still lying on his bed-sheets; an imprint where his head pressed on the pillow; his footprints in the clay around the veg patch; a half-sketched picture on a bread-shop wall . . . And when you see that it is hopeless to hold on, instead you dip your bowl into a dappled pool and drink long and deep and jealous: you remember how, when he was a baby and all yours, only you knew what would make him laugh when he was tetchy; how only you knew how he liked his sop bowl—sweet and not too sappy; how only you knew how to bring him around after a nightmare.

When Dinah's scowl began to waver, when it looked as if she might begin to howl, Dyspeptic Joan diverted them with some tale of that new button woman in Horn Lane having the exact cloth-covered button that she needed for her best dress for the Barby Fair on Saturday.

Ruby in the kitchen broke the surface for a moment and looked up from the Almanac: Dyspeptic Joan was mystified, alarmed and, Ruby thought, distressed. "I doe see how her come to have that button there. It ay as if I bought that dress up from a shop. There ay no others like it in the world. Made it out of Mabel Foley's curtains, I did. Stretched and pinned the buttons up myself."

That afternoon, a thought landed on Ruby like a fly on meat. Her Boat Fund—all the wages from the chip shop she'd been saving, these three years—she could give that to Nan Annie to pay down a bit of the Blick's debt. Leaving her with no means of escaping Cradle Cross.

Captin was at Hunting Tree that evening. Not his night for coming with the supper, but he was up there, nonetheless, standing on a ladder, with Annie holding steady at the bottom; his arms slick with old compacted leaves, and clearing out the gutter.

Chapter 10

No matter what other accounts may say, Mary Mayde was not plucked from the wide maw of the ocean. The mermaid found the infant sitting on a rock a mile from shore, sucking on her salty middle fingers, in the light of a full moon; the mermaid duly scooped her up and held the infant to her in a crooked, muscled fin; she fed her with salty milk until she shone, plump-cheeked and replete.

"The Making of Mary Mayde," *Tales of Severnsea*

News of Maison Hester's desecrated wall spread round Cradle Cross through Thursday evening into Friday, beyond to Nether Cradle, up to Lapple and high into the Leans. Ruby, in the bread queue Friday morning, felt a splinter of a doubt in Dinah's raw assertion that it was Isa Fly who'd done it ("Glenda says as someone saw that white one from the button shop in here, dressed up in black so that her udn't show . . .") but the splinter of a doubt was sunk so deep in Dinah that it would hurt her too much to extract it and examine it and see what it was made of, and Ruby didn't even dare to try. Dyspeptic Joan was still relishing the Mystery of the Covered Button— "How did her come to have it?"—passing her bemusement up and down the queue. People smiled and nodded absently, indulgent, but took more notice, Ruby thought, than they would have done had

Dinah's mural not been tampered with. (No harm in this one button, but in the next few days there would be more lost things, precious tokens, set out in Isa's window and she'd be condemned not so much for displaying the lost things that somehow made their way into her hands—chance? Theft-magic?—but for being cruel; provoking beyond malice.)

Joan Dyspepsia and her button story soon lost its meager power to divert and didn't even reach the Bastock lot, but by the evening other news was spreading. Come the sounding of the final Bull, the crowd of buttoners did not flow freely from the gates and up Horn Lane and into Captin's or the Leopard or through the folds back to their kitchens and their tea. The horn-slicers, the polishers, the hole-drillers and carders began the climb up the Lane, but then they slowed as they checked through their brown wage packets that seemed lighter than they should be. Swiveled round toward the high green gates. At the low end of Horn Lane, behind them, people clotted round the gates; stood, clustered, and undid their packets and shook them into waiting hands beneath and pushed the coins from one side of their palms to the other. Questions, moving freely for a while between heads bent over envelopes—"Tommo, me packet woe come right." "Ar? Mine's short, an all."—then coalescing in discontented clusters all along Horn Lane. *Every* envelope was lighter than it should be. Ruby watched and listened from inside the fish shop; rubbed newspaper against the glass to fetch the shine up in the Friday clean.

"Noticed, they have." She picked her bucket up and took it through into the back, where Truda Cole Blick sat at Captin's table with clean sheets of newspaper set before her for the peelings and a high pile of potatoes in a bowl. One tea towel fixed to the back of Truda's collar with a dolly peg; another neatly laid out on her lap.

"I *said* as they have noticed." Ruby opened up the grate door with a folded cloth and dropped her window papers in, pushing them in further with the poker.

Truda did not look at Ruby. She peeled in long, swift strokes, turning the potato, and let the peel unwind before she dropped it in the bowl. More competent at this than Ruby would have guessed.

"I thought they might," said Truda.

"Set you working, has he?" Ruby nodded at the sink where Captin, with his back to them, was stirring lumps out of a vat of batter with a wooden spoon.

"Captin," Truda said the name as if it were a rope between her teeth, "kindly said that, yes, I could lie low here—although I believe Isa exhausted her powers of persuasion in convincing him he should take pity on a *Blick*. Still, his distaste for me might just work in my favor. The fried fish shop? The last place they would think to look for me! Captin says that I may stay as long as I do more than distract Isa when she comes—"

Captin twisted at the sink. "I day say *that,* our Ruby!"

"—*and* I must not suck all the vinegar from his fancy pickled eggs. *I* said that I was quite prepared to help him, but I would not do bones. No skins, no disemboweling fish. In short, no blood. I am not good with blood."

"Yo ay bad wi potatoes." Ruby sat down at the table and took up another knife.

"Praise indeed." Truda half twisted back toward the door through to the shop. "Lord. The pack *is* baying for my blood. Maybe I could daub myself in fish guts from his bucket"—she nodded toward Captin—"and go out there and counterfeit self-slaughter to demonstrate the scale of my remorse."

"Theym not *animals.*" Captin, gruff, banged his spatula against the vat to slap off the last drips of batter. "Theym just *angry.* They got to put some supper on the table. Just how short did yo leave um then, Miss Blick?" Captin lifted up his batter vat, leaning back against the weight of it and Ruby held the door for him while he staggered through into the shop.

Truda tipped back on the hind legs of her chair and called over her shoulder. "Evidently short enough for them to notice." She let the chair fall forward and dropped her voice. "Thing is, Ruby, I haven't cut the packets short *enough.* Isa says that I should proceed with confidence. But I lost my nerve."

"Stay put back there, I ud for now, Miss Blick," called Captin from the shop. "Go out there and they ull have your guts for garters."

Ruby closed the door behind him. "How come he's so pally wi yo, Truda?"

"We are considering a tentative alliance, Ruby. A fragile pact that serves both our interests." Truda looked past Ruby to the door onto the towpath. "Isa's taking her time. Maybe she can't get through. Maybe the good doctor isn't answering. You didn't see her out there, did you Ruby? She *said* she'd see me here."

A spark of glee in Ruby.

"I'm not sure what is worse," Truda went on. "Hiding out with gallant Captin *without* Isa or facing up to my etherless evisceration on the cobbles of Horn Lane. And the Hatchett Harpies were *already* poised to hoist my innards out with crochet hooks."

Ruby sat down across from Truda and took up a potato, trimmed off an edge so it sat flat against the wood, and cut it into slices, finger-thick. "*Tell* um, yo could, why yo ay gid um their proper pay."

"Lord, Ruby!" Truda's knife clattered against the peeling pan. She yanked the tea towel from her lap and threw it on the table. "You think I didn't try? I posted up a bill for them, explaining all of it. This morning in the courtyard. Well, Isa did it for me."

Captin put his head around the door from the chip shop. "Opening up the front, I am now, so yo might want to turn it down a bit." He twisted an imaginary knob at the corner of his mouth. "Unless yo want to gid yourself away."

Truda's features creased up in a scowl, but Ruby smiled as Captin pulled the door to. "Well, Truda, true it is. Yo sound . . ."

"I know. Distinctive. I'm a Blick. Blicks don't *blend in*." She strode over to the window, heaved up the sash and, perching on the sill, took out a cigarette, but didn't light it. Cast a glance around as if she looked for a new subject to distract her. "So, Ruby, will you miss it, do you think?"

Ruby's knife slipped, sliced a chip too thin—sappy and translucent, it would crisp to nothing in the fat. How did *Truda* of all people know about her plans to leave and go to sea? Irritation surged in Ruby—Isa must have told her, and although Ruby'd never said to Isa Fly that going to the sea should be kept secret, it wasn't something to be handled, handed round like farthings, palm to palm.

"You won't lament the loss of long nights steeped in fat and vinegar?" Truda tapped her cigarette against the wall and bit at her thumbnail, head cocked and expectant.

"Lament the loss of *this*?" A thrill displaced her irritation that Isa had shared her plans: this lent substance to their scheme, and Ruby was elated. "I woe miss it. Not one bit."

"Really? Isa tells me you've been working here with Captin, what, three years? No residue of sentiment in you, then, Ruby? Maybe you're too young to be nostalgic. When the customers find out, I anticipate a lynching."

"They woe miss *me*. They doe notice me!"

Truda wasn't listening. "Perhaps I'll hide myself away," she went on. "Somewhere high up in the Lean Hills. Do you think St. Barbara's Priory would have me for a nun?" She folded up her hands, mock-pious, and bent her head, demure.

Ruby laughed. "Soror Truda? Yoom taking it too far!" But this all made no sense to Ruby and she wondered if she'd misheard what Truda said before. *Will you miss it, do you think?* (Ruby turned this over; tried to find another way of reading it, but she'd only find out later what she meant.) "Folk woe care *that* much if I ay here on Friday nights to shake the salt over their chips."

"Perhaps not." Truda took her matches out and turned the box in one hand. Held it to her nose and sniffed the striking strip. "I wonder if one relinquishes tobacco on taking a soror's vows."

"I doe know what yoom on about," said Ruby. She liked Truda when she joked with her like this—it did not diminish her or deride her in the way that Captin did when Isa was around. "Ud *yo* miss all this, if *yo* left?"

"Lord, Ruby, don't speak to me of *leaving*." She put her matches into her trouser pocket and tucked the cigarette behind her ear. "I would *love* to up-sticks. Shake the dust of this place off my feet. Make camp far away. Florence, maybe. Oslo. Mexico. Did you know that in Milan, men have these little satchels and they carry them on straps like schoolgirls? And Neapolitans wear pressed linen without neck ties?" Truda's hand went up to her own neck—she still had that old tea towel pinned up there, a tatty gray against her shirt, sleek, tailored, cobalt blue. She tugged the cloth free and rolled the peg like a cigar between her fingers. "Cuba, perhaps. Peru . . . But I am tied to Cradle Cross, as long as Blick's is here . . ." She shook the cloth out and folded it up small and square and pressed along the folds.

Ambushed, Ruby was, by a fierce compassion for the baroque Miss Blick. "Ay there no one yo could pass it on to?"

"I am the last Blick in the line. I owe it to my forebears to keep the Blick's beast on its weary feet. And that's what I find most hard to bear. These Hatchett Harpies and their kind, they'd have it that I'm stripping Blick's down to its carcass, when *they've* sucked the blood from Blick's for decades. Feasted on the factory like pigs snuffling at the udders and never once lifted up their fatty heads to thank us . . ."

"Strange idea of pigs, yo got." Ruby swept her chips down from the table into a pan on her lap. "Pigs, sucking blood."

"Well, *milk,* then. Don't be so tediously literal."

"Pigs doe eat meat. Peelings, they eat. Scraps."

"Which is what we'll all be eating before long if I don't conjure up a way—"

Ruby looked up. "A way to what?"

But Truda wasn't listening. The back door had swung open and Isa Fly was there, knocking her shoe dust off against the step, her bag in one hand and a folded piece of paper in the other.

Truda dropped down to her knees, mock-pleading. "Save me, Isa, from this girl and her contempt. My figures of speech are too tangled and erratic for her liking."

Isa laughed and crossed the room to Ruby. Crouched before her, held her chin, gentle, in one hand and twisted up her finger in the spoon cord with the other. "Don't listen to a word that Truda says." She looked over her shoulder toward Truda, and Truda, sitting, leaned back against the wall like someone who, after being long pursued, had finally reached safety.

"This was left for you, pinned to the factory gate. Those children were paying it some close attention. I thought I'd better rescue it before one of them ripped the paper."

"For me?" said Truda, craning. "Hate mail, then?"

"Not for you. For Ruby."

"Oh, share it, Ruby, do!" said Truda, pushing herself up onto her feet. "Are you being summoned to a tryst?"

And before Ruby could slip the note into her pinny, Truda plucked it from her. Ruby jumped up and in her haste she knocked her chair down backward to the floor. She snatched at Truda's hand. "Gi it here!" But Truda, laughing, held the note high up above her head and each time Ruby leaped for it, Truda jerked it higher, out of reach.

"Jump, Ruby, jump! She's like one of those Jack Russells at the circus with a ruff about its neck!"

"Gi it here, yo snotty cow!"

Truda climbed onto a chair and held the note up higher. "What could possibly be in here to send you wild like this, you little yahoo?"

"Truda, come on. Let her have the note."

"She likes it, Isa, truly. This is how the puppy gets her exercise!"

And while Ruby pawed at Truda's arm and tried to pull it down, Truda passed the note between her hands and read out, with mounting incredulity, " 'Ruby. Your dad gave me your message. Here is my answer: these are my reasons for not liking Isa Fly. Foremost, she is afraid of what is true. Second, she is cruel. Third, she lays waste to those around her.' Who wrote this maleficent junk? 'I have written to my Cass down at St. Shirah. Cass will find the truth about why Isa Fly is come to Cradle Cross. Keep watching her and tell me what you find out. Do not be fooled by her.' Keep watching her? Do not be fooled?" Truda frowned down at the note. "Ruby?"

Ruby's hands dropped to her sides. Isa stared at Ruby, scratching at the corner of her eye. Ruby's insides pitched and lurched.

"Good Lord, there's more . . . 'This is from the heart of Isa Fly: "Belle Severn is a bastard—" ' "

Ruby glanced at Isa and reached up for the paper. "I doe think yo should read it. It woe be very nice."

"I should say." Truda held the paper out before her, out of Ruby's reach.

> " 'Belle Severn is a bastard,
> Mermaid without a tail.
> Her mother was a sea-whore,
> Her father a sperm-whale.
>
> Her mother was a sea-whore
> Who trawled the shore for men.
> She sucked them in and spat them out
> Until they came again.'

"Ruby, it's obscene!" Truda slapped the paper, and Ruby reached to snatch it back from her.

"I told yo not to read it!"

"And you're in correspondence with the person who wrote this? You're spying on Isa?"

"No! My dad's mending her boat. Her knows Isa. Her doe believe as Isa's here to find her missing sister. That's all it is! I ay a spy!"

"This is that woman from the Cut the other night, the singing, isn't it? 'The father was a sperm-whale, Who spawned the mongrel, Belle—' I'm not reading any more of this." Truda tore the paper into scraps.

Isa stared at Ruby. "Yes. I know the rhyme. 'He took one look at what he'd done, and turned and swam to Hell.' Tell me, Ruby: does knowing such a verse mean I must be complicit in its writing?"

The door between the back room and the shop cracked open, just enough for Captin to fit through his head. "Ruby. Need yo, I do, out here wi them chips." He stopped and took in Truda, still standing on a chair, and Isa, frowning, fixed on Ruby. "Am yo three putting on a play or some claptrap out here? Yoom loud enough, whatever yo am up to."

Ruby stayed out in the shop for the remainder of the evening, although Captin said she could go out the back, with it being quieter than usual—less money to be spent with Blick's wage packets being lighter than expected. Edgy and unsettled, Ruby scrubbed the counter, and then she lined the jars up and rubbed oily prints from the fingerplate on the front door and cast glances back toward the kitchen as she did so. For the first time since the night, just one week back, when Ruby saw her come in on the narrowboat, Ruby was afraid of Isa Fly.

Chapter 11

The mermaid took the child to be her own, and taught her
mermaid-manners in the slow tides where the Severn meets the Sea.
"The Making of Mary Mayde," *Tales of Severnsea*

That night, Ruby could not settle. She'd tried to tell them how the
Blackbird had pursued her with all her doubts and questions, but they
hadn't listened. Every time she sloped off toward sleep, she was
pecked and flicked on one side by the Blackbird, brandishing her
threat to hold her down beneath the surface of the water, and on the
other side by Isa Fly, who'd scratched so fierce at the corner of her
white eye when Truda read that note. She'd stared right into Ruby
and inside her had seen the Blackbird's doubts, the Blackbird's questions; taking root in Ruby, growing, wild.

Ruby took up Isa's angling book and propped it on the pillow next
to her and let her eyes pass over it until she drifted into an uneasy,
shifting sleep. And when she slept she dreamed that she was singing
out to Jonah from the rocks off Sawdy Point; he was scuttling on the
seashore, back and forth between the rocks, the sea, and bent up like
a crab, his arms crooked round his head, and Ruby's song fell from
her mouth and took the shape of a black eel, an oiled rope of muscle
writhing for the land. It pulsed and twisted at the water's edge, and
Jonah stumbled as he tried to retreat. Isa stood above him, on the

cliff-top, shouting urgently into the wind, but the wind carried her words away and Ruby could not hear what she was saying.

As soon as it grew light enough to work, Ruby rubbed at her dry face and wet her mouth with cold tea from the pot and took a knife out to the garden. She hid herself among the trees, looking out for apple-scab, cutting out the cankers, easing off the softened, wasted fruit where brown rot had got the better of the tree. The leaves hung heavy with the weight of this air, hot and pressed. Above, a slate of cloud. The pigs were squealing, shifting round each other, slapping flanks. There'd be a storm today.

She worked till her hair dampened, frayed, and pushed aside the thought of summers past when, days like this, before that trip Halfway-to-France, she would have gone down to the tube-works with her friends and fished for newts and kicked her feet and felt the still, green water cool her skin. She rubbed the worm-scar on her wrist and flattened down her hair.

Nan Annie, on her way out to the Lean High Road, called out, "Put a clean pinny on when yo come up!" The Barby Fair was starting up this morning, outside the priory gates, and every year Nan Annie sold their onions and their apples from a barrow.

Ruby loved the story of St. Barbara, the saint the fair was named for: a girl who'd kept her faith despite her persecution. St. Barbara spent her childhood locked up in a tall tower by her father to keep her faithful to his Roman gods and safe from Christian influence. When she professed the faith he loathed, her father swore that she would die rather than live a heretic, and raised his sharpened ax to smite her. Before his ax could realize its arc, the holy Barbara called down lightning from the sky and struck her father dead. Spirit-magic tricks to save her neck. (Ruby often wondered if he smelled like roasted horn.) Miners and firemen claimed St. Barbara, as if she would walk out in front of them and take the brunt and shield them from the flames.

No need to leave for the fair just yet. Ruby cast about the garden for other tasks to keep her here, to push out thoughts of Isa and the Blackbird. Set to, plucking out the weeds around the path, pinching out weak flowers on the sweet peas, deadheading roses past their prime, unwinding a long rope of bindweed that was strangling a bush.

It grew dark, though still early in the morning—not yet nine. When at last the cloud cracked and the rain began to spatter, Ruby tweaked the pegs clear of the sheets hung on the line and bundled them up loosely in her arms and dropped them inside on the clothes basket beside the grate. Went straight outside again and stood before the porch, palms up, and tongue bobbed out to taste the rain. She wanted to be eaten up, eroded by the rain like a sugar mouse, so that if Isa or the Blackbird came for her with questions or with threats she would already be dissolved.

The rain seeped into veins cut deep into the cracked clay. It pooled in the foot-worn treads around the apple trees. It coursed along the thin furrows between the rows of beans and spluttered on the tin roof of the pigsty. The rain coming so hard now Ruby had to close her eyes against it. It could leave pocks and indentations, this rain could, and now she bowed her head and watched the water gutter from the slick tips of her hair and from her fingers while the rain bore on her bent neck like tacks beneath a hammer.

She stayed there in the garden till the rain sputtered and slowed, until the spent clouds dispersed, disheveled. In their place, a clean, scoured, breezy warmth, not like the febrile heat of these past days and nights.

Ruby's shirt was sodden and it licked and lapped her skin. She went inside and closed the door behind her. Left a trail of drips across the floor. She peeled her clothes off and dropped them in a slack heap. Took up a rough towel from the grate and rubbed at her skin until it prickled. Stood scrubbed and shivering at the basket, the spoon cold on her chest, sorting through the laundry underneath the sheets until she pulled out her good dress and dry knickers and a pinny.

Ruby was grateful for the Barby Fair, this morning. She stepped into an underskirt and smoothed it with her palms. Stilled, she felt, and safe around the sorors. Glad she didn't have to go down the town. No bowl to be taken for her dad—Captin had said, last night, that Ruby looked wored-out and when he'd offered to take fish and chips down the Deadarm the next day, she had clamped Captin in a fierce embrace and fastened up her fingers tight behind his back. "My best Captin, yo am." Captin had held her head against his chest for a moment and then tried to push her, gently, from him. "That fat is getting hot."

"Yoom *my* best Captin." Ruby'd pulled him tighter.

He'd put his hands up to her shoulders and pushed her, firmer now, with a sharp edge in his voice. "Let me go now, Rube." And she'd remembered how he'd used her for a joke with Isa, how he didn't see her anymore if Isa Fly was in the room. Ruby'd turned her back on him and lowered a new basket in the fat, and while the fresh chips hissed she said to Captin how it was kind of him to let Truda hide, with Isa, out the back.

Strange, then, how it happened that just as Ruby reached behind to fasten up the hook and eye around her neck, thinking how she had been barbed and cruel to Captin in the shop last night, there should be a knocking at the door, and that when Ruby opened it she should find Isa standing, dripping, in the porch. And so Isa took her off her guard. Behind Isa, Truda Cole Blick in plus-fours, truculent, hair pasted to her head, and kohl smeared below her eyes. She had a stick over one shoulder with a bundle swinging from it.

"What am yo, Dick Whittington?" Ruby sniggered. A best-boy, with a one-eyed, white-haired puss cat lapping at his boots.

"I didn't want to come here. *She* insisted." Truda took a wilted packet from her top pocket and pulled out a flaccid cigarette. "Some picnic breakfast this turned out to be."

"Her matches are all wet," said Isa. "Would you spare a dry one, please, for Truda?"

"Yo come here to get *matches*?"

Isa said that no, they'd been caught up in the downpour on their way to Parry Lean and they'd come to borrow towels and dry off, if Ruby's nannie didn't mind.

In Cradle Cross they made up rhymes for different ways to die, and there was one for this:

> *Thomas Tenter caught a chill*
> *Walking over Leanin Hill*
> *Without a scarf to wrop his ed.*
> *Come Monday morning he was dead.*

So Ruby let them in, and despite last night—the Blackbird's note and Isa's eye on Ruby—the thrill she felt at having Isa as a guest elbowed her anxieties aside. "Nan Annie ay at home. Her's gone up to get ready for the Barby Fair. Her woe mind." But even as she said this, Ruby knew Nan Annie surely would. "Get yo clean towels, I will, from upstairs. I ull put the kettle on, when I get down, if yoom wanting tea."

"It's not a social call," said Truda. "We're not staying." But as Ruby flicked the latch up on the black door to the stairs, Truda called out after her, "I need something to warm my blood before I catch a chill. You won't keep coffee in this house, that I do know, but might you have a brandy?"

"We doe keep brandy in this house either, Truda," Ruby said. "Weem Primitive Methodist."

"*That* I can believe."

Ruby snorted, her hand still on the latch. "If yoom *that* cold·yo can go out in the sun, or yo can stay in here and have warm milk when I come down." She shut the door behind her, ran up for towels and came so quickly down the stairs she nearly slid. Found Isa barefoot, with her stockings on the grate, and Truda untying her stick-bundle and setting out its contents on the table: new bread, figs, a small paper parcel.

"Strange day to try a picnic," Ruby called back from the larder. Came out with a jug of milk and filled a pan. "Day yo see the sky set for a storm?"

"See?" Truda picked up the bread and broke it into pieces. "*This* is why I didn't want to come here. I have stomached such a glut of raw hostility, these last days, and after last night . . ." She turned to Ruby. "If you insist on knowing other people's business, we *fled* Horn Lane this morning." She unwrapped the paper—cold meat—and peeled off a thin slice. "I'd rather not eat here, but I am ravenous." She rolled the slice of meat. Devoured it, with the bread.

"Why was yo *fleeing*?"

"Persecution," Truda said, through bread.

"What, was they stood in Horn Lane shaking placards, wanting what yo left out their wages?" Ruby took the pan over to the grate and set it on the hot plate. "Was they pelting yo wi bad eggs? Is that what I can smell?" There *was* a foul smell in the room, something rank and damp, and Ruby went to weight the front door open.

"I think that's me." Isa pulled her mirrored skirt up high enough to smell it. "That's how tallow gets when it's wet."

Ruby stood unmoving at the front door. Looked down at her bare foot poised to shunt the doorstop into place. Was this a test? Was Isa Fly inviting her to ask, "What tallow?" And what would Ruby do, then, if she found out for certain it *was* Isa who had ruined Dinah's mural? Ruby, with her finger on the spoon, turned round to face her. "What tallow is that then, Isa?"

"My skirt's infused with tallow smoke." Isa took up a towel and rubbed it around her neck. "It's nothing."

"Nothing?" Truda choked, spat crumbs. Ruby fetched her water and Truda drank deep, nodding thanks, and raised a hand up as if to keep a marker in the conversation. "Last night. When you went home. Did you see anyone outside the button shop?"

Ruby thought back. "Just a courting couple twined up in the doorway." Giggles as they pulled back deeper into shadow. "And some kids looking in the window. Why?" She took cups down from the hooks above the grate and set them on the table.

"But you are saying that you saw nothing strange?"

"I ay *saying* nothing except what I saw. Or day see. Am yo accusing me of sommat? What is it as I am supposed to of seen, anyway?"

Truda slammed her glass down on the table. "And *that* is how it goes in Cradle Cross: people vowing they've seen treachery or cowardice where there's none, eager to leap two-footed into judgment and leave bandages on doorsteps, but when somebody *is* threatened, nobody has seen a thing . . . No smoke. No skulking. No one looking shifty."

"Truda . . ." Isa crossed the room and put a hand on Truda's arm. "Ruby didn't do this to us."

"What yo mean, somebody's threatened?" Ruby lifted up the saucepan from the hot plate with a cloth around the handle, and tilted up the pan to pour the milk. "What's been done to yo?"

"Someone broke into the factory."

"Was sommat nicked again? Did they take something else out of your bag?"

"Not this time, Ruby." Isa, calm and steady, looked at her (*into me,* thought Ruby). She remembered Isa with her fingers primed and ready around the priest. "They dragged a sack of horn into the middle of the yard and set it on fire. And then they pushed a burning tallow rag through the letterbox into the button shop . . ."

Ruby smiled, relieved. The tallow stench did not disclose Isa's guilt, but quite the opposite. It showed that Isa Fly had been attacked. She took the cup and fished out silks of milk skin with a spoon, then put the cup onto the table before Truda.

Ruby's smile infuriated Truda. "You find this amusing do you, Ruby, burning rags?"

"We were fortunate," said Isa, quickly. "We discovered it before it had a chance to take, but the smoke was rank enough. It's seeped right in."

"Fortunate?" Truda was almost shouting. "There is no *fortunate* about it!" She sat down at the table, but stood up, prompt, pulling at the damp seat of her trousers; too soggy to sit down in any comfort. She marched over to Isa and addressed herself to Ruby. "I accept that you didn't do *this,*" said Truda, plucking up a swathe of Isa's skirt, "but that note I intercepted last night—it laid *bare* the fact that you are corresponding with this dredger who for some reason I cannot understand has taken against Isa."

"I tried to tell yo last night. I ay spying for her!"

Truda dropped the skirt, nose wrinkled. "Isa Fly, you cannot wear that thing all day. You stink like wet sheep." She looked up at Ruby. "Do you have something dry about the house that she could borrow? Something that doesn't smell like rotting mutton?"

Ruby went into the parlor, where Nan Annie had hung up from the picture rail some of the clothes she hadn't taken yet to Baitch's to be hocked: her grandfather's old shirts, long, loose; his good suit; and just one dress, outmoded, ankle-length, in cream cotton with raised polka dots in red, speckled around the skirt. She stepped up on the couch to reach the hanger. As she unhooked it and laid the dress out, careful, on the couch, Ruby wondered why it hadn't, long before, been picked apart and made up in another style like all Nan Annie's old things, or made up into a dress for *her,* or at least cut down and made up into pinnies.

She went back into the kitchen. "Found something in there and laid it out, I have. If you take that one off," she pointed at the mirrored skirt, "I ull soak it in carbolic. That should fetch the stink out."

With Isa in the parlor, getting changed, Truda paced, sullen. "She made me promise that I'd not be cruel to you. She believes you are susceptible, that you are readily beguiled . . ."

Ruby flinched at this; felt foolish, and it brought to mind something she'd read last night in Isa's fishing book: "It is a very pleasure to see the fair bright shining scaled fish deceived by your crafty means and drawn on land." Her fingers wrapped, protective, around the ribbed scar on her wrist.

"Isa says she has few friends here and wants to keep them. If you are her friend, that is."

"I am! Of course I am!" *I've found my lie,* she thought, *my rock to hide behind. My cool place on the river bed.*

"The loyal Captin, I never saw a man so exercised—banging on doors, demanding to know who did this with the rag . . . I understand from the gallant Leonard—and it's superstitious tripe, of course—that the burning of a tallow rag is meant to ward off witches. They're saying it's revenge for Dinah's mural."

"I told yo that! I told yo people think as Isa did it!"

"And while the loyal Captin's marching about town defending Isa, *you're* trysting with this hateful dredging woman behind Isa's back!"

"I ay!"

Truda stood and took up the cigarette she'd set to dry above the grate and lit it with a fierce stroke of a match. "You're claiming that you *haven't* spoken with the dredger, then?"

"I day say that. I tried to tell yo this the other day but yo day listen! I *did* speak to her."

Truda strode across the room, but stopped short of Ruby, jabbing the cigarette in her direction. "About Isa? So you admit you are colluding?"

"No, because I ay! Ask Isa."

"She said you'd fed her some tale of how the dredger frightened you." Little sparks flew from the cigarette and landed on the table. Truda extinguished them with a swift press of her thumb.

"It wor a *tale*! Her said as her ud hold me under water."

"I concede that Isa asked you to keep a close eye on the dredger. But you deny you're keeping tabs on *Isa's* movements for the dredger? That note as good as said so!"

"Her wants me to, the Blackbird does, but there ay no movements to keep tabs on! Far as I know," Ruby jerked her thumb toward the parlor, "her ay left Horn Lane for a week! All as her does is telephone the doctor now and then and come back and tell us as her dad is ranting! Her ay *doing* nothing, Truda. Even if I was reporting back to Belle Severn there ay nothing to report! Her's supposed to be here on some big mission for her dying father and her's sorting buttons!"

"You'd swear, then, that you've not been telling tales on Isa? Ruby, this isn't someone passing notes in class."

Ruby, exasperated: "What has I got to tell?"

Truda sighed. "God, Ruby. I don't know . . ."

"Dun yo believe me?"

She glanced at the parlor door; spoke in a violent whisper. "Isa's got this dying father; the delightful folk of Cradle Cross are saying she's a vandal; there are rumors about Isa stealing things; and now these noxious implications about witchcraft. Burning rags and sacks of horn? Don't think that you're exempt from all this, Ruby. I hear the kids, their chanting: even if you're trying to hedge your bets, *they've* bundled you and me and Isa up together."

"If *they* can see as I'm standing up wi Isa, why cor yo?"

Truda shrugged. "Your point has merit, I suppose."

"Yo doe think it's them kids as set the fires?"

"Lord knows. I should keep a pail of water handy, Ruby. The cowards will be shoving lit rags through your door soon enough."

"Don't talk to her that way!" Isa, in the parlor doorway, wearing the polka dotted dress. It fitted well, but she looked sickly in it. She held out her mirrored skirt before her. "Truda, look at her face: you're scaring her."

"Scaring her? I'm frightening myself! When we get back to Horn Lane I will grab those children one by one and hold their thumbs against the horn slicer until one of them tells me who thought it such a hoot to start these fires. Warding witches off!"

"I do not care about the tallow rags, the witch-talk."

"Well, I do. I've had more than my share of intimidation, Isa. I'm not brooking this. I'll telephone the police when we get back."

"No!" said Isa, then, more quietly, "There is no need." She turned to Ruby. "You said you had carbolic for this skirt."

Ruby twisted up the spoon cord at her neck. "Her should call um, Isa. Her should call the police."

"You see, Isa? Even Ruby agrees with me, though I'm still not utterly convinced of her allegiance."

Isa dropped the skirt into the pail. "You should not call on my account."

"In that case I will call on *my* account. This was not a prank, Isa."

"There wasn't any danger of a fire."

Ruby poured on water from the kettle and shook in carbolic powder from the box.

"The rags just smoldered, Truda," Isa said.

"It is criminal damage. I know persecution when I see it—"

"And you think that I don't know persecution?"

"I didn't say that."

Isa crouched down by the bucket and said nothing.

"I have experience of this," said Truda. "Of the cruelty of cowards."

Isa used the stirring stick to lever up a section of the skirt. "Anselm helped me sew these mirrors on."

"What?"

"We thought that they would keep me safe . . . We thought that these mirrors would trap sea-devils if they got too close to me and saw their own reflection, when I walked the shore. We put broken nutshells in our pockets, too, so sea-demons couldn't settle down to sleep in there. We even made up songs for shouting when we walked along the beach, to drown out siren-song and stop us being lured into the water. You would have thought, the way I talked to Ans and Anselm talked to me, that we had a firm, unflinching faith in all these things. But Anselm never quite believed. He said that I invented them, to keep him feeling safe and unafraid." She shoved the stick into the bucket and stood up, looking around her for a towel to dry her hands.

Truda gathered up her bread, her meat, and wrapped them roughly in her blanket. "What are you suggesting? That we keep those who'd inflict harm on us at bay by crushing nuts and singing hearty songs? These aren't the creatures of your young imagination, Isa Fly. This was a tangible assault! I am not brave like Hector. As a girl, I could not stomach bandages on doorsteps, and as a grown woman, I will not stand for this."

This Truda, gawky, uncontrolled, and looking in this moment so much younger than her years; Ruby would not have been surprised if she'd stamped her feet.

"That," said Isa quietly, touching Truda's forearm, "was not my point at all."

Ruby moved around them, silent, taking up the drained cups and the saucepan, relieved that Truda's indignation was no longer trained on her. Went to the sink and did not look around lest the movement should catch Truda's eye and she should start on Ruby once again.

"Am I to understand that you, Isa, of all people, would choose to sink down in the mire of reminiscence and let this persecution pass unchallenged? I'm sorry, but you simply can't compare your fear of— what was it—sea demons—with attempted arson. Notes nailed to doors, slander; accusation. And horn sacks set alight?" Her voice cracked, straining with her rage. "How can you tolerate such cruelty?"

"Me 'of all people'? Truda, you assume a knowledge of me that you simply do not have."

Ruby had not seen Isa like this until now: her dark eye flashing and her jaw clenched. She turned to Ruby with a calm that seemed affected. "Would you hang that skirt out in the garden?" She didn't wait for Ruby to reply, but strode from the kitchen and out of the house.

"For God's sake, Isa!" Truda tied her blanket in a knot around the stick, and slung it, violent up over her shoulder. She had not tied it well enough: the bundle slipped and fell open on the floor. She knelt to gather her spilled things, and Ruby bent to help her. "They set a fire, Ruby. Am I supposed to retain my composure; let this pass?"

Ruby hung the skirt up in the garden, and they caught up with Isa on the Lean High Road, stippled with sunlight. Isa spoke, but did not turn around; did not stop walking. "You think I am indifferent to cruelty."

"Now, come on, Isa," Truda said. "I did *not* say that."

Ruby looked between them, almost running to keep pace.

"One day, Miss Blick, my brother did not come home from school. My father had taken to his bed. He kept me home some days to make his soup."

Ruby thought of herself taking bowls to Jamie Abel.

"The school was in the bay, behind the sea wall. We were supposed to come the long way back, around the inland path, but Ans . . ." She breathed in sharp but let her breath out fast. "He was not biddable."

Ruby looked at Isa. "What yo mean, he wasn't *biddable*?"

"It means Anselm didn't like to do as he was told . . . It got late and it was getting dark, so Moonie sent me down to look for him, in case he'd cut across the quick way, by the steps carved in the rock face, and up across the cliff."

"How old was he?" Ruby whispered, awed at Anselm and his daring.

"It was his first term at the school. No more than five, and I no more than six. Not strong enough to pull up Anselm, if he was stranded somewhere on the cliff."

"But Moonie sent yo out to find him on your own?" Ruby found a new list forming in her head: *Reasons Why I Don't Like Moonie Fly.* "Did yo find him?"

Isa nodded.

"Where was he?"

"I heard him calling out before I saw him. Blindfolded, he was, and ten feet from the cliff edge, and calling out for me. On his knees and elbows, inching forward, his fingers stretched before him feeling for the grass, and filament tied tight around his wrists."

Truda gasped. "Who would do that? And to a child?"

"When I got Anselm home, my father blamed the merymaids—he blamed them for every last misfortune." Isa Fly fell silent, and Ruby looked down at the road, hard-packed clay and sandstone, dense and certain and unyielding, underneath her feet. "But we knew, Anselm and I."

"And what did you do?"

"What *could* I do, back then?"

"So the perpetrator got away with it?" said Truda.

"I was a child!"

"Then *Moonie* should have put a stop to it. The brutality! What kind of man *is* he to let this pass unchallenged? Not to even try to find the culprit!"

"I tried to tell him," Isa said, "but Moonie swore that they were merymaids. He said the police could do nothing against them, and it would get worse for us if we tried to take revenge."

"So you— You and your father *knew* who did this to your brother," Truda, incredulous.

Isa nodded. "This, and other things."

"What 'other things'?"

"We knew persecution, Truda, and we know it still."

"And yet nothing was done?"

Belle Severn is a bastard, Ruby thought. *Mermaid without a tail.* "I know who did them things." Ruby spoke with certainty. "It was the Blackbird. It was Belle Severn, wor it?" She looked at Isa Fly for confirmation.

Truda put her hand on Isa's arm to stop her. "The dredger? *She* is your tormentor?"

"One of um," said Ruby. "Was Cass the other one?"

"What has Belle Severn told you about Cass?"

"Just as her's wrote to her to ask her why yo am really here."

"That's all?"

Ruby nodded.

Isa turned to Truda. "Whatever you think of me—" Isa broke off and stood still. She held her hands over her eyes. "My Anselm . . . I tried so hard to protect him."

Isa was raw, exposed. Ruby flushed and flattened down her hair and, panicked, cast about for something she might say to comfort her. "I ull find a honey-cake for yo when we get to the fair."

Truda looked at Ruby. "Find a honey-cake?" There was a catch in Truda's voice, and Ruby thought that Truda might just cry. She slipped her arm through Truda's on one side and Isa's on the other (though this was awkward, carrying her basket) and led them up the Lean High Road together.

.   .   .

It was not a large priory though the lands held by the sorors were ex-
tensive; saddle-shaped, and straddling the spine of Parry Lean, the
grounds ran down the hill as far as Hunting Tree. Twenty-four sorors
in all: eighteen worked within the walls, six were apostolic. The
founding sorors had cut blocks of clay themselves out of the fissure in
the flank of Ludleye Lean and wheeled them down the hill in barrows
to the brickmakers' for firing. With brick and loam and oak, they'd
built the steady, well-paced priory: the infirmary with its three towers,
the simple domicile, the chapel. The sorors fed themselves: they worked
a five-cow dairy herd, three fish pools and two hectares of hard-
cultivated arable.

The fair was held outside the priory gates (the plain, coarse image
of St. Barbara with her firebrand carved into the wood) on that gently scooped-out swathe of ground around the east edge of the wall.
From tables set out underneath the oaks, tarpaulins stretched between the branches, the sorors traded honey, bacon, salt-fish, kiln-
fired tiles and pots and trivets. An old trade fair, this, where goods,
not shillings, were exchanged, and it drew people in from all around
the Leans: from Rodeleye, from Muckeleye, and even from the new
towns of the marches; nailers from the Cradles bringing s-hooks, hob-
nails, rivets; glassmakers from Brierleye with twice-wrapped three-
inch panes. Games and stalls and ham-poles (boys shinning up a
greasy pole and grabbing for the ham), and then at night the bonfire,
on the crest of Parry Lean.

(Eliza, Ruby's great-grandmother, who left the refuge of St. Barbara's only once a year, would be coming to the fair. She would not
stay long this year, and in the days that followed she would swear to
Ruby that she'd seen the ghost of Ruby's mother Beth out walking in
the hills.)

Ruby gabbled up the steep, larched hill, till they broke out from the
cover of the trees and up onto the thin, bald ridge that ran along the
highest part of Parry Lean. A sheer slope to the left, and down it, to
the valley and up the other side, ferns that had turned early with no
rain for weeks—all russety, dry gold. The sky now clean-blue, lucid.
Set out before them, St. Barbara's Priory, the clay path dipping down

and swerving around the south wall. Shouts and laughter drifted from the fair, and Ruby could not help but be excited. She broke free of Truda and of Isa; she broke into a canter, but a few feet on she stopped herself and turned back to face them. "Best not be running. Eggs, I got in here." Walking backward, Ruby lifted up the basket on her arm. "And lavender, to trade for honey-cake." Isa didn't even nod or show she'd heard, and Ruby felt ashamed of herself, and chewed her lips to keep them shut. She walked on, slower now, trailing her hand against the priory wall. The noise from the fair grew louder and as the wall curved around they saw it laid out in the shallow dip scooped from the hill: white canvases like sails strung from oak masts, taut strings of dancing flags; below them, barrels, trestle tables, barrows. Ruby hopped from foot to foot, but Truda put a firm restraining hand on Ruby's shoulder and said she couldn't face it; all those people. There'd be pointing, whispers about wages. And anyway (she scuffed at the ground), she had to make her peace with Isa Fly.

Ruby waited; watched as Truda and Isa walked back around the wall towards the ridge. She followed at a distance, but they did not look back, and at the ridge they turned right onto the valley path. Six steps in and Isa Fly and Miss Blick were plunged into the valley, hidden by the ferns.

Ruby spent the morning beside Nan Annie, scooping potatoes from the sack, and placing onions, gentle (as if they might be bruised), in proffered baskets, until their barrow was empty but for a few slips of papery skin. The rest of Ruby's day passed by too quick: in cheering sack races, in sitting up against the base of an old turkey-oak to eat her honey-cake, in taking trays of tea from one stall-holder to another, in shaking cloths out that had gathered crumbs, in talking with the sorors who had known her since her birth, what with all her visits to Nan Eliza. Besides the sorors, Ruby knew few people here by sight and fewer still by name, as many of the people down the town did not venture further than Crux Coci, and others, being chapel, were suspicious of St. Barbara's. There were a few Ruths, though, who had some dealings with the sorors: she spotted Joan Dyspepsia in her best dress-made-from-curtains, bending, prim, over a stall; Trembly Em beside a folding table with her good-luck trinkets set out on a tray.

The sun and breeze and honey-cakes engendered such a good humor in Ruby that, seeing how Em sweltered, she asked if she could mind her stall while Em found a shady place to sit. Em dabbed a swabbed hankie underneath the locket at her neck; said, "Bless yo, Rube," and Ruby set Em's chair down on the far side of a cedar so that she could sit in quiet, looking down into the valley, bright with ferns.

Ruby took her place beside the stall. Em had laid her trinkets in neat rows; some were curved like little shields, some long like thorns, some crossed like open scissors. (Ruby wasn't sure what they were meant to figure.) No one came to buy: *Who would?* she thought. Where was the charm in these? The workmanship was poor, and who'd hang something quite so grimy around their own neck, much less around a baby's? She picked up an iron thorn and took a hankie from her pinny to give it a little polish. She couldn't bring the iron up to a sheen, but could at least lift off a bit of dirt. She noticed that the thorn had a small hole near the top, as if it should be threaded on a string, and an indentation halfway down: a little circle. At first she thought it was an imperfection, but when she turned the next charm over, she found another circle—same size, same shape—halfway down, and another on the next. Something had been pressed into the iron before it cooled—the head of a nail, perhaps? Ruby felt a sudden stab of pity—to think that Em considered these rough creations worthy of a kind of maker's mark!—and this lent a condescending vigor to her efforts as Ruby worked her way along the tray.

She lingered at the fair all day. Captin had said last night that with trade so slack (what with the wages cut), he'd manage down the chip shop on his own, so Ruby stayed into the evening for the spit-pig and the bonfire. (The wood pile had been covered with tarpaulin for the storm, and only built up when the sun had burned the damp off.) No cloud to keep the heat in, so when the sun began to dip below the far Black Mountains, the air cooled quickly. Ruby joined the darkening crowds drawn in toward the bonfire, ten-foot high, their noise, raucous and jovial, lost in all the vastness of the sky. Vi Cope was here, and she heard the older Bastock girls, but they didn't pick out Ruby. With Nan Annie gone already and no grown-up faces watching out for her, Ruby—free, divested—bounced lightly on her toes and wrapped her arms around her, full of a gladness that for now (and just for now) was more compelling than the anxieties about Isa and the Blackbird that had settled, heavy and insistent, in her gut.

Someone dropped a hot parcel of grease-paper into Ruby's hands: in it, a jacketed potato, skin slippy with salt-butter. She stood a little way back from the fire to eat it up, scooping out the flesh of it with her fingers and folding shut the emptied skin to keep the last bit of butter in, then bending down to wipe her sucked fingers on the grass. She would go home soon, Ruby thought, while there was still a bit of light to walk back by. She was not scared of darkness (at least, not in the hills) but there were open drains and ditches on the way and if in the pitch-dark you missed your footing, you'd twist your ankle, if you didn't drown. So Ruby worked her way toward the fire to throw her taterpaper in. As she grew closer, a new urgent tone was cutting through the babble. People were jumping up to get a look at something Ruby couldn't see. Being smaller than most people in the crowd, she slipped between them, dipping under elbows and shunting sideways through the cracks until she reached the front.

A man was tugging at the tunic of a soror, and pointing down to where the fire burned brightest. Others were crouching, squinting, trying at once to shield their eyes and look into the flames. At first Ruby couldn't see what had alarmed them. A call for water rang out; shouts to put the bonfire out. The outer branches of the fire had not yet taken, and people began grasping at their ends to pull them clear. There was something—someone—lying in the fire. Although at first it was impossible to tell what was the firelight and what was its reflection, but then as the fire began, limb by limb, to break apart she saw reflected in its heart not just the frantic sway and pulsing of the crowd but her own dark eye; then Isa's; then, most sickening, most certainly, her mother's.

While she stood before the bonfire, a fragile net of meaning formed about each dark and blinking eye within the fire and if someone had not pulled her from it, she might have plunged her bare hands deep into the flames.

She was pushed, rough, backwards from the fire and Soror Brigid caught her as she tumbled; urged her to go for water, and Ruby ran, half-stumbling, up to the gates of the priory. She hammered out an urgent thoc-thoc with her fists until she felt the gate giving a little, the bolt inside pulled clear. The gate had planed the clay into a smooth flat plate and it slid freely out over the ground. (Each week Soror Ursula, the gatekeeper, rubbed the wood with flax-seed oil; dripped castor oil along the bolt shaft to keep it running clean.)

They brought out water from the trout pools by the bucket, hand to hand, and rakes and forks to split the fire apart. For a while it seemed that all of Parry Lean had caught alight, and Ruby was pushed back once again when she tried to get in closer, and told to join the other children stamping out the little fires that leaped clear of the branches from the stack. The children's shouts were all of who was being burned up in the bonfire, and if they would be dead already or if their skin would just have peeled off and how strange it was that burning people smelled like roasted fish. But when the fire was all but out, they sighed in disappointment, shoulders sagging: no body lying in the embers, just a few charred trout that had been thrown on with the first buckets of water, and the remnants of an effigy in straw, dressed up in a blackened membrane, a vestige of a skirt sewn all round with a thousand glinting mirrors.

Chapter 12

It is a very pleasure to see the fair bright shining scaled fish
deceived by your crafty means and drawn upon the land.

TREATISE ON FISHING WITH AN ANGLE

DESPITE ELIZA'S florid claim that she had seen the ghost of Beth
wandering in the hills, there was no doubt in Ruby's mind, nor can
there be in ours, that her mother was dead. She had neither cause to
question this, nor cause to tend a weary hope that Beth might one day
return, unlike older children in her class whose fathers, uncles, brothers had gone missing at the dogged end of the War, and, being "missing," might one day be retrieved. Ruby had one photograph of Beth
(with Jamie Abel, home on leave) pasted in the back page of the Almanac, and in it she looked light and spirited, and yet Ruby never
longed to resurrect her. For chained up inside Ruby, dungeon-deep,
she guarded a grotesque fear that, had her mother lived, she might in
time have got like her Nan Annie, who hard-pruned the tender shoots
on Ruby; who tied and trained her lest she grow too wild.

In those bleak months that followed Jamie Abel's move down to
the Deadarm, Ruby, left alone, exposed, with her Nan Annie, flitted
like a butterfly, frantic, to and fro between the houses of her school
friends in the town. She lit on every mother and found the sweetest
quality within her and sucked it up, extracted it, like nectar. The

mothers didn't mind (most of them had known Beth, and they'd liked her) but their daughters (Vi, and Lorna Rudge among them) became jealous, irritated, and it was not long before, one by one, the daughters stopped inviting her for tea.

Then, on her eighth birthday, Jamie Abel crossed his drawbridge and gave Beth's Almanac to her. Pressed his hands around it as if he imbued it with himself, as if it were a surrogate for parental protection. She read it each night till the light went, trying hard to hold the book ajar and not to crack the flimsy spine. (Before the trip Halfway-to-France, Jamie Abel had read with her each evening. While she sat placid at his knee, he would trace the swirling on her crown, twist it up and flat it down.) When Jamie Abel went back to the Deadarm and left this book for Ruby in his stead, she read it with a finger in her hair, twisting tighter with the pages' kinks and coils. She read the notes that Beth had written in the Almanac as if Beth had put them down for *her*, for *Ruby's* eyes; she added to Beth's lists of "What I Will Need to Take With Me to Sea"; she knew that in her plan to get to sea she was finishing what Beth had once begun. And in the Almanac, she found her mother, young, and a companion.

A new thought, though, had taken shape in her, since meeting Isa Fly. A week from now, as Horn Lane burned, the Ruths and the Naomis would tut and say, *"Poor Ruby! That unmothered girl, her never had a chance!"* They'd say that Isa Fly uncovered Ruby's yearnings, like rudimentary figures scratched on an unlit wall, and used her still and gauzy eye to make her own sense of them. They'd say that in the dark mirror of her sighted eye, Isa Fly reflected back to Ruby what the girl so yearned to see: the light and spirit of her mother. In that long summer week in Cradle Cross, Isa worked her spell up against Ruby Abel Tailor like she worked a hook up from a needle: "When the hook is bended, put it in the fyre again and give it an easy redde hete . . ." The summer bonfire tempered Isa's barb, and when Ruby saw the shape of Isa buried in the fire, *she* was hooked; pierced through to the marrow, where Isa Fly extracted her allegiance.

There was no way of building the woodpile again that night. The air was sour, heavy with a chill that shouldered through the crowd. People broke up in disappointment with bitter talk of "pranks" and "foolishness"; the waste of a fine fire. The talk among the children was more incendiary, piling up a little stack of guesses about who it was made up into that effigy, and did it work like wax dolls stuck with pins, and did her feel herself grow hotter with the flames? Ruby shook her head and walked away. She stood beside the charred skin of the skirt, held intact by the mirrored web of thread, and stared, intent on understanding what she had seen in the flame. Then, while nobody was looking, she snatched it up and ran.

It was darker in the shadow of the long wall around the priory, away from spitting firebrands, but when Ruby reached the ridge she stood and waited with the skirt-skin draped across her arm, twisting up the spoon on its red cord, until her eyes became accustomed to the night, until she could make out where the path on one side dipped down into the valley, through the ferns, the shortcut to the spring, and where the larched slope on the other side dropped down toward Lean High Road, and her home. The fern path would be quicker in full daylight, but in this twilight Ruby was more certain of the larch side, shunting down it in a crouch, and when she skittered out into the clearing she stood and stretched and brushed off the needles and the scraps of bark that had been caught up on her own skirt (*kindling*, Ruby thought). She was not late home yet—not yet ten o'clock, judging by the last midsummer light still undrained from the sky—and Nan Annie would not miss her: normal Saturdays, Ruby would still be working in the chip shop down the town. So Ruby turned sharp right, back on herself and followed the Lean High Road up round Parry Lean until she reached the lich-gate that marked the entrance to the chapel grounds. Stepped through the thin windows of light thrown out across the graveyard from the chapel (fat candles on the high sills, always lit), toward the larch-wall, and the gap. She stopped, still, at the top end of the path that fell down to the dip where (last year? the year before?) she had found Nan Annie's losslinen hung up on a tree. That was not where she was heading—even with the spoon around her neck to keep her safe, she did not want to risk missing her footing in the dark and slipping, unseen and unheard, into the pool.

She moved slow along the path between the gravestones and Ruby held her right hand out to touch each one as they passed. The fifth one was Beth's marker; her fingers grazed the stone. Before the bonfire, Ruby would have known her touch would not invoke Beth's spirit. Now, not so sure. And Ruby did not want to feel alone.

She stopped there for a moment, and then turned, passed beneath the lich-gate and back down onto the road. A group stamped by; women, men and children with loaded baskets from the fair. She stood to one side to let them pass, but the widest of the women, at the back, turned round and called to her, "Am yo all right, chick?" Ruby nodded, but this little kindness made her want to cry.

She kept to the middle of the road, flanked by the dark woods. A wood pigeon somewhere above her, sending out its somber, pulsing call.

Almost dark, but she was nearly home. She knew this stretch of road—the curve before the steep descent, and then her house at Hunting Tree, set back in the clearing on the left. She knew to follow the curve fully around and not be tempted to take the shorter, straighter line—the road edge crumbled down toward the stream. She knew the crouching shapes the bushes made; stopped; stared into the dark forms crowding at the edges of the road. *Changed, they have.* Ruby pressed her finger so hard in the spoon's bowl that it slid against her skin, clammy, cold. The slap of wet feet on dry clay; a linen shuffle; a rustling of branches pushed aside.

Now Ruby knew fear well, but did not call it that. Through all the years since she'd been out Halfway-to-France, she had been strung out tight, fear fizzing on her tongue and prickling in her fingers and settling in her belly as a low persistent ache. But this was Ruby-with-her-spoon. Her unaccustomed boldness did not fit; she shunted in it like a small girl in big shoes, clumsy and determined.

"Who's there?" She pulled the spoon from underneath her dress and wrapped it in a fist. The darkness in the verge dense, thicketed.

"You never came down to the Deadarm like I asked." A dark shape, displacing branches; Belle Severn in her blacks, climbing up toward the road. "Have you found out why she's really here? When Cass writes back and tells me what she knows, you'll be sorry that you chose to stand with *her.*"

Ruby tried to walk on past the Blackbird, but the Blackbird stepped into the stream and she kept pace with Ruby. The heavy fabric rasped and Ruby knew she should act on her fear and run away, but instead she licked her drying lips and scratched her palm and felt for the spoon to keep her sharp and brave. "Was it yo as nicked Isa's skirt from out my garden? Was it yo as made it up into a guy and put it in the fire?"

"Someone's burned her skirt? I'm not so good with fire. My ways are with water."

"Ar, I know. Her's told me some of what was done to her, to Anselm."

"What has she told you?"

"All them things as Moonie blamed on mermaids: cutting nets and holing hulls and leaving Anselm tied up on a cliff."

"Is that all?"

"Is that all?" Ruby, enraged, flung out her arms; possessed the road. "Yo *persecuted* Moonie Fly and Isa! Yo tormented them!" And now, she thought, *you're spoiling things for me.* She wanted to send fists of flame into the treetops and set fire to the scrawny woods, the thickets. She stamped her feet to set off sparks. "Why cor yo leave her to herself? Why cor yo let us be?"

She could see the Blackbird now; the undergrowth thinned out; she'd sat down on the culvert, one foot dangling in the shallow, sun-sapped stream. She turned the sole of her other foot to rest it on her leg. Her skin bright against her blacks, even in the dim light.

"We had our reasons."

How brazen, Ruby thought, *to do such things and then not trouble to deny them.*

"We swam beneath his boats to frighten off the fish. Should he chance to hook a fish when he was angling, we would steal it from his side when he was sleeping and wrap it in a finger-cage and let it slip back into the water. We poured salt-water on his herb beds while he was sleeping."

"Isa said that something held her underneath the water. Moonie broke his fingers when he pulled her free. And someone threw a stone at her, her said."

"And Isa said that I did that to her, did she?" She scattered her words, light, like seeds from a loose hand.

"Her day spell it out. You blinded her, and Moonie blamed the merymaids. That must of suited yo."

"Some nights we called to the Flys from the rocks off Sawdy Point." The Blackbird dipped her toes under the water and kicked up a little splash. "We waited for the boats that Moonie Fly had made, and we would go for them. And in the mornings we would watch him pace the jetty, throwing up his arms. We fed on his despair and we were happy."

Ruby recalled something Isa had said and her skin prickled: Anselm had been lured to the beach and killed during an air raid, and Moonie had blamed merymaids for that. "Some nights in the War?"

"What?"

"You sang out from the rocks, you said." Comprehension, almost like delight, surged in her belly. "Did you do that sometimes in the War?" This delight ebbed away as quick as it had come, and in its wake were jutting, awkward forms so obvious that Ruby wondered that they'd only just now come to her attention. They were not questions—nothing so precise—but certainties as old and obdurate as rocks along the shore, all yet to be examined and explored. One certainty: the flint-edged, blinding hatred that Belle Severn directed against Isa through the years. This hatred had not been eroded over time. Its edges were still scathing, still unblunted. These cruelties—pressed down, heated, calcified—shaped the landscape Belle and Isa moved in.

"I came up here, in the War. Cass sent me inland."

But not, thought Ruby, *until you'd lured Anselm to the rocks off Sawdy Point.* "Why did yo come here, then? Why come inland when Cass is there, and when yo love the water?"

"Cass thought that I'd be safer . . . Safe! Here! Wiping blood from soldiers on a boat moored so close to all the lights of Muckeleye and all the little fire-pits of the Cradles!"

"Safer? That ay why her sent yo here. War work? Her wanted yo out the way. So no one could match yo up wi what happened to Anselm."

"No one was going to match *me* up with *him.*"

Ruby tried to stifle her delight. "*Yo* think as Isa's come to get yo back."

"It was the War, Ruby! There were always bodies, parts of bodies, on the beaches."

"Yo think her's tracked yo down. Moonie's dying and they want to get revenge for all yo did to them and Anselm before Moonie dies!"

Now Ruby knew this couldn't possibly be true: she had seen Isa's shock and fear when she first saw the dredger; her nervousness about the second priest. But if *Ruby* was certain Isa hadn't come here for vengeance, for all Belle knew, Isa Fly had been looking for her from the crown of Wytepole Bridge. *And best of all*, thought Ruby, *Belle believes me.* "What am yo waiting for?" mocked Ruby. "If yo done those things to Isa—blinded her and held her under water and then got her brother killed—yo ud easy pull her in the Cut and hit her with your dredge-spoon on the head. There's always someone saft enough to get drowned in the Cut. Then Isa ud be done for and her could never bother yo again."

The Blackbird's plumes danced as she shook her head. "If she is here to get revenge then why hasn't she taken it?"

"Her is biding her time. It's what yo think, ay it? Yoom scared of her!"

"Cass will write back. She will know what Isa's doing here."

Ruby jogged backward, on tip-toes. "Her's coming, Belle. Her's coming to get yo!" She turned and ran for home.

Belle Severn stood up, shouting after Ruby. "She's a witch of a woman. She's enchanted you, and the Blick woman, and that Captin. Although I think I might have disenchanted him . . ."

Ruby stopped; spun round. "Captin? What have yo done to him?"

"I haven't blinded him. I haven't holed his hull, if that's what you mean." The Blackbird crossed the road—the stream passed underneath it—and stepped into the other ditch.

"What do yo mean, you've disenchanted him?"

Belle Severn did not answer, but sang out as she walked:

> *Isa Fly has got one eye—*
> *Her father pawned the other.*
> *And then he cut her heart away*
> *And fed it to her brother.*

Ruby kicked the ground. It was too late to check on Captin now. A moment ago she had thrilled at her own cunning, and Belle Severn had dulled it. She wanted to recoup the hard, shrill pleasure she'd felt in the Blackbird's agitation. *I scared Belle Severn,* she insisted to herself. *I was brave, and I was very clever.*

These last yards home were down a sheer, quick stretch of road; it carried her with a jolting momentum. The spoon tapped at her breastbone. Ruby wondered: if she'd had one all her life—not *this* spoon, of course, but maybe one of Em's iron thorns or shields—would she have grown up fearless and quick-witted? She'd ask Nan Annie why she, Ruby, didn't have one. Did all iron keep you safe and make you bold, or was it because Isa Fly had done the giving?

At Hunting Tree, the door was weighted open and a sallow light spilled out into the garden. Inside, in her nightdress, Nan Annie counting coins out at the table. Ruby lingered outside for a moment. Her nan looked fragile, Ruby thought, in her absorption; more exposed. Ruby pressed the spoon, light, through her dress. She'd scared the Blackbird: *could I scare Nan Annie?*

Nan Annie hadn't mentioned the red cord at Ruby's neck; Ruby had long since given up the threading of odd buttons onto string for amulets, but maybe Nan Annie saw the red cord as another Ruby-fabrication and didn't see the need to question it. And Ruby knew far better than to *tell* her Nan about the spoon: she'd cite the Bible—"The borrower is servant to the lender"—and insist that Ruby give it back.

Ruby left Isa's burned skirt in the shelter of the porch. She sat down at the table and they talked a little of the fair; what had sold well, and who'd left with barrows full as when they'd come.

"Them trinkets as Em makes," said Ruby. "Her doe sell many."

"Her mostly gives um out." Nan Annie made a pile of ha'pennies.

Ruby would later tell herself that it was Isa's spoon that made her imprudent—she'd yet to calibrate this newfound bravery; to distinguish between *reckless* and *courageous*. There were tracts of ground between Ruby and her nan where, by tacit agreement, they knew never to tread. But now Ruby took a spade and dug the earth.

She asked if Em made good-luck charms for Beth and baby Grace. Nan Annie nodded, lips pressed together.

She asked if Em made one for her, Ruby: Em said her charms kept children safe from harm, from wicked influence. "It ud make yo feel brave to have a thing like that."

"Yo doe need one." Nan Annie flicked the coins into her cupped palm, under the table edge. She wrote a number down in her account book. "Precaution is what keeps yo safe, not bits of scrap iron strung about your neck."

"But if my mom had one, and Grace, why day Em make me one?"

"Because I never let her."

"Yo day want to keep me safe, then, Nan?"

And that's when Ruby knew she'd dug too hard. Nan Annie moved the block across the porch and pulled the back door to. Ruby stood up; moved around the table. "I day mean that. I meant—"

Nan Annie stood, her back against the door; arms folded high about her chest. She spoke quiet and controlled: had the thorn around Beth's neck kept her safe? No; she was burned up by a fever. And Grace? Had the Severnsea Bore declined to smash the *Lickey Bell* to pieces because there was a baby on board with a lucky spoon? ("A spoon?" said Ruby. "The baby had a spoon?" But Annie didn't listen.) "I lost my girls in spite of them things slung about their necks, so doe yo go putting trust in scrappy charms in iron and thinking as yo can walk on water if yoom wearing it! There ay no magic in um. I doe believe in luck, Rube, so why ud I believe in trinkets? But if I did indulge in that way of thinking, I'd say as they was cursed. So doe take it as a mark of neglect that yo never had one. Take it as a mark of sommat different."

She dreamed that night of Isa, then herself, spooned rigid from the Cut and dropped into the belly of the dredge-boat, their bodies blackened, scorched, held intact only by the mirrored sheath of cotton binding them like flies on a spider's web. The dredge-boat inching through the bowls and narrows of the Cut down toward the shore, toward the open sea. The Blackbird had stolen Ruby's spoon, and she was poised and gleeful at the helm.

Chapter 13

Tea, *v.* colloq. trans. To supply or regale with tea.

THE SUN was already high above the Leans when a voice under Ruby's window jolted her awake; Nan Annie barking out a brief good-bye.

Ruby had slept fitfully last night; a pain in her chest had woken her some time in the dark hours—she'd been lying on the sharp lip of the spoon. She'd slipped it off and hooked the cord over her bedstead, but her thoughts had been too skittish and unruly to let her sink back into sleep. When it got light she'd gone downstairs. Not yet five by the mantel clock, so she'd taken a cup of water back to bed and read her Almanac to ease her into sleep. She began with the pages she'd transcribed from Captin's prize book, *Ashore and Afloat,* about a breed of women not afraid of water, a breed that didn't seek to conquer it or plunder; mermaids who would cluster around a shipwreck not to pick over the spoils but to gather up the children who would otherwise be drowned. They did not save the adults who, too cynical to be taught water-ways, would rather choke on the water. But children are susceptible and therefore can be taught, and these children were named for the water they were found in.

She read the paragraph on *médecins de mer,* the mermaids skilled

in healing: should a man in all knowing do a good deed to such a mermaid with no expectation of reward, she would turn his goodness
back upon him, multiplied: not only would she heal the maladies that
ailed him, she would also gift him her capacity to heal. And she read
about the curse that mirrored this: should a man in all knowing *harm*
a mermaid, she would turn his ill-will back upon him, multiplied: not
only would she aggravate the maladies that plagued him, she would
also plague him with the ailments of the sea. "His skin will bleach and
blister," Ruby read, "with the acid from the belly of a whale, though
he has not been swallowed up. His flesh will swell with fish-bites
though no fish have bitten him. His eyes will see a tempest though the
water's still. His abdomen will distend as if he has drunk brine; his
throat will chafe and burn with thirst and this thirst will not be
slaked."

She rubbed her face; creased, she was, and parched from her salt-
dreams, and though she couldn't dig it out, there was some truth preserved within them. She went downstairs without brushing her hair
or getting dressed, straight out into the garden, barefoot, in her
nightie. Ruby worked the handle of the pump and bent to let the
water soak her neck, her face, her hair.

"Yo ay bothering wi clothes today, then, Rube?" Nan Annie,
crouching with a trowel, half-hidden in among the canes of beans.

Ruby, alarmed, stood up too quick and banged her head against
the pump. "I thought as yo had gone up to the sorors."

"Your dress is in your bedroom, then, is it? Hanging up and ready
to be wore?"

Ruby frowned and pushed her hair back from her face.

"Em was here. Her told me yo been free wi other people's clothes,
Ruby, so I take it as yo gid your own away." Nan Annie hacked at the
earth with her trowel.

Ruby bit her lip. The polka dotted dress. "I ud of asked, if yo ud
been here. I thought as it was going down to Baitch's."

Baitch's? Nan Annie said. Did Ruby think she'd give away the one
thing she had left of Beth?

Too late, Ruby remembered where she'd seen the dress before: the home-leave photograph of Beth and Jamie Abel, stuck in her Almanac.

"Eggs, and ends of bread; bits as I was keeping in the larder—all week things am going missing." Nan Annie sat back on her heels. "I says to Em yo wor brung up to steal, but Em's been telling me some more about this half-blind girl who's made a pet of Truda Blick. Her says this girl is using your two hands to do her thieving."

"Her cor blame Isa! Got soaked in that storm, her did, and needed sommat dry."

"Yo took it and yo never asked: yo *stole* it. Yo was so caught up wi your fancy for this stranger that yo gid her sommat that wor yours to gid."

"I forgot as it was Beth's."

"Yo forgot?" Nan Annie stabbed the trowel so hard into the ground that it stayed there, fixed, upright. She stood, her hands pressed on her thighs, and marched past Ruby to the porch. "Forgetting is a luxury yoom blessed with, Rube, so doe delude yourself that yo has got it hard." She kicked her shoes against the scraper. "Yo cor miss what yo never had." A grubby cloud loitered across the sun, and Ruby, wet and chilling, followed her nan back into the house. She didn't care, Nan Annie said, if this Fly girl got herself chased out of town with dogs and fire irons; it was *Em* that she was bothered for. And Ruby shouldn't shame her, by asking for the dress back, by putting it around that Annie Nailer Tailor would strip the clothes from off a stranger's back: "Just tell this blind girl to leave Em well alone."

Isa Fly had waylaid Em, said Annie, on the way home from the fair. She was waiting for her at the gap to Kenelm's Field; confronted her with one saft question hard after another about some lad Em knew back in the eighties, back when she was Ruby's age. Nan Annie'd settled Em before a fit took her, this time, at any rate.

"Upsetting an old woman, making her ill? That warrants guys, it does."

Ruby lingered at Hunting Tree till Nan Annie had gone up to the priory, and by the time she reached Horn Lane, she found that there was no one in the button shop, and when she tried to get to Blick's, the factory gate was locked. She stepped back onto the cobbles and called up at the high window, but no answer. Once more she pulled and pushed the gate within its give, and panic rose and clamped her throat. (She had the mirrored skirt safe in the basket of the bike, still smelling of the fire. Those dreams! Skin, blackened, red and stretched almost translucent, shiny around the roasted belly of the spit-pig . . .) She bent to shout in through the crack between the two wings of the gate and took a few steps backward till she was outside Captin's. She scratched up shards of stone, loose on the putty between cobbles, and hurled them up toward the high window. Her aim was skew, and some stones rattled on the bowed window at Captin's. He barged out of the shop but stopped short when he saw that it was Ruby.

"Rube! What am yo playing at?" Gruff, he was; and shambling. He seemed smaller, older. *The Blackbird,* Ruby remembered. *She's disenchanted you.* She decided to test Captin's loyalty, to see what damage Belle Severn had done.

"Did yo hear about the Barby Fair, last night? Someone made a guy up out of Isa's skirt and put it on the bonfire."

He turned his back on Ruby and fiddled with the lock.

"Did yo find out who it was as lit that tallow?"

"Kids, it ull of been. Kids messing."

What did the Blackbird say to yo? she thought. *What did her do to yo?* Captin, in shadow. Captin, whom Isa Fly had lit up from within, was dimmed and simmering.

"Ruby!" Truda called out, hoarse and low, an ineffective whisper from her window. "Was that *you* hurling stones? Stop, will you, before I have to call a glazier. I simply can't afford it. Not this week, anyway." She threw a key down on a ribbon and Ruby caught it in cupped hands. "Use this, would you? Cleaner. Cheaper. And be quiet, will you? Isa's sleeping."

Captin cursed under his breath. "Am yo going up there, Rube? I cor see what business yo ud have in Blickses on a Sunday."

"I got the skirt for Isa. Her's up there, ay her? That's why I'm going in." *And I want to tell her not to worry about Belle.* "I scared her for you, Isa," I will say. "I scared Belle and her woe come for you now."

Truda hissed from high above Horn Lane that Ruby should be sure to lock the gate behind her, but Captin pulled her, rough, into his doorway, his words flecking and fierce. "Yo wants to watch how much time yo am up there wi Miss Blick. Her influence, it ay all for the good."

Ruby frowned and loosed herself from Captin. He shook himself and brushed away imaginary dirt. "See yo later, I will, up at Hunting Tree."

"Why? Am yo coming up?"

"I got to talk to Annie, and I got things to do."

She eased the bicycle with great care across the lip of the green gate, and leaned it, inside, up against a wall. She lifted out the package from the basket and laid it across her upturned palms to carry it upstairs, as if it were a cushion with a crown. The office felt bleak and grimy; stale despite the opened windows, and at first Ruby could not see why. Fewer piles of papers, and more orderly. Cleared floor, too— enough, at least, to cross the room without stepping over ledgers or displacing invoices. And then she noticed that the photographs had been taken down and stacked up in three apple crates along one side of the room. On the walls, picture hooks in pale squares were framed in grime, marking out where the photographs had hung, till now.

Truda, standing at the kitchen-closet, saw her looking but said nothing. She worked at the stuck lid of a tin with a knife blade and nodded at the couch where Isa lay: Isa hadn't slept until first light, Truda said, and finally succumbed only when Truda stirred a powder in her milk. "We heard about the guy up at the bonfire, but I don't think that's what did for her. She was already unsettled. I wondered if she was anxious about Moonie, but when I said she could call home I only made it worse."

"Am yo going to get the walls painted?" Ruby looked round speculatively. "Is that why yo took the pictures down? I can gi them walls a good wash with some sugar-soap, if yo want. Come up nice, they will."

"And fiddle while Rome burns?" The lid came free, and Truda held the tin just below her nose. "Is this tea? It smells of metal. Dust and metal. Tastes that way from what I can remember." She held it out for Ruby. "Have a sniff."

Ruby smelled the contents of the tin. "Old tea, mind, but that doe matter. It doe go off. Since when do yo make tea?"

"Why? Don't you want tea? I thought that it would be your drink of choice."

Ruby thanked her. "What did yo mean, fiddle while Rome burns?"

Truda dug a spoon deep into the tin. "It means no, I won't be painting it . . ." She shoveled tea leaves from the spoon into the pot. "Will this be too strong?"

"Doe yo know how to make a cup of tea, even?"

"It's years since I've made tea for anyone, so do be kind to me. I last tried it at college and I do recall that I was mocked for being too—what was it? Not 'vulgar' . . . it was neater and more spiteful. Ah! *Marchand!* That's it. I was too *marchand*."

Ruby shrugged.

"It's French. It means 'merchant.' "

"It doe sound that bad."

"They didn't simply mean that we sold things. They meant my family was sullied, because we Blicks *earned* our money."

"How else yo going to come by it?"

"Ah, well. Ask that question and you reveal that you, too, are *marchand*, Ruby. Money," she moved her hand around in a mock-gracious wave, "isn't in the ether that *we* breathe, you and I; it's in our pockets. Or in my case, it's not. And as I learned to my cost, you do not, Ruby—let me make this as plain as my face—you do *not* put the milk in first if you want to look soignée. It marks you out as aspirant."

"That sounds like a good thing to be."

"It is!" Truda breathed deep and leaned against the sink. "At least that's what I was taught to think."

Ruby cast about her for something else to say: Truda, sad, and Isa not awake to make it better. "Why *did* yo take the pictures down?"

Truda sighed and absently shook more tea in the pot. "It's their blasted *eyes*, Ruby. The eyes of my dead brothers; the eyes of my dead uncles; the eyes of Hector and my grandfather and my mother . . . They watch me, every day. Watch over me."

Ruby thought they had looked kind, and said so.

"Oh, I'm not scared of them! Benevolent, they were, all of them. Brave. *So* kind. Industrious. Competent. I don't want them to see . . ."

"See what?" said Ruby.

"All this!" She swept her hand across the room. Pressed her palm to her forehead. "The swift disintegration of all that they constructed! The hastening demise of Blick's, under my incompetent and ineffectual governance!"

"How long yo had the factory?"

"What?"

"How long is it since Mr. Blick died and yo had to take it over?"

"I don't know . . . two weeks?"

"Exactly! Yo cor of mucked it up that bad in two weeks if the mess wor there before."

Truda looked perplexed at Ruby, at this new thought, then shook her head. "It doesn't work like that."

"But what difference does it make, taking their pictures down?"

"I thought, perhaps, foolish as it sounds, that if I were not being watched, I might just feel a little freer to do what must be done."

"What is it must be done?"

"Drastic measures to save their factory, somehow. To save their legacy . . . It sounds gallant, don't you think? Almost chivalric . . ."

"And do yo?" Ruby said. She took the spoon and tin away from Truda—this tea would come out thick enough to spread.

"Do I what?"

"Do you feel freer, now yo've took their pictures down, to do what yo got to do?"

A short, cold laugh. "No, Ruby, I do not." She cast her eyes round at the emptied walls. "I feel alone."

They stood there for a moment, saying nothing, Ruby watching Truda with a cautious and benevolent recognition: a fellow solitary soul.

The kettle whistled and Ruby started forward. "Ud yo like *me* to make the tea? I doe mind."

"Thank you," Truda said, and Ruby saw that she was glad to be relieved of such a slight, inconsequential task.

"A bit too much leaf there is, in there." Ruby spooned some back into the tin. "But see how it comes out, we can. If we need to, we can put the kettle on again to make it weaker."

They made the tea together, setting out the bronze tray on its legs; cups, saucers, milk jug and a little tea strainer with its own stand, and sat down on the winged-back chairs to drink it. Truda chose a record for the gramophone, but lifted the needle back into its cradle when Ruby put her finger on her lips and pointed at Isa, still asleep.

The news, said Truda, from the broken bonfire had reached the town last night before the fish shop closed. "You were up there, then, were you, at that fire last night?" Truda asked, wincing as she sipped.

"Ar. And I know as it's saft," said Ruby, spooning sugar in her tea to blunt the tannin, "but I had this dream as Isa had been burned up at the same time as her skirt." Still queasy with relief, she was, that Isa was not scorched or scathed.

"You need not have worried. She was here."

"So?"

"Do you think that I would have stood by while Isa started smoking at the edges?" Truda reached into the back pocket of her trousers for her cigarette tin. "I would have chucked a bucket of water on her at the least."

"Yo wor so blarsey about that tallow rag when yo was up at my house yesterday."

"Well, Isa convinced me that I should let things settle. All these changes, here, since Hector died . . ." She swept her hand around the office. "People are about to lose their livelihoods. I suppose I can't blame them for seeking a whipping boy."

"Her changed your mind?"

"It's not that I've discarded all of my concerns for *Isa's* safety—"

"Good!" Ruby stood, putting down her cup so quick that it chinked against the saucer, slopping tea. "Yo day see um at the bonfire! They was excited, some on um, looking round for pikelets to toast while they waited for a body to be fetched out of the fire." Ruby marched over to the stairwell to fetch the toweling bundle she had left there. "And yo know what the Ruths and the Naomis ull be like," she said, easing up the rolled towel, "when they hear about it. All 'I said as her'd provoke someone if her wor careful.' "

She took the towel back over to the fireplace, where she knelt down and unrolled it. Inside, another layer of soft cloth. She peeled back the folds. The charred skin of Isa's skirt, its mirrors dulled and blinded. Gentle, slow, she lifted it and stood up, taking great care not to tread on it or knock it. Still, dark flakes were dislodged with the movement and drifted to the floor. She held it up. Waited for Truda to be shocked. "I saved this from the fire. I brought it back for Isa."

Truda struck a match and lit her cigarette. Glanced at the charred skirt then looked away. A gray wash through her skin, but Truda said nothing. Ruby laid the skirt across the back of a bare chair; picked up her cup and saucer and took them to the sink to tip out the slopped tea. She sipped at the tea left in the cup. Too rough, too strong.

"It's not their style though," said Truda, bringing up the teapot for more water. "All those chapel widows: I can't see them burning Isa at the stake. They'd rather stare her to death in the queue at Maison Hester's while she was trying to buy bread." She twisted round to Ruby and made her eyelids spring back, whites like peeled eggs, to demonstrate the stare. Ruby snorted, spraying tea.

"Here. Clean yourself up." Truda handed her a pressed white handkerchief from the pocket of the jacket that hung on the back of the desk chair. Her monogram, a flourish in the corner.

Ruby turned the hankie in her hand. "Am yo sure? It's such a good one. It ull stain."

"Keep it . . ."

Ruby dabbed around her mouth and on her skirt where she had spat the tea, and tucked the hankie in her pinny.

"You were very sweet to even *try* to drink my tea. It strips the tongue. I feel like the Ancient Mariner. 'Water, water, every where . . .' " Truda emptied out the kettle on the leaves. Gave them a cautious stir. "Does this look any better? Can it be salvaged?"

Ruby peered into the pot and tilted it so that the liquid caught the light. She shook her head. "Best chuck it. Make a fresh pot, but warm it round with hot water first, yo should."

"What would I do without you, Ruby, eh?"

Ruby smiled. "It's only tea."

"It is *not* only tea. It's . . ." But whatever Truda was about to say, she swallowed it. "You *will* keep working for me, won't you, when Captin's gone?"

"When Captin's *gone?*" A cold surge from Ruby's neck, all down her spine.

Truda misread Ruby's confusion as reticence. "Of course, if I succeed in salvaging some vestige of the business, I should be able to pay you in shillings one day, not in Loan of Bicycle." Truda tipped the water from the teapot. Slopped tea leaves in the sink.

Ruby frowned and took the teapot from her. She laid out a pad of newspapers and tipped the tea leaves on it.

"It *has* occurred to me that you might want to look for other opportunities when you finish working in the chip shop. Away from Horn Lane. I don't know . . ."

"When Captin's gone?" Ruby repeated. Pressed her fingers in a scoop and slid them around the sink to gather up the tea leaves. "What kind of gone?"

"What kind of Cradles double-talk is that?" Truda laughed. "There is only one kind of gone. Left. Vamoosed. Departed."

"When Captin's died?" Was Captin ill, and hadn't told her?

"Lord, Ruby, no! When he's sold up and gone wherever it is he's off to. Whalemouth, is it, where his family is?"

No, she thought. *It's not. His family is here, in Cradle Cross. Up at Hunting Tree Hundred, me and my Nan Annie, that's where Captin's family is.* "Sold up?" The chill extending down her arms and freezing up her fingers. She rinsed them. Wiped them on a towel looped around a rail inside the door.

"Well, technically it isn't his to sell, I know. Hector gave it him rent-free. Wanted to make sure people ate all through that War and those lean years afterwards, even if it was a few fish bones dipped in batter."

Ruby worked the frozen knuckles in her palms, bending all her fingers in their turn. Thought that they might snap off if she didn't knead some warmth and flexibility back into them.

"I'm not buying him out, exactly . . ." Truda went on, washing out the tea cups, unaware of Ruby stiffening beside her. Ruby did not know of any other woman besides Truda who didn't want to knit a warm jumper for Captin, or invite him round for something hot on Sundays.

"Paying him off, perhaps. I've made a little deal with him. One of Isa's strategies for getting Blick's back on its feet."

Ruby swallowed. Rubbed along her jawline where her face had stiffened. "*Isa* thought of this?"

"No, not exactly. The principle was hers: if the bank won't lend, then I should cash in some assets. So Captin vacates the chip shop and surrenders any right of tenure, liberating me to sell it on as a going concern, or to parcel it up with our other properties in Horn Lane. We don't anticipate substantial proceeds from the sale. Enough, perhaps, to carve away a bit of debt and buy in a few batches of horn. I haven't told her yet."

"And what does Captin get out of this bargain?" Quiet, Ruby spoke. "He loses his home, the place he's worked in all his life . . ." But even as she spoke she knew she lied. *I mean the place he's worked in all* my *life*, thought Ruby. *He had a life before mine and now he'll have another.* And Captin had never lived above the chip shop. *Ferret* was his home, and he would leave in her.

"What does *he* get out of this bargain? The shove he needs to leave this place, that's what . . . From what Isa's said, he wanted to leave thirty years ago but got *stuck* here instead. I put it to him first on Friday, I admit, but he wasn't sure and I was not about to take his business from him. But then he took me aside last night. He came to *me*, Ruby, determined to be shot of it. I didn't hold his thumb by the horn slicer."

The chill in Ruby splintered. Captin, disenchanted. She pressed her nails into her palms.

"Has he said precisely when he's leaving? I know he won't be here *much* longer," Truda said. "A week, is it, or two at most, he said?"

Ruby said nothing. Her eyes flicked, frantic, counting tins along the shelf. She sucked her tongue. She squeezed her toes inside her shoes, and kept the tears stopped up. Felt Truda's eyes on her, but could not look at Truda.

"God, Ruby, I'm so sorry." Truda smacked her forehead. "I thought you *knew* about all this. We talked of it in the fish shop. I asked you if you'd miss it. What did you think I meant?"

Ruby shrugged.

"Down in Horn Lane, this morning . . . He looked so grave! So Captin didn't tell you he was going?"

Ruby shook her head.

"Well, he is a fool to treat you quite so shoddily."

Ruby felt a rage surging inside her. "It ay just *Captin* being shoddy here, Miss Blick: yo never liked him and yoom getting rid of him."

"Come on, Ruby. That is hardly fair."

"Yo just said he was a fool! How come yoom the only woman in this town who cor see what a good man Captin is?"

"He isn't quite my type."

"Isa likes him. That's why yo want him off and out your way."

"Isa *humors* him." Truda walked over to the couch where Isa lay. Her feet were bare and so, crouching beside her, Truda eased the blanket over Isa's toes. "She knows how to make an old soul feel— How can I put this?" She let her hand rest light on Isa's ankle. "More alive; a little younger." Truda's voice was gentle, tender, even, and this enraged Ruby further.

"If Captin was younger yo ud *still* think yo was too good for the likes of him, when yoom Cradle-born just like the rest of us. Yo live here, work here—yoom stuck in the Cradles just as sure as I am."

"*In* the Cradles, dear," she said. "But hardly *of*." She stood up and strode back to the kitchen.

"In um, of um—Captin doe mind being from the Cradles. It's where he belongs."

Truda reached up and took a tin down from the top shelf. Gently shook it. "I'm not compelling him to leave. As I said, Ruby, your Captin came to me." She turned to Ruby; sighed. "I have no doubt you will miss him at first. But one can get used to that."

"It ay just that," said Ruby, petulant. "He's leaving. Getting away. I doe want to be stuck here!"

"Me neither, but I haven't any choice. Don't be so self-indulgent! You're not indentured, Ruby, it's a bloody errand job. I'm not asking for life service."

"I doe mean stuck at fogging *Blickses*."

"Ah." Truda bit her lip and closed her eyes. "The small-town itch."

Ruby glared at Truda. "Yoom mocking me."

"I'm not mocking you, Ruby."

"I doe want to be stuck here."

"Nor do I."

"I cor live out my life in Cradle Cross."

"Lord, nor can I . . . Shall we join a traveling circus, you and I? No, let's form a troupe and take our show to Morecambe every summer."

Ruby found that she was grateful for this diversion, swift and sharp and confidently rendered, and she grinned. "Morecambe?"

"We'll put Elizabethan ruffs about our necks," said Truda, lifting up her own chin, then Ruby's, with the point of her index finger. "We'll have a tent, striped red and white. We'll pitch it on the beach. We'll live off whelks and cockles that you pick from the rocks and we'll save the profits to buy us a coracle. We'll row to Reykjavik and pitch our tent below the frozen cliffs and draw a crowd of girls named after goddesses. Freya, Sif and Ilse, hair white as Arctic ice, with ruddy cheeks. We'll dazzle in the cold."

"What about Isa?"

"Ah, we must have Isa to bewitch the audience for us. One word from Isa and they'll be queuing at the tent flap to bring us sealskin coats and salted fish and take us home to warm our fingers around. their fires . . ." Truda broke off and glanced over at the charred skirt. Chewed her lip. "You know that I agree with you, don't you?"

"About what?"

"About these fires. The tallow and the guy. This animosity that Isa seems to garner. *Isa* might pretend that it is nothing. I cannot." Truda twisted off the lid of the patterned tin and held it close to her face. "Biscuits from St. Barbara's, with stem ginger and honey. They sent them down for Hector, now and then." She breathed in. "Ah. God bless those sweet-toothed sorors. Two left. Would you like to try one?"

They sat down by the empty fireplace, and while they drank their weaker tea and ate their gingered biscuits, they traded details of their growing skepticism about Isa's search, giggly with relief at their confession, and forged a tight, giddy alliance. (And Ruby built a wall around the news that Captin would be leaving her behind, so that it would not seep through all of her and leave her sodden and bereft. Penned up within the wall: her shame at being told of his departure and not knowing; Truda's glee, and Ruby's indignation that he should think of leaving and not consult her first; her jealousy that he would soon be free of Cradle Cross and living by the ocean. These currents pulsed against the walls, but Ruby twisted up her spoon as if it were a key to lock a gate against the tide, and kept these currents harbored.)

Ruby nibbled at the edges of her biscuit. "Dun yo think as these fires am caught up with Isa, maybe, looking for this daughter, for her dad?"

"What, for old Lear, 'mad as the vexed sea'? I confess that I am wholly unconvinced by her Cordelia . . . I'm not certain, yet, if it's this inane search for missing daughters that's getting somebody worked up into a lather, or simply someone taking against Isa. The old story of wary townsfolk tilting at the stone-blind stranger, come to plague 'em. Either way, we'll work on her together. Get her to renounce this search and live a quiet life."

All this trouble, Ruby said, for no purpose: Isa was no closer to finding Lily Fly (for Captin had read Ruby's list of "Men Who Might Be Moonie" and, like Glenda with the Lilys, accounted for them all). Ruby told Truda of her notion that Isa hadn't come to find a sister, but instead to get revenge on Belle Severn, but Truda dismissed it— "Isa, avenging angel?"—with no comment on how inventive Ruby was, how brave.

They moved, back and forth, through their objections: even if this lost daughter existed and they somehow found her out, why should she believe this tale about a dying father? And if she did, then what on this earth would move the girl to leave behind her home and family to go with Isa to the sea? Why would she want to visit a man she last waved off when she was, what, two? Three?

"And the final strand," said Truda. "If we stretch the bounds of our belief yet further, and the lost daughter agrees to go with Isa, what happens then? She grants him her forgiveness and lets him touch the hem of her garment and wins him a reprieve from whatever damnation he has brought on himself. Then what? Does Isa Fly imagine he'll get better? God, no. He'll die of disbelief that she was fool enough to go forth at his bidding. Or he'll die of disappointment that there was no last reprieve, no Gospel-cure. He'll die anyway. That'll be what happens. We all bloody do."

"But what ull Isa do then, if her cor find the daughter? Go home? Her dad said as he ud jump down off the cliffs if Isa went back before her'd found her."

"God, no, Ruby, we couldn't send her home! She must come with us to Reykjavik . . . We'll pluck a random woman from the queue at Maison Hester's and slip her a tanner to claim she's the missing daughter and absolve Moonie Fly."

They hadn't seen Isa sit up, slipping off her blanket. They started. Ruby flushed and Truda stood up, quick.

"Isa, honey. You catch us in the midst of our conniving."

"I heard." Quiet, Isa spoke, and clear. "I have no desire to win my father a reprieve, nor expectation that I'll bring him any peace."

Truda's awkwardness at being caught conspiring twisted into a raw indignation and as Ruby watched she thought that Truda might dart forward and slap Isa—one, two—hard across her pale, impassive cheeks.

"Then what on God's good earth," said Truda, throwing out her upturned palms in question, "are you *doing* here?" More quietly, "And why can't you tell *me*?"

Ruby moved to Truda's side. "Yo doe seem to like him, even, Isa! He ay looked after yo, he ay stood up for Anselm or for yo. He ay like anything as yo might in reason want a dad to be . . ."

Isa looked across from Ruby, and to Truda. Back again to Ruby. "So unlike your own attentive father, Ruby."

Ruby shrank back behind Truda, but wanted at the same time to run across to Isa, to hide behind her polka-dotted skirt, to have her calm hand pass across her head and soothe her.

"There's no call to speak to the girl in that way!" Truda, barbed. A dot of scarlet on each cheek. "She simply does not wish to see you harmed, and nor do I. This mock-quest, Isa, for Moonie's absolution . . . it's unconvincing. You *despise* your father, Isa! You talk of him with barely obscured hatred! The premise of this enterprise is to save him, to procure a little peace. I fail to see why you would protest loyalty and filial devotion."

Isa tugged her dress straight, rubbed her face. "I'm going to see Len. He would not laugh about a dying father when he thought that I was sleeping."

Truda frowned. "We haven't finished here." She reached for Isa's hands and turned them over, pressing her thumbs into Isa's palms. "Just listen, will you? Please? For the sake of argument, you're here to find this daughter for your father." Her tone was pleading now. "He must see how much you loathe him—all right, if loathing is too strong, what little *affection* you have for him . . . What power does he have over you to compel you to leave your home? To forbid you to return? And is it worth the ill will? This tallow rag, and now this effigy?"

"Do you want to be rid of me?" Isa pulled her hands away from Truda's. "Does it trouble you to have me staying here? Am I too difficult? Do I attract too much attention?"

Truda strode across the room to the chair where the burned skeleton of skirt lay. "You *know* I do not think that way!" Hasty, rough, one-handed, Truda plucked the skirt up from the chair. "*This* is where he's brought you, Isa! This is in the nature of this place to which he's sent you! Does it not make you *afraid*? Round here they think anyone of unknown provenance walked in from the woods with a fat sack of spells." She brandished the skirt. "You're not trusted even if they saw you emerge squalling from your mother, and your mother from her mother before that. And even place-of-birth's no guarantee . . ."

A flurry of dark sparks fell from the mirrored net. The thread that held the skeleton together came undone and the tiny mirrors reeled and spun across the floor, skittering and clicking on the wood.

Ruby cried out, "Saving it, I was, for Isa!"

"Presumably," said Truda (who, too late, laid the skirt down gently on the desk), "you had a point you wished to make."

Ruby ignored her. Dropped down to her knees and scrabbled for the mirrors. She pinched them up; she shepherded them into a pile with the edge of a cupped hand. One last mirror slipped into a deep crack in the floorboards before she could catch it. She remembered with a stab how last night in the ebb-flame of the bonfire she had seen that wrenching flash of Beth and Isa caught up in the mirror. She pressed her nose against the floor and looked along the crack, then, growing frantic, slipped the spoon from around her neck and shoved the handle down into the groove, slicing up and down and gouging out a waxy curd: old dirt and beeswax polish.

"Get up, Ruby," Isa said, and Ruby heard restrained exasperation. She collected up the other mirrors in her palm and shuffled on her knees across to Isa. She held them up in cupped palms, like an offering.

Isa rested her hand on Ruby's head. A brief touch, gentle, and as Isa scraped the mirrors from her palm, Ruby looked up at her face. Isa dropped the mirrors in her pocket, and as she did it seemed to Ruby that Isa Fly retreated. As if both eyes grew gauzy and were blind to her, and Truda. Her words were worn, as if from repetition. "My father is afraid of obligation. He runs from his mistakes, from all his duties, and I will not be like him. *You* understand that, Truda. That's why you're here, amidst all this." She swept an arm around the room. "Against your will. To fulfill your obligation to your forebears. I am compelled to be here. I would not—*could* not—linger with my father when he willed me elsewhere. I go when I am told to go. You're right. This isn't loyalty, or filial devotion. There are imperatives that bind tighter than these. And yes, I am afraid."

And that is when it became quite clear to Ruby. Isa did not leave home on a heroic quest. She had been expelled.

Chapter 14

Mermaids are like trout: where the water is brackish, their scales
wink and shimmer, green and gold. Inland, in fresh water, their
scales lose their sheen and become dull as mud.

TALES OF SEVERNSEA

OUTSIDE the button shop, Ruby sat down across the doorway with
Truda's satchel undone on her lap and the broken fish-priest in her
hand, using the splintered end to draw slow patterns in the ash. Isa
had locked herself inside, though Ruby had no doubt Isa had seen her.
But instead of coming to the front to let her in, Isa had failed even to
acknowledge her; she'd pulled the middle door shut, controlled but
conclusive, and left Ruby, fingers gently drumming on the glass.

Her skin still prickled with the shock of it. (And Isa had left Blick's
so hastily. When Ruby had asked Truda if they should follow, Truda
didn't answer; no trace left of their earlier ebullience; all evaporated
in the heat of the exchange with Isa Fly.)

Ruby's throat was tight; her stomach twisting in discomfiture that
she and Truda should have been caught out by Isa in the throes of in-
fidelity. *No!* thought Ruby. *We was not unfaithful. We was right to
share our doubts.* Isa had built them half a tale, and they had simply
shaken it to see if it was sturdy. Frail, it was, and flimsy, but Ruby's
faith in Isa Fly was solid and Ruby winced to think that Isa might be-

lieve that she and Truda had been mocking her. So Ruby, on the doorstep, drawing circles in the dust, told herself that she was waiting out of kindness and tried to think of ways she could help Isa not to be afraid.

But her own fears kept intruding. *Captin, going?* She did not want to see him; did not want to go to him, did not want to hear him say that yes, he would be leaving. *How will it be for me with Captin gone?* she thought. *My home's all ready sticks and kindling. How will it be without our Captin striding in to tread out Nan Annie's fires when she's combustible?* She couldn't stay in Cradle Cross without him: Isa *had* to take her to the sea. But Isa was absorbed in something Ruby had no way of understanding; Moonie had banished her, and Belle Severn was making her afraid.

She turned the broken fish-priest in her hands. Its loss had mattered terribly to Isa, although it had no function Ruby could determine: despite the name she'd given it, this *couldn't* be for priesting. It was more broom-handle than club, and if you tried to whack a fish with it, death would be messy, inefficient. So why would Isa keep it? Not to be mended, surely—even if you cut a tailored joint, snapped wood like this could never be repaired. It looked raw, skinned, as if the top layer had been stripped, except for a blotch, darker, halfway down. Ash, she thought, and wiped it on her skirt, but the mark didn't lift. She ran her finger over it: it was not a blemish on the surface, but a charred circle branded in the wood.

Perhaps if she, Ruby, relinquished it and told Isa that the dredger didn't steal it, then Isa's fears might start to dissipate; this could make a little clearing in her head. Room to think of finding Lily, or getting back to Severnsea, somehow.

Ruby stood up and shook the ash from her skirt hem. She put the broken wood back in the satchel and knocked, decisive, at the door again. "It's only me, Isa. I got to talk to yo."

Isa unlocked the door but only opened it a little.

"Can I come in? I got something for yo."

Isa left the door and went directly to the stool behind the counter. She took up a pair of scissors and began snipping buttons from their cards.

Ruby leaned her palms flat on the counter and bounced on her toes. "If yoom afraid of Belle Severn, yo ay got cause to be."

Isa didn't answer.

"I saw the dredger last night. Her stopped me in the lane just by our house. Yoom not here just for Lily, I told her. Truda thinks I got it wrong, but I reckon that doe matter. Not if Belle Severn believes it."

Isa twisted a button on its card and slid the scissor points around the cotton. "Believes what?"

Ruby grinned. "Her thinks yoom here to get revenge on her, for what her did to Anselm. Her's scared of yo. I told her as her should be, and her is." She waited for Isa to look up and to smile, to say *well done*.

Isa put her scissors down. "You told her that I've come here for revenge?"

"These songs her sings; the note her writ . . . it's all bluster. And—" she reached into the satchel, "—her never nicked *this*." She smiled, biting her lip, and pulled the piece of wood out with a flourish.

Isa stared. "Belle Severn didn't steal this from my bag?"

"I took it." Ruby twisted up a finger in the spoon cord. "I day nick it, though. It's more I sort of took it by mistake."

She waited for the reprimand, or at least a frown, a look of disapproval, but Isa simply told her to wait. Puzzled, she watched Isa go through to the back: if Isa wasn't cross with her, she wasn't relieved either. Ruby turned the wood and placed her finger in the imprint. "What's it for, anyway?"

Isa didn't answer. She came back with the travel bag and set it on the counter.

"Yoom not cross wi me?"

"No." She took the broken wood from Ruby—almost snatched it—and, with a quick glance through the window at Horn Lane, she rolled it quickly, tight inside the nightdress.

"I thought as yo'd be angry."

"Well, I'm not."

"The dredger is. I think her's angry cause I worked it out."

Isa pushed the bundle to the bottom of the bag. "You should not provoke her, Ruby."

"Her day try to hurt me: her only said her disenchanted Captin."

"Disenchanted him?"

Ruby shrugged. "I doe know how her did it, but it worked. Her disenchants him and suddenly he's moving down to Whalemouth."

Isa stopped fastening the clasp. "No." She stared at Ruby; shook her head. "No, no."

She wanted Isa to say something sympathetic about how bereft she must feel, losing Captin: but then, she thought, why would she? Isa herself had worked loose the knot between them. Captin, not her grandad; Captin, not her kin. "It's all right for yo, Isa! When yo go back home, yo ull be neighbors. Yo can go and see him when yo want!"

"When I go home? Ruby, you do not understand. How did she disenchant him? Len, going to Whalemouth—" She broke off; her hands covered her face.

"Doe worry, Isa!" She read Isa's distress as homesickness, anxiety, perhaps, about a dying father who, in his madness, had banished her. "We ull find your sister and then yo can go home." She leaned over and tried to peel Isa's fingers from her face; Isa allowed this, but bowed her head. "Soon Isa, yo ull be going home." Ruby rested her hand on the back of Isa's neck. "Captin ull be waiting down at Whalemouth. It woe be long till yoom back there."

Isa raised her head and shook off Ruby's fingers. "Where will he be now?" She stood up; grabbed her bag. "I have to talk to him."

"He said as he had things to do. I doe know what they was. He's going up to our house, later, to tell my nan he's going, I suppose."

Isa paused at the front door. "If you see him, Ruby—"

I don't want to see him, Ruby thought.

"Tell him that I don't want him to go. Tell him—" Isa pressed her hands against her eyes. "Tell him if he goes to Whalemouth, I am lost."

It was awkward, tiring work, carrying the crate of photographs from Truda's office up to the Blicks' house. Ruby'd used the towel and muslin from the burned-up skirt to wrap some of the pictures, but even so, she progressed slowly with the first crate, careful not to jolt it on the cobbles. The weight of it pulled at her shoulders and she thought she had a splinter in her palm.

Up Horn Lane and round onto the Breach, went Ruby, past Maison Hester's and, at the corner, left on Islington. She picked her way along till Tenter Lane veered up, sharp, off to the right. The streets were quiet: those not in chapel had stayed indoors, pretending that they were. Besides, the Leopard didn't open until noon. Just past the nailers' cottages, Ruby found the rough track that led up to the house. Till now, she'd never ventured further than the gateposts, even though the gates were never closed. She almost passed them without notice; so deep were the gates lodged back within the hedges—high, untrimmed, untidy—that they would need to be cut free in order to be closed. The tales that kept the Cradles children distanced from the button factory also kept them hopping, wary, at the mouth of the Blicks' drive and Ruby felt excitement trickle cold between her shoulders as she marched past the high gates, with permission, for the house.

It was cool in the shadow of the hedges, but the track was steep and rutted, and Ruby had to stop three times and let the crate rest on her knee before she reached the top, where the track emerged to bank around the scuffed edge of a wide lawn (tufted, thinning—thirsty in this heat), and sloped yet further, up toward the side of Truda's house. Ruby put the crate down and stood for a moment, pushing back the damp hair from her forehead. She had imagined this house often, a house fit for the Blicks: something turreted and Gothic; something lavish and malevolent and cruel.

It was grand; it was arresting; it was not a handsome house. Its hipped roof, trimmed with looped ridge tiles, slid forward here, retreated there, with windows tucked beneath it. (This spoke of many floors, inside. Two steps to a landing, six steps down again; a house to lose yourself in.) Beneath a half-timbered gable end, a wide bay window jutted out beside a narrow slit of window, both askew. No symmetry about it. No coherence. But being so ungainly, so lopsided, the house was more inviting than imposing and Ruby, eager, took the path around at a faster pace, past Hector's rhododendrons, to the side door underneath a cautious, shallow arch, just as Truda had instructed. There would be no one home (the hard-nosed housekeeper had sniffed decline in the air after Hector's death and had already found herself a new position). So Ruby put the crate down and felt in her pinny pocket for the key.

Inside the door, a small and shabby room: a rank of rubber boots along one wall, beneath two offset lines of coat hooks, empty but for a slack green mackintosh that Ruby recognized as Hector's. There was a narrow table set against the other wall, and it was here that Truda had said she should leave the crates.

She extracted the muslin and the towel, still carrying the stink of the charred skirt, and, before she left, she tried the door that led into the house (curious, she was, to know how Truda lived), but it was locked, and although she had the keys, she didn't linger. Two more crates to collect, and Truda had been clear she wanted them moved out as soon as possible, by hand because her car would be too jolty. She had heaved the first crate into Ruby's arms as soon as Ruby went back to the office. A residue of their new-forged comradeship re-mained: Truda promised Ruby she would buy her iced cream, when she'd taken the last crate, from that Italian who parked his cart in Stower Street on hot afternoons; this in return for sending Ruby out on heavy work in the full heat of the day. So Ruby, thinking of her iced cream, worked as quickly as she could to get the crates removed from Blick's.

The third crate was the hardest and, it seemed, the heaviest, and Ruby struggled up the Breach, a burning coursing through the mus-cles of her arms. She was pausing outside Maison Hester's, shunting the crate gingerly from one knee to the other, when she saw Trembly Em and Glenda move around the corner, both bending at the waist, both scanning the ground around their feet. They did not see Ruby yet, and she did not relish an encounter with them, not while she car-ried a crate full of photographs for Truda. She wondered, too, if word of Captin's treacherous plan had yet reached them (and indeed if it had yet reached Nan Annie) and if Glenda would trap her and tease out the little that she knew of his departure. She looked about, but there was no way of evading them, so as they drew nearer Ruby called out, "What am yo looking for?"

Glenda stood up straight and tugged at Em to do the same. Em was a little out of breath and held one hand to her throat and pressed the other into the small of her back. "Her's lost her locket, her has," Glenda said, nodding toward Em with her dark eyebrows arching in exasperation. "Put that down and help us look, will yo?"

"I ay lost it," Em corrected her. "It's been took."

"Lost, took . . ." Glenda, impatient, trying not to be, screwed her face up, scrubbed her hand across her cheeks. "At any rate her ay got it and her wants it back. I said as I ud help but I cor be looking for it all day, cause we got the Ruths and the Naomis later and I ay cooked a thing and me mom ay good for much, still, after all that with the mural. So glad, I am, as we happened on yo."

Ruby hesitated. Wanted to say no, she couldn't help, she had these pictures to deliver and then there was the matter of her iced cream. Em was always losing things: the Mission keys; her purse; once she had even lost the whole basket of losslinen. (How *that* had set the Ruths and the Naomis scurrying!) And Ruby had used up whole Sundays walking in between the dark and shut-in houses Em might just have visited to feel on the floor around the chairs, or crawling on the cold stone of the chapel to squint under each pew. She looked at Em, whose eyes were veined with pink and fixed on Ruby, whose skin was slick and mottled in the heat, and thought with some revulsion that if she had her iced cream she would have to offer Em at least a lick, or if she couldn't face that, not have one at all. At the thought of giving up her iced cream, Ruby's throat, already dried, grew raspy. And nobody but Truda would know that she had given up her iced cream, and Truda might just think she didn't fancy it, so there would be no reward for such a sacrifice . . .

"What yo got in there?" Glenda, curious and glad (thought Ruby) to be distracted from searching for the locket. She lifted off the towel that Ruby had pressed down between the pictures and, like a magician, plucked a picture out and held it out before her. Her eyebrows caved into a frown. "A Blick?" She scowled. She shoved it back in; pulled another picture out. "Yet more Blicks? What am yo doing, Ruby, with a box that's full of Blickses?"

"Taking them to Truda's house, I am."

"Why?"

"Her doe want them at the factory anymore, that's all."

"Oh, *cold,* her is, that one!" She thrust the photo back into the crate and Ruby heard the grating of the frames. "I always said as her day have a natural emotion in her bones or in her blood."

Ruby flinched. Remembered how, back in the War, it had been Truda who'd told Hector that there was no more flour or sugar down at Maison Hester's, and this injustice against Truda made her bold. "Yo cor say that about her!" Fury built in her, and she was almost cross enough to cry. "Her's *grieving*! It ay much above a fortnight since her lost her uncle and her ay got *anybody* left."

"What then?" Glenda bristled. "Her doe want to be reminded of what the factory *was,* before her and that Fly girl grabbed it by the neck and shook the life out of it?"

And even though she knew that Truda had not *meant* to damage Blick's, Ruby could not honestly refute this, not in full, so she bit her lip to keep it from letting any lies out and she shook her head.

"What else as her got yo removing? What, planning to run off, is her? Sell up from under us and leave us faithful buttoners behind? Them Blicks, they care about themselves, they do. And *this*." She rubbed her fingers and her thumb together. "Take their blood money, they do, and they run wi it."

There was no reasoning with Glenda with her anger fully cranked and set for Blickses, and Ruby did not know how to distract her from her fury.

"Em ull tell yo," Glenda went on, gesturing toward her, "as Samuel Blick—he was the father to that Hector and the others—he day count the lives lost in a war by *names* of men. Counted it, he did, in buttons on their coats and on their trousers. Tell Samuel Blick how many men was killed off in a battle and quick as lightning he ud say that's so-and-so new buttons for Blick's to make. 'More uniforms, more buttons,' he ud say. 'And someone's got to make um.' "

Ruby glanced at Trembly Em. She wasn't listening to Glenda. Her eyes were bloodshot and tears were lapping at the rims but there was something fearful in the way she looked at Ruby. Or, not so much at *Ruby,* but her chest, and as Ruby followed Trembly Em's gaze, she realized that she had not put the spoon away, not since she took it out at Blick's to try to get that little mirror from the crack between the floorboards. Exposed, she felt, with the spoon dangling there, but with the crate that she was carrying she could not slip it back inside her dress.

"Help yo find your locket, I will," said Ruby, quick, "as soon as I got rid of Truda's crate. Come straight down and help. Ten minutes, probably not that much, I ull be, if yo can wait."

Em stared, still, and did not answer Ruby.

Glenda blew her breath out, her anger against Blick's unwound by her relief that someone else would take on Em. "Well, I better go and get them custards in the oven." She pulled a key out of her pocket and took the steep steps down to Maison Hester's. She paused at the bottom. "Look at this!" She shook her head and turned the key in front of her as if it were strange to her and she wasn't sure what she should do with it. "Weem locking every time we go out, after all that wi the tallow." She worked the lock and turned to ask Em if she'd like to come and wait down in the cool for Ruby to come back. But Em still stared at Ruby's spoon, so Glenda shook her head in mock-despair and arched her brows at Ruby. She turned toward the door then slowly back to look at Em because, like Ruby, she had seen a shift in Em's demeanor that she did not understand.

With Em still staring, Ruby gabbled. "When did yo last see it—your locket?" She shifted the weight of the crate and did it clumsily, hoping that the noise might draw Em's eye, or make Em tell her to be careful. "Was yo wearing it up at the Barby Fair, because I cor remember noticing if yo had it on. Did yo have it on yo, yesterday?"

"Sommat that precious? Her always has it on her, Ruby," said Glenda, watching Em. "Doe yo, Em. Your locket."

"I had it at the gap to Kenelm's Field." Quiet, Em spoke, and firmer than Ruby'd ever heard her talk. "That I know for sure cause that's when that Fly girl come for me." Her fingers flew up to her neck. She traced the length of it, from her chin to her throat, her fingers resting in the little well above her collarbone. "I hope as yo day set her on to me."

Glenda looked from Em to Ruby. Could not brook exclusion, so stepped forward and shouldered her way into their dispute. "Well, I saw her on the Breach calling after *Captin,* of all folk, just this morning." Ruby saw her lick her lips, relishing the tale. "Looks like her ay been frighted off, then, by the burning. Stubborn, her is. Staying put when her's not wanted."

"Sometimes fire's the only thing," said Trembly Em, stepping closer toward Ruby. Ruby took a small step backward. "The only thing," said Em, "as shifts a stubborn pestilence."

"And what is it as they say about the plague house?" Glenda, experimental, posited her words as if she tapped a powder from a vial and watched for a reaction.

"Raze the plague house," Em said, "and the town will live." Em leaned across the crate to Ruby. "Let us have a little look at this thing, Ruby."

Ruby held her breath in. Em's girth was pushing on the crate, and the wood pressed into Ruby's belly. She set her legs wide so she wouldn't topple. The loose hairs of the raffia that circled Em's good hat were jabbing at her chin. She could not reach up to the spoon to touch it and be bold and she realized how much she, this past week, had relied upon the spoon to keep her safe. She could light on no good reason to stop Em from looking at the spoon, but it was as if Em's gaze was desecrating Ruby, and she grew cold and trembled.

She strained her head away as if this could stop Em. She looked, pleading, to Glenda, but Glenda leaned back against the shop door with her arms folded and, raised eyebrows, twitching smile, watched Em, and Ruby, discomposed.

Now Trembly Em, who (you will remember) had, when younger, fallen from a tree, was thought of as saft-headed, and others of the Ruths and the Naomis often called on her believing that they did her a substantial kindness, each thinking that she demonstrated quite how generous she was to spend her time with such a saft-head, each leaving feeling nourished by the sweet milk of her charity spilled into poor Em's cup. Each gifted her with secrets, believing that saft-headed Em, benign and bruised, would feel so grateful for the private packages they unwrapped in her presence. Em gave little in return, but no one expected much: a vacant smile; a fist of leathered cabbage leaves; a good-luck trinket, maybe, when a child was born. She knitted things for children that she favored. Ruby's drawers were filled with things that Em had made for her and for her mother and for her grandmother before her: a crocheted comforter; a winter bonnet that tied under the chin; a new pair of gloves, half-fingered. It was Trembly Em who, years before, had made the beaded shawl for Annie's sickly baby; the shawl that wrapped itself around the wreckage of the *Lickey Bell* and that was laid out with the salvage of the wreck on a trestle table in a damp, ill-lit church hall down at the Shoulder.

Ruby had long despised Em for her musty, pressed affections. But now, recoiling from Em's bent head at her chest, she knew she'd welcome them in place of this too palpable, too curious attention. For Ruby, too late, might protest that she knew nothing of the provenance and the power of the spoon that Isa Fly had kindly given her, but she could not pretend an ignorance of its effect on Em.

Em, galvanised, intent, slipped a damp palm underneath the spoon (as if to catch it, should it fall) and with the other hand she ran her plump fingers around it. She pulled the spoon to turn it in the light and with each twist, the cord cut into Ruby's neck and she felt it tighten at her throat.

"Watch the girl, Em! Doe strangle her!" Glenda, cool. Intrigued more than alarmed. "Her woe be much good for looking for your locket if yo've garroted her!" Glenda stepped in close and peered at the spoon. "Looks like one of yours, Em."

"Well, it cor be. I only made the one."

Ruby felt the cord slacken: Em found, or felt, what she was seeking. Her fingers formed a fist around the shaft and then she dropped it, almost threw it, against Ruby's chest as if the iron burned her.

"*Her* woe be helping me," said Em. "There ay no use in looking anymore."

Glenda protested; she shouldn't give up easy.

"I woe find it by looking, Glenda." Em, contemptuous. "Other ways, there is, to find who has took it." Em looked, sharp-eyed, at Ruby. "Tell your friend, Ruby, tell that Fly girl what I says. And doe bother coming to the Ruths this afternoon. Yo ay wanted."

When Em had huffed and blustered up the Breach and out of sight, Glenda offered Ruby, who was flushed and jittery, a cup of tea to cool her down or warm her up—either way, to undo what had been done to her out standing in the sun. And though Ruby knew that Glenda wanted to pick at her for gleanings, she willingly went down the steps, one at a time and sideways with the crate, and set it down inside. Glenda said that Ruby shouldn't mind Em; that she was just un-raveling at the edges and wanted time to knit herself together. Told Ruby, she did, that Em had got herself all tangled about that white girl, Isa Fly, and her locket. That Em was going on and on in chapel about people dying of grievous deaths who shall not be lamented and how they should not suffer witches to live on among them, and that's why Glenda took her out the chapel meeting early with the guise of looking for the locket, because it might just quiet her a bit. "But," said Glenda, "I ay never seen her so provoked."

Ruby couldn't offer Glenda any tale of substance to explain why Trembly Em was exercised and more alert than they had ever seen her. She swallowed down her tea and took the crate to Truda's, and as soon as she was rid of it, she slipped the spoon from round her neck and turned it in her hands to find what it was about the spoon that had so animated Em. Frowning, she found an indentation, a tiny full-moon dimple halfway down the handle, just like the mark on Em's iron shields and thorns.

She took the steep lane from the Blicks' house slow and kept in close beside the hedge; picked off flecks of privet, savoring the cool slick of a shadow that spilled all down the lane; bending, stretching her sore arms and rubbing where they felt tight after carrying the crates. She resolved to go to Isa with a warning: to tell her that some-how Trembly Em had got it lodged deep in her head that Isa Fly had took away her locket; she'd show her, too, the little marking on the spoon and, together, they could work out what it meant. Ruby would take the warning down to Isa as a gift, an offering to show her she was sorry if she'd caused her some offense, for a warning about Em, of all the people Ruby knew, would show that she was acting out of love. Costly, it was, standing firm with Isa against Em (and Ruby did not know yet just how high a price she'd pay). For all that Ruby had over the years shrunk back from Trembly Em and balked at her staunch, scented embraces, Em had been a refuge, a defender more than once: that time when Ruby got wet fetching water from the brook for that brew that Cradle girls made in the autumn (claywater and conkers, mixed with sticks—they called it Bloody Soup), Em had sat her by the fire with warmed milk; spent an hour ironing damp out of her skirt. And that time one summer: some girl, meaning to be teasing, pushed Ruby as they teetered on the wall around the cooling pond and Em had said to Annie it was *her* fault Ruby had got wet, and bashed out some clumsy story of a bucket being spilled. She remembered these things, now, of Trembly Em. Remembered too how Em had looked at Ruby as she all but threw the spoon back at her chest. Em's disgust had been acrid as bone-smoke and the memory of it made Ruby blink; her eyes smarted, brimming full. She felt, quite suddenly, how bare, exposed her own landscape would be without Em, without Captin. Faithful, they had sheltered her, or tried to, since Jamie Abel went down to the Deadarm.

Jamie Abel. A gnawing in her belly. Ruby started to run down the Breach, her knees, her ankles jarring on the stones. Jamie Abel. She hadn't brought his dinner down from home. She could *see* it up there, sitting on the table, a bowl on a square of muslin, waiting to be wrapped: cold meat cakes; a slop of butter pie. She would call on him and tell him she was sorry she'd forgotten, and then she would cycle home, quick as she could, to fetch it down.

Sunday mornings, when she took his dinner before chapel, she sometimes found him sitting cross-legged with his boots off on his island, rubbing at his shrapnel-shredded foot; spread out before him, weighted at the corners with his boots, the correspondence pages she'd saved for him from Captin's *Muckeleye Gazette*. This morning, and Ruby now so late, he would be hungry and that might prompt him into wondering where she was, and Ruby took a fervid, glowing pleasure in the thought of Jamie Abel alert and itchy, prickling with worry for his girl. She did not feel resentment, not today. For, unlike Em, her father never came in close enough for Ruby to be repelled by things she did not understand, and unlike Captin, her father was not going anywhere, and today Ruby was thankful for his island.

She slipped, eel-quick, between the folds toward the Deadarm. Stepped across the legs of boys reclining in cool entries, rolling marbles at chalked targets on the walls, waiting to be called in for their food. Passed girls framed in dark windows, laying forks on tables; a mother, sleeves rolled, scraping broth out of a pan.

Midday, high summer, there is a tautness and precision in the light: all things—bricks, nettles, fingernails—are saturated with the fullness of themselves; all things are generous in the yielding of their detail;

they are laid bare, as by pain, before the cruel scrutiny of light. Such dry, refining heat there was that day; not the indolent and sticky kind that renders skin and bone so slack and heavy, like sodden unwrung clothes. A clarifying heat, it hard-fired thoughts that had till now been unshaped, supple and compliant, that till now had been like well-kneaded clay and therefore could be molded into something more appealing. Such a thought had Ruby passed between her hands each time she approached the Deadarm, ever since the trip Halfway-to-France. The thought was this: *What if, this time, when I get down to the Deadarm, my father isn't there?* Each time she drew near she'd press this thought—an empty crucible—and pulp it; try to make it take some other shape. But Trembly Em had shunned her and Captin was leaving and this fierce heat had hardened Ruby's fear of Jamie Abel leaving, and now it would not be refashioned.

She could not see her father. Not at first. Her eye was drawn directly to a woman seated at the right side of the island, her ankles bared, her feet furling and unfurling, stuck out above the Cut. She could not see the woman's face: bent forward, she was, hidden by the hair that sprang in gold-red coils all twisting to her waist, and working with a slow comb at a knot. Ruby gripped the spoon's bowl through her dress, watching from the mouth of the high gulley. Unsettled, Ruby was, not so much by this unknown woman's presence (how could she be alarmed by someone combing through her hair?) but rather by the manner of her combing. Alert, absorbed, she combed her hair with fine, distilled attention. A rare attention, this, and there was something heady and compelling even at this distance, even in observing it. A refined attention, it commanded the full focus of the gaze—a state that can only emerge when there is no distraction, no effort needed to maintain even the most meager of defenses; when you feel safe; and all the world around you may dissolve. This woman was at home, there on the Deadarm, and Ruby was alarmed.

She heard her father calling, and if you'd asked her at that moment Ruby would have sworn it on the spoon that he'd said, "Beth!" But it was not a yearning call, or a cry of despair. Modulated, it was, like a question; confident, and waiting for an answer: "Beth?" He called again, emerging from the workshop stripped to the waist, his hair slick and dark from being washed. Ruby stepped forward, out into the sun, but hesitated before calling out to him. He did not look, to Ruby, like a man maddened by hunger. He was not watching for his daughter, or his dinner. A knot in Ruby's throat. Legs rickety, she leaned back against the warmed brick and tugged the spoon free of her dress and slipped her fingers around it. Watched Jamie Abel crossing, in his syncopated gait, over to the red-gold woman combing out her hair. Watched as he bent to part her hair from around her face and watched as the woman leaned back on her hands and tilted her chin up and Jamie Abel rested his lips, slow, against her forehead. The woman's white skin shone. Ruby's breath swelled in her and she could not let it out.

Ruby was not sure quite how she drew attention to herself. Maybe her spoon caught the light. But something drew the woman's eye, and she turned to look at Ruby. Her father looked up too, and started back and with his hand against his crown he stared, uncertain, up at Ruby. He raised his fingers in a cautious, awkward wave—a skewed salute. Ruby, eyes narrowing against the light, did not acknowledge him. It was not Beth whom Jamie Abel called for. Ruby saw that now. Belle Severn rose and (watching the ground under her bare feet) walked around the edge of Jamie's island until she stood across the Cut from Ruby, and Ruby felt her throat grow tight and dry. She tucked the spoon back in her shirt.

"Doe worry, Ruby." Belle Severn curled her toes around the edging of the island. "I said you'd be too occupied to bother with his dinner. I told him you had no doubt been summoned to the side of Isa Fly."

Ruby did not bother to correct her. She looked beyond Belle, back to where her father fumbled in his pocket for his baccy, and she searched his face for some pain at her neglect of him. Easier to search this out than try to make some sense of what she saw: Belle Severn and her father moving easy round each other, water over rock.

"Don't worry about dinner," Belle went on. "I won't see him hungry. I promise you that he has been well fed." She gestured to a cloth laid out beside the fire-pot; on it, emptied bowls, a bottle, the round end of a loaf. Something disconcerting, Ruby found, in this mock-mothering of Jamie Abel. She looked back to Belle and tried to work out why she had not recognized the Blackbird straight away. Saw that Belle had shed her blacks (they roosted, hanging from a nail, like sleeping bats) and, undisguised, she wore instead a cotton shift like verdigris, unbuttoned at the neck.

"You're staring like I'm naked. You didn't think that I was always done up in them blacks, now, did you, Ruby?"

A leaden pulling, down through Ruby's belly like a plumb-line, down through her feet, and Ruby felt she'd never move again except to deepen, hour by hour, the indentations that her shoes made in the clay. Dumb, she stood, and hollowed by her hunger and her grief. Even through his self-elected isolation, Jamie Abel must have seen that his girl needed to be moved by him and called out, "Dun yo want some dinner, Rube? We got enough left for yo, if yo want some."

He did not wait for her to answer but busied himself, stooping down to wipe a bowl out with a cloth, and spooning something from the pot; hasty, flicking up his eyes to check on Ruby, to see (she thought) if he could find approval or displeasure in her face. Sloppy, he was, and Belle Severn laughed and took the spoon from him and wiped up all the spills. "Now then, Ruby, how *shall* we get this to you if you can't cross water and your father says he won't?"

Ruby, whose emptiness was pressing up against the walls of her, did not want to eat here with her father—not with Belle. But Belle cocked her head and frowned and said, "Don't say that you don't want it when I've gone to all this trouble!" And Jamie Abel folded up his arms and gave a small embarrassed smile.

"Good it is, Ruby. Fish broth. Not too heavy for this heat."

Ruby jolted down the steep bank to the towpath as if Belle Severn pulled her on a string. Watched as Belle Severn placed the broth bowl in the bottom of a bucket and looked about her; took up a broom leaned up against a post and pushed it through the handle of the pail. Jamie Abel laughing as Belle held the broomstick out across the water, the bucket swaying underneath. *You don't know,* thought Ruby, *how we are being scoffed at by this woman. How she is using you to harbor her.*

"Reach out!" called Belle. "I'll slide it down toward you."

Ruby stretched her arms out, still a good foot from the water.

"Need to be a bit closer than that, you will, if you wants your dinner!"

A plunging in her belly. Her skin stinging, prickling. She shuffled closer to the blunt edge of the Cut.

"I'll teach you ways to walk on rocks, Ruby!" Belle called. "But you *will* need to walk nearer the water!"

Ruby, giddy, stood, yet felt that she was swaying, her toes lined up against the Cut-edge of the towpath, the broom-handle a foot or so away.

"Reach out now, Ruby!" Jamie Abel, this time, mocking her, and this enraged Ruby. Her cheeks flamed, and she swiped for the broom-handle, but Belle jerked it higher, out of reach.

"Higher, Ruby, higher!" Her father, face creased and pink with laughter, one hand slapped to his cheek, the other beckoning her forward.

Ruby reached forward, eyes fixed on Belle Severn, and her rage spilled out in hot tears on her cheeks. She swiped at her face with her sleeve, as if she were dispatching summer midges.

"O, Ruby! Don't say that I've upset you! Are you taking lessons off that Isa One-Eye? You want to be careful, Ruby! That Isa Fly can cry a dry well full!"

Ruby remembered Isa, blinded, and her brother lured down to the beach. She did not need to take a warning about Em and stolen things to Isa. How could she have thought, last night in the dying light, that Belle was scared of Isa? Ruby needed to keep Isa, and her father, safe from Belle. Her fingers closed tight around the curved butt of the handle and she did not release it.

Belle would swear to Jamie Abel later that she did not yank the handle back in, quick, toward her. Whatever Belle intended, Ruby tumbled forward, deep into the Cut.

Chapter 15

Standing water is but a prison to fish. And they live for the more part in hunger like prisoners, and therefore it is the less maistrie to take them.

Treatise of Fishing with an Angle

She went up to St. Barbara's. There was nowhere else to go, nowhere else to dry herself in safety: Isa was not in the button shop, nor Truda in the office up at Blick's; she *couldn't* go to Trembly Em, and as for home—even if Captin was up there (and she wasn't sure of that), even if he'd stand between Ruby and her nan, she'd pay for getting wet when he was gone. She walked the long way, up through Owley Fields, so she wouldn't pass near their house at Hunting Tree and risk meeting Annie, wet. Around the west side of the hill, she went, where the sorors had cut good paths in the clay. Breath short, toes sliding in her shoes, a film of diesel slippy on her skin. Her dress smelled of Cut-cack—her own father's rank filth. She tugged the dress loose where it slapped against her skin and took the path up through the fern valley. No shade, but even if this sun sucked all the wetness from her hair, her dress, her seams, she knew she would still carry with her the Cut-water like a stain, and Nan Annie would scrub it out of her. She wanted to be cleaned and dried and, as she walked, imagined herself laid out on a scrubbed slab in the smoke room round the back end of the dairy, there with all St. Barbara's trout and ham. Waiting for the smoke to cure her and the salt to dry her out.

When she reached St. Barbara's she would go to Soror Brigid and ask her if she'd take her Almanac through to the kitchen and lie it on the dry-rack up above the stove. As she walked she peeled the pages back from one another; recited Beth's lists and her annotations— "What I Shall Take to Sea"; "Places I Will Go When I Have Got a Boat"—to make sure that each item was remembered lest the pages had been glued together by the Cut and would not be unstuck. This, it was, the dunking of the Almanac, that had wrung snarls out of Ruby as she panted, dripping, on the towpath on her hands and knees. Not her father's lips pressed on Belle Severn's carved white brow; not even Belle stood at her father's elbow, sniggering behind her hand. "Beth's book!" Ruby had screamed at Jamie Abel. "Look what her's done! Her's ruined my mom's book!"

She had almost reached the high ridge at the top of Parry Lean (*some Fairy soap and two spare vests; a small packet of tea*) when her ankle tilted in a pit of leaves. She stood up and tried to brush the dried leaves from her dress, but she was slick, all tacky from the Cut, and the fragments stuck to her legs and to her palms. Her ankle burned— with every step, hot splinters—so when she at last had knocked the priory gates, she sank to rest beneath a turkey-oak where spring-moss made it soft, and waited for the soror. She glanced around her, watching in case Nan Annie should crest the slope of Parry Lean. Saw where the earth was charred from last night's fire and looked up, quick, instead. Fat green acorns clustered like dulled jade on crabbed fingers. An old lady of an oak, all knobs and splits and bulk. They'd let it stand when they were culling forests for the War, since turkey-oak's no fighter. It bends and warps and wanes—no good for boats. *And how I want a boat,* thought Ruby, *to take me to the sea . . . a square of towel; a pair of pants; some sugar lumps; a blanket.*

Soror Ursula, it was—wide and full and the rope around her surplice straining to gather her in—who drew the gate back with one hand and, when it was fully drawn, weighted it to stop it closing. She took her time, did Ursula. (Captin always said of her, "Her doe hold back at teatime." Said that the sorors put her at the gate on purpose to show this "wor one of them Houses that was all punishment and famine.") Ursula had been opening the gates to Ruby since Ruby was a bundle in Beth's arms and she knew well how it was with Ruby and with Annie. A slow, broad smile at Ruby, rancid, damp: yes, Annie had already been up to Eliza just that morning but was long gone home, if Ruby wanted her. This was their joke, a code between them, and Ruby forced a smile. She struggled up, but fell back down as soon as she tried to step on her sprained ankle.

"Oh, Ruby! What you done to yourself, precious girl? No, don't you try to step on it. We shall sit here a bit and let you get your breath, and then I'll walk you in to get it looked at."

She put a hand on Ruby's arm, and for a moment they gazed together down the falling hill toward the town, across to Crux Manicata and beyond.

A bit of ham, a net of apples and a paring knife . . .

"Now let me help you in. For lovely girl, you stink."

The sorors kept a set of rooms for visitors, still and white. They used the old word, *gestr:* a bathroom and a bedroom and a room for studying. Soror Ebba, capable and trim, drew the water and reached across the tub to open wide the window. "Don't add the cold if you can help it. Best to have it hot as you can bear. Call me when you're finished."

Ruby peeled off dress and pants and underskirt and dropped them, sopping, in a pail. Beside the bath, a wooden stool. On it, carbolic soap, a square of flannel and a steep-sided tin jug. A hard-hair brush, long-handled, for her back; a short one for her nails. She lowered herself, wincing at the heat, slow and careful, down into the water. Stretched forward to depress the tender flesh around her ankle. Scratched out flecks of cack and weed lodged in between her toes. Streaks down her neck and on the insides of her wrists. She scrubbed them with the flannel, hardly flinching, and then filled the jug and poured it down her back. Reached behind and scrubbed down the gauche nubs of her backbone as far as she could reach, then up the other way. She used the handle of her spoon to eke out compacted little crescents from the towpath—dung and clay—from underneath her nails, then worked them with the brush till they were all but flayed. She took the spoon from round her neck and lay its cord along the wide lip of the tub and, with a finger, rubbed soap along the length of it. Worked the soap in with the brush, then rinsed it with clean water from the tap. She didn't linger longer than she had to in the bath—as it was it took too long. She had to stand up when she'd taken out the plug and pour fresh jugs of water down herself and around the tub to sluice the scum away, and as she scuffed and sanded her skin dry with a rough towel (checking in the creases of her elbow; in the tight well of her ear) she worried about getting her dress clean and dry enough for going home for tea. So when Soror Ebba came in (Ruby, dried, and sitting in a borrowed linen shift), with warmed milk and a bowl of blackberries-in-syrup, glinting like dark jewels, Ruby pressed her, anxious and insistent, lifting up the bucket, asking Ebba if she could think of anything to help her with her dress.

"What, like this, you mean?" Smiling, Ebba tilted up the bowl of blackberries-in-syrup. They slopped into the bucket. Ebba, eyes round, let her jaw drop in a pantomime of shock. "Oh dear, Ruby. I seem to have spilled something on your dress . . . *Goodness*, child, we'll have to launder this for you this instant, Ruby! And blackberry so tricky to wash out. I'll write a note for you to take down to your nan. I'll explain that I *insisted* that you took the dress off straight away to put hot water through the stain." She handed the milk bowl to Ruby and, fixing her with clear, lit eyes, pressed her own hands around Ruby's. "There's *nothing* in that Annie can contest."

Ruby sipped at the milk while Ebba knelt and bent her leg back at the knee and cautious, firm, probed all the flesh around the foot to check for swelling. The same leg, this, that Isa Fly had patched up at the knee. And now that she was clean and knew that Annie could not beat her for the Cut-stink in her dress, Ruby's fear released her and in its place, a serrated hunger clamped her, growling in her belly.

Soror Ebba glanced up at her. "Hungry? I'll find some bread and cheese when we have finished." She raised her eyebrows. "Or blackberries, perhaps?" Ruby smiled. Felt Ebba's breath, warm, fresh, against her shin. "This hurt, Ruby? This?" Ebba kneaded at the skin around the ankle, faster, but still light. "Cold dough from the larder, this, my girl. We'll see you right as rain." Ebba sat back on her heels. "So tell me, now. What happened to our Ruby? How did she end up filthy as a dog?"

So Ruby told about the broom-handle; the dinner in the bucket; Belle Severn teasing her and feeding fish broth to her father; the Almanac, all wet (her voice caught in her throat when she said this); and as the tears flowed slow and steady, down her cheeks and to the corners of her lips, she cursed herself aloud for being saft enough to bother, but said that she was worried by the Blackbird; that *everyone* was blaming Isa Fly for thieving things and rubbing tallow onto Dinah's picture and for all the trouble down at Blick's; that Captin Len was leaving; that it was Isa's effigy that had been burned and Trembly Em was saying it was Isa took her locket, and the loss of it was making Em get cruel and strange with Ruby . . . She felt the spoon-cord damp against her neck but did not mention Isa's spoon—*her* spoon—and how it was the spoon more than the locket that had turned Em clear against her.

"It's just a saft old locket. Her's *always* losing things." Ruby, petulant, impatient, and smudging off her tears with a brisk hand. "I doe see why as Isa Fly should get the blame."

"Hunger's chased away your kindness, Ruby." Ebba stood up; lifted Ruby's foot to rest it on a pillow. "*You* need to be fed."

While Ruby ate up bread and cheese and a sliced-up pear, Soror Ebba rubbed a minty liniment into her ankle and bandaged it in crepe and told Ruby a story: a girl from down the Cradles, Ruby's age, bit more, rounded out and swelled beyond all hiding. When her father noticed, she ran up to St. Barbara's and (not knowing she'd be welcome at the gate) climbed a tree beside the wall. She'd pulled herself across the thickest branch that overhung the wall then let herself fall, like ripe fruit, into the soft ground. They kept her safe, the sorors, with her bruised belly. The warmest cell. Brought her settle-tea and blankets. Rubbed her feet. The child was born too soon and though no one was surprised when the boy died before his mother even caught her breath, they gave him all the rites and wept with her as if she'd lost a full-fledge. They took a little lock of hair before they buried him and put it in a locket, and the girl, Emily, sat with the locket in her palm, keening through a day and night by his new-cut grave and cried out for her baby.

Ruby, twitching, tried to hold her itchy feet quite still. She twisted up the spoon. Directed all her will to make it look as if she listened to the story. She'd heard Em's history—or much of it—before, but Ebba told it with a new inflection and she didn't use it for a cautionary tale. As if insight and understanding could be pressed like an apple into Ruby's hands. Ebba seemed to Ruby to expect a particular response, and Ruby, willful, fidgeting, resisted. Her hands were full already: Captin leaving; Belle Severn sharing dinner and the Deadarm with her father; Isa burned in effigy; and Trembly Em's raw loathing directed against Ruby. She needed to get down to Isa—she had yet to warn her that Trembly Em thought she had took this fogging locket; that she, Ruby, had underestimated Em, and Isa should take good care that *she* did not discount her. For if saft-head Em had kept a pyre burning fifty years, all for a baby she had only had two days, what fevered culpability would Em now hurl at Isa Fly?

"Yo done this up too tight." She slipped a finger underneath the binding. (Ruby did not notice that even as she stepped around the reason for another person's pain, set out so plain before her, Ebba did not rebuke her or insist that she should try to stretch out her compassion—taut and limited, just now—to encompass Trembly Em.) She leaned forward to scratch at the bandage round her ankle. She didn't think about concealing *this*: Nan Annie wouldn't reprimand her for a scratch, a sprain, a fall—unless it was a fall into the water.

"Best keep it strapped up for a day or two," said Ebba. She held the pot of liniment to Ruby, on her palm. "Put this on your ankle before bed, and keep your weight off it as much as you can manage, for today. There's bruising, but it should ease tomorrow. Go now, and see Eliza. She knows you're here. She's waiting."

Ruby stood and, tentative, tested her weight on her ankle and it held. Soror Ebba held the door back for her. "And watch where you're stepping, Ruby."

Ruby didn't want to go and find Eliza. She wanted to leave *now* and seek out Isa. She put a hand up to her crown to flatten down her hair, but found that it was damp, of course, and Ruby couldn't leave before it dried and risk encountering Nan Annie.

Ruby knew just where to find her Nan Eliza: round by the trout pools, where she always sat. Since her fingers had become too crabbed for threading silks in needles, Eliza Trent had claimed a new job for herself; shooing off the rat-cats from the trout pools with a stick. Brows fierce, sitting bent up, knitting holey shawls and scarves and socks, licking her finger, counting stitches; or nodding in a jerky sleep, her fingers twisted in the loose plait that gave her a look of a sad child, bewitched into being old. Always cold and always cross; always underdressed.

Her great-grandmother tried to stand, at first, when Ruby walked toward her, pushing on the bench to ease herself up, her thin mouth splitting her face with its wheeze, but then when Ruby got close enough, Eliza grabbed at her and tugged her down, her fingers caught in Ruby's tunic like a claw.

"The sorors say as there ay ghosts but I saw Bethy bright as light among the wych-elms yesterday."

Ruby sat beside her. "Hello, Nan." On good days, Nan Eliza looked weathered in a fine way, like good wood. On bad days, like today, dried up, she was, and very old, and Ruby longed to water her till she grew plump and full, pink-cheeked again; to watch her brim and spill with gickling, to have her tickle Ruby till she doubled. She took Eliza's cold hand between her own, but Eliza huffed and pulled it free and plunged it in the pocket of her shift.

"How's our Annie?" Eliza drew a crust out of her pocket; nibbled at it and, licking at the corners of her mouth, broke another piece to crumbs and threw it for the fish.

"Yo saw my nan today," said Ruby, gently. "The sorors said as Nannie come this morning."

"And I saw our Beth, an' all. Yesterday, I saw her, when I went out there for the fair." She swiped her hand toward the wall beyond the pool.

Ruby sighed. "Wearing a long dress by any chance, was her—your ghost? A long dress all in white with red spots all about it?"

Eliza took up her knobbed cat-scaring stick; jabbed it toward the pools. "Them pools," she said. Eyes fearful; rounded out. "Doe look in um. Yourself, growed old, yo'll see in um. *I'm* in there, all growed old." She stood up and moved crab-wise toward the nearest pool and, without looking at it, lowered her stick down toward the water. "Keep stirring it, I do. The only way to stop the old hag settling."

"Yo ay a hag," said Ruby, gentle. "Come on. Sit down by me."

"And if I sit who ull see to it that the old hag, her doe settle?"

Eliza's chin was up, defiant, the tendons pulled tight underneath the give of loose, soft, sagging skin. Remembered, Ruby did (when she was small enough to climb up on Eliza, and Eliza strong enough to hold her without snapping), reaching up and tracing with her finger that silky sag of skin, that bit of us that's velvet as a newborn to the end. Ruby stood to take the stick from Nan Eliza's hands. Stood, as she did each visit, stirring Eliza's pool.

"*Yo* think I'm saft-headed an' all." Eliza tapped, rapid, at her temple, like a woodpecker. "All this wi the ghost—Annie day believe me, neither. Why would her? Her ay never believed a word I said."

Ruby watched a red squirrel race across the capstones of the wall beyond the pools. "A woman, it was, Isa Fly, who borrowed Beth's old dress."

"It was the *image* of your mother, Ruby Abel Tailor, with all the color bleached from her, and on this matter yo ay got a *spit* of knowing. Dun *yo* remember Beth? Dun *yo* remember what her looked like? Dun *yo* remember how her eyes was, or her smile?"

Ruby sighed. When Eliza fixed on her course she would not be diverted.

"If that wor a ghost, that woman stole something of Beth," she went on. "And this ay about a dress. Keep stirring, now! Doe stop! I ay been walking round in little circles, looking for a way to call her up, if that's what yoom thinking. I doe *want* to see your mother, love her though I did. Gone, her has, and them that's gone should not be seen again. *I* day bring her on. I doe believe as ghosts ull be called up with chalk scribbles and charms. But means something, it does, a ghost appearing, and yoom fools, all on yo, if yo pretend it ay Beth come to see us."

There was no use, Ruby knew, in reasoning with her. Eliza had a way of throttling all counter-argument with her rumination; a live, sinewy flex, it was, strangling like bindweed. But she *could* be distracted by a story from the town, as long as Ruby worked it carefully and laid it out as some poor soul's misfortune, and not gossip, nor a chance to pick off bones.

"Em Fine-knee Bacon saw someone wearing my mom's dress, too. Her's in a state." She lifted up a slick of pondweed with the cat-stick.

Eliza turned her head to stare at Ruby, ardent and inquisitive, like a hungry bird that's seen a worm. "What sort of a state?"

"Her says as someone's took her locket."

"Took her locket?"

"Yo know," said Ruby, scraping lines into the clag around the pool edge, just below the surface of the water. "The one as has the hair in from her baby. Telling me all about it, Soror Ebba was, just."

"Her told yo all about it, did her?" Eliza pressed a crust against her dry lips and forced it in as if she was being fed against her will. "Who ud be so cruel as to take a lock of some dead bab's hair? And yo ull know as Em had her bab around the same time I had Annie."

Ruby shook her head. It didn't matter to her but she knew she had to wait here in the priory until the sun had burned the damp out of her hair, so she put her mind to listening to Eliza. "No. I day know that."

"It's—what, fifty years? But I can see it clear as yoom stood there. I was twenty-one, but Emily was only fifteen, still a girl, and her was grieving up here with the sorors, with her bab just out and dead. I was heaving, down at Hunting Tree, with the after-pains and all me lifeblood pooling on the floor. The midwife had to reach inside to pull out the placenta. Mother-meat, her called it. Her arm up like her was delivering a calf." She turned her head as if she took the strain.

Ruby felt her stomach clench and roll. She put her hand against her belly; tried to soothe it. "That ay what's *supposed* to happen, is it, Nan?"

Eliza shook her head and laughed and threw her crumbs toward the pool, but they settled on her shoes and she bent, breathless, to brush them off. "These wise-women, they straddle life and death. Sometimes they deliver both . . ."

Eliza would let raw and streaming talk like this flood from her, time to time, and Ruby knew to stand still and keep stirring.

"That midwife, her collected women's birth-blood in her tins to feed the herb beds. Vervain, her grew, to keep the devil where her wanted him; buckthorn for a purgative; allheal; coltsfoot and centaury. Her had enough of my blood to grow a garden. A year, it took, of stout and greens and beef for me to get enough blood flowing through me to stand up. And all that time, Em Fine-knee Bacon nursed our Annie for me. Gid her the milk as her had made *her* baby. But he was buried, so her fed our Annie for me like her was her own. Everything, her did for Annie."

Ruby'd watched Em in their kitchen, each September: a nub of pencil clamped between her teeth; one end of the tape measure held gentle at the nape of Annie's neck; Em huffing as she bent to check the inch-mark at the root of Annie's spine. And then by All Saints' Day, Em would come back up to Hunting Tree and she'd slip Ruby into long-sleeved yellow vests (conscientious, scratchy) and swaddle Annie in a bed-jacket with ribbon threaded through the scalloped edge, sugar-almond pink or baby blue. Em's surrogate embraces, stocking-stitched, to warm them from her distance through the winter.

"Feels bad, Em does," Eliza went on, "because her tried to warn our Annie off him."

"Warn her off who?" Ruby lifted the stick and let the water settle. Spoke light, she did, to disguise her interest, because despite herself she was now curious and knew Eliza would clam up tight if she thought that she was trading tattle.

"Warn Annie off the one who *done* it to her. The one who got Em shinning up a tree and over walls."

Ruby held the cat-stick just clear of the water. Watched a drop form at the tip and slip into the pool.

"Our Annie, her was too proud of catching him. Her day know as it was *him* who'd done the catching. Our Annie thought as Em was playing jealous, so her day pay Em any heed . . ." Eliza stood up. Shuffled next to Ruby. "But when it come to it, it's *me* what should of tried to put her off him! Too well I knew what kind of man he was! I should of tried the harder! Chased him with a stick! God above knows how many girls—and it *was* girls—as that man spoiled, how many babies as he spawned afore he drowned!

"Em saw it, and I saw it, how he looked at Annie, licking his lips, and Annie six months' short of sweet sixteen. Told him, I did: 'Yoom twice her age: yo leave her well alone.' I even put myself his way to try to draw his eye from off my girl."

Ruby watched the ripple forming on the water, like shocked lips falling open in an "O."

"But Annie ud not listen, and her ud not believe me when I said her was a fool to trust in Jonah. Even when our Annie saw the proof of it—me, her own mom, twined up with him in the bed—her says as Jonah must of took me out of pity, or he was the loser in a wager, because I was too old to win him any other way. Thirty-six, I was. And Annie still fifteen."

Eliza took the stick from Ruby and thrust it at a scraggy cat that was creeping out from underneath a bush and looked intent on fishing.

"But I suppose if Jonah *had* of listened, if he had of let our Annie *be,* her ud never of had our Beth, ud her, or Grace, that little soul . . . And wi'out Beth, there ud of been no Ruby." She took a pinch of Ruby's cheek between her fingers. "So *some* good come of Jonah Nailer Tailor, eh?"

Ruby forced a smile. She'd heard enough, for now. She started to stand up, to say good-bye, but Eliza clawed her hand around her neck and pulled Ruby in so close that their foreheads pressed together. "Yo think I'm saft. I know it. It's writ over your face." Spittle on Eliza's lips. "But I ay as stupid as yo think, and nor is Emily. Her treated Annie like her own. Even gid her a good-luck charm as her'd made on her furnace for her bab. Day work though, did it? It day bring Annie luck . . ." Eliza released Ruby's neck but hooked a finger underneath the cord and before Ruby knew what she was doing, her nan had yanked the spoon from underneath the shirt and pressed it to her lips in a hard kiss. She whispered, eyes tight closed, "Em makes all these with love, Ruby. I'm praying this one brings *yo* better fortune."

Ruby tried to move away. She told her nan it wasn't one of Em's, but Eliza said she knew when she saw Em's work and Ruby couldn't tell her otherwise. *Yes,* thought Ruby, *and you see my mother walking in the hills.* But Nan Eliza gripped the spoon and Ruby couldn't move without jerking the spoon free of Eliza's fist.

Eliza told Ruby how a spoon like this was meant for a child conceived too soon and inclined from her birth to be too hasty. It was hung around her neck to help her savor life one tiny mouthful at a time. And if her impatience, demonstrated by her reckless scramble from the womb, should lead her to take too much of life too quick, the spoon was there to rap her knuckles. Taste this moment. Slow, now.

Eliza took another crust out of her pocket; pressed it against Ruby's lips and worked her finger and her thumb in till she'd pushed the bread inside. Ruby tasted, on her fingers and her nails, salt and clay.

Chapter 16

Some nights the child wept because she could not breathe below
the water. Some nights she wept because her feet hurt on the land.

"The Making of Mary Mayde," *Tales of Severnsea*

RUBY FELT TROUBLED, queasy, heading home: this latest knowledge of her grandfather—more than a debtor; lascivious, prolific—sat
bitter on her tongue. Uneasy, Ruby stepped side-on down the larched
hill, leaning on the slim trunks to keep steady. By the time she reached
Lean Lane, pain flickered in her ankle and she stopped to dampen it.
She wanted to take off her bandage, slip her fingers round the skin
and rub some pink into the white and puckered hatching where it
itched, but Soror Ebba'd said she shouldn't shift it. She sat down on
the bench-strut of a stile and bent to hold her ankle very tight between
her palms and press it with her thumbs, slow-working at the itch as
Ebba'd shown her.

Not far from Hunting Tree now, and Nan Annie, Ruby pulled taut
the skirt of her dress—the dried stain of Ebba's blackberries, her alibi,
still there. She stroked it, smoothed it and then moved slowly down
the dappled lane, stepping in each little pool of sun as if she could
soak up all its heat to keep her safe and dry. Instinctive, as she reached
the low gorse clumps that edged along the boundary of their land,
Ruby's fingers moved through her hair and checked for damp.

The crack-shot of a newspaper, shook out; Ruby started.

Captin, it was, sat on the fat roots of a turkey-oak just below the clearing, legs out, with his *Muckeleye Gazette*. He folded up his paper and laid it on the ground between his legs. Pushed a thumb slow across his forehead, flattening his frown, and trying to smile. "I wondered when yo'd come."

"What yo doing out here? Nan Annie kicked yo out?"

He sucked deep on his pipe and blew out a cloud of sweet, thick smoke. "Yo ay far off wi that." He spoke so low that Ruby had to pass her house (glancing up to check for her Nan Annie) and crouch down low to hear him, but her ankle couldn't stand the strain of that, so Ruby lowered herself down onto the ground.

"Stayed, I did," he whispered, "to warn yo as your nan . . . well, her ay in the best of tempers. I bought her up some news."

"Go on." Ruby scuffed the red dirt with a twig.

"Yo ay heard yet? I thought maybe Miss Blick . . ."

I will not make this easy, Ruby thought. *You can bear the pain of telling me you're leaving.* "Miss Blick what? Yo thought as her did what?"

His mouth clamped in a line so tight that she could see the knobbing of his jaw bone underneath his beard. "Your nan wor always like this, Ruby."

Like what? thought Ruby. *Rasping; hardened; cruel?*

"Light, her was, and limber. Ready as a new boat in a cradle." He smiled, wry, caught up in his own sweet smoky fug. "We was going to follow Dil down to the Severnsea ports, me and Annie. Soon as her turned sixteen, we ud be *off*! We had our plan: a seafront villa. Clean paint, and our own skiff. Annie on the doorstep in her pinny, calling in our children for their tea . . ." His pipe between his teeth, he pressed against his temples with his hands' heels, then scrubbed his face with dry hands.

These old people, Ruby thought. She took her stick and scored out a circle in the clay. *Laying out their histories; their excuses. What they should have done, but never did.*

"Should of took her, I should, when I had the chance. Stowed away. Not waited round for Jonah to get his fingers into her."

"*This* ay news, yo hankering for Nannie." Ruby scratched the circle deeper. "Followed her, yo have, for all the time as I have been alive, and long before. A runty pig, yo am, that's wanting scraps. *This* talk," Ruby made her hand a quacking duck, "of all yo should have done when yo was a young man, *this* ay what has put her in a temper." Spit-livid, Ruby was, and at the same time all she wanted was for Captin Len to hoist her up and over and to land her safe and square up on his shoulders, but Captin did not look at Ruby. Stood up, he did, and knocked his pipe against the tree. Swept his hands against his trousers, brushing off clay-dust.

"Them debts as yo was worried for, theym pardoned. Yo ay got need no more to worry about debts to Truda Blick. I did a deal wi her. I gid up the chip shop—rights and tenancy and all on it—without a fuss, without gidding her trouble."

"And what's her gid yo?" said Ruby, puzzled. Blick's was being stripped, and Truda, she had nothing left to give.

"I *said* it, Rube, already! Ay yo been listening?" Captin, scratchy, flustered. "I thought as yo ud know all this already. Her's let your nannie off the debt her owed to Blickses. That money Hector gid her to pay off all them bills when Jonah died. Yo said as there wor no one else to bear the debt for yo. Well, there yo am. I done it."

A sweet coat, but the medicine was still too bitter to swallow. "Wanting thanks, am yo," said Ruby, "for fogging off and leaving me wi Annie?"

He did not say much more: just that he'd like it if she'd help him in the coming days to give the chip shop a good clean before it finished. That she'd be welcome down at Whalemouth, any time, with Annie's say-so. (A twist in Ruby's guts: he *knew* she'd never grant her this permission!) Before he walked off down toward the main road, Captin held his paper out for Ruby. "Not many days, now, and yo ull have to buy your own."

When it came to it, Ruby didn't need the dark stain in her skirt. She found Nan Annie bent forward in the grate-chair over sewing, her cheeks rare and pink. On the table, Annie's alibi—a bowl heaped high with onions, slithers so thin that they'd make you weep yourself raw with the slicing. ("Doe bother me wi prattle about dresses, Ruby,"

Annie said, not looking up. "Cor yo see I'm busy and them onions
wants cooking for a pie, still?")

Ruby, fearful, kind, brewed her nan fresh tea, then cooked the
onions in the copper pot till they were sweet and brown. She cast a
glance from time to time at Annie, and threw out questions, once
she'd said them in her mind to test out that they'd not lead too close
to Captin, and while speaking, Ruby pressed her finger through her
dress against the spoon.

"What am yo working up?" Ruby scooped out flour onto the
bronze dish on the scales, careful not to spill it on the table.

"A new piece of losslinen," said Annie, a white pillowcase laid out
across her lap to help her see the needle's eye for threading.

Ruby sliced lard to squares and set it on the stove to soften up.
Her belly's roof was taut, pulled high; her breaths were nipped-in,
corseted. A bleak fantastic thought flew at her: *what if Nan Annie's
sewing one for me?*

Annie clicked her tongue against her teeth. Ruby held herself in,
waiting. Glanced over at Nan Annie, who held her needle high
against the light and drew the end of cotton through her wetted lips.
Nan Annie looked at Ruby; nodded at her ankle and asked what
Ruby'd done to get a bandage, but when she said she'd slipped up by
the trout pools, she knew Nan Annie wasn't listening; she didn't even
offer a rebuke. Ruby took a teaspoon to the jar of baking powder and
scraped a flat-edged knife across the spoon to level it. Her hand shook
as she tipped it on the flour, and the teaspoon clinked against the
bowl.

"A new piece? I day think as yo'd finished up your last one."

"Who says I finished it? The basket has been took."

"What has? The basket wi the losslinen in it?"

"Can yo believe it?" Nan Annie laid the linen on her lap and held
her needle and thread out for Ruby. "Do this for me, ud yo, Rube?"
Still light outside, but even with the casements wide and the door
open to entice in a bit of breeze, it was never bright enough inside the
kitchen.

She took the needle over to the window. She dabbed the cotton at
the eye, and with her back to Annie, Ruby let her breath out, slow.
This was safe enough: Nan Annie, inviting her to share her incredulity

at the losslinen, stolen; inviting her to stand beside her and be shocked.

And in that moment, as she took the needle to Nan Annie (eyes too sore, too full to thread up her own needle; hands laid quiet, redundant, in her lap) Ruby felt that Captin was too cruel; that the price for buying Annie out of Jonah's debt was too high; that it was Annie forced to pay against her will. Captin, going! Captin had walked Beth down the aisle and passed her hand to Jamie Abel; he'd cradled Ruby her first night at Hunting Tree and built a low, wheeled dog called Bobby for her out of wood scraps, flat-head nails, old leather for his ears. Unspoken promises, there were, weighty and paternal, resting in these acts and they were much too precious to be broken.

So Ruby was attentive while Nan Annie sewed her stitches in her blank new square of linen and told how Trembly Em had been up this afternoon and how the Ruth and Naomi Thursday Club had sat down ready to start stitching, and Dinah had gone upstairs to fetch the losslinen from where she'd put it for safekeeping on her tallboy and come down to tell them that it wasn't there and made Glenda go and look in case she'd missed it. While Annie spoke, Ruby rolled her pastry flat and lifted it above a flat round tin; pressed it, gentle, with her knuckles, close into the rim. Shook out split peas to stop it scorching and put it in the oven for blind-baking.

"*Anyone,* is there," said Annie, squinting at her sewing, "so cruel as to steal a basket filled of losslinen from grievers?" She laid the linen in her lap. Ruby glanced at her. Nan Annie was pinching herself in the soft crook of her elbow.

Ruby knelt before the stove and shook her head (a borrowed gesture of dismay); a tea towel round her hand.

"Em has an idea as her's testing, but her day gi a name. Her thinks it will come out as it's the same one as took her locket."

Too hasty, Ruby dropped the door onto its latch. The metal grated and Nan Annie, starting, pricked her pointing finger. "Now look what yo done!"

No point in trying to run. Ruby stood and watched the bead of blood (too flagrant and too eager) form on Annie's lifted finger. The blood-bead swelled; it split and spilled itself, a black-red drip against the white of Annie's skin. She waited for her nan to surge, to swallow her, but Annie's rage abated just as quickly as it came; a pulsing wave against the harbor wall.

" 'S just a little prick." Nan Annie sucked her finger.

Still, Ruby stood there. Held-in, she pressed the spoon against her chest; felt cold iron branding her with Isa's seal and leaving her a scar-circle of thick skin and a baying, full-moon boldness.

"Sorry, I am, about Captin going."

Another blood-bead rolling from her finger. Nan Annie pulled a hankie from her pinny and pressed it to the tip. "He told yo, did he, then?"

Ruby nodded.

"I never thought as Len ud go and leave me . . ." On Annie's hand-kerchief, a neat unfolding bud; blood-bloom. "Len, of all men! Stepped back, he has, his whole life from decisions set before him as if they was a cliff edge! Still, from what Em says, this Fly woman has gid him a big push . . ."

Ruby chewed her lower lip.

Nan Annie pressed a fresh fold of the handkerchief against her fin-ger and looked up at Ruby, eyes gleaming like cut coal. "Why is it, Ruby, as the men leave us, yo and me? Len and Jamie Abel. Jonah. Why do these men leave us here at Hunting Tree?"

Ruby flinched. Later, she would understand why these words pierced her, but for now she felt she'd left herself unguarded. She had allowed Nan Annie to draw a circle in the clay around them both: *We two, within it: an all-but orphan and a widow, both abandoned.*

"Come on, Nan. Me dad ay left me!" Ruby tried to make a space between her and her nan, for Nan Annie's bruising would spread into her, she knew, generous as a rotting apple at the bottom of a bowl.

"Really, Ruby? Your dad ay left yo?"

"I see him every day!"

"Except the days as yo forget his dinner." Annie's eyebrows arcing, cynical. "Yoom very loyal, Ruby. A loyal fool."

"It's oney Captin, leaving! Me grandad, it ay as if he *left* yo, is it?"

Annie took up the sewing from her lap and shoved it in the cloth bag hanging from the chair. And yet Ruby went on, wanting to reason with her nan who saw a pattern where Ruby only saw the knotty dan-gling threads on the rough side of the cloth.

"Yo cor say as drowning's leaving."

Annie looked up at the ceiling, the heels of her hands pressing to her temples. Quiet, she spoke. "I know when I been left. Get out."

"What?"

"Yo heard me. I doe know what yo think as yo am playing at, stood there! I cor be doing wi this chitter! Hens there is to see to." She swiped an arm toward the garden. "Pigs to feed. Slugs to pick off beans." She bent to pick up her fresh losslinen. "I need to get on, and wi'out your prattle. Get out!"

Ruby went. Knew better than to stay. Bemused, though, Ruby was, that Nan Annie had tossed her out this once and had not reeled her in. She did not feel relief at her expulsion: this was not unconditional release and, as Ruby swept up cacky straw and shook out corn and cut slim slugs in two with the sharp thrusting of the spade (that summer was too dry for slugs to fatten), she tried to call to mind that other time when she, triumphant in false-freedom, had swum off from Nan Annie; that time that Ruby'd thought herself unhooked. She rubbed the worm-scar on her wrist. The memory was too slippery to catch.

When she'd finished with the hens and pigs and slugs, she crept unshod past her Nan Annie, creased up, dozing in the grate-chair, and tried to get across the landing to her room without exacting creaks and yawns. (She couldn't trust this house not to betray her.) She undressed and pulled her nightie on, but did not go to bed—she knew she would not settle till she heard the cough downstairs, the scraping of the chair across the flags, and Annie's slow step up the curving stairs. And besides this, Ruby had her work to do. She eased her sore leg up onto her bed (her stooped image reflected in the black gleam of the window) and set out her scissors and her ink pen and her Almanac. The pages of the Almanac were undulated now; Cut-damped, soror-dried. Brittle, too, they creaked with every turning. The lists, imprinted as they were in Ruby's mind, were not lost to her— confident, she was, that she could ink them over where her own hand and her mother's had been blurred to incoherence. (Later that night she would write out in a clear, emphatic print her amended list of

"What Shall I Take to Sea." She'd write it on the central pages of the Almanac, the pages where it fell open quite naturally when untied. She'd put a date to it. She'd sign it.) In some parts of the Almanac, Ruby's pasted scraps (and Beth's) had worked loose. The lists; the maps; the three years' close-accounting of her Boat Fund; these Ruby pried free with the flat blade of her scissors, slow, precise, and slipped them in between the pages of the "Treatise on Fishing with an Angle," and weighted Isa's book down beneath her wash-jug ("when you have taken a great Fish, undo the mawe and what you find therein, mayke that your bait, for it is best").

But she could not save the stories cut from Captin's *Muckeleye Gazette,* or from the *Tales of Severnsea* that Dil's girls sent. Some had dried up, folded on themselves in pulpy creases. Others flaked off in her fingers. Some had been dissolved altogether, or had left a mirrored imprint on the facing page. And if the paper scraps themselves could not be salvaged, they were tricky to decipher, these flecks of text reversed and overlaying Ruby's scratchy blotted sketches (a fly for catching grayling; a fly for catching trout). She had no mirror in her bedroom, so she held the Almanac up to the darkened window and, tilting the book, she read in the reflection, " . . . LEYE'S SOMME HE-ROES IMPERIL . . ." She took up her pen and wrote the headline out in full. Remembered too well when she'd first read it: that night when, back from their trip Halfway-to-France, Nan Annie'd shook the paper in her father's face, and slapped it on the table. " 'Storm in English Channel,' Jamie Abel!" Annie'd shrieked. " 'Muckeleye's Somme Heroes Imperiled!' It doe say nothing about daughters, though, doe it? It doe mention the *children* as was put into harm's way!" And then Annie had pulled Ruby (blotch-eyed, doped with sleep) into her; she'd pulled her roughly by the shoulders and hooked her close in to her belly with a crooked arm. Ruby remembered how she'd tried to ease her nannie's arm away, struggling to breathe . . . "It doe mention Ruby, daughter of Somme Hero, imperiled!" Nan Annie, incensed, flaring. She'd thrown kindling across the room and hissed at Jamie Abel, slapping down a dare for him to leave. Ruby, sobbing, frantic, tugging at their sleeves, had tried to damp them down. She'd never seen her slow, mild Jamie Abel spark at Annie (or at anyone) like that: all crackle and barb. (Later, someone doused her nan—Trembly Em perhaps—but neither she nor Jamie Abel ever seemed to smolder sorrow or remorse. But Annie would send Ruby down the Deadarm every Christmas with a plate of sweetbreads and cold pork.)

She finished inking in what she remembered of the cutting, and then held up another fragment to the window. (The worm-scar on her bared wrist, white and grainy, flecked with blue.) She *knew* this story, and as she wrote out SEVERNSEA BORE TAKES SIXTY SOULS, marking in the serif-strokes like newsprint, the memory that had slipped from Ruby's fingers in the garden sank its hook into her now and yanked her backward with a force that left her light-headed and winded.

She was back there, treading nervous and uncertain through those taut, strained days that followed on from her father's departure. Nan Annie: braced, composed, as if she held herself together. The old rules reasserted and augmented, laid out with quiet command: "no going *near* the water. No crossing it. No paddling. Do not, do *not* get wet. Too many of my family have been drowned." Ruby had not believed that this was binding. Nan Annie'd settle down. She worked herself up too much over things.

But Ruby worried more about her father: he'd not taken much with him down to the Deadarm, and his clothes would be damped through with these blunting nights that followed from the clear, wide-open days. She'd taken him a comforter, some thick socks and a guernsey that Trembly Em had knitted him last winter. She didn't want her father catching chills.

He didn't *ask* her down there (she'd never know if Nan Annie believed this) and Jamie Abel had been shocked when Ruby's voice came at him through the darkness from the town side of the towpath. He told her to get fogging home, for God's sake, to stop her nannie worrying; she'd refused. Said she'd be back in time to take her Friday bath. Insisted on giving him his woollies, Ruby had, and fumbled with the mooring for the drawbridge. Her foot somehow got snagged up in the ropes and she was tugged into the water and the wooden bridge slammed down on top of her. *The waters compassed me about, even to the soul: the depth closed me around about, the weeds were wrapped about my head.*

Scooped out, she was, and laid like a seal skin, stiff and raw and coated with Cut-sludge, over her father's shoulder. He carried Ruby home and tried to shield her from the sharp malicious chill that hacked through to their bones. Her arms swung free; her wrists bashed against his back. The fingers of her left arm tingled, distant, but they weren't cold like the fingers of her right arm. Slick and hot, they were, and only when he got her in the light of the kitchen up at Hunting Tree (the kitchen steaming with a tub for Ruby's bath; sweet apple wood fast-burning in the stove) and only when he laid her on the table (Ruby flopping like a china-headed doll with perished joints; loosely sagging limbs ready to unthread) did he and Ruby and Nan Annie see that Ruby's wrist was gaping, torn wide by something jagged in the water.

Nan Annie wouldn't let him stay. She stripped Ruby of her clothes, thick and reeking, hardening with mud, and lowered her into the bath to warm her through. Annie knelt beside the tub and held her head clear of the water. Ruby retching, coiling forward. A cloud of crimson pinking through the water; blood flooding from her wrist despite the cloth Annie had used to bind it. The lamplight, reflected on the surface of the water: it bore into her; made her raw eyes ache. Nan Annie's apron purpling in the wet. Nan Annie hooked her underneath the shoulders and heaved her, slopping, angled, from the tub, but Ruby's heels caught on the rim. The tub upturning, flooding all the flags. One hand gripped beneath her chin, one hooked around her shoulder, Nan Annie'd tried to lift her, drag her over to the table, find somewhere dry to lay her down, but Ruby slumped, unwieldy, and underneath her shifting weight, Nan Annie must have buckled, feet slipping on the slick, and lost her grip, for Ruby's head slammed on the stone. Lips numb, she'd gaped at Annie, vacant as a caught fish, and with a slow stone-weight her eyelids, rasping, closed. And then Nan Annie frantic, slapping cheeks to wake her up. Ruby, calm, floating from Nan Annie, in dark waters . . .

A jolting. Lying against Nan Annie, a cup forced between Ruby's lips. Ruby biting on the china; choking on the hot, thick tea; spewed tea running steaming down her chin and staining brown the towel that Annie'd wrapped around her. Annie smearing Ruby's eyelid up and open. Flecks of curd, she saw, floating idly in the cup below her chin . . . Days of rags and iodine; tansy paste that stung inside her wrist; blood leaching through the linen. Dizzy months when Ruby could not stand. Nan Annie cool, attentive, every day intoning in a whisper words that would, for nearly seven years, keep Ruby Abel Tailor tight-tethered to the land: "Slice yo, I will, Ruby Abel Tailor, if yo go in the water. Bleed yo, I will, like a pig, till yoom so weak as yo woe have strength to leave the Hunting Tree and find yourself a water to be drowned in. High and dry at Hunting Tree, I'll keep yo."

Landed, with the Almanac before her, Ruby felt sick and giddy. She fell back on the bed and the spoon around her neck shifted against her. She closed her eyes. She still had Isa Fly. She still had Isa's spoon to keep her safe. She felt along the shaft. She would not stay. She would get to Severnsea and wait for Isa Fly. She pressed the indentation with her finger, and Ruby made a vow to stow away.

Chapter 17

Tenter-hook, *n*. 1. A hooked nail or spike. 2. *fig.* That on which
something is stretched or strained; something that causes
suffering or painful suspense.

SOME THINGS, once lost, will never be retrieved, but there were
those among the Ruths and the Naomis who took as their exemplar
the widow who has lost her piece of silver, and, diligent, persistent,
they duly swept out all their corners till there were no more left to
sweep. If a Ruth or a Naomi had suspicions that her lost thing had
been stolen, she would watch the window down at Baitch's Hock
Shop lest the thief had swapped it for a farthing. (Shady Baitch, they
called him, as so much of his stock was hot.) But if the Ruth or the
Naomi knew her lost thing held no monetary value, and knew beyond
a doubt that she'd not left her precious object on a window sill beneath an opened sash, ripe for the stealing, then she might suspect that theft-magic had snatched her lost thing from her. And with
Isa Fly in Cradle Cross (and Dinah's sole memorial to her lost boy
cruelly desecrated), what else could explain the disappearance of
these sacraments—the locket, the losslinen—that would not fetch a
farthing down at Baitch's?

There were ways to find the one who had used magic in her thiev-

ing. The best way known to the oldest of the Ruths and the Naomis
was as follows:

> Open up the Bible on the Book of Ruth at Chapter 1 and
> Verse 16. Take up your door key, knotted with a ribbon. Place the
> key flat on the Bible, so that the threaded end stands well clear of
> the top edge of the page. Shut the Book and wrap it tight up in a
> scarf. Let it hang loose from the ribbon. Speak out slow the names
> of those who are suspected of the theft. Be attentive. The Bible
> will turn when you speak the name of the one who used her
> arcane trickery to steal from you.

Thus furnished with this Bible-proof of the witch-thief's identity, the
thief-finder had further means, more visceral, of winning back the object she had lost: a heated bottle filled with urine, nails and hair.

And if this witch-bottle failed to elicit the return of the lost thing,
there was only one recourse. The witch-thief should be punished with
a burning.

Ruby kicked at dry stones as she walked down to the town on Monday
morning; not too fast, with her tender ankle, plucking ears of meadow
fescue from the roadside and shredding off the seed. Nan Annie had dismissed her—said she'd do the washing on her own. Pale and strained,
she was, her eyes receding; a dot of crimson coloring each cheek.

Ruby needed to retrieve her Boat Fund; now that Nan Annie's
debts were paid, she could acquire the items on her sea-list. And she
needed to go through the waxy packet of cuttings Captin had set
aside for her—those emptied pages in the Almanac had gaped at her
in shock and accusation: *O, Ruby! How could you have permitted
our depletion!* And she needed to find Isa and exact from her some reassurance that Isa would return soon to the coast, with or without the
missing daughter; they needed to agree to their trysting place. (Ruby
had a bright-eyed vision of the three of them—herself, Isa, Captin—
sat around a table with their fresh-dipped Friday fish.)

As Ruby turned into Horn Lane she recalled what Isa'd said in the
Blick's office. She'd talked of obligation, of being frightened, of Im-

peratives, and though Ruby hadn't fully understood what Isa meant (as perhaps Isa intended) she'd felt the sense of it. Something was binding Isa. A threat, maybe; an incantation, like the one that Nan Annie had woven around Ruby compelling her to stay dry. Moonie Fly had made threats to Isa, Ruby knew. He'd told her that he'd jump down off the cliffs if she returned without the daughter. But just as Ruby knew, bone-deep, that she'd return to Isa through her years like sea to shore, she knew, bone-deep, that Isa wasn't bound by *Moonie's* threats. But if Ruby did not comprehend the nature of the threat that pressed on Isa (exiled her!) she nonetheless was buoyed up by a carefree confidence that she *would* come to understand it, just as Ruby had recalled the incantation Nan Annie'd used to bind her to the land (for Ruby believed that in the act of recollection, she'd undone it). And when she understood how Isa's rope was knotted, Ruby would untie the killick that kept Isa anchored here and she would slip free from the dead-weight of these Imperatives.

Ruby applied her clumsy logic, earnest and uneven, like a child with too much butter on her knife. It was fear, she reasoned, that was restraining Isa, the same vicious breed of fear that had, till now, held back Ruby. But the spoon had lent her boldness, and it was Isa's spoon. Maybe it was time to give it back.

Ruby, frowning, twisted up her finger in the cord. It wasn't that she *asked* the spoon, or at least not directly; she did not believe that Isa's spoon imparted knowledge to the bearer. Yet when she cast her question out: *"What frightens Isa Fly?"* the answer slapped at her feet, hooked and landed: "Isa Fly's afraid of mermaids who throw stones and slice through nets and call out in the night from Sawdy Point."

Horn Lane was strange this morning, and it took Ruby a moment to work out what was missing: no music spilling out of the Blick's window. (Later that day she would learn that Truda's gramophone was stacked up with the rest of her possessions, ready for the Muckeleye auctioneer. Lot 7, of 52.) But the Bastock gang was there, writing things with long sticks in the dust, and as Ruby approached, Lorna Rudge spoke clear and loud so she could be sure Ruby would overhear: "Ar, her's used a spell has Isa Fly to nick that locket off Trembly

Em, and if that wor enough her's took the losslinen an' all!" The Ruth and Naomi Thursday Club had got themselves the proof of it, they said. At their meeting, yesterday, they'd done the Book and Key to find the thief, and Dinah's Bible turned on "Isa Fly."

She felt her stomach lurch at Isa being caught up in their skeins. She needed to help Isa loose herself from Cradle Cross, or the Ruths would whittle Isa down for kindling.

Isa let Ruby in, and locked the door behind her. With Isa staring at them through the glass, the children outside scattered.

"Have you seen Belle Severn today?" Isa, trying to speak light.

"No, not yet. But yesterday her made me fall into the Cut. I ay in no hurry to see her." Ruby lifted the spoon up and began to loop the cord over her head. "And I think as yo should have this back."

"No." A crack in Isa's voice. "Don't take it off." She laid her hand on Ruby's to stop her. "I do not want it back. I gave it to *you*."

"A loan to make me bold. It's worked, Isa. Braver, I am, than I ever been before. But yoom troubled, Isa. Yo been getting more fretful ever since yo gid the spoon to me."

"A spoon to keep anxiety at bay . . ." Isa tucked the spoon back into Ruby's dress, but hooked a finger in the cord. She bent her head and looked hard at Ruby, and Ruby felt helpless, suddenly, and younger than her years. "Is this your way of telling me you're no longer prepared to watch the dredger, to find out what she says? She made you fall into the water, and you don't want to be bold Ruby any longer?"

"No! That ay it at all! It's just as I can see *yoom* scared of Belle Severn."

"She does not frighten you?"

Ruby thought of Belle Severn, laughing on the Deadarm; her threats to tangle Ruby up in nesting wire below the water. She chewed her lip. "I think I got it wrong. I'm sorry, Isa, but I doe think as I *has* scared her off. Her woe leave yo alone." Her eye was caught by something, a bottle, half wrapped in a muslin cloth, set on the counter. "What's this?"

She reached out to lift it free of the cloth, but the glass was hot to touch. She leaned close and examined it.

"I found it in the fireplace when I came in."

It was filled with amber liquid. Ruby used the muslin cloth to lift it to the light: thin strands, there were, floating in it, and a dozen four-inch nails at the bottom; a witch-bottle. "Was the shop locked last night?"

"I thought it was. I must have been mistaken."

But this couldn't have been put in the fireplace last night, she thought: *the grate was clean and swept, but the glass was still warm. Someone had heated it this morning and brought it to the shop.* She ran to the door and wrenched back the bolts, then ran back to Isa. "Come on." Ruby grabbed the bottle with the muslin and with her free hand grabbed at Isa. "Theft-magic? I woe stand for this! Weem going to see Captin."

Isa allowed herself to be pulled along by Ruby. "Captin? What is he to do with this? You cannot think that Len—"

"What? No, Captin day do this. He's been disenchanted, but he ay been turned into something wicked."

"What can Len do, Ruby? There is nothing to be done."

As Ruby strode, the hairs inside the bottle rose and danced. "I doe know. We got to tell someone. Come on."

The moment they were stood there in the chip shop (at least, Ruby was inside, but Isa stayed behind her, waiting at the door) Ruby wished she hadn't taken Isa there. She'd hoped that the witch-bottle would be enough, that Captin would be gallant once again, that he'd rage up Horn Lane, calling on the bottle-maker to come out, to face him. But Captin, unsmiling, gave Isa Fly a single nod and stared down at his feet as if it hurt his eyes to look on her directly. Captin turning his back, getting on with chips. Ruby all but shaking the bottle: "But look, Captin. Look what they done!" and Captin saying, gruff, that he could see as it wor nice but it must of been them kids who kicked about outside. When Ruby turned to look back at the door, Isa had already gone, and when Ruby tried the button shop, she wasn't there.

She went back to the fish shop. She did not blame him for his curt manner with Isa: the dredger had disenchanted him; he should not be held responsible. If she could find out what words the dredger used, then she and Isa would undo them and he would be her warm and gallant Captin once again . . . But Captin had retreated out the back; she could see him, stood on *Ferret* with his pipe, affecting to arrange a rope; he only went there in the day when his mood was crabby. She knew better than to try cajoling answers from him now. The Cut was busy—tubes and cokes and barrels, and horses on the towpath. She retreated, giddy with relief—the strength had seeped out of her legs and left them hollow, rickety, at watching Captin out across that deep black slit of water in between the towpath and the boat.

She turned her thoughts to their life together (once she'd undone what Belle had said to him). Ruby, Captin, Isa at the sea. She needed to take money from her Boat Fund. She knelt down at the sink and reached beneath it. Felt against the bricks until she found the loose one; unlooped her spoon and slipped the handle in and out the crack around the brick until she'd eased it free. She set the brick down on the floor and reached into the cavity behind; pulled out a steel tube— just longer, thicker than her forearm. She carried the tube over to the table. Both ends of it seemed closed in, welded shut, but Ruby knew just where to twist, and separated the tube into two. This was Captin's bottle-safe where he used to hide his vinegar and, for the last three years, where Ruby'd banked her Boat Fund. She held the open tube under her nose: hope; the prospect of escape—these smelled like vinegar to Ruby. She tipped her coins onto the table, but didn't count them out. She'd just take a shilling for today; more than enough for buying soap and tea. More than that and Grocer Foley would put it all about that Ruby Abel Tailor, clinking rich, had emptied all the coffers up at Blickses. (A few days later, bruised and bereft, she'd think back to the shadow that fell on the table as if someone on the towpath darked the window, and she would know for certain that someone had been watching as she tucked the safe away.)

Captin came in as she stowed the tube back in its place and he greeted her, a little wary, with tense, assumed exuberance, and said how glad he was that she'd come back and that he'd make them both a cup of tea. And with her Captin back, lightly affectionate, attentive, she couldn't bring herself to ask about the dredger, what she'd said. Ruby smiled back at him and put the kettle on, and, as a profession of her faith in him, her almost-kin, and making her home down in Severnsea, she asked him for a bit of flour and water, and made it up into a gluey paste. She sat down at the table; careful not to mention when he asked, with genuine concern, what happened to her book, that it was Belle—she just said that she had dropped it in the water, and laid out all the salvaged papers and pasted them back in.

Outside, the Bastock gang had skulked back and started up another skipping rhyme.

> *Make a guy of Isa Fly*
> *And put it on the bonfire, high*
> *Watch Isa burn, watch Ruby cry!*
> *So long, Isa-with-one-eye!*

Ruby glanced at Captin, cleaning his chipping knife, to see how he'd react, but he coughed as if to cover up the words and, moving to the grate, said, too loud, "Doe yo forget the packet Dil's girls sent you." He set it on the table next to her.

Usually she loved these waxy packets sent from Severnsea and slit them open just as soon as Captin had sorted the post, but she'd left it unopened—what, four days? Who needed bits cut from the *Whale-mouth Post* or snipped from magazines when there was Isa-from-the-sea to tell the stories?

She eased out the cuttings from the waxy packet and spread them out before her. Captin across from her, cutting a last bowl of chips. "A recipe with kelp to soften the skin and improve the complexion," she read; DR. FRANKLIN'S ADVICE TO SWIMMERS; an ink sketch of a half-surfaced wreck at Gleed. She set these to one side, for a headline caught her eye: A GRISLY CATCH, she read, her finger twisting and untwisting Isa's spoon; THE MYSTERY OF THE BODY IN THE CAVE:

> They were searching for lost farthings, but beachcombing brothers Ernest and Alfred Simkin found more than they sought when, at low tide on Wednesday, they ventured into caves beneath the cliffs that loom at Sawdy Point, St. Shirah, Severnsea.

Ruby drew breath, sharp, and Captin said, "Rube?" but Ruby shook her head to dismiss him.

> "I thought it was something fallen off a ship and pushed into the cave by the high tide," says Ernest Simkin (aged 10 years).

"Something was shining," Alfred Simkin (aged eight) adds. Yet it proved to be no treasure that enticed them deep inside. Drowning is too commonplace at Sawdy Point. Many in despair have chosen to meet Death by leaping from this cliff, but the Simkins had not stumbled on a suicide.

A swell of nausea, swilling in her belly. Moonie Fly. There was no date, no way of telling how old this story was—when had the packet come? Had Isa called home since then?

The body—or what remained of it, for it was horribly abused by being left for days in water—was wrapped up in a fishing net and the torso pierced right through with a fishing spear (or, more accurately, a portion of a spear: the shaft was snapped in two). Perhaps it was the steel tip that had caught the light and lured young Alfred and Ernest?

The Detective-in-Charge confesses that he is perplexed. No local person has been reported missing in the last fortnight—and the police surgeon estimates that the body would show yet more severe signs of decay had it been in water any longer. The case, so far: no witnesses; no evidence; no hope of identifying the ill-fated victim. All that is known is that the poor soul was a woman.

Ruby blew her breath out. It wasn't that she cared a spit for Moonie Fly, but she was glad that Isa would be spared this.

Stories are already spreading, and to urbane inlanders these tales must by their nature seem too strange, too primitive . . . The Simkin boys believe them. " 'Tis not an ordinary murder," Ernie says. (Perhaps we should be chilled by such words dropping from the mouth of one so young!) "Nets and spears," adds Alf, "is ways to kill a mermaid." A grisly catch, indeed.

She spread the paste on the back and pressed the paper on her Almanac, trying to stick it flat, but the page beneath was buckled. Another piece, an inch long, about the body in the cave: the police were questioning a local man, aged sixty-six. Another piece, under the

headline, SPEARED BODY IN THE CAVE: DEVELOPMENTS. They had released him for now, but the inquiry was still open. There were rumors
of another suspect, someone that the police wanted to question. They
were conducting searches of the beaches, the cliffs, the fields above
the bay; they hoped to find the other portion of the weapon.

Not a broken fish-priest, Ruby thought. *Not a broom-handle.* She
glanced, furtive, into the front where Captin was checking on the
chips, and slipped these further clippings in her Almanac and laced it
up, tight shut. She called out, "Captin, can yo manage wi'out me for
a bit?"

"Oh, Rube, the Bull's just gone!"

"Please, Captin. I ull come back to wash up. I never ask."

She was barely through the door when a hand snagged her and
dragged her to one side. Glenda, ahead of the Blick's crowd.

"It's that white Fly, ay it, Ruby? It's her as gone and sucked all
sense out of our Captin and talked him into going off wi her!"

"No! Isa doe *want* him to leave."

"Doe gi me that!"

"Her doe!" And Ruby saw clearly now why Isa didn't want him
down at Severnsea. She saw why Isa'd been so furious with Truda. Because Captin, who read the *Muckeleye Gazette* from front to back
each day, would doubtless switch allegiance. He would read these stories in the *Whalemouth Post,* and there'd be more. *Police hunt
woman,* Ruby ventured, *white-haired, with one eye.*

But it was Belle she needed to find now, and in her haste she didn't
trust herself not to give Glenda a hard shove and move on. The
spoon's edge cut into her chest, and she was bolder than she'd ever
been with Glenda.

"Wanted, Captin has," said Ruby, "to go to the seaside since Dil
went. That's his sister. He wants to be wi Dil's girls, and their children." Proud and taunting, Ruby flaunted this, her secret wisdom
about Captin, but then as Glenda (eyes flicking over Ruby) garnered
it and glowered, Ruby wished she could retract what she had said and
added, quick, "He's a growed man, is Captin."

"A growed man on a leash!"

"Isa Fly cor make him go if he doe want to."

"There ay no saying *what* her can make folk do. Theym saying as

Isa Fly has got the Blick girl forcing Captin out and fetching his lease out from under him. Now tell me that ay true, our Ruby! Yoom thick wi um, ay yo?" Nodded her head, sharp, toward the factory. "Tell me that ay true."

Ruby glanced up at the high window. "Why cor it be as Captin wants to go and see his family, like he says? Why is it as yoom always ready to believe it's Blickses as should be blamed? They cor be blamed for every little loss! Yoom too ready to believe all as yo hear."

"I cor believe *this*! Annie Nailer Tailor's stock has spit to call me credulous! Her from the family of True Believers."

"What's that supposed to mean?"

"Nothing as yoom ready to be hearing . . ." She dusted down her dress front; pulled it straight. "Well, all right then, Ruby. If Captin says that's why he's leaving, it must be so. He's going there to be wi Dil's girls." Mocking, Glenda sang this out, acerbic. "He's going there to gid his nieces piggybacks. He *ay* going cause he's been sweet-talked into it and promised a dip in the sherbet by a woman he ay known above a fortnight!"

"Yo think as Isa's tricking him to go? It ay right, Glenda, speaking of her that way. It ay just wrong, it's . . ." She groped for a word grand enough to convey her meaning. Thought of Truda Blick, imperious, and loyal to Isa Fly. "Slander, it is." She held her shoulders straight and lifted up her chin. "How dare you talk about my friend that way?"

"How *dare* I?" Rough and urgent, Glenda pulled Ruby by the shirtsleeve through the crowd and into the alley between Horn Lane and the Cut. Cool in here, but thick with piss-stink. "I dare cause there is them in Cradle Cross has known this woman longer un a fortnight." Glenda spoke low, hissy and insistent; her nails pressed deep into Ruby's arm. "There's them as know her's cunning, her conniving."

"Yo mean Belle?" Ruby squirmed under Glenda's clutch. "Yo doe know her like yo think yo do. Yo doe know what her's done to Isa Fly."

"Belle warned me this might happen, and now I seen it for myself: her wins people round, does Isa Fly. Her makes um think as there ay nobody in the world but her. Some controlling effect, her has, as makes some folk think as they should drop their other obligations and tend to her. 'Entreat me not to leave thee,' her says, wi that seeing eye, 'or to return from following after thee . . .' "

Ruby shook her head, and her dismay was not all invented. "That ay what her does!"

Glenda softened. Ruby knew that look. *Poor Ruby, wanting for a mother.* "I ay saying as her *means* to do it, Ruby. Some wicked influence was planted in her, perhaps, and her ay had no choice about its growing."

Isa Moon. Tugging them, releasing them: her tides.

"Yo *think* yoom fond of her; yo think her's fond of yo. But her has blinded yo and Captin and that Blick girl . . ." (and for the first time Ruby heard Glenda say Truda's name with something like concern) ". . . and this woe end well for yo."

Ruby wriggled to shake Glenda's fingers from her arm. "I got to go."

"Where? To Isa Fly?" Glenda shook her head and released Ruby. "Watch as yo doe make your pledge wi her, Ruby. 'Where thou diest, will I die, and there will I be buried.' "

Ruby's throat grew tight. "I ay going to Isa." She was going to Belle Severn. She was going to find out if Belle had had a letter and if Belle had discovered, yet, what Ruby had just learned: why Isa Fly had fled here, from St. Shirah.

Chapter 18

A witch-bottle will bring great anguish to the thief who has used wicked esoteric methods in her crime. The thief will be afflicted with such heat and agonies, as if she herself were being stabbed and burned, that her torment will be visible to all who look on her. The witch-thief, thus afflicted, will return the stolen object forthwith in the hope that her great guilty pains may abate.

Uncommon Remedies

It was too still in the Blick's yard when Ruby shut out Horn Lane and closed the high green gate behind her. Yes, the Bull had gone for dinner, but Blick's was never usually this quiet in the day, what with furnaces to tend and carcasses to be stripped for the ovens. Where were the furnace-men? Why were there no fires in the deep arches opposite the gates, no horn sacks piled against the railings? How familiar she'd become with Blickses, Ruby thought, to know that this was strange! A week ago she'd shied away from this place, kept at bay by tales of blood and bone, but now there was a body in a cave and Isa Fly was too scared to go home.

Ruby stopped at the bottom of the stairs to Truda's office and slipped her Almanac from the satchel; she unlaced it and checked once more to see that the cutting was tucked safe inside.

She'd found Belle Severn sitting confident and at ease at the

Deadarm. Belle had offered to make Ruby tea (Jamie Abel, Belle had said, was worn out and was having a lie down). She could hardly ask if Belle had heard about this body in the cave at Sawdy Point; if Belle, like Ruby, had yet drawn the line between the Grisly Catch and Isa-on-the-run; if this was how Belle disenchanted Captin. So Ruby'd simply asked—trying to be light, ingenuous—if Belle had news from Cass, and asked once more what she had said to Captin. Belle had mocked her: said she was too young to understand the nature of the spell Isa had wound round Captin and therefore just how easily it had come undone, and when Ruby had played saft and petulant and said that she "wor too young," that Miss Blick gave her the important jobs, that Isa trusted her, Belle had thrown back her head and laughed and said that Rube was easily deceived.

"You want someone to plait your hair and bring you sugared tea, Ruby, and God knows you deserve a bit of sweetness and affection after having that dry lemon Annie Nailer Tailor bring you up. And that's what's so sad about this, Ruby. You've been sucked in by them two and by their false attentions. If you go back there now, up to that office, behind that bolted door, they won't be looking for a missing sister. And that's all I told Captin: Truda Cole Blick comforting Isa Fly and Isa giving comfort in return—that's a sight as would put any man to flight."

The Blackbird had expected her to be despondent, to feel that she'd been made to look a fool, so Ruby's head dropped forward and she'd twisted her toe in the clay and hoped that she looked wounded. And although Ruby failed to understand the power of what Belle had said to Captin, she was satisfied that Belle didn't know—not yet—about the body in the cave. "I doe want to be made to look a fool. And yo udn't try to fool me, ud yo, Belle? Yo ay heard from Cass?"

"I'm expecting a letter any post. Three weeks I've been waiting, thereabouts, so it'll be a long one."

And that was when her stomach lurched and Ruby was as sure that Cass was dead as she was certain of the spoon about her neck. And Isa would not go back to St. Shirah—never, willingly—and Ruby would not meet her at the sea.

As she made her way back through the folds, she heard another rhyme.

If yoom wiser, doe cross Isa
or her'll split un splay un splice ya.

She pulled the lace up tight around her Almanac, slipped it back into the satchel and headed to the office.

"Is that you clattering up my stairs, Ruby, you great rhino?"

Truda sat behind the desk; before her, a stack of papers; a typewriter; an open ledger.

"Where's Isa?" Ruby said.

Truda did not look up but nodded toward the ante-room; one finger keeping her place on the ledger, the other hand twisting up her kiss-curl. "Got any villains in the family, Ruby?"

"Villains?" Ruby shifted from one foot to the other. "Well, me Grandad Jonah was a rogue, from what I know."

"Would he don a hood and come round here with a can of paraffin, do you suppose?" Truda took up a pen and chewed the end in mock-consideration.

"Doubt it. Unless you can summon up his bones from off the seabed."

"Ah. A drownèd villain. No good to me." Truda tilted back in her chair and pointed her pen at Isa as she came in through the door. "Aha! That one can fish! Theym saying her's a witch . . . How about it, Isa Fly?" She let the chair fall forward with a thud against the floor. "Any good at underwater exhumations? Could you summon up a drowned soul from the deep?"

"Admire her spirit, Ruby. Don't hold her to the letter." Isa placed her hand on Ruby's shoulder. "Have you eaten?"

Ruby shook her head, but could not look at Isa. *She will read this in me with her white, white eye: a spear, a net, a body in a cave.*

"I'll find another egg."

Ruby watched her leave. She fiddled with the broken satchel buckle.

"Sit down, will you, if you're staying? Or at least don't fidget so."

Ruby moved a pile of letters from the chair and could not help but read the first few lines. "Lay-off letters?"

"What choice do I have?" Truda picked up more papers and

squared them up against the desk, and Isa laid out forks and spoons and salt and bread-and-butter on the copper table.

"Do you want *me* to deliver them?" No sooner had she said this than she wished she hadn't: laying off was worse, even, than debt-fetching, but it was too late to retract it.

Truda held bent fingers up to Ruby's cheek. "Don't be kind, for God's sake, or I'll weep."

Ruby slipped her satchel strap over her shoulder and pressed her hands down on the clasp. She tried to keep her eyes fixed on her lap; Isa was watching from the table. She did not want to be afraid of Isa, so instead imagined Isa Fly afraid. *How scared Isa must be; my Isa-as-a-fish,* she thought. *She's lost her lie; she's naked in the stream; she's waiting to be landed with a hook.* She found a new list forming in her mind: Things We Need for When We Run Away. They'd go abroad, she thought; one of the places Truda longed to visit, or maybe just the Western Isles; there was a farm Truda had mentioned; long-haired cattle yielding a rare kind of horn.

"Yo could leave Blickses." She twisted the spoon at her neck. "Yo could leave Cradle Cross. Yo could take me wi yo. And Isa."

"Become a fugitive?" Truda lifted up her chin and breathed out at the ceiling. "That would be preferable to *this.* I did not want it all to end this way, to end in such a dreary fashion! A letter from the bank, of all things! I would have preferred something more colorful; dramatic. An old score to settle, maybe. An old enemy of Hector's with vengeance in his heart and explosives in his pocket. God, even some ex-lover of the degenerate Miss Blick laying a fuse and waiting for the saltpeter to blow. But . . . no. 'This is the way the world ends. Not with a bang but a whimper.' "

"What's brought this on?" Ruby spoke to Truda, but it was Isa who replied.

"The bank has refused to honor a loan agreement it made with Blick's, and so this week Blick's will not be able to pay out the wages."

"Dear strange, beguiling Isa Fly, that's not it at all." Truda pushed her chair back from the table. Walked over to the window—stood to one side so that, no doubt, she could watch the street and not be seen from outside. "The bank's refused to make a loan to *me*. They would have made one to dear Hector. They did it all the time. They simply don't trust Hector's *niece* with Blick's business. And so Blick's Fine Horn Button Manufactory ceases trading in its one hundred and seventy-fourth year, thanks to the unbankable, unbackable Miss Blick."

Ruby chewed on her lip.

"Did you know," said Truda, watching Horn Lane, "that if in any part of England . . . not just England! Alaska. Norway. Corsica, for God's sake! If a man should look down at his cuff, a woman at her *peignoir*, a child at the placket on his nightshirt, there'll be a button there and that button probably came from Blick's. They won't know that it's from Blick's. There's no name etched on the reverse of the button. Unless they live in Cradle Cross they won't have heard of Blick's. The only way they'll know about the sad demise of Blick's is when their tailor brings around a new shirt and they find their fingers clumsy and surprised around the buttons. They'll feel a difference, but they will not know precisely what has changed. There's quite some skill in making buttons that will do their job then ebb into the seam. You see, they know, without knowing that they know, that it is Blick's that makes the best buttons . . ." A bitter, broken laugh. "I used to mock my brothers and my father and my mother for being so committed to this factory. Before the War, that is. Before I *lost* them. When I was younger—younger even than you, Ruby—I would lament their risible lack of ambition. 'Why bother with a button when there's so much that needs doing in the world?' I'd say. 'Why not hooks and eyes?' God, how dear Hector would lecture me. He'd line up his favorites on the desk: a robust tiger stripe; Russian buffalo horn; delicate little West Australian ocean pearl. 'They have *function*,' he'd say, and he'd push them out toward me with his finger. 'They have *beauty*. They have *grace*.' But he would say that once a good button is in place it becomes invisible, unless it's lost, and then its absence is more eloquent than the four raised prick holes left behind. 'You pay scant attention to the precise little round that holds your decency intact,' he'd say to me. 'But if you lose this button from your shirt, the yawn in the silk when you reach forward for another egg custard will summon the attention of the women seated around you as effectively as a stage whisper . . .' He liked to joke, you see, that one day I would join the Ruth and Naomi Thursday Club and eat cake with Dinah and the other Hatchett Harpies."

Ruby could see the Ruths and feel their nudges. She folded up her arms, being Dinah. " 'Her's that *lazy*! Her cor even sew a button sose it stays on and her *Doe Care*!'

"Ah, that eloquent little yawn where the button should be . . ."

" '*And* her's havin' another custard.' "

"Indeed . . ." Truda twisted on her heels and left the window. "Well, *we* have no custards, but we do, I think, have bread. We have *some* butter—just a little. We have salt. And, I do believe, thanks to the bountiful Miss Fly who knows our every need, we have boiled eggs and, now that Captin no longer brings battered fish in paper, some species of sprat that she has conjured from the Cut. Eat 'em while they're hot."

But Ruby found she had no appetite. She could not join them at the copper table; she could not look at Isa, and even when Isa asked her if she felt quite well and why she looked so pale, she could not meet her eyes. She offered to make tea (a chance to turn her back on Isa's watching) and tried to work a list up—*a towel, a slip of soap*—but other, awkward items found their way into the list: *a spear, a net, a body in a cave.* She looked over at Truda, who was teasing meager flesh from her Cut-sprat, not eating it and talking about 18 Tenter Lane and how the agency had found someone to buy it, but their offer was far lower than she'd hoped for, and how her broker had sold off her shares and how she'd pared down her allowance to the bone, and Isa asked what Truda planned to do when it was over, and Truda said despite it all she couldn't think beyond the bloody lay-off letters and how Glenda and the harpies would be when they received them. "That said, I favor Ruby's plan." She raised her fork to Ruby.

Ruby stirred the pot. *They found the body rotting in a cave.*

"Get away from this lot," Truda nodded at the window, "with their piss-bottles and chants and stinking rags . . . And while we're talking about persecutors, I have a little letter for the dredger." Truda wiped her fingers on her hankie. "And this letter alone gives me some pleasure." She crossed to her desk and pulled out a letter from the pile. "It appears that Blick's have, until now, supplemented the dredger's earnings with a generous and regular gratuity." She rapped the letter. "We thank her for the vital service she's performed but sincerely regret that we are no longer able to express our gratitude in monetary terms . . ."

There was a broken spear lodged in her belly.

"How d'you think she'll take it?" But before Isa Fly or Ruby had a chance to reply, the telephone rang out in the ante-room and Truda, cursing, went to answer it.

Ruby stirred the leaves, slow one way, then another. Her satchel was still hooked around her; the strap was tacky and it pulled against her skin, but she could not take it off, not with the Almanac and all the cuttings safe inside. She did not look around but was certain should she turn that she'd find Isa staring into her.

"You're certain you won't eat?" Isa, suddenly, was at her side, scraping fish bones onto a newspaper.

Ruby shook her head.

"Not even a piece of buttered bread?" She fetched the plate and set it on the desk. "We won't clear that yet, in case you change your mind."

"I said as I ay hungry." She looked over her shoulder. Truda had shut the door.

"Your neck is marked. It's red."

Ruby lifted up the satchel strap and eased it to a new position. "It's fine." She poured the tea while Isa made a parcel of the fish. This careful, mundane folding paper around flecks and bones, it irritated Ruby. "What am yo going to do wi them?"

"There is a cat, a stray, that lives along the Cut."

"Yo put bones out on the step?" The swell of irritation rolled through Ruby. "Rats ull come, *and* more cats than just the one as yo invited. Captin woe like that."

"The cat will see the rats off. And if she doesn't—"

"What?"

"Captin will be gone soon enough."

"Ar. Captin ull be gone to Severnsea."

Isa said nothing, and her silence angered Ruby. Anger, long distilled, ignited in her, lit by her flint-edged disappointment. No sunwarmed Anvil Rock and Isa's fingers, nimble, teasing knots out of her hair. "Yo promised yo ud take me to St. Shirah. How could yo make a promise when yo never had a moment's thought to keep it?"

"Ruby, I would not have promised such a thing."

"Yo said as yo ud teach me how to angle. I been learning, Isa. 'A tench is a good fish and heals all manner of other fish that are hurt, if they may come to him.' That's one thing I learned. 'The angler maye have no colde nor no dysease nor angre but if he be causer himself.' All of it, I know. 'You can not bring a hook into a fish mouth without a bait.' Yo said as yo would take me out into the water with a rod!"

Isa laid her hands flat on the counter. "I did not say those words."

"Yo gid me the spoon to stop me being frightened of the water. Yo gid me the spoon so as I could go to sea, and been working, it has! I ay so frightened. When I fell in the Cut, my nan day hit me. Her day even notice I'd got wet."

Isa rubbed the corner of her eye. "And you believe the spoon did that for you?"

"Yo must of known it from the day as yo got here. Yo must of knowed yo never ud go back."

Isa shook her head. "I *cannot* go, not now . . ."

"What, not until yo found the missing daughter? Is that what yo was going to say? Well, *that* ay why yo woe be going back and yo knew it from the first time as yo said it."

"And why is it, Ruby, that you think I will not go?"

The door slammed behind Truda and she marched back to her desk. "Isa simply has to go back home." Her cheeks were marked with kohl smears. "No, Isa!" She held up a hand to forestall any protest. "I've been a selfish fool to try to keep you here."

There had been some friend of Hector's on the phone. Some old friend in the trade who'd heard that Blick's was going under, but hadn't heard that Hector Blick was dead. "He said he'd heard about the bank; that they were being beasts. He's offered to have words with our suppliers." The words caught in her throat and Truda looked up at the ceiling. "John Hawkins; an importer. Haven't seen him since I was a girl." Truda wiped at her cheek with her sleeve. "I said that I was grateful that Hector didn't have to suffer; better to be pinched out like a candle, quick. John said in the sweetest way that I should not deceive myself or try to deceive him."

Isa's hand pressed light on Truda's shoulder and Truda twisted up to look at her. "He's right. I am selfish beyond measure. I would have countenanced Hec's suffering—some prolonged illness, a few days' reprieve—if it had given us a chance to speak again." She pressed Isa's hand and then lifted it free. "I'll drive you back tonight."

"What am yo on about, go home?" Ruby shouted. "Her cor go home!" There would be men, she thought, waiting to meet her, spread out in a line across the cliffs; one stepping forward with a piece of splintered spear. "*That's* selfish, wanting her to go!"

Ruby kept her eyes stitched close and tight to Isa's face. Truda was insisting that Isa should go home and tell her father that there was no Lily Fly in Cradle Cross. If it would offer some consolation, some incentive to go back, Truda would take on the search for the daughter. She would hire a detective, someone to cast the net more widely, someone with resources who could track the daughter down.

Ruby's words slipped out. "But her day come here looking for a sister." Her finger rested on the spoon; Isa watched her.

Truda stood. "Ruby, you have been so diligent. With all the groundwork you have done, we may find her yet."

"How, Truda? Yo think there's other places we could look? Stones as we ay yet turned over? Because it ay like it has been a proper search. 'Do you know a daughter of a man named Moonie Fly? No?' " She dipped in a mock curtsy. " 'Well then, thank you for your time.' " A rage swelled up in her. "Her says, Truda, as Moonie's dying and her come to find his daughter to say sorry, but if this was *Hector,* ud yo not be bold—brash, even, and go knocking around at every door to find this last thing as he wants, this last thing as might make him well again? Ud yo not stop all the women of an age and ask um if they know their father? If her said yes, her knows her father, then yo ud press her. 'Am yo sure of him?' yo ud say. 'Dun yo share his features? Am yo sure as he ay a proxy father? Sure as your blood-father day leave yo to be brung up by another? Doe yo suspect that your mom might of been unfaithful to her husband and that yo am the product? Has yo ever thought perhaps that yo was got out of wedlock; that your blood-father was feckless like my grandad and he udn't marry her and so her had to turn to some other man to make her good again?' "

"Ruby, are you delirious? I'm not sure *that's* a line I shall pursue."

"I'll say it in words yo understand! HER CANNOT GO HOME!" She banged her fist against the table with each word.

"I am not banishing her, Ruby! She will be free to come and see us when it pleases. The House of Blick is crumbing around me no matter how I try to prop it up and I would like to do this one good thing, this one unselfish act, and send Isa home to see her dying father. Tell me, Isa, that you'll go."

"But that's just it!" Ruby, exasperated. "Her *woe* be free." She walked over to Isa, gripped her hand and held it tight. "If yo doe tell Truda and her finds it out another way, her ull think as yo been using her to harbor you."

Isa stared at Ruby with a fearful clarity, as if her blinded eye had cleared and snapped clean open. She said nothing; sank into a chair and Ruby dropped down to her knees and tried to animate her, rubbing reassurance into Isa's cold skin with her thumbs.

Truda drew her tin from her top pocket. "Isa, you've been too long in my company. Why should I harbor you? You look as if you're farded up for Hallows Eve! With these theatricals, we'll admit you to our troupe."

Neither Isa Fly nor Ruby looked at Truda. "I got my Boat Fund, Isa. We can take you somewhere safe." Urging her words onto Isa's fingers like warm breath on clouded windows. "We ull find another place, a hiding place where they will never catch you."

"Somewhere safe? So cryptic, you two." Truda spoke low, uncertain. A dry voice; luster gone. "Is this about the witch-bottle, Ruby? A jar filled with urine and old nails? Surely not enough to scare off Isa Fly."

"Yo can teach me how to angle," Ruby said, "and we can watch the boats and I ull fry up all the fish we catch."

Still Isa Fly said nothing.

"Come now, Ruby. Elucidate, would you?" Truda tried to pry her tin open, but her hand shook. She jacked the lid up with her thumb, too rough, too quick, and the tin jolted, scattering cigarettes across the desk. One landed on a plate; one in a cup; one on a piece of bread and butter. She pinched it off and tried to wipe the grease away. "Fag sandwich, anyone?"

Ruby gripped Isa's forearm. Shook her a little. "Doe be afraid." She tried acting practical, and sat back on her heels. "Now, Belle Severn doe know yet, I doe reckon; her said as Cass ay written in three weeks. But her ull find out soon enough and then yo better be long gone from here."

Isa stared at Ruby.

"All those years of learning!" Truda gripped a cigarette between her teeth; spent three matches in trying to light it. "Drinking gin and eating toast and translating the dirty bits of Pliny." She crouched down beside Isa and Ruby; examined them, head cocked, as if they were a sculpture at an exhibition. "And yet I still have no idea what you are saying. Is it a private language? Will someone furnish me with a translation?" She walked around them. "Isa?"

Isa spoke, quiet and hoarse. "How did you discover it?"

"A story in the paper Dil's girls sent. I got it in my Almanac." She took it from the satchel and slipped the cutting out. "And then Belle said as Cass ay written." Her hand shook as she gave Isa the cutting.

"They found her?" Isa whispered.

"Found who?" Truda said.

"The sea-whore," Ruby said. "Moonie's merymaid. The one that persecuted um, along wi Belle."

Isa held the cutting up to Truda, and her eyes were full. "They found her, so I cannot go back home."

Chapter 19

List, *v.* To careen, veer or incline to one side.

THROUGH THE DREGS of the afternoon, Ruby sat beneath a tree and sank into the shelter of her Almanac. Isa, brandy-oiled, had at last told them what had truly brought her here, and questions advanced on Ruby; they formed ranks, demanding her attention, but Truda would not let her stay to ask them.

That evening up at home, Captin came to share his Monday supper; tried, and failed, to pull her into conversation.

When she slept that night she dreamed of Isa Fly and Moonie in a fishing boat, flinging green nets into sullen waters. Their catch keel-hauled, hefty and inert: Truda, Belle and Ruby.

Ruby went straight to the Deadarm in the morning. (Nan Annie would chastize her if she forgot to take her father's dinner yet again: "Has we come into money as I ay aware of, Ruby, for yo to be so profligate wi food?") She did not linger there: her stomach heaved and rolled at the eggy stench of Cut-dregs, warmed and rancid on the water. She wondered if it would be this or something like it that drove Jamie Abel from his island to the land; the Cut so choked with cack and weed and sticks that Cut-men and women would abandon their stuck boats, and firms would move their freight onto the roads and he would get no more boats needing patching. She couldn't see her father, so she called out that she'd left his dinner and didn't wait for him to answer.

She held two lists in contention: "What We Need to Run Away with Isa" and "What I Need to Stow Away with Captin," and did not know which one of them might yet win out. Either way, the substance of each list was just the same and Ruby needed the distraction: thoughts of Cass-in-the-cave and Belle-set-for-revenge and Isa-on-the-run reared up before her; she needed to be working on her lists. She stood in Grocer Foley's queue and sank her hand into her satchel for the Almanac. No room in front, behind; the early queue packed tight along the counter. (She could, she thought, have done without the satchel.) She felt inside it, but—no Almanac. Slick-palmèd, she felt through her satchel once again, then through her pinny pocket. (A handkerchief, she found. Her little coin pouch with her money from the Boat Fund safe inside it. A pear stalk and a pencil.) She scoured the floor about her in case the Almanac had somehow tipped out of her pockets, and set Nan Annie's basket down beside her on the floor.

"Em Fine-Knee Bacon says they have took measures . . ." Dyspeptic Joan, further up the queue, with Nancy Lupus. "*Measures,* they am taking, Emily says."

"Oh, ar? Her ay found her locket, then?"

"Nor the losslinen ay turned up, neither."

And now, thought Ruby, *my Almanac is lost,* and with its loss, a raw gaping growing where her belly ought to be.

My Almanac. The shape of the loss bigger than the neat dimensions of the book, the lists of sugar lumps and apples, tea leaves, ham. *I will search all up the Breach and up the Ludleye Road and up the Lean High Road. I will walk again through all the places I have walked this morning.* But even as she tried to hold herself together, Ruby smarted and her eyes stung with a sudden and astringent understanding of Trembly Em and Dinah and all the Ruths and the Naomis who had lost their precious things—the locket and the mural and the losslinen. Until now Ruby had not given much thought to the losses that had left these women casting all about them for a thief.

"So Em says as we should pay attention . . ." Joan Dyspepsia, winching up her eyebrows, "cause if these measures work, the thief ull come to light . . ."

"Like a moth to the moon," said Nancy Lupus.

When it came to her turn at the counter, she was careless, forgetting who was in the queue and how they listened. She had intended, Ruby had, to buy just three things she remembered from her list—the tea, the sugar lumps, the inch of Fairy soap—but when she stood before the counter without her Almanac, she was immoderate and hasty and asked for too much. Ruby put her coins down on the counter and pushed them toward Grocer Foley.

"Nice to see as somebody's got money," Glenda called out from behind her. "The rest of us woe be paying down our strap too quick just now, Mr. Foley, what with Blickses laying us off. But I doe bear a grudge. Good, it is, to see as Miss Blick's looking after yo, at any rate, Ruby!"

Flushed, eyes down, Ruby left the grocer's with the basket pulling on her arm, its handle pressing ridges on her skin. She was dismayed that she had drifted so far from the modest and considered intentions listed in her Almanac. *Ginger biscuits! A twig of licorice! A twist of raspberry kali!* She went straight to Horn Lane to stash her basket, checking the gutters and the doorsteps and the gratings as she went, in case her Almanac had perhaps fallen there. These seven years, she had never been without it. Skinned and smarting, Ruby tried to peel the edges of herself back in and seal herself up against the loss.

There was a lorry in Horn Lane (HEATH OF MUCKELEYE, BEST HORN BUTTONS painted in red on the wooden flank) backed against the open gates at Blick's. Men in pale brown overalls were laboring beneath the weight of a squat steel machine and a man with a pencil in his ear was guiding them backward up the loading ramp. More men in brown were easing steel shanks of die-cutters and heavy presses out across the yard and up onto the lorry. She found Truda just outside the gate. With her, a man was ticking off the requisitioned items as they passed. "Heath's" embroidered in that vigorous red script across his apron. Truda held a finger up to indicate that Ruby should wait for just a minute, and as Ruby stood beside her, she slipped her free arm through the crook of Truda's elbow; kept it there while they watched the button presses being carried off. She waited till the Heath's men had closed up their loading ramp and Truda had signed the papers, then asked Truda if she could leave her basket with her for safekeeping while she went looking for the Almanac.

"Five of our twenty presses left, Ruby," said Truda. "Five of eleven drills . . . A preemptive move to keep my creditors at bay."

Ruby squeezed on Truda's arm. "Where's Isa?"

"Not in the shop?"

"I day see her there. Has her decided what her's going to do?"

Truda frowned and looked about her; said, too loud, "What's in your basket? Apples? Spuds? I can't offer safekeeping. I will have sold them, along with my soul, by lunchtime."

She wanted to find somewhere to sit quiet and write lists: "What Isa Should Do Next"; "Ways to Help Her to Escape a Hanging." Her head was full—snared bodies in dark places—but without her Almanac she had no means of retreat or of evasion, and as she searched, could only think about what Isa'd told them up in the Blick's office.

One morning, Isa had said, about three weeks ago, her father came in bloodied from the beach. He never ventured in the open sea, but when the tide was low he liked to trawl the edges of the tidal pool round Sawdy Point for crabs and minnows. He always took his fishing spear with him—it acted as a stick for steadying. There'd been an accident, he said. He was panting and abstracted. He'd gone too near the ocean and he had slipped on seaweed; lost his spear, and Isa, he insisted, must retrieve it.

She found it in the cave below the cliff, just as he said, but he had failed to mention that the spear was pinning down a woman's body. She told them how the woman, Cass, was still struggling to breathe when Isa found her, cold hands rigid around the spear, eyes urging Isa Fly to pull it out. "The spear shaft snapped." She'd put a hand across her mouth. "It was that, I think, that killed her in the end."

Moonie had shouted at her when she came back with a portion of the spear; wild and coarse, enraged. He said it was deliberate: that Isa

Fly had broken off the spear; that all of Severnsea would know it to be his; that she wanted him convicted of the murder.

"He would not talk about what happened in the cave. He denied being in the cave at all. I asked if Cass attacked him, if he had swung for her in defending his life, but he wouldn't answer.

"I went back down to Sawdy Point that night. I had to swim—the tide was at its highest. I took his fishing net, thinking to wrap the body in it and pull it to the beach; I planned to alert the police. I would explain it all to them: Anselm's death, the years of persecution. I would tell them how his mind had been worn thin, and I would explain that I had killed Cass Severn, trying to save her.

"But I could not move her body, and when I reached Two-Fish Cottage, my father was out waiting on the step. His illness was taking hold already: the thirst; the stains upon the skin. He blamed me for all of it."

Moonie had always chided her, she said, by holding other daughters up against her. He'd say how other daughters would have known how a father should be treated. "Other daughters would have known when to put pepper in his soup and when to make it salty; when to fill his pipe. Other daughters, Moonie said, would not have let him take his fishing spear down to the shore when he was in a rage . . .

"He said that I believed the worst of him; that since I was a child I always asked how *he* had wronged 'them merymaids' instead of seeing quite how they wronged him; that I had betrayed Anselm, thinking that he was killed in a bombing, when it was Belle Severn who'd lured him to the rock and let him drown.

"He ranted through the night about the vengeance of a stubborn, bitter god. He said God wanted him stuck back in Cradle Cross, patching boats. He said God punished him because he disobeyed, because he tried to make a new life in St. Shirah. He said that I should go to Cradle Cross and find his daughter out. I should go back and tell his daughter that he hoped she was satisfied. He hoped that she was happy with what he'd come to; that it was down to her he'd come to this; that it was down to her there was a body rotting with his spear stuck through the belly. That he had paid enough; that he had paid enough for leaving her behind."

"So there is a daughter, somewhere?" Ruby'd asked. "Yo day make that bit up?"

Isa had nodded. "He often speaks the truth when he is cruel. But all the rest of it: repentance forced upon him in the face of retribution? Moonie, making recompense to those he had abandoned? The pair of you were right to doubt—what was it Truda said?" A half-smile toward Truda. "My loyalty; my filial devotion."

Truda had thrown her hands across her face. "Don't listen to me! I am a verbose fool. I'm tart and cynical and you are sweet, sweet Isa!"

"I was not born a skeptic." Isa had pulled her knees up, rested her chin on them; rubbed her legs to generate some warmth. "As a girl I thought my father was the moon. I thought I could take a ladder to my father and climb up to his shoulders to reach this moon and touch its surface. All those broken promises, when every month the old moon was renewed. Why did *he* never try to start again?"

"But you can, Isa!" Ruby had cried, and she blushed at the memory. "You could still go to the police."

Isa shook her head. "I tried. I told Moonie that I'd go, if he did not. But he said that the saftest constable would see how I was trying to slide my blame onto him; that he'd be compelled to tell them how I came home with a portion of his spear. He said he couldn't trust me, that if I stayed at home I would betray him, but if I left, he'd keep his own counsel."

She pressed her finger up against her eye. "They have questioned him. Brammeier says that they have looked at all the marks on him; the blisters, this skin corrosion; this thirst, he has, that cannot be slaked. My father told them he's been persecuted thirty years by this merymaid, that he wanted to be rid of her, that he is glad of her death, and they have concluded that my father is not in his right mind. That even if he were in his right mind, he is too frail and too ill to have carried this out on his own, and they have stopped their questioning."

Truda spoke up. "And what has Moonie told them?"

A sudden cold had sluiced through Ruby's shoulder, through her belly.

"I don't know. But Brammeier says they want to question me."

.   .   .

Ruby went door-to-door, along the Breach and all down Islington to ask if anyone had found her Almanac. "It's all as I have off my mother," said Ruby. To those who didn't know her, Ruby added, "and her's dead." A heavy brick of sympathy to weight open each reluctant door. None of them confessed to finding Ruby's book, but behind each door was someone who insisted that she knew who was to blame for this and all the other cruel losses Cradle Cross had endured through this past week. There were questions about Blick's: "I seen yo wi Miss Blick. Is it true as Heath of Muckeleye is gidding work to them most skilled of Blickses? The rest am going cap-in-hand to Rudge's and to Bissell's, or getting on the bus to Muckeleye." And people had it sewn together: Isa and the thieving and the demise of Blick's, and behind each door was someone who insisted that "her ud get her dues."

Without the Almanac she felt distracted, unsecured without it weighing down her pocket; she risked drifting off course. *My lists, my maps, my seven years of making ready for my journey, Ruby thought. Without them, can I ever go to sea?* She still was rehearsing lists with desperate urgency when Jamie Abel called across the water, "All right, Ruby?"

"Yo seen my Almanac?"

"Your what?"

"Beth's book. My book," she reprimanded. "The one as yo gid me when I was seven."

"Yo lost it?"

"That, or it's been took."

"Send it round, I will, if it turns up."

The offer sounded strained and stilted; awkward in his mouth. Questions followed: "How's Eliza? And Annie—is her treating yo all right?" Her replies were clipped and trim, as if he were a pastor or a teacher, because *her* father didn't talk like this and she wasn't certain how she should respond. Before Isa Fly had come to Cradle Cross, he'd never asked her questions, and Ruby never prompted him to ask. Too much risk in answering. How could she bear it if Jamie Abel found out that she was in some kind of danger, but did nothing to mitigate the risk? If he discovered that his girl was in despair, but left her standing on the town-side of the towpath and did not cross the water to embrace her?

But today he walked out to the Cut-edge, watching her, and as he scrutinized, Ruby shifted weight from one hip to the other to ease the aching in her swollen ankle.

"The Blackbird ay here today, then?"

"I finished working on her boat."

A bitter taste in her mouth (the Cut-stench didn't help): he was lonely without Belle Severn. *That's* what this was. Jamie Abel didn't care for Ruby. He was lonely.

"Her'll be round," she called out, caustic, but Jamie Abel shook the comment off him like a wet dog.

"Her woe."

Ruby arched her eyebrows.

"Her woe, Ruby. Doe look at me like that. Her's gone."

"Gone where?"

"Doe yo believe me? This morning, her went."

Ruby shrugged and twisted around her spoon.

"Look at the Cut, Rube!"

"Ar?"

"Does it look like it's been dredged?"

A prickle at the back of Ruby's knees. "Where is her?"

"Her ay heard from her mother. Her's worried. Her's gone back home to see as her's all right."

"Her's gone back home?" She grabbed the spoon and held it tight within her fist.

"Saint-something. Severnsea."

"Dad, I got to go."

But before she could make her way back to the tunnel, Jamie Abel called out after her, "Captin come down this morning. Told me as he's going. Yo knew this already, day yo, Rube?"

"What, am yo cross as I day come and tell yo?"

Jamie Abel shook his head and shifted his weight.

"What, then? Dad, I got to go!"

"It's just that wi Len gone . . . He does a lot for yo. Yo and Annie."

She flushed. *I bought Captin Woodbine's and a Western paperback. I have licorice to sustain me on my journey.*

"Yo know as yo can always come down here if yo needs to, doe yo, Ruby?"

"What, to live wi yo?"

He shook his head once more. "I mean if things am bad up at the Hunting Tree, yo can come down and tell me."

She could not bring herself to offer him a nod.

The door to the button shop was propped back, but Isa was not sitting at the counter. *How could she open up a shop,* thought Ruby, *when there is a body in a cave? And now Belle Severn's gone to see her mother.* But it was soothing and distracting in there; the scrubbing and the snipping and the sorting; the slow closing of a heavy door, cloistering the quiet.

She found Isa cramped up, fevered, puking on the stairs.

Truda was in the Blick's office, packing cards of buttons into crates. Ruby explained how the witch-bottle had done its work on Isa—the sharp pain in the abdomen, excessive heat within the bowel—and what should Ruby do, because Isa needed help, and Belle had gone—

But Truda interrupted. "Oh do please shut up, Ruby! Witch-bottles?" She flung her hands up to her forehead and grasped her sleek hair in her fists. "Don't badger me about her! Stop quizzing me for answers that I simply do not have! You're clucking like an idiotic hen. I've tried, God knows, to reason with her, to go straight to the police, but if she wants to act the guilty fugitive then that is her prerogative. She has chosen this. Now get out, would you, and leave me to dismantle my inheritance?"

But when Truda realized that Isa Fly was ill, she sent Ruby up to Dodd's for belladonna, and up to Tenter Lane for fresh sheets and clean nightshirts.

Ruby sat with Isa later while she slept on Truda's couch in the Blick's office. A new skip-rhyme, shouted more than sung, down in Horn Lane below:

> *Ruby Abel Tailor stuck close to Isa Fly*
> *With glue boiled up from Blick-bones,*
> *Blood-pudding and fish-eyes.*

Miss Blick slid up to Isa, and said to Isa, "Honey,
I'm in the spit, I'm sinking quick, cause
Blicks runned out of money!"

Rube and her sticky fingers crept around the town and nicked
A locket and some linen
And she pawned it for Miss Blick.

The next morning, Wednesday, there was a locket laid out in the window of the button shop. And when she saw the locket, Ruby (cold, her hand gathering the spoon up at her throat) wondered how long she would have to wait before her Almanac was laid, ingenuous, on the middle shelf beside it.

Chapter 20

The wise seafarer does not look at the full moon, for there are stone
jars on its surface, filled with the broken promises of men and
should he stare too long, the seafarer is absorbed in a futile longing
to turn his stone jar over and start his life again. Moon-blind, he
neglects his course and, too late, discovers he is set for rocks and
certain death.

"Ancient Advice to Seafarers, derived from Lore and Legend,"
The Coastal Companion, Severnsea, Almanac for 1899

IF RUBY FOR a fleet, bright moment thought that the reappearance
of Em's locket would calm down the Ruths and the Naomis, she was
soon corrected. Blick's was still sacking all but a dozen workers;
someone had been marking doorframes with a knife; the Cut was silt-
ing up; besides all this, the locket had been emptied; it no longer held
the fair curled lock from Em's short-lived, long-loved baby. In the
bread queue, Maison Hester's, Wednesday, Glenda and the others
piled up the fragments they'd collected since "them Measures" had
been taken yesterday—and Ruby knew for certain that "them Measures" meant the witch-bottle she'd found in Isa's grate. They did not
speak the name of Isa Fly, but it was clear to Ruby who they meant.
"The Wax-work," they called her, with shifty sideways glances toward
Ruby. "The Wax-work melted down," they said. "Her's gid the locket

back, but the heat woe pass from her, nor the pain that's got her folded up around her belly; her woe get well until the losslinen is back."

It was Dinah Hatchett Harper who spoke out to stop them (and Ruby's eyes had jerked up in surprise to meet with Dinah's). Dinah's voice was dulled—more pumice, now, than caustic. "At least Em *got* her locket back. Cor that be an end to it, and a cause to be grateful?" Fuel on their fire! Their indignation burgeoned: it burned gaudy—talk of proxy-dolls and sticking pins; it burned rank—talk of holding tallow close against a flame. "How *can* there be an end to this when the losslinen is still stolen? When Blickses is being shut? When someone's leaving her mark on our doors?"

Neither Dinah, blunted, grayed, nor the freshly whetted Hatchett Harpies, nor our sad Ruby, clouded by her longing for her lists, could know that they would be united with their lost things soon enough. And when it came to Saturday, some of the Ruths and the Naomis would, too late, take Dinah's part and say that things had gone too far; lost things were found, so why was there a need to set a witch-fire? (Because there was still in Cradle Cross one precious stolen thing left unreturned, one account left unreconciled, and that was a tiny spoon.)

And so the reappearance of Em's locket rocked the Cradles more than it settled them. It was a week of strange corollaries—some of them quite predictable, but nonetheless surprising. The Blackbird's flight from Cradle Cross did not (as Ruby might some days ago have hoped) leave calmer waters in its wake. Belle, absent, looking for her Cass; Ruby's unease was more unsettling than the fear she felt when Belle was present, preening in the Gutter, or threatening frogbit, or writing notes denouncing Isa Fly; this unease traced out great looping circles in the skies above her head; it swooped at her when she did not expect it.

She took half a pound of fresh bread up to Truda's, in case Isa Fly was well enough to eat. (It was supposed to be for Jamie Abel but, she thought, he'd go well enough without.) In her satchel, a soft brush for Isa's hair (because brushed hair could make you feel a little better); clean flannels; a dozen sprigs of mint for making tea.

The office was orderly and still; a low wall of crates along the edges, a single ledger open on the desk. Truda looked up as she entered, her finger urging silence at her lips. She sat with bare feet propped up on the desk, shirt open at the neck—the room was hot; charcoal in the grate and coffee on the stove to purify the foul air of a sick-room.

Isa lay unmoving on the couch, coiled in tight around her knees with her back to the room. Despite the heat, a blanket rested on her. A pail sat on the floor beside the couch. Ruby leaned; peered over: Isa's mouth dropped open slightly in a little snore; her blind eye had grown sticky; the lashes thick with cuckoo spit.

Truda summoned Ruby and held three cards up before her like a dealer. Each card had five half-inch buttons stitched to it, close in tone and pattern. "Pick a card." Her voice low, clear, controlled.

"Have yo packed?"

"Dappled pinbow; tiger-stripe; tree grain. Which has the most appeal?" Truda fanned the cards out on the desk.

"Has her said yet?"

"I favor the tiger-stripe, myself. Good for sports jackets and outerwear."

"Has her said yet what it is weem going to do?"

Truda held the buttons to the light. "I asked her if she'd let the doctor see her, but she's having none of it. *Enquire Within* says orange peel and cardamom for fever and bicarb for the bilious attacks. Mind you, it says bicarb for everything."

"But the Blackbird! Her's been gone two days and it woe have taken more than one to get there."

Truda picked up her cards and put them in the drawer. "Ruby, Isa's either limp and barely conscious or cramped up around a bucket spewing bile. She's hardly in a state to run away."

"How come yoom so calm? Belle *must* of found out about Cass by now. Her ay saft—her ull put it all together. Her'll tell the police that Isa's here, or more likely, her'll come to finish Isa off herself!"

Truda shrugged. "I've pressed her—gently, mind—to go to the police. Preemptive; before they come for her. I've given her until first light Friday morning."

"What yo mean, *yo gid her until Friday?*"

"If she's still not capable of making a decision, I shall sling her over my shoulder and drop her in the backseat and drive her down to St. Shirah myself."

Headlights scooping out a tunnel through the trees; moths battering the rear lamps, Truda singing loudly in the front, and in the backseat, Ruby cradling Isa's head and stroking her white hair. "Yo mean we will."

Truda shook her head. "No, Ruby, I don't."

"Yo ay going without me! I got a map of Severnsea—" But then Ruby remembered with the force of a sharp blow: she had no Almanac, and neither lists nor maps. She had nothing to guide her to St. Shirah. "Yoom leaving me behind?"

Truda stood and walked around the desk. "This isn't some tall yarn in a penny comic. We can't solve this with coracles and Morecambe." She laid a hand on Ruby's shoulder. "If she does not go back, then she looks guilty. She didn't do it, Ruby, and we're not fugitives. We cannot live off berries in the forest."

"Captin's going." She stared down at her shoes. "And Isa Fly. And yo."

"I'm flattered, Ruby, truly, that you'd miss me. But don't be anxious, child: I shall return."

"Why?" Ruby wriggled free of Truda's hand. "Why ud yo? Yo ay got cause to come back to—what is it yo call it?—Clay-Dull-Cross. Blickses has fell apart. So why ud yo leave Isa by the sea?"

But Truda had cause to return: John Hawkins had made an offer. A buyer ("he insists") had let him down; he had two tons of horn that needed shifting. He was offering the horn and what he called a modest little loan; enough to pay a dozen buttoners for a month. "I have to try, with kind, kind John behind me."

"So yoom leaving her to come back to save Blickses?"

"I won't be *leaving* Isa. She will visit, I am certain." All bluster, Ruby thought, but no conviction. "Once this ghoulish mess is all cleared up."

"Yo think as her ull come back here to see us?"

Truda tapped her pockets for her tin.

"Yoom safter than I gid yo credit for. And once her's gone—" Ruby broke off and pinched inside her elbow.

"Should she choose not to return, then at weekends I'll hound her in St. Shirah." Truda lit a cigarette and looked at Isa. "And consider squandered all my other days."

The telephone rang, and when Truda had closed the door behind her, Ruby rushed to Isa Fly, still sleeping. "Her says as I cor come wi yo, but I woe take no notice," she whispered, leaning close to Isa's ear. "There is words for this. 'Entreat me not to leave thee, or to return from following after thee; for whither thou goest, I will go.' " She twisted around the spoon to seal the promise, " 'and where thou lodgest, I will lodge.' Except I woe be following. If her's taking yo down to St. Shirah, I ull be there, waiting, when yo come."

Captin wanted help to clean the gut-room ready for his leaving, and she took with her the basket of provisions and stowed them underneath the kitchen sink. There was not much to do: throughout his tenancy he'd kept the fish shop brushed and scrubbed. And he had few possessions to collect. She did, however, fold up his crocheted blanket from the couch and imagined herself throwing it around her shoulders, stood on *Ferret*'s bow. (No contention now between her lost lists: tomorrow she would stow away with Captin.) She took out a long-caned duster and as she stood up on a stool to clean the picture rail, she told Captin about her missing Almanac, and grinned into the wall as gallant Captin promised he would find another one for her on his first full day in Whalemouth; he would put the parcel in the post the moment that the inked address had dried. He made her supper. No Isa: just the two of them out in the back room like it used to be. (He said that he'd asked Annie, but she wouldn't come, so Captin wrapped a fish for Ruby to take up later for her nan.) When they had finished eating, Captin took down his prize book, *Ashore and Afloat*, from the shelf above the grate, and pushed it across the table toward Ruby. That, and the twisted branch of driftwood. Said he knew she loved these things so she should keep them to remember him when he was by the sea. And Ruby felt ashamed that she was smiling as he pressed her to his chest; she could not confess to him her plans to stow away, but she did not want her Captin thinking that she cared more for the acquisition of this book, this twisted branch, than for the loss of him.

"Doe worry, Captin. I ull be wi yo, all the way to Whalemouth," Ruby whispered into Captin's shirt. Breathed in vinegar, tobacco. Her grip tightened round his middle. "Yo cor leave me behind."

"Ar." He sniffed, and Ruby, caught up in her glee at talking straight but being thought symbolic, did not hear leave-taking in his voice.

The next day, Thursday, she went back to Captin's to finish waxing up his cutting table. She'd asked him why he wanted her to do it now when he'd be working on it later, gutting fish. Captin, brisk, yet not unkind, said if *she* didn't want to do it, that was fine. He'd do the job himself. Fastidious, accountable . . . yet Leonard Salt was leaving her unguarded.

She did not want to do the Thursday teas at Maison Hester's for the Ruths and the Naomis; she wanted to stay up at Blick's, but Truda shooed her out: Isa needed sleep and soda water and not Ruby hopping up and down, demanding when *precisely* they would leave. Ruby did not want to listen to the Ruths and the Naomis: there would be more talk about Captin, lured to sea by the promise of Isa; more talk about the tearing down of Blick's; more oblique babble about Measures, she was certain, though nobody would speak the word "witch-bottle." One of the women there had saved up her own piss and mixed it in with hair, and this had made Isa ill. But Ruby promised on the spoon that whatever was said, she'd keep her own close-counsel through the meeting. She would make tea while Isa Fly was vilified.

She primed herself instead to ask Glenda if she'd had any news from Belle, and to ask if anyone had come across her Almanac. She prepared herself to be mocked by those who didn't know its provenance. ("Weem grieving for our losslinen and look here! Ruby's fretting cause her's mislaid a blessèd book!") Such admission of a loss would align her, Ruby knew, with the aggrieved women of the Ruth and Naomi Thursday Club. As Ruby climbed the Breach, she dashed away the thought of Glenda Hatchett Harper, brows raised, looking down at Ruby; sly, triumphant.

She tried the door to Maison Hester's, but it jarred against its bolt. (She recalled, now, how she'd heard Glenda saying as they'd keep it locked outside shop hours, what with the tallow on the wall.) Ruby knocked and peered inside, her cupped hands round her face against the glass. She was first here, the other Ruths slowed down by bringing a chair each and carrying it high to keep the legs clear of the gutter dust. Dinah's four chairs from her kitchen were already set out in a row beneath the mirror. When all the women got there, the chairs would form not so much a circle as a tight, thin ellipse and Ruby was glad that she'd be out the back and on her own, with the door open. Her ankle was too sore to stand for long and wait for Dinah (maybe she'd need to beg a chair to use while she prepared the tea), so Ruby sat down on the middle step to rest it and bent across her knee to ease the bandage up and slip a finger in to carry off the itching. Leaning forward, Ruby noticed something on the bottom step. Too dim, the light down here, to see it clearly, but it gave off a cloy, meaty smell. She felt her skin grow clammy. Heard Dinah puff and strain to shift the top bolt.

Dinah held the door wide. "Come in, then. Too hot for custards it is, Rube, so I thought as I'd make jellies for a change, but it turns out it's too hot for um to set."

Ruby stood up, but did not step inside. Distracted, she was, only for a moment by this Dinah, softer and confiding.

"What dun yo think, Ruby? Mix um up, shall I, wi a bit of Carnation, and call it sommat different?"

Ruby jabbed a finger at the bottom step. "We'd best get this cleared out of the road, first, before the Club comes, stepping in it."

"Get what cleared up?" Dinah frowned and peered. "A dead thing, is it, fell down off the road?" She nudged it with her shoe.

Ruby crouched down, tentative, but did not want to touch it. "I doe think as it's a creature."

"Well, whatever. Yoom right. We cor leave it there for folk to tread on. Get sommat, I will, for us to shift it."

Ruby, head tilted, examined the bundle. This close, it looked like wet rags, badly dyed in crimson. Dinah came back with the coal shovel and eased it underneath. "Let's take it out the back where we can see it." She held the shovel at arm's length before her, checking underneath to make sure that nothing dripped or fell from it. (The floor still wet, in streaks, where Dinah had just passed the mop across it.)

Dinah's house, like all those on the Breach, was built upon a slope, and while you had to step down from the street into the front end, the back end opened out on level ground. Ruby followed Dinah out into the yard. Dinah tilted up the shovel and let the bundle slop onto the ground. "I doe know what to do wi it, I'm sure. Dig an hole, I s'pose, and bury it."

Ruby crouched to peer at it again. "I doe think it was living. Rags, it is, I reckon." She unlooped the spoon from around her neck and, using the handle, tried to tease an end of rag out, but it slipped free; slapped back onto the bundle.

"Oh, gi it here, if it ay dead," said Dinah. "If its rags, put um in the scrap bin, I ull, and let um rot down." She bent and scooped the bundle up with both hands. "Though why someone ud leave a mess like this on my doorstep I cor fathom . . ."

As Dinah held the knotted mass above the scrap bin, one rag dangled free, and this one was not stained all over. Ruby saw a pattern in the corner and looked closer: a cursive, tangled monogram. She clapped a hand across her mouth. They'd found the losslinen.

Ruby pushed the Blick's bike up the steepest section of the Ludleye Road. A question set her rhythm as she walked: *the locket found, the loss-linen, and next my Almanac?* She'd have her lists again, her maps, her Twelve Impediments, all ready to take to Severnsea . . . She waited for the joy, heady and light, to rise in her, but it wouldn't come. *The empty locket and the bloody linen: what has happened to my Almanac?* So Ruby spoke her lists out loud—she'd write them out so neat, so careful, in her Almanac—and shouted down the clamor in her head.

She stopped at the Crux Coci and reached into her pocket just to check that it was there: Nan Annie's losslinen. She drew her fingertips (still tender—all that dipping in cold water, and red from all the scrubbing) over Annie's stitching: the nubbed forget-me-nots; the spindled rosemary; the loops and swirling of the monogram. She held the losslinen above her, arms outstretched, squinting up to see against the sun. The substance of the stain was still there and she knew she'd never shift it.

There had been no formal meeting, after all, and Ruby learned that finding a lost thing could be more testing, more distressing than learning to accommodate its loss; that there might be but an *instant* of rejoicing, swift-extinguished, and then a greater sorrow than before. As they teased out the linens and matched each piece up with its stitcher, the bitter grief of all the Ruths and the Naomis filled them up, spilled over. Nan Annie hadn't come down for the meeting. ("Her wants to keep herself shut up," said Glenda, "what with Len Salt leaving her tomorrow. And her's best out of *this*.")

Ruby had retreated to the back step so that Glenda and the others couldn't reel her into talk of retribution. She sat with Annie's linen, a slip of soap, a bowl filled with cold water and a brush. She used her spoon handle to swirl the linen in the water; watched it pulse, unfurl, until the water pinked. She twisted up the linen in an oozy rope and greased it with the soap; let the rope unwind and lay it on a board across her lap; took up the bristle brush and scrubbed at the not-yet-broidered parts and rubbed more gently with her finger at the stitching round the seams; poured water through the linen square again, and rubbed at it. Twisting, scrubbing, careful not to let the bristle catch; pouring, two, three more times, until the water ran through clear. She wrung the linen, pulled it flat. She folded it and put it in her pocket. The linen, found—it couldn't cancel out the loss of Captin, Ruby knew. (She told herself Nan Annie wouldn't need to be consoled for losing *her* when she had stowed away with Captin.) But it might offer a glancing consolation.

Some of the women tossed their linen into Dinah's range for burning. Some wrapped it up in paper and took it home to bury it. Some, in the quiet of their kitchens, tried to wash it out as best they could, for Dinah, Trembly Em and Glenda had not seen the wounds that carried off their Horace and their Robert, their Alfred and their Jack. They knew that there was blood; that you don't die, in war, from bruising. And among them in the quiet of their kitchens was a pained but purposeful endeavor; working at the boards and bowls until once-crimson water ran out clear.

By the time she turned off the Lean High Road, Ruby's breath came swift and shallow and her ankle throbbed, but she dropped the bike and almost ran into the house, pulling out the linen as she called out to her nan. She slipped off her shoes; pulled off her socks to feel the smooth cold of the flags. In the dim light of the kitchen the losslinen did not look much of a prize. It had gathered dark flecks; lint; grown grubby in her pocket, and the stain that looked pale enough against the sun was, in here, more like shadow. She rinsed the losslinen under the cold tap. The latch clicked at the bottom of the stairs; she twisted round to face Nan Annie in her apron with her hair covered, for dusting. Saw Annie's eyes on her discarded shoes.

"Me shoes ay got wet." She scuttled across to pick one up and held it out to Annie. "It's just me feet was hot wi coming up."

Annie said nothing as Ruby took her shoes and set them by the door, and Ruby, wary, watched Nan Annie turn to face the stairs and with an unaccustomed care, lift up the latch and press the stair-door shut, two hands, and lower the latch, slow, behind its hook. She stood there for a moment with her back to Ruby, and Ruby cast about the room to see what she'd forgotten. Her hand went to her spoon, but it was covered up and out of sight. Her hair was dry. She'd taken her dad's dinner. And yet the air in here was thick with accusation.

"I found something for yo." Ruby held the losslinen stretched out by the top corners. "It ay come clean but I can tell yo it looks better un it did." She spoke with a strained cheer. Nan Annie turned and looked at her, disdainful. "Put it on the grate, I ull, to dry."

"I doe know how to thank yo, Ruby." Nan Annie's tone was flat, gray, veiled, and Ruby sucked her lip in as she laid the losslinen across the rail, not knowing yet what her nan was withholding.

Nan Annie reached into the pocket of her pinny. "Ud this help, dun yo think, wi saying thank yo? I got something as I heard as yo bin looking for." She held out a book tied with a shoelace. She set it on the table and, with the same controlled precision she'd used on the stair latch, undid the knot that kept it shut. The book fanned open on the table, and Annie waited for a moment till it settled, then laid the shoelace between its pages.

Ruby stepped forward to look closer and a thrill surged through her. "Yo found my Almanac!" Flooded, Ruby was, by a sweet, rushing delight that swept away all caution, all the flinching and hard-garnered circumspection that she'd mustered these past seven years. Isa was not harboring the Almanac (*I never thought her was!*) and it would not, like the locket, be laid out in the window of the shop and, now she had it back, she did not care where it had been, only that she had retrieved her history (scrappy and unstuck though it now was) of all her lists, and Beth's; of all Ruby's desires; her aspiration.

She went to pick it up, but Annie plucked it from the table and pressed it in between her own hands.

"I cor tell yo how pleased I am, Nan, to see it!"

"Doe thank me, Ruby Abel. I day find it."

"Who did, then? Tell me so as I can tell um thank yo. Who gid it yo?"

"Someone who cares more for yo than yo have merited."

Ruby watched Nan Annie pass the Almanac from one hand to another. She wanted to feel it weighing down her pocket; wanted to run her thumb along the spine, but her caution was returning like cold fingers playing on her neck, so Ruby did not ask if she could have it back, not yet. Nan Annie had taken possession of the book and would not readily surrender. *Maybe,* thought Ruby, *her has read inside and seen as it was Beth's and her's forgot how it was passed from her, through Jamie Abel, down to me. Maybe her thinks as it ay mine to have.*

"Me dad gid me it one birthday," Ruby said. "I day take it, I day."

"I ay accusing yo of taking it."

What then? Ruby thought, her fingers round the spoon. *What is it, then, as yoom accusing me of doing?*

Nan Annie wet her thumb and smudged through pages by the corner until she found the one she wanted—"Now, where is it?"—spread them open and, in a chapel voice, she read, " 'What I Shall Take to Sea. Some Fairy soap. Two vests. A small packet of tea.' "

Ruby pressed the spoon against her chest. So here it was: her guilt, laid out in groceries. "Nannie . . ." she began, but did not know how to continue.

Nan Annie glanced up in her direction but did not catch her eye. A practiced reader with the Gospel at the lectern. " 'What I Need to Stow Away with Captin.' Nice, it is, to see yoom practicing your writing. It says here it was just last Sunday as yo wrote this bit out. See, here—yo've writ *this* neat." She held the book out toward Ruby, and ran her pointed finger underneath the words. " 'A square of towel,' her's writ, 'a pair of pants; some sugar lumps; a blanket.' Yo dun this for an exercise at school, ay yo, our Ruby, because I know as these lists am all for make-believe. Sure I am of this, because yo ud not torment me wi running off to *sea* of all places as yo could choose to run to." Nan Annie crossed the room toward the grate. "Yoom looking clammy, Rube. Yo need a cup of tea."

Nan Annie dropped the Almanac into her pinny pocket, and as she passed by Ruby, she tilted Ruby's chin up with a finger. "Yoom playing. Yoom pretending. We know that. Yo ud no more run off to the sea than jump into the Cut." She shook the kettle; held it out. "Fill it up, Ruby, ud yo, while I see to the fire."

"So can I have it back, then, Nan?" Ruby said, light as she could, "sose I can do more practice-writing?"

"Yo doe want *this* book, Ruby!" Nan Annie, kneeling on the rug before the grate, plucked the book from her pinny once again. Flicked through it. "Scraps of *this* and bits of *that* stuck in it. And these pages ripped! A mess, it is!"

"Ripped?" she said, indignant. "I ay ripped it up!" She walked over to Annie; knelt beside her.

"What dun yo call this?" And Annie pointed out a narrow jagged flap where a page had been clumsily torn out. There was still a portion of a cutting pasted on the flap; this was the page where she'd stuck THE GRISLY CATCH.

"I day do this," she said.

"And here?" Nan Annie thumbed through till she found another ripped-out page, where SPEARED BODY IN THE CAVE: DEVELOPMENTS had been. "And here? And here? Yo day do that either?"

Each torn-out page had held a cutting about the killing, or the notes recording Ruby's speculation about Cass.

"A mess, it is," Nan Annie said. "Tell yo what. I ull buy yo a new notebook for your birthday. One wi nothing in it, sose yo can write on *clean* paper wi nothing printed on."

"But I like *that* one, Nannie." Ruby, urgent and cajoling. "Me mom wrote in it too. A picture of her, there is, in the back." She showed her Beth's and Jamie Abel's photo. "See?"

Nan Annie sat back on her heels. "Who gid yo this?" Not sharp or rough, her tone (and indicating danger), but thick, as if she needed to cough her gullet clear. She held the book out at arm's length so she could focus properly.

"In it, it was, when my dad gid me the book—the photograph."

"Go on."

"He said as Captin took it when Jamie Abel come back from the War."

The photo fell out; fluttered down to Annie's lap. "Well, yo ay stuck it in right, Ruby. I ay sure as yo should have sommat like this, if yo cor see to it as it doe fall out."

Ruby wanted to protest that it was Belle's fault; that Belle had pulled Ruby into the Cut, and the Almanac was wetted in the fall and the photo had worked loose and that it was not her doing. She sank her nails into the soft crook of her arm and knew she could not offer this defense.

"Hard it is, at your age. Fourteen, bar a week or two. Yo ay responsible" (Nan Annie waved the unstuck photograph and tucked it in her pocket), "but yoom too old for make-believing. Too old for writing around the edges of a book. Yo need to gi it up, now, Ruby. Planning pretend journeys; shopping lists . . ."

A jabbing in her heart: Ruby's hand flew to the spoon and formed a fist around the handle. The sharp lip pointed inward, and Ruby dug the spoon into her chest as if she could scoop out the barbed, hot coil that writhed beneath her ribs. A fervid boldness coursed through her and she pushed herself up from her knees and rested, ready, crouching on her toes. She looked straight at Nan Annie. "It ay pretend."

"No." Nan Annie shook her head, but did not look at Ruby. The dull thunk of the fire-door, opened and set back. "Yo like to *think* it ay pretend, but we both know as yo ay going to the sea! Yo *tell* yourself as yo ull go there one day." Contempt had hardened Annie's face.

"Yo make your lists. Yoom giddy wi the thought on it, but yoom like me, our Ruby. Yo woe do anything about it. Yo'd never do a thing like that to me. Good Ruby. Loyal Ruby. Yoom Cradle, yo am, like me, to the grave. Besides, I checked wi Captin—just to be certain as he ay planned to smuggle yo off wi him down to Whalemouth. He said as yo ay mentioned leaving to him, Ruby."

The fire yapping, gold. Later, Ruby cursed herself that she had not moved more quickly. But how could she have known what Nan Annie would do? Ruby pushed herself up on her feet; Nan Annie in between her and the grate.

"Joked about it, we did," Annie said. "Said as he'd best check as yo doe creep on overnight. Well, I satisfied myself. There ay no danger of yo stowing, Ruby."

What will her do to me to keep me here? Ruby twisted up her finger in the spoon cord and moved back toward the door. *Cut me, will her? Will her bleed me dry?*

"He day want to tell yo. He day want a good-bye, but—what is it?" She craned to check the time on the mantel clock. "A quarter before five? Len, on *Ferret;* he ull have left the Cradles by the hour."

And then the flames snapped out as Annie tossed the Almanac deep into the oven.

Ruby wondered later if she should have tried to pull the book out of the fire; instead, she had stood silent in the doorway, steadying herself against the jamb. She watched Annie, with a cloth around her hand, lift up the fire-door and ease it shut; Nan Annie moving around the kitchen, making tea. The tap of Annie's shoes against the flags; the water coming to the boil; the mantel clock . . . Her nan was saying how she wouldn't let the pot sit; how she'd make it weak, the tea, what with Ruby looking clammy, looking pale. This Annie, not veiled now, but unguarded, cruel, her words tumbling out of her as if she'd secured a treaty after long negotiation and no longer needed to be careful what she said. Annie, swaggering and bountiful; victorious.

Her thinks her has me. Ruby pressed the spoon against her skin. Watched Annie at the table, pouring tea; those bird-bones on the insides of her wrists; the skin stretched not-quite-tight between them.

Her thinks her's done enough to keep me here. She glanced up at the clock. Not ten to, yet, and two miles to the Cut.

Annie, in the larder. As Ruby left, she heard her nan say that there was a bit of cake left, if she fancied.

Ruby had never seen Nan Annie run before; she didn't see her now but she could tell her nan was running down the Lean High Road after her by the way her shouts advanced and then retreated; advanced again, retreated with the rising and the falling of her feet. Ruby did not look back but cycled hard, her bare soles flinching on the pedals, although the pedaling had no effect here with the road sloping so steep. Annie could not catch her, Ruby knew, but Annie's calls, raw, hoarse, distraught ("Doe go, Ruby! Doe leave me!"), followed Ruby down the road and stayed with her all the way down to the Cradles.

There was a note on Captin's table, thanking Ruby for all the gifts she'd been so kind as to leave him. "I will take the licorice and kali to my nieces for their girls, but I will eat the ginger biscuits on my way." She felt inside the cavity below the sink. Her safe, her Boat Fund, wasn't there.

Chapter 21

Mark, *v.* To notice or keep the eye upon; to ascertain by observation.

SHE SAT on Captin's couch till it grew dark. A small indignant crowd of people wanting chips had gathered at the front (she was not the only one who'd been led to think that he would leave tomorrow), so Ruby let herself out through the back, and with one hand trailing on the brick of the Horn Lane houses and one hand fixed around the spoon, she walked along the towpath and under Wytepole Bridge, toward the Deadarm. She had nowhere else to go. She'd knocked at Isa's and called up at Truda's window, but no one answered and there was no light inside. She'd beaten at the green gate with her raised fists, her forearms, but no face appeared up at the office window.

There was no traffic on the canal after dark and so the towpath was not lit, but shards of light fell from the windows of the steelworks onto the surface of the water. The Cut glinted, its surface cluttered and undredged. Flimsy rafts of twigs and reeds had matted at the water's edge and Ruby kept the fingers of her right hand on the wall to stop herself from stepping out and testing them to see if they would hold her. The Cut narrowed to a chasm here, with high bricked walls on either side. Somewhere above her, somewhere to the right, a roar burst out and rang around the Cut—that great shouted groan, it was, that a gathering of men make when they're disappointed. *Some game with betting in the Leopard,* Ruby thought, and this led her to think of Captin, going for his Bass, and this thought was like a tight hand at her throat.

It was darker as she turned off for the Deadarm. No tall, bright windows here; no furnaces still burning. A few casements were lit in the house-backs that loomed six feet above the towpath, opposite the Deadarm, but the light from them was meager and constrained. Ruby looked up along the house-backs for the gully that ran through the folds and back out to the Breach.

The workshops down here were squat shacks or open sheds; the men who worked them went back to their families or the Leopard in the evenings. Except for Jamie Abel. She found his island readily enough—the only one with a dim, sickly light leaching from a lantern on a nail. It was only now she wondered how she'd get across, but then remembered Jamie's town-side gangplank. He never used it, Ruby knew, and polite visitors, if they crossed at all, would wait for him to lower down *his* drawbridge, but regulation meant he had to have one anchored to the land.

When she had wiped her toes, cacky, against the grass on the slope below the gully, she walked along the towpath a few feet until she stepped on wood instead of clay. His narrow bridge was fixed at one end—hinges, brackets—a foot in from the Cut-edge and the length of it sunk across the towpath so that horses wouldn't trip on it. Her pulse quickened and she pressed a finger on the spoon. Seven years, it was, since she had tried to set this gangway onto Jamie Abel's island, and last time she had tried to get across he'd had to pluck her, bleeding, from the water, and that was when it had all started with Nan Annie. Ruby glanced toward the island, but she could not see her father—by now he would have settled for the night on the horn-sack mattress underneath his workbench. If she did this quietly enough he would not know that she was coming until she was on his island, and then he'd be too late to try to stop her.

She'd never raised the bridge herself, but she'd stood beside her father every working day and watched him do this. Every day, before he left her. She crouched down and felt along the plank until she found the unfixed end and eased it up to rest on her left shoulder. She stood, pushing up against the wood. A dangling length of rope slapped hard against her. It was secured, she recalled, to a ring set in the free end of the plank, and she remembered how her father (in the days when he slept up at Hunting Tree, in the days when they came here together) taught her to check that the rope hung clear behind you as you raised the bridge up, that it wasn't tangled up about your feet. She walked forward till the plank was all-but vertical. It stood taller than her by a good yard, and Ruby set her feet wide and turned her shoulder in to bear the weight of it. Just a foot or so now between her and the Cut-edge, but Ruby, with the bridge leaning against her, could not think too much about this. That night when she'd brought the jersey for her father, the bridge had been too heavy and the rope had slipped and burned her hands and she'd been tangled in it. But she was older, now, and stronger. She held the rope taut; let the bridge swing forward a little out across the water, then, leaning back against the wood-weight, kept the rope tight; paid it out, hand over hand, until she held the bridge above the edge of Jamie's island. Too heavy now to hold, it was: the rope slid through her palms and out across the Cut, the wood clapped on the stone. She did not wait: the falling bridge had probably roused her father like a loud thump on a door. With her arms stretched out for balance, leaning forward, Ruby shuffled out across the black and shifting waters of the Cut.

Ruby did not find her father standing in the doorway with a hammer raised to knock out the intruder; she did not want to call him, to alarm him, and Ruby, thrilled by what she had accomplished, found she liked being here alone. There was a sallow light cast from the lantern, good enough to see by, enough to ensure she was not afraid of tripping up and falling in the water. She played with the curving shadow that she cast against the hull of the once-beached, cradled boat, flinging her arms wide as if to hold it. Jamie's ladder was still there. *I will lie down in this boat,* she thought. *I'll lie flat beneath the shutts, and I will stay there till the boat is on the water.* She climbed up and peered over the bow into the belly of the boat. It was filled up with a pitch-thick dark, so she climbed down again.

She stood in the pooled light outside her father's workshop; imagined that she'd find her father sleeping. In the morning she would bring him tea and he would say, "What's this, Rube?" and Ruby would tell him how Annie'd burned her Almanac; remind him how he said as she should come to him if things got bad at Hunting Tree.

But Ruby didn't find her father sleeping. She found him standing by his workbench with his coat on, flicking an unlit Woodbine from finger to finger, and, sitting on the spindled chair beside him, her Nan Annie, with Ruby's shoes sat squared at Annie's feet and ready to go walking.

As they walked home, Nan Annie's hand locked round her wrist, Ruby pinched her belly through her shirt, cursing herself (*Yoom fogging saft!*) for waiting all that time at Captin's and losing her best chance to get away. Why had she not run west along the towpath when she'd seen that Captin had already left? Why had she not run round Blickses Kink and up toward the lock? *Ferret* could have been stalled there for a good twenty minutes and Ruby could have hidden herself in among the children who lingered around the lock gates; she could have jumped down to Captin's boat as she came out on the low side of the lock. Why had she not, instead of sitting in the dark and pulling horsehair from the couch, begged a passing boatman to let her travel on with him to Ludleye Port? Why had she not run back across the drawbridge instead of standing slack-jawed in the doorway at the Deadarm while Jamie Abel said that it was Belle who'd found the Almanac—Ruby must have dropped it by the Deadarm—but he who'd sent it up to Annie, not wanting their Ruby to come to any harm? (And at the thought of Jamie Abel standing with Nan Annie, Ruby felt a sob roll in her, rising like a breaker.)

I did not do these things, she thought, *because my nan is right. I am like her. I ay got the nerve to leave the Cradles.*

The moon emerged; dispersed a thin and grudging light, enough to steer them clear of ditches, to keep them on course in the middle of the road. They did not speak. Nan Annie went a step or so ahead and tugged Ruby up the hill behind her, not because Ruby dragged deliberately behind, but Ruby's ankle throbbed and she could not take the steep hill any faster.

Nan Annie did not take her straight to Hunting Tree as Ruby feared, but pulled her off the road at Kenelm's Field, along the rutty track and toward Trembly Em's. This did not give Ruby any comfort, and she called out to her nan, "A bit late, ay it, for a visit? Woe her be in bed?"

Annie stopped and turned to look at Ruby as if she had forgotten she was there. "Expecting me, her is, so we am going."

Slow, they skirted round the field, Nan Annie picking her way, peering at the ground before her lest *she* should turn an ankle, lifting her feet high before the next step; and Ruby saw her nan and thought of Belle and her bird-gait. She and Annie edged along the field and Ruby watched for where the ground pitched down toward the Gutter; thought of the Blackbird, down there with the satchel; the Blackbird and her frogbit-threats to Ruby; she thought of Isa, blinded by a stone thrown on a beach; of Anselm, Isa's brother, blindfolded and bound high on a cliff. Nan Annie was not malicious; was not brutal like the Blackbird, Ruby thought. *All as her's done is make me frightened of the edges.*

The air was dense and fuggy in Em's carriage, the windows clouded with the steam from something boiling on the hotplate; a scraggy stew with dumplings that Em ladled onto a tin plate for Ruby, careful not to let the juices spill.

"Yoom starving, I bet, since yo missed your tea."

And indeed, Ruby found that when she sat down at the narrow table, bolted to the floor, her belly snarled as if it had been startled. She watched the women as she ate: Nan Annie was sat rigid on the couch, and fiddled with the flimsy crocheted cover on the arm; beside her, Em had taken out a box of good-luck trinkets, and, lifting out the odd one, polished it up on her pinny, held it to the light. They had things to say to her, they were waiting, and when her hunger had been blunted, Ruby's belly twisted up in apprehension. She stood up and carried her plate to the tin bowl on the washing stand, but Em told her not to bother with the crocks.

"Sit down. They can wait."

Relieved, perplexed, she saw that Em regarded her with some of her old familiar affection. Mollified, Em was, and Ruby, unnerved, looked back and forth between the women. She sat back down. Waited.

It was Trembly Em who cleared her throat as if to bring them all to order, Trembly Em who spoke first, loud and sure. She set her trinket box beside her; laid a hand, protective, over Annie's knee; addressed herself to Ruby. "Your nan come here to see me when yo went off after Captin on that bicycle. Her day know if her ud see yo again, Ruby. Her doe know what's got into yo. But 'Yo ay got cause to worry, now,' I told her."

"Yo told her what?" Her nan had seen the Almanac: she'd found out Ruby's plans to stow away. What more was there to know? Anxious, wanting for some courage, she felt for the spoon through her shirt, and then, seeing Em's eyes twitch toward her fingers, dropped her hand into her lap.

"I told her," Em said, sitting up the straighter, "I told her as yo've good as been bewitched, and as we ull see to that."

Ruby twined her hands together in her lap to stop herself from reaching for her spoon; Isa's spoon. "Bewitched?" She creased her frown in what, she hoped, looked like confusion. Not that Ruby thought that Isa had been weaving spells to draw her in; not that Ruby had been charmed by her (for Isa Fly was strange rather than charming). Not so much what Isa Fly had *done* (a gentle shielding pressure, she remembered: Isa's hand, curved around her crown; Isa bending with a bandage and a needle, mending Ruby's gashed and bloody knee); but rather what she *was* that fascinated Ruby. For something deep in her had chimed with Isa, binding and expectant as a rhyme.

"Yes, Ruby: bewitched. Your nannie knows all as has gone wrong in this town since that Fly girl come to plague us. The precious things her's played wi, took away; my locket." (Her fingers flew up to her throat to check that it was back there.) "The losslinen, and Dinah's picture spoiled with that tallow."

"Yo got your locket back! And the losslinen! And how can yo be certain as *her* did it? My *Almanac* was lost, but Isa day take that!"

Annie's head snapped up. "I cor hold her accountable for stealing your book off yo, but I can look to what yo put down in it! Yo put as yo ud stow away, and I cor think as *yo* dreamed that up on your own! Em says as it was Isa Fly, it must of been, who goaded yo to run away to sea! Isa Fly who said as her ud take yo wi her!"

Ruby frowned and said she hadn't written *that* down in her book.

"Oh, Ruby, yo day *need* to!" Trembly Em was watching her with a head-tilting sympathy, her jowly nod saying, I *know, of all women, how it is to be beguiled.*

On and on went Trembly Em, setting out her evidence against Isa Fly and Ruby countering, and all the while Em fiddled with the trinkets in her box, laying them out in a jostling line.

Ruby pressed against the spoon to give her boldness. "Yoom pledging friendship wi each other every week, all of you in the Ruth and the Naomis! But it's only when a stranger comes as yo show what yoom made of. Yoom all suspicion, trading tattle! Branding Isa Fly a thief when no one has the proof of it!"

Annie looked at Ruby, but she did not chastise. Tired, she looked, pulled tight. "Em says her has proof."

"What proof?" Ruby said, and anger against Em and all the other Ruths flared up in her. "The witch-bottle, yo mean?"

"It got this back for me!" Em fondled the locket at her neck.

Nan Annie turned to stare, incredulous, at Em. "A witch-bottle? Yo *day*!" And Ruby felt a shift in Annie's attitude to Em; an uncoupling.

"That's proof, is it?" said Ruby, folding her arms high around her chest like she'd seen Dinah do when she wanted convincing. "Heating up your wee on someone's fire and then all watching? Someone gets a fever and yo take it as a proof that her's a thief so as yo can convict her of theft-magic!"

Em shook her head and spoke with such a resolute authority as Ruby'd never heard in her before. "That spoon around your neck, Rube: tell your nannie where yo got it from."

Ruby put her hand over the place where the spoon lay underneath her shirt. Thought of Isa, yanked out of a rock pool by the spoon cord. "Someone gid it me to keep me safe in water."

"Someone?"

"Isa." Ruby said, and seeing a look pass between the women, added, quick, that Isa hadn't used the spoon to put a charm on her; she'd given it from kindness. Ruby looked, pleading, at her nan. "I told her yo was worried about me falling into water. Her said as it ud keep me safe, Nan, that was all. And her was right. It worked." Her finger was twisted so tight in the cord that the tip of it was growing numb. She let it loose and the blood rushed back into her finger. "I fell right in the Cut last Sunday. I day tell yo. But I day drown, day I? I'm here. Dry, I am, and safe."

"Safe?"

Ruby's belly tightened. "Safe." Cautious, Ruby spoke. "I'm safe."

"That spoon did not keep yo *safe*!"

Ruby, defensive, wrapped a hand around it through the cloth.

"Yo thought as iron ud keep yo from a drowning?" Nan Annie's knuckles locked across her head; white, taut, straining with the effort of keeping all her anger in. "I see her, Ruby. Every time I am near water I see my child wi'out her mother to protect her. There is worse things than being dead. Lost and alive and pecked at on a rock. Gulls feeding off my baby's soft, soft cheeks. Fish jumping up to nibble on her toes . . ."

Ruby blew her breath out; *that* spoon hadn't worked, she said, but this one—the one that Ruby wore—had saved Isa Fly when she was little, and now it had saved Ruby.

"Doe speak as if I'm saft! As if I'm simple!"

Em patted Annie on the arm to calm her down. "Come on now, chick. The girl doe understand."

Ruby looked between them: what did she not understand?

"Isa Fly gived yo a spoon," Em's words were slow and even, "that was not hers to gid."

"Yoom saying as her stole that spoon an all? Yoom saying as there ay no more spoons but *this* one in all England?" She tugged at the cord around her neck.

"Did the Fly girl say where her had got it from?"

"From her Dad, Moonie. Isa said as Moonie gid it her."

Em shook her head violently. She braced her fingertips against her temples, as if she hoped to hold her head steady between them. "Well, that cor be right . . ."

Ruby, loud and sharp, knowing she took advantage of Em's sudden and aggressive discomposure, demanded to know who the victim was, who Em thought Isa Fly had stolen from.

"Me." Annie, head bowed, pinched herself in the soft crook of her elbow. "That spoon was made for Gracie. For my baby."

"Yoom saying Isa Fly took your dead baby's spoon? The same baby who drownded thirty years ago when her was wearing it?"

Annie nodded.

"That's saft! How can yo say as it's the same?" Ruby shook her head. "Yo might as well say Isa Fly's that dead baby raised up from the waters!"

Em, shocked, drew herself together: that witch was no more kin to Annie than Em was, and Ruby was a fiend to dare to say it.

"Washed up, it could have been, from out the wreck, and turned up on the beach or anywhere!" Ruby thought of treasure seekers, down at Sawdy Point. Thought of the body, caught up in the cave.

Bleak, Nan Annie looked; bewildered. She said she didn't care how Isa Fly had come by Grace's spoon, but she would like it back.

"Look at the mark, Annie." Em wiped at her ruddy cheeks with the edge of her sleeve. "That's what yo come for."

"It's Isa's spoon and her gid it to *me*."

"Look at yo, Rube! Yoom under her sway! Since yo got that spoon about your neck yo've even got a *look* of Isa Fly!"

Ruby wrapped her fingers around the spoon handle as she saw Em struggling to get up from the couch.

"Show Annie!" Em lurched toward her and, seeing that wild anger in her eyes, Ruby thought that Trembly Em might slap her, bite her, take her head and shake it from her shoulders. Unsteadied, Ruby was, and all the life was seeping from her legs. She pulled the spoon up slowly by its cord and laid it, light, against her shirt. It was just a circle, she told Annie, and no circle could prove that Em had made it. Nan Annie stood before her and Ruby felt the breath against her face as Annie, gentle, slipped her palm under the spoon and let it rest there; traced the length of it with a finger; turned it over. And Ruby saw, rather than heard, the sob rise up in Nan Annie, rough and sudden, as if it shook her by the shoulders. "It ay a circle, Ruby." Annie said. "It's a moon."

"So?" said Ruby, rough. Then, more gentle, for she'd never seen her nan so thinned, so emptied, she added, "What's that prove?"

"Her puts a moon on all the things her makes, Em does. Her always has."

. . .

Later on that night, when Ruby, spent and leaching, feverish, was laid out in the tower at St. Barbara's, the sorors watching over her would try to work out how it came about that one of these two women who, they knew, loved Ruby most in all the Cradles, had sunk a whetted blade into her shoulder. And, not being certain that it was an accident, not being certain that they wouldn't come for her again, the Sorors kept the door to the tower bolted through the night.

Soror Brigid, it was, tall and striding, who carried Ruby all along the cloister to the tower, lit by little votive lights in niches scooped out of the rough plaster; Brigid's hand pressing Ruby's head close to her chest to keep Ruby from jolting, to keep the shoulder-gash from splaying itself wide. Queasy, Ruby felt—this Priory air too clean, too sweet, too rich with lavender and thyme.

Soror Ebba tried to staunch the wound; Soror Alethea bound her shoulder, tight around the chest and underneath her arm. Thumbs on Ruby's forehead, breath warm on Ruby's face; their fingertips pushed through her hair and pressed on her neck to check for lumps and swellings. They sponged her with a flannel soaked in borax and warm water to flush the flecks of dirt from Ruby's cut. With warm, firm hands, they laid her out in bed, and Ruby feebly bucked and flinched and flexed against the pain. They laid her down so gently, did the sorors, trying not to bruise her. By then the night had already begun to ebb away, and Ruby slid into a gauzy sleep.

She heard Trembly Em and Annie in her dreams; she felt the pressure of them on the bed, against her legs, even though the tower was locked against them. She saw Em once more take out a long, thin nail and hold its head with trembling hands against the little indentation on the shaft of Ruby's spoon. Saw, once more, how snugly it had fitted. Heard her nan cry out, and Em declaiming, "Her has stole more than my locket, more than spoons!" She'd taken with them a look of each child they were made for; that was the blackest witching, Em said, and it needed punishing.

.   .   .

A linen rustle woke her, a scuffing on the tiles; Soror Ebba taking round hot milk. Too quick, she opened her eyes and the room tipped and lurched before her. Seasick, Ruby was: yanked in and pulled back, drawn by her fever too close into all that lay around her; a stubbed quill of goose feather stabbing through the pillow-case; through the window, larch tops flicking in the wind; parched, baked clay and charcoal from the burner working on the other side of Ludleye Lean; smoke writhing up from Soror Eva's kiln like a signal Ruby couldn't understand. Such insistent, tyrannical lucidity. The baked earth floor below her, dried, compressed, and dried again. Ruby felt that she was drying, too, with all the life-blood seeping from this deep crack in her shoulder. Felt as if she could split right down the middle. Thought of her Nan Annie with her hands pressed to her head as if to hold herself together, and wondered if she worried about cracking, too; if this was a flaw that ran through all of them. They were clay-made and they were cracked and all the time they were just smoothing bits of sand over these cracks with their feet.

Even in her sleep she held the spoon tight in her good fist in case Em should try again to take it from her. Em had insisted Ruby give the spoon back to her nan: "It's all her's got of her lost baby and her's due it." But Ruby had protested, telling Em how Annie'd burned the Almanac: "Beth's book's all burned, and that was all *I* got of my lost mom." And then Ruby'd asked what good it could do for her nan to have it back: "A spoon woe bring your baby back to yo."

They lifted her to change the sopping sheets for dry ones smelling of burned wood and lavender. Ebba held her like a baby on her lap; pressed a bowl of sugared milk up against Ruby's lips; cradled the back of Ruby's head with a steady hand, and Ruby's tongue lapped at the corner of her mouth as one long drop ran curving down her chin.

.   .   .

She woke later that same day when the sun was high, giddy after her thin, scratchy sleep. Nan Eliza was beside her and on her lap a glazed plate, glossy as a cherry. Two cobs of oat bread; one neat, round as a doorknob, the other broken down to crumbs; a curving scoop of butter in a spoon. She tried to raise her fingers to the plate, but felt a deep tug in her shoulder, and so Eliza fed her, crumb by crumb.

She dreamed, again, of Trembly Em and of her knife. (Or maybe just remembered it, but in her fevered state she couldn't really tell.) Ruby hadn't seen Em snatch it up, and nor, she thought, had Annie. (For watching fear and horror spread through Annie like a stain, Ruby knew that her nan never *could* have carried out the threat she'd made to bleed her if she went near water, years before.) "Her's due the spoon," Em had insisted. "It ay Isa Fly's to gid and Isa Fly ull pay for thieving it!" Again and again, Em called out all the things they'd do to Isa Fly now it was proved that she had stolen these things from them. She'd tried to cut the cord round Ruby's neck, or so Ruby had thought . . . Annie'd tried to ease the knife away, but Em's fingers had grown stiff around the knife and Annie had struggled to wrest it clear. Ruby, sick with fear, had tried to run past to the door, but Em had reached past Annie and that was when the blade, aimed for the cord, sliced into her. Someone had slipped a scream in through one of Ruby's ears and as much as Ruby shook her head the screaming was tight lodged there and she couldn't work it free . . . Annie, grappling with Em and trying to pull her clear. Em's shaking fit had taken hold of her and she was felled. She'd brought down Annie; Ruby with her. Ruby had pulled her legs free, scrambled backward and, before Annie could extricate herself and catch her, Ruby escaped through the carriage door, making for the sorors.

When Ruby woke again, Eliza was still sitting close beside her and the sun was low and Ruby cooler. Ebba lifted up the compress and smiled and thanked her god and said that Ruby's wound was gumming now and that she had stopped bleeding. Worn and sore and rusted, Ruby was—the wound-side of her nightdress was stiff and crusted red. She took her time in moving; unbent her thumb, unwound her fingers from the spoon and, when Ebba had moved off, she turned it to show Nan Eliza the full moon; the mark that proved to Em that Isa Fly was guilty of theft magic.

"*This* is what it was as got me cut," she whispered. "Em says as this is her moon marked on here." Her tongue was thick and all her mouth was dry as she explained what Em had said about the spoon and about Isa stealing it. Eliza held a glass up to her mouth; a handkerchief below her chin to catch the drips.

"Ar, well. Em's always said as yo cor trust the moon." She whispered to match Ruby. "Comes and goes, he does. But still, yo cor resist him. Yoom sucked in like the tide and then spat out. One night he's flooding yo wi all his light and just a few nights gone his light's all spent and yoom left in the dark . . ."

"But what if it *isn't* a full moon?" Ruby reached her hand out and laid it on Eliza's lap. She made a circle with her thumb and forefinger. "What if it's just a round, a nail head?"

"Her *meant* it for a moon." She lifted Ruby's hand and moved it gently like a lamed bird back onto the bed, stroking it. Nan Eliza told her that Em first put the mark on the trinket she'd made for her first baby. She knew that Jonah wasn't to be trusted; that some of him—his fickleness, his unfaithfulness—was living in the baby's blood and in his marrow. Em lived by superstition, and her reckoning was that you couldn't have more than one moon in your life: she thought if Jonah's children had one strung about their necks already, they'd be free of him and all his influence.

Jonah knew about the moon-mark: it was the same mark that he used to brand his tools, and Em didn't shrink from telling him exactly what she meant by putting it on Grace's little spoon. He thought that she was mocking him and hated her for it, and Annie too, for putting that spoon around Grace's neck.

"I still doe get why it has to be a moon," said Ruby.

"Ay yo seen a picture of your grandad? That big flat face?" She bent in close to Ruby and Ruby felt Eliza's lips dabbing at her ear. "Em didn't want her father to find out that it was Jonah who had

messed with her and got her throwing herself out of trees: he swore
he'd kill the boy. Em didn't want *that* sitting on her conscience. So Em
gid Jonah an ekename. Besides him, I am the only one as knows it."
Eliza fingered Ruby's spoon. "Doe tell Em I told yo . . ." She pressed
a finger onto Ruby's lips. "Emily has always called him Moonie."

Chapter 22

Net, *n*. A moral or mental snare, trap or entanglement.

RUBY WAITED till she was certain Nan Eliza was asleep. Ebba'd tried to talk Eliza into going back to her own bed, but Eliza swore she'd stay, and now she was slumped down in the chair at Ruby's side. Eliza's lashes flickered; jaws tight, knobbed out at the hinges; eyes moving like bare knees beneath a sheet. Ruby waited till the others were, if not sleeping, then calm, stilled—just two patients, besides her, in the tower room that night; an elderly soror who took apoplectic turns and opened her eyes only when Ebba spoke sweetly in her ear and smoothed almond oil into her hands; a younger woman from the other side of Muckeleye who, when she wasn't pacing round the tower, lay with her face against the wall. Ebba had retired for the night and Soror Alberta, after checking on her charges, had slipped out with the jug, perhaps to bring back more milk from the kitchen, and locked the door behind her.

Ruby swung her feet round to the floor and crossed to the nearest window, leaving toe-prints on the baked-earth tiles that glinted for a second by the stovelight and then faded. She rehearsed the news she had to take to Isa: *Jonah was called Moonie;* and the second part, its mirror (for Ruby was as certain of this now as she was of her own re-flection), *Moonie Fly is Jonah.*

With her good hand she eased one heavy drape toward her and a sail of moonlight swung into the room. Quick, she slipped behind the cotton twill and pulled it closed behind her. The window, set low in the wall, was open wide and straining for a breeze.

She sat on the sill, swung around her legs and gauged the drop below her: ten foot or so. She couldn't lower herself down by her arms, not with her shoulder split, but neither could she linger here till morning and go out through the door, for Trembly Em was set on harming Isa, and there was only Ruby who knew this and would warn her. No reason to suppose that Em would go for Isa Fly tonight—and Isa (she remembered with a stab) might already be out of reach, half the way to Severnsea in the back of Truda's car . . .

Soror Ebba had prescribed that Ruby needed bed-rest for at least a week while they augmented her depleted bloods with beef and greens and stout. And Brigid had stood by Ruby's bed that evening, her fingers resting light on Ruby's knees, and said that they wanted to be satisfied that neither Em nor Annie had *meant* her harm, that it was safe to let her leave; that there had been an accident. The sorors would be firm in this, she knew; she did not doubt that they'd keep her locked in until her cheeks were ruddy and her blood was rich and plentiful again.

But Ruby had made her vow: she'd follow Isa. So when Alberta's key clicked in the lock again, Ruby jumped, her good hand on the spoon.

A hollow leaping in her belly, then the hillside rushing at her knees and tipping her; she fell forward into bracken, and a searing, white-hot, branded Ruby's shoulder.

A ditch ran like a dry moat around the tower wall, and Ruby followed it, her fingers trailing on the brick. Brambles snagged the thin skin on her ankles; stingers brushed her fingers, raising little swollen discs like Braille.

She had been overwhelmed by it at first. Knocked flat, winded, she had fallen back against the pillow: this notion that her grandfather had not drowned in a wreck but had made himself another life as Moonie . . . and each significance had unrolled over her like one wave unfolding itself on another, and between them, Ruby could hardly catch her breath. The lost daughter that Isa had been dismissed to find was Jonah's daughter.

Ruby had asked Eliza if they'd ever called Beth by a different name; she'd barked a short, harsh laugh and said that Jonah liked to set himself apart. He didn't call her Beth; he had his own name for his daughter, and Annie hated it. He called the baby Lilibet or Lil. Now she, Beth's daughter, would make a present of herself to Isa: *it is me you have been searching for. I am the child of the lost daughter, and you at last have found me. Take me to the sea and to your father, and I will make a peace with him, for Beth.* And beneath it all, this new current that buoyed her up and tossed her, light and giddy: *Isa Fly is half an aunt to me.* And Trembly Em was wrong: Isa Fly had not *stolen* a look of the babies with the moon-mark around their neck. They'd shared it with her, and with their white-faced father.

"Isa is my aunt," she said, aloud, and tipped her head back to direct her whispered declaration to the stars, to the full moon. And then her belly lurched, remembering how she had come to learn this—Em's mark on Ruby's spoon—and how Trembly Em had sworn not to suffer witch-thieves to live . . . Em was unhinged and Ruby had the proof. "Look what her's done to me," she'd say to Isa when she found her. She would find a boat and she would stow away. New blood seeped through the right arm of her nightie where the cut had come unknit with the wrench of the fall. "My aunt will sew me up," she said out loud. *If, that is, she hasn't left already.* And as she followed the ditch round the tower and up toward the moonlit ridge of Parry Lean, she made up a new rhyme for her aunt to keep the thought of Isa gone at bay:

> *If yoom wiser*
> *Go to Isa*
> *And her'll mend un stitch un hide ya.*

She chanted this beneath her thinning breath, stumbling down the Hollow Way, avoiding the Lean High Road and her nan at Hunting Tree; avoiding Kenelm's Field and Trembly Em.

.   .   .

There was no call for people to walk down Horn Lane that Friday evening, not now that Captin's chip shop had been shut, so it was almost dawn when Truda came on Ruby in a bloodied heap at the Blick's gate. Truda cursed, and peeled up Ruby's eyelid. *Miss her, I will*, thought Ruby, *when I have gone to sea.* Her tartness and her pithy declamations. "Am yo back?" she said to Truda, but could barely raise the air to make it sound.

"What, child? I can't hear you!" A jerk as Truda tried to lever Ruby from the ground. "This blood!"

"I will miss yo . . ." A coarse and brittle whisper.

"Lord, Ruby-girl, what is this? Don't give me dying words, child, I can't bear it."

Ruby felt Truda's arms slip underneath her, Truda rocking back and up to lift her. "Has some Infernal Being put a curse on me, that everyone I care for has to die?"

Ruby's smile was slight as Truda held her to her chest and, jolting, cursing, carried her through Blick's gate and up into the office. "Was that a shadow of a smile I saw then, Rube? You find my feeble jibes to be reviving? I've plenty more of 'em." Ruby's eyes cracked open; saw linen, egg-yolk yellow; peacock blue.

"Am yo back?"

"Back?"

"From the sea."

"The sea? Dear girl, we only got as far as Tenter Lane."

She let her head fall into Truda's chest and rested there till Isa came to mend her.

Speculation flourished like maddocks in horn sacks in the shucked and ashen days after the fire. Fingers pointed at the scorched high window of the Blick's office: where was Truda Cole Blick? Blick's had floundered these past weeks, since Isa Fly had exercised her influence on Miss Blick . . . How could Truda's critics know that with her uncle's death—a clear fortnight before Isa Fly arrived—the suppliers had seized their chance to withdraw from Blick's Fine Horn Button Manufactory and hastily reeled in their credit-lines? The price of horn was going up; the trade routes were more tangled than they'd been, and these past months the tariffs for getting shipments through the customs men in Danzig were prohibitive. The Russian horn magnates saw easier returns in grinding up their horn to spread directly on their fields round Petrograd, and brokers in England saw that button futures lay in casein; cheaper, cleaner, easier to press. But Truda's detractors had seen none of this: they saw how Truda had dismantled Blick's, had laid them off, had emptied the factory of everything of value, and now she'd fled, or at least nobody was quite sure where she was. The conclusion? (Wrong, as it turned out.) That the peculiar Miss Blick had set fire to her factory, praying that her underwriters would pay out.

It was quiet when the evening Bull woke her. When Ruby moved her head, it rattled; an old cart on rough roads. She was half-reclining on a bank of pillows, a blanket pulled up to her neck, and dressed in someone else's shirt, mull and soft. The windows were wide open bringing in a breeze. Truda was working at the desk, piling papers into neat bundles, tying each up with a lace, and hurling others at the grate for burning later.

"Where's Isa?" Ruby's voice was cracked and dry, but Truda's grin was broad on hearing it, and, standing up too quick, she knocked her chair onto the floor.

"Telephone." She crouched by Ruby and peeled back the blanket. "I was thinking that you would need a trip to the QV—"

"The hospital?"

"But Isa's stitched you up while you were sleeping, neat as any surgeon." She looked at Ruby's shoulder, grimacing. "And the bleeding's stopped. I have a tea you're supposed to drink. It's bitter, but Isa says it's good for stemming bleeding."

"Is her better, then?" Ruby struggled to sit up. A deep tug in her shoulder and she sank back down again.

"She is well, or well enough."

"What's her going to do?"

Truda, impatient, shook her head. "There's time enough for that."

"But St. Shirah—yo was going to put her in the car."

"Sadly, Ruby," she leaned forward in a mock whisper, "I have missed that boat. Now that she has her strength back there is nothing that I can do to compel her."

The door opened and Isa came back in.

"Ah, Isa! Ruby is sufficiently revived to interrogate me, which brings me some relief." Tender, muted, Truda spoke to Isa without her customary flourish. "I couldn't stretch to paying gravediggers this week, not with all my other creditors."

Isa pressed the heel of her hand into her eye.

"Lord, Isa, what did Brammeier say?"

Isa shook her head. "I did not speak with Brammeier. But all that can wait." She knelt on the floor beside the couch; one hand on Ruby's cheek; the other pushed a curl behind her ear, and Ruby felt a warmth bloom through her. "So tell me: a gashed shoulder; collapsing at the threshold before dawn? Truda said that we should take you up to Hunting Tree, but"—she ran her finger over the worm-scar on Ruby's wrist—"I thought it best to wait until you woke, to find out how this happened . . ."

Hot tears started up (*How well Isa knows me!*) and this time Ruby did not try to stop them. She would claim Isa for her own; tell her that she knew, now, why she'd seen Beth's eye and Isa's and her own reflected in the mirrors at the bonfire.

"Dun yo think I got a look of yo?" She tilted her head.

Isa gave a little shrug.

"I cor see it, except Em says I got a look of yo, but her thought it was the spoon that gid it me." She raised her hand to take the spoon from round her neck—this tiny spoon, a gift to instill patience. As if words like these could be measured out and not tipped quick like sugar from a scoop! But the spoon was not there, and Ruby panicked. "Did her get it? Did her come when I was sleeping?"

"Who, Ruby?"

"Em; Trembly Em—Mrs. Fine-knee Bacon."

Isa frowned and looked, concerned, at Truda.

"Did her come for my spoon? For *your* spoon? Her tried to cut it off my neck: did her come back to get it?"

Isa shook her head. "I took it off you when we dressed your shoulder."

Behind her, Truda crossed to the desk and pulled open a drawer. She took out Ruby's spoon and gave it back to her. "Em Fine-knee Bacon slashed you?"

"Nan Annie tried to stop her."

"Your grandmother was there?" said Isa, quickly.

"Em says I got a look of Isa Fly."

"And that's why Emily attacked you with a knife?" Truda threw her hands up to her head. "Exorcism? She thinks you are possessed? That primitive was trying to *bleed* resemblance out of you?"

Ruby ignored her; talked instead to Isa: Nan Eliza swore that she'd seen Beth's ghost in that spotty dress, when it was Isa that she'd seen up on the hills. Em thought Isa stole, not just the spoon, but a look of Ruby's grandad by some witchcraft, and that's why it had ended up with this (Ruby glanced down at her shoulder). "Em's got it all wrong. I got a look of yo because of Lil. I know who Lil is."

Isa moved as if to stand, but Ruby reached out and took a thin pinch of her sleeve. "Stay by me!"

Truda spoke at Isa's shoulder. "I thought we had dispensed with this. We abandoned it, the Quest for the Lost Daughter. I thought we had established that her father did not so much *dispatch* Isa as *banish* her with grave threats at her heels."

"Yes, but we was looking for the wrong person before." Ruby reached for Isa's hand, despite the heat that screamed like flares through her shoulder. "It wasn't Lily. My mom was Beth to everyone but her dad; my Nan Eliza says he called her Lil. Which means yoom kin to me."

And what had Ruby hoped for? That Isa Fly would gasp and fall upon her neck? That their salt tears would mingle and that Isa Fly would knit their fingers up together and swear to her that she would never let her go?

Isa sat quite still; a pressure on Ruby's fingers, slight and fleeting as a pulse.

Truda raised her eyebrows. "Ruby, this is some queer game that you're playing: *you* claim you're kin to Isa in the hope that I consent to take you with us when we leave?"

"Doe listen to her, going on," said Ruby, tugging Isa's hand for her attention. "Your dad had a different name when he was here. Jonah, he was called. It was Trembly Em as gid him the name Moonie. Her didn't like him much. He'd gid her a baby when her was my age, but her baby died, and by the sounds of it he, day treat her too kind."

Truda's hands were planted on her hips. "But she said nothing of this when you first asked her?"

Ruby shook her head. "Her said as God had took him." Em was so definite about him being dead, so distressed that Ruby never questioned it.

"I pressed her," Isa said. "And she insisted that her Moonie was dead. She wasn't lying, Truda. She believed it. And I had no reason to doubt her." She rubbed Ruby's cheek with her thumb, and asked how Ruby had discovered this.

"Em made a charm for Moonie's children and put a little mark in with a nail, to figure for a moon. He used to brand a circle on his tools, but Em had it as a moon. It was to mock him, partly. And her wanted it to work against the sway as he put over folk." She turned her spoon to show Isa the mark. "The moon, here, see?"

"And this is your proof? A mark on a spoon?" Truda's hands, flung wide in disbelief. "Em Fine-knee Bacon has some tale about a moon, a nail, a spoon, and you deduce that your mother and Isa shared a father? And this, the same Emily who was quite certain that Isa stole her locket because someone put it in the window for the owner to reclaim? And she maintains that your Jonah and Moonie Fly are one and the same?"

Ruby shook her head, impatient. "Em's too busy wi thinking about how her wants to punish Isa. Her cor see the bridge between um."

Truda raised her eyebrows. "Nor, frankly, can I."

Anger knotted up in Ruby's belly. "Yoom saying yo doe believe me, ay yo? Well, Miss Blick, go up to Hunting Tree! Go and fetch a photograph of Jonah and Isa can say if it's Moonie Fly!" A new thought shattered and spilled through her, like milk from a dropped bottle. How would she tell her nan that Jonah ran away; that he had made himself another life elsewhere? (And while she tried to work out how to handle such a jagged, broken pain, she could not see her nan already knew this.)

"Has Trembly Em determined how Isa took possession of the spoon?"

"Her thinks her got it by witch-theft."

Truda rolled her eyes. "Isa, do you have time for this?" But Isa held her hand up to still Truda.

"Let her speak. The spoon, Ruby . . ."

She explained that her nan had a second baby, Grace, and it was for Grace that Em had made the spoon. Grace had been sickly; she'd had sticky lungs, and Nan Annie wanted to take her to the sea. Grace was wearing the spoon when the *Lickey Bell* was wrecked; Nan Annie had come back living, but Jonah let it look like he had drowned. "He must of wanted it that way. There was a telegram. Captin told me: 'Delivery imminent. Come now.' That's why Jonah made the journey. Captin thought it was to do with business, Isa, but it wasn't. He was coming to your mother. The *Lickey Bell* sank on the day that yo was born."

"And the spoon?" said Truda. "It wasn't lost with Grace?"

"He must of got the spoon off Grace's neck before her drowned. He must of kept it and then gid it to Isa. He leaves the Cradles; he runs off to the new life he's been working up in Severnsea."

Her grandfather, like Jonah in the Bible, crouching in the bottom of a boat set course for Tarshish, eyes squeezed shut and imitating sleep, trying to will the storm away.

Isa moved to one end of the couch and took up her bag from underneath. She pulled out the broken spear and handed it to Ruby. A circle branded in the wood; a moon; Jonah's mark, and Moonie's.

"My father branded all his tools this way so that if he lost one it would find its way back to him. That is why he wanted it retrieved."

"God's sake, Isa!" Truda dropped down to the floor beside them. "You kept it?"

Isa took the broken spear from Ruby and held it lightly. "This fortnight I have scrutinized myself. I've tried to conjure up some strength of feeling for my father; to find some reason why he shouldn't hang for what he's done. He would not act when Anselm was tormented as a boy, when I was taunted; blinded. And now he's made me an accessory to murder. He never bears the blame if he can find another soul to carry it for him. And I've thought about Cass Severn; Belle. The stone-throwing, the net-cutting—that was testing, but we bore it. Spent our days stitching nets back together. But then, when we were older, they took my brother."

"Took?" Truda's hand was resting on her throat. "I thought you said he drowned."

"Anselm and I were on the way back from a long day in the shallows with our rods. We cut across the beach to take the short way home—the moon was full enough to take the cliff steps. And then he saw a winking light across the bay. All the lights were meant to be extinguished in case they showed the enemy where to fire. But Anselm was so brave! I see him in you," she smiled at Ruby, "for all your borrowed fears . . . He wanted to be certain it was not a landing craft with the Hun crouched on board. And then we heard them calling out from Sawdy Point. Not so much a calling as a song. Sirens splayed out on a rock, they were, false-pleading for our help, saying they'd been stranded by the tide. I recognized the mocking in their tone—I'd heard them taunting Moonie time enough. But Anselm was too credulous. He said he'd take the skiff and bring them safe back to the shore, even though the Zeppelin bell was being sounded. In the morning they were watching me—Belle Severn and Cassandra—watching from Sawdy Point when I found his body on the beach. He was not quite sixteen. Belle Severn wrecked our family, so I should have no compunction about Moonie wrecking hers . . . I have tried to conjure up some strength of feeling for Cass or for Moonie, and I find that I am dry. I can't summon a sentiment."

"Fine, then. Death to mermaids." Truda took the broken spear from Isa, brandished it. "But why not be rid of *this*? You could have chucked it in the sea, or burned it! Why bring it here with you?"

"He said that the sea was set against him; that if we tried to throw the spear away it would come right back in on the turning tide." She eased the spear from Truda's hands and pushed it back inside her bag. "*He* wanted to burn it, but I took it from the fire before it caught."

"Why would you do that, Isa? To protect him?" Truda said. "To incriminate yourself?"

"No." She released her hand from Ruby's and pushed herself up from her knees. "I have spoken with the police in St. Shirah. They are expecting me tomorrow." She brushed the dirt from Beth's spotted dress. "If I don't arrive by sunset they will issue a warrant for my arrest; they'll send search parties. I've told them you'll escort me there."

And though Trembly Em would never come to learn it, the moonmark on the spoon had accomplished its preventative intent. Moonie's child resolved to stand fast; she would not wax and wane like Moonie; would not, like Jonah, try to flee. They would drive down to St. Shirah in the morning.

Chapter 23

Blick [a. Ger. *Blick, sheen*], The brightening or iridescence
appearing on silver or gold at the end of the refining process.

RUBY WOKE UP in the dark; it took a moment to determine where
she was. This scrawny mattress; piled tea chests; it smelled of cottonseed, of Captin. The room over the Fried Fish Shop. Truda had
brought her here to rest ("Lock yourself in. No one will come looking
for you here.") while she and Isa went to pack their bags. *But what
things,* Ruby thought, *will I take with me to sea?* She tried to count
off items from her lists but found she had forgotten them and that
there was relief, release in this. She'd have to go with nothing but the
spoon.

They'd left her with a picnic on a tray—bread, cold ham, a three-
inch bit of toffee and some milk. Ruby folded the bread around the
ham and ate it hurriedly; she was ravenous, and didn't pause till
everything was eaten. Besides, she wanted to build strength up for the
journey. They'd changed their minds about going to St. Shirah in the
morning: it was not as if they'd sleep; they might as well drive down
there through the night. And Truda would not hear of leaving Ruby
in Cradle Cross without them—"These women who take knives to
Ruby's neck!"—but would deliver her to Captin, down in Whalemouth. ("I'll tell your grandmother you've gone to convalesce. I'll

come and fetch you when—and only when—Em Fine-knee Bacon has been charged with the attack; when I've satisfied myself you're in no further danger.")

There was a burst of singing somewhere, and Ruby took her milk cup to the window; strained to hear it: "none of the ransomed ever knew how deep were the waters crossed . . ." It sounded like chapel, and Ruby was confused: it wasn't Sunday, was it? How long had she slept? The singing pitched and lurched; it was a favorite of the Ruths and Naomis, and Ruby did not know that Dinah Hatchett Harper had requested this especially for *her;* that the Ruth and Naomi Thursday Club had gathered in an unscheduled service to say prayers for Ruby and her safe return. For since first light the news had dispersed through the Cradles, swift as blood through water, that Ruby Abel Tailor, injured, had vanished from the Infirmary at St. Barbara's. No one was quite clear about her injury—there was word from Trembly Em that it was all tied up with Isa Fly, a spoon. The sorors—who loved Ruby but underestimated her determination—said she could not have gone far, weakened as she was by fever and blood loss; she must be somewhere close on Parry Lean.

So all that Saturday, the sorors and the Ruths and the Naomis and Ruby's chip shop regulars and chain-boys and nailer-girls went searching with long sticks all through the dips and trenches and the beds of brittle ferns around the high walls of St. Barbara's Priory. (While Ruby'd slept at Blick's that afternoon, Glenda had come knocking at the gate. "Asking, in effect," said Truda, "if I'd scaled the tower walls and kidnapped you, dear Ruby. I lied, of course, and said I hadn't seen you. Well, they're brutish creatures. Let 'em sweat!")

Those that were not fit to search (with lanterns, now, as dark was coming in) had gone down to the chapel in the town to plead at the mercy seat of God for the lost girl's safe return. Em Fine-knee Bacon was among them, waiting at the back, and singing, "How dark was the night that the Lord passed through ere He found His sheep that was lost."

Ruby knew this hymn from the Thursday Club, and flushed, she was, by an unexpected yearning—dragging, melancholic—for all she'd leave behind. Her picnic lent her strength; she slipped downstairs and checked the fish-shop clock. Half-past nine. They weren't leaving till sometime after ten. She unlocked the front door, but felt unnerved. Why were they singing this late in the chapel? What if they finished just as Ruby reached the top end of Horn Lane; the Thursday Club, with Trembly Em among them?

So Ruby took the back steps to the towpath.

The Deadarm was in darkness when Ruby reached it—no lantern on its high nail. She kicked a stone into the darkness; a test to see if Nan Annie was there with Jamie Abel, for noise out on the Deadarm, perhaps someone falling in the water, would draw her nan straight out.

She did not kick it far, but it hit the water. No light, no movement over on the island. Another stone; she winced and threw another.

A voice came hard and hollowed, back across the water. "Who's out there?"

Ruby felt a lurching in her gut. These past few fevered hours had so consumed her, she'd forgotten Belle. Now Belle was back, but where was Jamie Abel, who had not for seven years left his island?

"Where's my dad?" Panicked, Ruby thought of Jamie Abel lying caught up in this foul and silted water. She stared across the Cut but could barely make out where the water ended, where the ground began. Ruby pressed a finger to the spoon. "Tell me what yo done to him!"

"You think I'd hurt your father, Ruby?"

Unsettling to be spoken to by someone hidden in the dark, across the Cut.

"Yoom saying as yo doe know where he is?"

"I'm saying I haven't seen him! Silas was up here, just, and locking up." Silas Tolley's workshop was alongside Jamie Abel's. "Si says that Jamie Abel has been up on Ludleye Lean all day, out with a party looking for you, Ruby."

Ruby drew breath, sharp. So she'd drawn her father from his island, finally. But she felt no thrill in this, no triumph, just a shrill anger. How could he know so little of her! Why would she have bothered to jump down from the tower at St. Barbara's, and then linger in the Leans? He'd misjudged her capacity, imagined she was like him,

like Nan Annie: a tethered dog treading the same path, same circum-
ference around the Hunting Tree . . . Did he imagine he could scoop
her this time, limp and broken, from a copse on Parry Lean and leave
her on the doorstep for Nan Annie and slink back to the dark hut on
his island? (But beneath her anger, Ruby felt a gladness bloom, invol-
untary and tender as a bruise, and for a moment she was pleased that
he had looked for her at all.)

"Find him, Ruby. Tell him you are safe."

She was unbalanced by this Belle who didn't mock, but chastened
her. She'd heard mothers like this; seen them cuffing girls, late home,
about the head and hooking them in close, angry embraces. But she
had not asked for Belle's concern on her father's behalf; it weighed on
her, unwelcome and audacious.

"*He* doe care about me being safe." Ruby put her hand up to her
temple where her pulse flicked, rapid.

"You *want* him to believe that you are lost? That you're drowned
in a clay pool on the Leans?"

Ruby swelled, defensive. A pounding in her head. These questions
left their mark on her like little tender blisters. "About time as he did
sommat to show as he's a father to me; showed some—" She fumbled
for the word Nan Annie used. "Some accountability."

"*You* talk to *me* about accountability!"

Ruby swayed a little, her head too heavy for her neck. That Belle,
of all people, should reprimand her!

She heard a rustling; Belle's black robes, rearranged.

"You broke your word to me. You said that you would watch her,
that you would find out why she'd come. Isa tracked me down, you
said, because of Anselm. Moonie's dying, you said, and Isa Fly's coming for revenge before he dies. I thought she'd at last found out where
I was, extorted it from Cass . . ." Some mewling, wounded noise
spewed out of Belle. "And all the while you knew that she had killed
her! You had it pasted in your notebook: 'THE GRISLY CATCH. THE
BODY IN THE CAVE . . .' "

Someone must have lit a lamp in one of the high windows, curious
perhaps with all this shouting, for a light flared above them. Enough
to show Belle's face, white and worn. The rest of her was shrouded in
her blacks.

"Tell Isa: this time I will not look on as a Fly dies before me. I will not stand above her; I will not *watch* her drowning. I will hold her head beneath the water and I will pin her dark eye wide so that she sees my face as she is dying."

Ruby's guts twisted in alarm. She stumbled down the towpath, back toward the main drag of the Cut to warn Isa. Behind, the slap of wood on brick; she slowed and looked over her shoulder, wincing as she turned, and saw Belle Severn poised on the drawbridge. She'd cast her blacks aside, and her arms gleamed white and sculpted as peeled sticks. "Tell her that I'm coming for her, Ruby," she called out. "Tell her I'll show her all the mercy that she showed my Cass." And then Belle Severn, mermaid-mannered, arced into the dark unsifted waters.

The lamps were lit at Isa's. Ruby fell up the stone stairs into Isa's kitchen, and, trying to turn the stiff key in the lock, screamed out for Isa, "Her's coming for yo!"

No time to notice the shrill, acrid stink of overheated oil that eked through the brick from next door in the chip shop. Ruby tried to drag the table up against the door but found it was too heavy with one hand; rushed around the other side and pushed and nudged the table with the weight of her until she'd wedged it tight across the doorframe, the wooden legs squealing on the clay tiles. The Ruths were still going: assertions of steadfastness, almost shouted: *"We have an anchor that keeps the soul steadfast and sure while the billows roll . . ."*

Ruby stumbled through to the button shop; the shelves and bottles seemed to buckle and to sway before her eyes. They could get out this way, thought Ruby, up Horn Lane and run to Truda's; maybe they would meet her in the car . . . But before Isa was halfway down the stairs, Ruby saw that Belle was there already at the front and hammering wild-eyed against the glass, rattling the door against its bolts.

Belle's elbow shattered the top frame of glass. (She had, you see, the strong arms of a dredger.) She plunged her hand through; reached for the top bolt, and inside the shop, Isa half-pushed, half-lifted Ruby up the stairs and into the bedroom that ran from front to back. They shifted the wardrobe up against the door, Ruby pushing with her back to it.

Her wound was bleeding freely once again, and, sapped and husked, she fell down on the floor. "Truda will come soon," said Ruby, breathless, while Isa worked her bandage loose. "Find us, she will. Help us." Ruby smiled; their Truda, valiant, scaling the gutter-pipe to reach them.

Isa took a hankie from her bag. Wadded it up; pressed it to the gash in Ruby's shoulder. "Look where I brought you, Ruby, with my running. Shut in an upstairs room, with all this blood, this fear."

"Yo day bring me to this." Ruby leaned back on Isa's shoulder. "Yo come here to help Moonie."

"You know that isn't true."

"For your sister, then. For me."

"I didn't come for you." Isa turned and, tender, cupped a hand beneath Ruby's chin.

"But I am glad yo found me."

"You are too generous to me." A long tear trickled from Isa's blinded eye. "Do not imagine that I'm good, or that I'm brave. Anselm was those things, and you are so like him . . . I came to Cradle Cross because I'm frightened. I came because I am afraid of being shut up behind a door without a handle on the inside. I came because I have no wish to be hanged by the neck."

Ruby lifted Isa's hand up to her lips. She held it there a moment, too tired even to kiss it; let it drop. *The sister to my mother.* Ruby's grief for Beth; a parcel in brown paper that had squatted unwrapped, these years, on her doorstep. Isa held her close, and Ruby wept.

They waited for the sound of Belle's feet on the stairs, her push against the door. But it did not come. Instead, through the rear window, they heard another song—not from the chapel this time, but a thinner, taunting rhyme, half-chanted and half-sung:

> *If you're wiser, don't trust Isa*
> *Or she'll split and splay and splice you.*

Isa lifted Ruby's fingers from her sleeve and eased herself up, quiet, from the floor. She moved to the middle of the room, her bag still slung across her shoulder, and, reaching up, she turned off the gaslight. Darkness dropped on Ruby like a hood; *the kind of hood they slip on murderers before they hang them.* She heard Isa cross the room. The darkness eased, and Ruby saw where Isa stood, to one side of the window.

Panic surged through Ruby, and with it a new strength. She pushed herself up, slow, awkward, and joined Isa near the window; held her hand. *Keep you ever from the water,* Ruby thought, *from the sight of the Fish . . .* Tentative, they peered into the dark.

"I can see you!" Belle called up from the Cut.

Isa stepped further back into the room, but Belle must have caught the movement, for she shouted, "Run, Isa, if you like! But be sure that I will find you: I will search for you and I will never cease."

For whither thou goest, I will go; thought Ruby, *and where thou lodgest, I will lodge.*

Isa pulled Ruby to her; spoke quiet, clipped, urgent. "Keep her in the Cut. Talk to her."

"What about?"

"Whatever absorbs her, makes her voluble."

"Yo do, Isa."

Isa nodded, brisk. "Provoke her, then. Invite her to talk about her loathing of the Flys. Keep her there and I will clear the door. Truda will come soon, and with her car."

While Isa tried to push the wardrobe clear of the door, wood scraping in a brusque, affronted squeal, Ruby sat on the low sill and, twisting, peered out of the window.

"Belle, am yo still there?" She heard Isa strain behind her: the wardrobe was heavy, and it had taken two of them to shift it. "Look what yoom come to, Belle! Yoom used to salty water. Clean. And now yoom swimming with the Cut-eels and the cack!"

"Cack will draw a Fly, Ruby. I'll wait."

"Why? Her's going to the police in the morning. If her killed your Cass, then *they* ull hang her. Yo doe need to get yourself in trouble. Yo doe need to come and get revenge."

"You know what she's done, Ruby: this didn't disenchant you? What would it take then, Ruby? What power does she have? You're prey to it—the Horn girl, the chip man—all of you. She has hooked you through the heart and landed you . . ."

Ruby looked over her shoulder. Made out the shape of Isa, still trying to shift the wardrobe. "Her cares for me. Her pays me attention."

A slap against the water. *"Her cares?"* A coarse cawing, somewhere between coughing and a choke. "Look about her, Ruby! Her brother, drowned; her father, at last, dying . . . Len Salt got away and he will thank me that I disenchanted him. But *you*—you're trapped in an upstairs room waiting to die. *Her cares?* No, Ruby: Isa Fly lays waste to those around her."

Isa was at Ruby's side, her fingers on her sleeve. She nodded back toward the wardrobe. "I can't move it on my own. It's catching on something." She stayed there, beside Ruby, and said in a low voice, "Why is she not coming for me?"

"She is a pestilence!" called Belle. "She spreads misery about her like a plague!"

"But Isa day kill Anselm, you did!" Ruby shouted out into the dark. "Yo cor blame that on her."

"I didn't kill him, Ruby. I left him on a rock. I didn't save him."

Isa scanned the Cut. "Why is she not coming? She can scale cliffs: she could scale the wall and climb in through the window."

"Did you hear me, Isa Fly? I left him to drown and that is merciful neglect. I didn't catch him in a net! I didn't run through his bowels with a fishing spear!" Her voice, distorted with disgust, with grief. "Bloated up like bladderwort, she was. My Cass! No eyes, Isa Fly! The fish had sucked them out."

Revenge for Isa, stone-blinded, Ruby thought. *For Anselm, blindfolded and tethered on a cliff.*

Isa's hand was scratching at her eye. "He was a boy!" she called into the dark. "He was fifteen! What did Anselm do to you to earn your *merciful neglect*?"

"You paint him like a saint, when you and he were hard as flint and cruel as the sea. 'Belle Severn is a bastard': which of you made that rhyme, Isa? 'Her mother was a sea-whore, Her father a sperm-whale'? I tried to tell you about Moonie but you wouldn't listen. I tried to tell you and you shut the door on me, and then you started up the rumors and the songs. You refused to see him as he was."

Isa planted two hands on the sill and leaned out of the window.

"And my Anselm deserved to die because we would not believe the tales you told us about Moonie?"

"What tales?" Ruby frowned at Isa. Ruby knew by now that Moonie Fly was capable of any cruelty. He'd used Em and discarded her; he'd left his debts behind, his Lil, and let Nan Annie think that he was dead. He'd killed Cass Severn with a spear and hoped to fix the blame onto his daughter. Done so much, and left so much undone.

"She has never listened," Belle called out. "But she will now."

("Why does she not *come* for me?" said Isa.)

" 'Severnsea Bore Takes Sixty Souls'—you had it writ out in your notebook, Ruby."

The *Lickey Bell* skewered; the splintering of the night; dead men, bloated. Her grandad and the baby, lost; Nan Annie, saved and grieving—she'd need to write a new ending, thought Ruby. That night, the waters rose up to swallow Jonah, running from his duty and his debts, and it was Moonie Fly who breached the surface.

"Cass was there that night," said Belle. "Waiting in the water a hundred feet from land. She knew the Bore was driving up the Shoulder. She waited as her breed do when there are storms or troubled waters, in case there might be children needing saving. She saw a man swim from the wreck toward the rocks. A child—me—clinging to his neck. She watched him pry my fingers from his neck and put me on a rock just feet from where my Cass was waiting. He didn't pay attention; didn't see her. But she watched him. He was not a drowning man. Time, he had, and strength to climb up on the rock and sit beside me. Time enough to take something from my neck: a charm, a little spoon looped on a string."

Ruby put her hand up to her throat.

"My Cass, she took me up and followed him past Whalemouth and found out where he lived. Two-Fish Cottage, St. Shirah. She taught me that man's words; she made me recite them every night so that I'd not forget: 'I'm taking this to gid to our new baby. My Flo is sweet and ripe, but your mother was sour. Yoom a sickly child and yo was never meant to live.' He put the spoon cord round his wrist and lowered himself back into the water. And then he swam away."

Ruby twisted up a finger in a cord. Grace had lived. A baby on a rock. Beth's little sister with the sticky lungs.

Isa was calling out. "You never told me."

"I tried," said Belle. "Every time I saw you on the sand or on the rocks or planting in your garden, I tried to tell you what he was, and what I was to you. You wouldn't listen."

Ruby looked at Isa. "Did her, Isa? Did her try to tell yo?"

"You taunted me," said Isa. "We were playing, me and Anselm, on the shore . . ." Her hand covered her eye.

"Yes, you and Anselm said I was a bastard, my Cass a sea-whore . . ."

"You threw a stone."

He is the canker in your belly, Ruby thought, *Isa Fly, and Belle: like a great whale you have swallowed Jonah up and carried him inside you, and Jonah has been eating up your soul.*

"I tried to question him." Isa, shaken; her words shot through with new uncertainty. "But Moonie said that Cass was one of them 'too keen to gid it out.' He said that she spoke only lies, could not be trusted. She was constant as a mermaid, Moonie said."

Jonah: waxing, waning, Ruby thought. *Jonah: constant as the moon.*

"The likes of her and you, he swore, would only bring bad fortune," Isa said. "And we should keep away."

"Cass *was* constant! Cass saved me! Cass took Moonie's words and promised she'd undo them: we would make Moonie wish that he *had* drowned."

"But Anselm?" A cry from Isa, bellowed out into the dark. "It was Anselm, not my father, that you drowned."

"Yoom no better than your father, Belle!" Ruby's voice was rasping. The air was rough and harsh; it made her cough. "Yoom just like Moonie Fly!"

Chapter 24

The only obstacle to improvement in this necessary and life-preserving art is fear.

Dr. Franklin's Advice to Swimmers

A FAT-FIRE is hungry; takes too quick. It licks up greasy walls; it laps with a hundred tongues where rendered fat has seeped into the brick. It eats the air, and Horn Lane air was rich with particles of bone, fine, powdered; prime dry tinder.

Dinah had been at the top end of Horn Lane when Ruby stumbled into Isa's through the back. Trembly Em had slipped out of the chapel, and Dinah had followed her. For Annie Nailer Tailor (who'd kept away from Isa Fly; who hadn't wanted to see Jonah's dark eye looking back at her) had sent word to her friend Dinah that Em had become unhinged, that she had wounded Ruby, that she had talked of hurting this Fly girl. Dinah had stood in shadow; watched Em come out of Captin's Fried Fish Shop; watched her sit down on the high step; Em ready, waiting.

And it was Dinah who first tried to put the fire out, who flung her good jacket across one of the vats. But by then it was too late for modest measures. And all the streets, the houses, were dried up that summer, ready for the fire; the sun had sucked the marrow from the doors and boards, from props and struts, from joists stretched out like ribs from one wall to another. Before Dinah Hatchett Harper reached the Blick's gate and the bell, the fire was eating up the fish shop and devouring all that lay on either side.

Ruby's eyes were stinging now, but growing used to the Cut-dark; she could see Belle moving—her white face, her arms—in the shifting light. A slop, a splash of water; Belle Severn striking out toward the side.

Isa twisted Ruby round to face her, her fingers gripping her arms tight. "When she finds she can't get in by the stairs, she will scale the wall and climb in through the window. Go now! The window at the front—climb out, go to the top end of Horn Lane and wait for Truda there. Tell her to come for me!" But Isa kept her grip on Ruby; did not let her go. Her eyes were on the Cut, for Belle had stopped short of the towpath. Laughing, she was, singing. And light—red, gold—was dancing all about her on the surface of the water.

> Isa One-Eye, Isa Blind,
> Cut her eye out with a spoon.
> Isa steals and says she finds,
> Isa No-Fish, Isa Moon.

"Why's her stopped?" Ruby's throat stung when she breathed. "Why ay her coming for yo?" Isa did not answer, but watched Belle, in the water, swim away for the other side. Shouts behind them, in Horn Lane. Not Truda, but the frantic, uneven clamor of a bell.

To those who heard the bell and first came rushing out the Leopard, down Horn Lane, it looked suspicious; Dinah Hatchett Harper emerging from the burning chip shop with her arms on fire. What would the ruminators say after the fire about this woman, whose only son had died in the World War *simply* because he was a button-maker? Fifteen years Dinah had clung to this belief, a flimsy raft, and her *simply* that anchored it. Easier to growl and hawk at Hector Blick, who'd held that button-making was not critical enough to keep boys working safe at home, than for Dinah to turn round and face the phantom at her shoulder—her dead Horace, who had died without permission. And the desecration of Horace's picture by Isa Fly, ally of Truda Cole Blick? Dinah hardly needed this incitement. Her fury against Blick's had been smoldering for years. The mural, smeared with tallow—her touch-paper. Never mind the truth, that Dinah had lit a rag in Isa's grate but nothing more. Who looked the likely culprit? Dinah, or the trembling old lady, Em Fine-knee Bacon, who stood and bleated, pointing at the window?

Ruby ran to the front window and tried to lift it up with her good arm; the floorboards groaning, hot beneath her feet. Isa came to join her. Behind them, Belle sang out that Isa would be smoked out from her lie, her rock, her safe place in the shadows. They strained at the sash together—couldn't shift it. They saw the crowd below, arms raised as if to catch them, and tried again to lever up the window. No give. And then they saw that it was painted shut.

Em took the sight of Ruby next to Isa as a proof that she had been right all along. As the crowd grew, spilling from the Leopard, from the chapel, she called out like a preacher on a corner that Isa Fly had stolen Ruby, along with all their other precious things, and look what she had done to Ruby now: put her beyond reach and beyond finding. Glenda Hatchett Harper shook her, rough. "Shut up!" she screamed into Em's ear (and no one but Em could hear with all the shouting and the clamor). "Look what *yo* has done!"

"Her brung it on herself!" said Em. "Those things her took from us! Our losslinen!"

"There ay no proof as Isa took that from us!" For much as Glenda wove her speculative threads up tight and binding about Isa, she suspected (rightly) that the basket had been taken for a dare: Dinah had retreated, wounded, since the tallow-on-the-wall and this past week Glenda had observed a fidgety disorder twitching through the children in the bread queue; they bobbed their tongues at Dinah when her back was turned; they mimicked her, hands planted on their hips . . .

just a short hop, brazen and electric, between this and snatching such a prize as Hatchett Harpy's linen. (One of the Rudge girls, making mischief, left the basket on the step at Isa's shop. But it was neither Lorna Rudge nor Isa who had doused the cloths in blood. For all her protestation, *that* was Em, who knew that she was seen to be saft-headed and was afraid that if she spoke out about the stolen spoon, no one would believe her. So she bought a quart of hog-blood from the butcher and told him she was making a black pudding.)

"But Dinah's mural!" Em spat, "*Her* done that!"

"It was gid out that her did, but no one saw her. They only saw a person dressed in black! It was Belle Severn told me her'd seen the Fly girl. Her told me her had sommat held against her and I shored it up for her."

"My locket?" Em said, fierce and desperate, her eyes fixed on Isa Fly and Ruby in the window. "Her took my locket, day her? Her took a look of that old fogger Moonie wi it!"

But Trembly Em had dropped the locket. Glenda had found it on the road by Kenelm's Field and left it at the button shop, implicating Isa. "For Belle's sake, I did it. I put the blame for all of it on the Fly girl for her. But setting a fire? Yo took it too far, yo saft old cow, and now yoom burning Ruby up wi her!"

She pointed at the window, but Ruby was no longer there. Trembly Em fell to her knees, and Glenda didn't even try to help her up.

They tried to move the wardrobe, pushing back against the side of it, feet slipping on the floor, but the room was filling with a choking, rolling smoke, the stench of bone and flame. Below their feet, reeds of light sheared in through split seams in the planks; through cracks; through vacated knotholes in the wood that stared like eyes that had been blinded and now reflected fire. Ruby heard her name over the groans and cracks and splinters of the fire, not so much shouted out as torn from the throats of all the anguished Ruths and Naomis who were watching empty windows, helpless, in Horn Lane. (And Lorna Rudge and Vi Cope were sorry that they'd stolen Ruby's metal money-tube from under Captin's sink and swore that if she got out alive, they would give it back. Besides, they'd not been able to get it open.) Ruby ran to the rear window; gulped in air, and saw Belle Severn splayed out, beckoning on the far towpath, calling them to come into the water.

And what of Truda Cole Blick? Only now was Truda entering Horn Lane, her car abandoned on the Breach. She'd packed her night-case, unhurried and precise (rolling her stockings in a tight whorl and easing creases with a flat hand from her silk chemise), strapped the case onto the luggage rack and nudged her car at a sluggish pace down Tenter Lane, down Islington, in no hurry to get Isa to St. Shirah. Only when she'd taken a wide slow-handed turn onto the Breach did Truda hear the bell, and even then she'd thought that someone mocked her; that someone rang the bell to alert Cradle Cross to Blick's swift demise under her direction.

Ruby sat down on the sill and swung her legs out.

"I believe you, Belle. I believe all as Moonie did to yo and Cass." Each word a harsh scrape on Ruby's tongue, her throat. "I want you to leave Isa. Her's your sister. Let her be."

She glanced behind her: smoke oozing in below the wardrobe and up through the floor. "Look, Belle: I got something of yours." She held her spoon out before her. "Can yo see? Look at me, Belle, and yo ull see Moonie in me. Yo ull see Anselm. Yo ull see Isa. Yo ull see yourself."

Isa put her hand on Ruby's arm.

"Annie Nailer Tailor was your mom in Cradle Cross. Moonie left her. His name was Jonah, here. Beth was his daughter, but Jonah called her Lil. Her's dead now, a long time, and I never knowed my mom but now I found two aunts which is better than no mother at all. It's Moonie did all this. Yo kill Isa, yo ull hang, I'll see to that. But doe kill her and there's a chance yo both might live."

Isa joined her on the sill, the floor too hot to stand on. No time for Ruby to twist her finger in the spoon cord and ask it one last time to keep her safe in water: Isa threw her bag onto the clay below the window and they jumped from the sill together; cleared the towpath; fell into the water, lit and shifting, dancing all about them, red and gold.

Truda smelled scorched bone, burned horn, repulsive as any Blick's roasting day, but smoke was not venting from the tall oven chimneys but rising unrestrained and blooming in dark plumes above the factory. She forced her way down Horn Lane through the swelling crowd. She stopped before the button shop, and as the shelves inside buckled and bowed, jars lurching, smashing, spraying fine horn buttons out across the floor, and as Ruby and Isa, unseen by Truda, threw themselves down into the Cut, a memory ducked under her defenses and presented itself brazenly to Truda.

A spring morning before lessons, and Truda crouches in the field beside the hawthorn hedge, cold water dripping from the catkins down her collar as she eases horn blanks and three-drills from the mud and drops them in a jar to keep Spy, her terrier, from choking when he goes rooting for rabbits. There's been an edict: "Scrap buttons—chipped, scuffed, incorrectly drilled—to be dropped into a bowl beside your station, to be counted at the day's end and summarily deducted from your wages." Short-lived, this edict is, and half-heartedly enforced, because buttoners have pocketed their scraps and, going home, have pitched them into fields, or at the Ludleye Gutter. (Besides, the War brings Blick's enough new business to tolerate such modest little losses.)

As the Blicks' house grows quieter (Lysander, Phil, enlisted; Uncle Archie, then her father, gone to War), Truda and her mother sit in the kitchen in the stretched evenings and pour Truda's scavenged scrap buttons, tipping and tapping, out onto the table, arranging them by type: Trust Mes (with holes too closely set, giving them a squinty, dishonest look; you could blunt or even snap a needle if you didn't aim true every time); Cyclops; two-drill; three-drill; chips; scratchings. Her mother, sorting horn blanks with chipped edges or scratched faces by firelight and pushing them into long rows with her finger, two rows dark, two rows light, for drafts pieces that sit cool and heavy in the hand. They sketch out solitary eyes, sheet after sheet, until they perfect the wide Egyptian stare with the iris spoked like a cartwheel. They make up labels—the Cyclops; Blick's Limited Edition Three-Hole Special; Blick's Ornamental Two-Hole—and paste them onto bottles.

But Truda could not see the bottles now, no matter how she cocked her head and rubbed her eyes: the windows were clouded over with black smears that pulsed and swirled before her. She stretched her hand out; wanted to rub this window clean so that she could see the labels she'd made with her mother. But there was no glass and it was too hot and someone was pulling on her arm and tugging her away. And Truda was in Horn-Lane-as-it-burned, and she was gagging, retching at the stench.

Someone was rubbing her between her shoulder blades, and a man—her foreman—bent low, twisted, shouting up into her face, "Miss Blick, Miss Blick, what shall we save, Miss Blick?" but Truda did not understand the question. *I'm sorry,* she said, *I am sorry,* and he shouted out again, "The presses or the horn, Miss Blick? What shall we try to save?" She stood straight and looked around, confused, scanning the heads about her for Isa's white, white hair, for Ruby.

Firemen from Blick's, from Tolley's, Bissell's, Rudge's had already pulled the gates back and run for the fire-pump fixed beside the water, had already sunk the feed deep into the Cut. (They did not see Belle Severn; did not hear her taunting.) Intent, they were, on rolling out flat loops of hose through the yard, on shearing through the crowd and up toward the two small houses. Truda stepped back out of their way; panic, harsh, acidic, in her gullet. A hand on Truda's shoulder. She spun around. "Isa!" But it was Glenda Hatchett Harper and she was saying something Truda couldn't hear at first, and nodding whey-faced at the button shop and pointing at the window up above.

As Ruby had predicted, Truda Cole Blick tried to climb the guttering. It was Glenda who ran forward and pulled Truda down and told her not to be so fogging stupid—"Them men have brung the water; they um setting ladders to the wall." It was Dinah Hatchett Harper who ran toward Miss Blick with arms outstretched but too burned to embrace her. So all the other Ruths and their Naomis did it for her; formed a skein around Miss Blick and bound her up firm, close, and joined with her in screaming out, "I'm sorry." Above, the foreman on the ladder slammed an ax into the window frame; below, a clutch of men were grappling with a button press to batter down the door. The Ruths and the Naomis released Truda, then. She cast her jacket off and joined in with the heaving at the door. In Horn Lane behind her, the Ruth and Naomi Thursday Club prayed on Miss Blick's behalf, and they called out for Ruby and they pleaded for Miss Fly.

The water took Ruby by surprise, and she flailed and lost her grip on Isa's hand. She felt the stretch and gaping in her shoulder; her own blood swelling warm around her chest. She closed her mouth against the flecked, fermented water; these unseen things that stirred about her in the dark; stroking, lapping, scratching at her legs. *Hear the word of God,* she thought. *The waters compassed me about, even to the soul: the depth closed me round about, the weeds were wrapped about my head* . . . Her spoon was floating upward—she could not see it, but it drifted against her face and Ruby knew the feel of it and, reaching up to grab the spoon, her hand broke through the surface of the water. Someone seized her, tight, about the wrist. She breached the surface, sucked at breath, a heated, pulpy liquor streaming from her nose. Belle's arm reached over her and locked about her shoulder, around her chest, and Ruby felt her lips move on her ear. She grabbed Ruby underneath the chin and forced her fingers deep beneath her jawbone. Ruby strained back, trying to see Isa. The oily waters lapped around her neck.

"Leave Ruby!" Isa shouted out with mettle in her voice, and Ruby saw her, dripping on the towpath, bent over her bag.

"Shall I choke her on the Cut-cack, Isa Fly, before I come for you?"

Ruby tried to twist her head to look at Belle, but Belle's fingers only sank into her neck. "It woe hurt Moonie, killing her. Yo know what he's like. He doe care for Isa. He's set her for a hanging."

Belle shifted her hold on Ruby. "She killed my Cass, so I'm obliged to kill her in return!"

"Yo doe have to! Yo ay bound up by it! Yo ay got an Imperative!"

Ruby felt the fingers loosening around her jaw, but Belle still held her tight about the chest, kept her mouth above the surface of the water. *Belle holds me close. She is my aunt. She will not let me go.* Isa was shouting from the towpath, urging words across the Cut, but the fire was spitting, creaking, groaning, and Ruby couldn't hear.

"Come closer!" Belle screamed out. "Or are you scared of being close to me?"

And as Isa lowered herself back down into the water, Ruby saw the glimmer of a hook curved in her hand. Belle saw it too; she laughed and called, "Am I a great fish, Isa Fly, that you will land? Will you catch me like you caught my Cass?"

Isa swam out toward them. She stopped some yards away, just out of reach, but close enough to be heard clear enough. "Anselm always said that mermaids shouldn't trouble us if we were kind to them," she called. "He was puzzled by you, Belle, by what you did to him. 'Dad calls them mermaids, but mermaids are supposed to heal,' he'd say. 'They have the gift of making people well.' He never understood why you would hurt him . . ."

Médecins de mer, thought Ruby. *But they will harm a person, if they're harmed* . . . She watched her clear-skinned, alabaster Isa. "Look at her, Belle!" And with each word she felt Belle's fingers ripple on her throat. "What happens when a mermaid's killed?"

"What do you mean?"

" 'The dying mermaid plagues her killer with all the ailments of the sea. His skin will bleach and blister . . .' "

Ruby knew this passage from her Almanac. " 'His flesh will swell with fish-bites though no fish have bitten him. His eyes will see a tempest though the water's still. His abdomen will distend as if he has drunk brine; his throat will chafe and burn with thirst and this thirst will not be slaked.' "

Shouting from the towpath; people running through the gulley, half-crouched, but not looking at the water except to fill their buckets in swift scoops while others took broom-handles, axes, sticks, to the rear window and the door. Ruby tried to call to them but Belle's grip slipped on her and Ruby slid beneath her arms and underneath the water. She twisted round and pulled herself up; used Belle as her ladder. Ruby hooked one arm about Belle's neck and with the other hand she gripped Belle's chin. "Look at her! Look at your sister! There ay no marks on her! Her father, it is, *your* father, Moonie Fly, who carries all the marks of mermaid-killing! Tell her, Isa! It's Moonie as is blistered and corroded!"

And for an instant Belle was still as still and staring over Ruby's head at Isa. Belle's eyes were lit; they shone like she was drunk on something. There's something heady, like lit spirit, in the truth, and now it flared in Belle.

Ruby urged her words into Belle's ear. "Yo cor blame your sister! Yo cor make Isa carry all the blame for what your father did . . ." And then she turned, her arm hooked round Belle's neck, and shouted out to the people clustered round the back door of the button shop. "We ay in there!" she called. "Doe look for us no more! Weem here, now! Weem all here!"

A shrapnel-shower from the blaze—glass and splintered wood—was falling on the water all around them and the people on the towpath raised their arms above their heads, around their faces. Belle pulled Ruby to her and tried to swim with her for the towpath, but something shifted underneath the water, tugged her under and Ruby lost her hold. Belle struggled, thrashed; her foot was caught up and she couldn't free it. Monstrous, she looked, rising from the silt and tossing up her head and flailing, straining against the thing that held her under; her mouth leaching at the corners, phlegmy strings.

But Ruby did not sink. *I have the spoon,* she thought, *to keep me safe in water.* Her feet had come to rest on something solid (a piece of Rudge's tubing, upended on the Cut-bed). She set her feet wide on it and reached out for Belle. Her fingers slipped on Belle's skin—this film of diesel, basting them—but Ruby held her aunt's head and tried to keep her nose, her mouth out of the water. Isa swam toward them, her hook raised and Belle looked, frantic, wild, between them.

Someone was lying out flat on the towpath, leaning out over the water with a broom handle, calling out to them to catch hold of it and be pulled to the path. Another crouched there, proffering a stick; another jumped into the water, while Ruby tried to tell them Belle was trapped; that's why she couldn't let her go; that's why they weren't swimming for the side. As Isa Fly drew breath and plunged below the surface, working with her hook at wires that kept her sister trapped beneath the water, Ruby slipped the spoon from around her neck. "This ay mine, and it ay Isa's. Your spoon, it is, Belle. Yoom Grace!" She looped the spoon around her aunt's neck. "Isa says your spoon is meant to keep yo safe in water." Ruby urged the words into Belle's ears. "Yoom meant to live!" And Ruby twined her fingers around the spoon and held her aunt till Isa Fly had freed her.

FOR ALL that happened in Horn Lane that night, only two lives were lost. The door to the button shop was torn clear of its hinges, and amidst the smoke and clamor, as men directed hoses at the flames, Trembly Em crawled unseen through the wild crowd, into the shop and up the stairs. She died on the landing on her knees, killed by the fire she had started, still searching for her lost Ruby-girl.

Truda wrapped Ruby in a blanket and sat her next to Isa in the back-seat of her car. She wanted to drive Ruby straight to the QV—her shoulder wound was dirty; it needed attention—and it's not that Ruby didn't give the proposition thought: Nan Annie and Belle Severn meeting at her bed; Jamie Abel tendering his blood to replenish that which Ruby'd lost; Captin on the early train from Whalemouth, praying that this time he wouldn't be too late . . . Then Truda driving every day to the QV with her best attempt at fresh tea in a flask; Dinah sending up a bag of custards . . .

Ruby shook her head. "No. I ay going to the QV, Miss Blick, and nobody can make me." She turned to Isa. "It's too late. I vowed it:

'Whither thou goest, I will go. Where thou lodgest, I will lodge.' If yo take me to the QV, I will climb out of that window an' all."

("And she bloody would," said Truda.)

"I will follow Isa all the way to Whalemouth. And do yo think I'd make it all that way, wi this?" Ruby gestured at her bloody shoulder. "Do yo want that sitting on your conscience: me, dead somewhere by the towpath, because I tried to walk down to the sea? Take me to Dr. Brammeier and I promise that I will not run away."

So Truda left them at the Blicks' house up on Tenter Lane, and while they waited for her to return, Isa cleaned up Ruby's wound and put on a dressing soaked in turpentine, and then used the Blicks' phone to call Dr. Brammeier with a message for her father: "Tell him that I'm coming home. I'm coming back to talk to the police. And be certain to call him by his true name. Call him Jonah."

Ruby knew how her grandfather's last hours would unfold; knew that Jonah would not be there when they reached St. Shirah. She'd read of this in *Tales of Severnsea; "Médicins de mer."* Jonah had killed Cass, and in return she'd plagued him with the ailments of the sea:

> As the tides are dragged from the shoreline, so the offender is
> dragged back to the place where he did harm, whether it be ten
> feet or ten miles from the land. And as he is compelled to move
> ever deeper through the waters, he pleads with the mermaids to
> save him. He revokes the curses he called down upon them; he
> begs their forgiveness for the cruelties he performed; he demands
> their mercy, but finds no mermaid there to show it, and whether
> he offers himself to the sea in bleak propitiation or whether he is
> swallowed by the waves, the offender has no power to leave the
> water, and he drowns.

So it would prove to be. When Isa reached St. Shirah six hours later, she would find that the police no longer wished to question her. They'd say they had no evidence, and Isa Fly would open up her bag to find she had no spear inside; for either Ruby or Belle Severn had taken it from Isa's bag on the towpath and hurled it deep into the Horn Lane fire. And the police would inform Isa that her father, Moonie Fly, had walked into the ocean and left behind a scrawled, ranting confession.

Following the rusted stream bed of the Ludleye Gutter, Belle Severn waded on the rocks to St. Barbara's Spring, where losslinen was hanging from a tree. From there she went with her spoon—Ruby's spoon—to Hunting Tree, and took with it a promise for her land-ma, Annie, that before too long their Ruby would be home.

~⁓o

THIS IS the tale of Ruby Abel Tailor, who could not cross the water but dreamed of an easy plenty by the sea. This is the tale of three separated sisters—one witch, one mermaid and one missing—and how Ruby was caught up in between. And this is the tale of Cradle Cross, circled round with water, and how Ruby Abel Tailor learned to cross it.

ABOUT THE AUTHOR

ANNA LAWRENCE PIETRONI grew up outside of Birmingham, England. She graduated with a first class degree from Oxford and worked for several years in the British prison system before turning to writing. This is her first novel.

ABOUT THE TYPE

This book was set in Sabon, a typeface designed by the well-known German typographer Jan Tschichold (1902–74). Sabon's design is based upon the original letter forms of Claude Garamond and was created specifically to be used for three sources: foundry type for hand composition, Linotype, and Monotype. Tschichold named his typeface for the famous Frankfurt typefounder Jacques Sabon, who died in 1580.

DATE			